T0149679

When a young Peace Corps volunteer is recruited for a "second job," we are thrust into a new heart of darkness—and light. A rich, thrilling LeCarre-esque journey into the tribal and geopolitical wars of 1960s Africa.

Kenneth W. Davis, Professor Emeritus of English, Indiana University

LAND OF THE SUN, LAND WITHOUT LIGHT

David Michael Litwack

LAND OF THE SUN, LAND WITHOUT LIGHT

iUniverse books may be ordered through booksellers or by contacting:

iUniverse
1663 Liberty Drive
Bloomington, IN 47403
www.iuniverse.com
1-800-Authors (1-800-288-4677)

ISBN: 978-1-5320-6431-9 (sc)
ISBN: 978-1-5320-6432-6 (e)

Library of Congress Control Number: 2019900388

Print information available on the last page.

iUniverse rev. date: 01/26/2019

.... they come not single spies, but in battalions

- Hamlet

FOR DONNA LU OWENS WITH ALL MY LOVE

ACKNOWLEDGMENTS

This work could not have been completed without the aid and comfort of Dr. Kenneth Davis. He is Professor Emeritus of English at Indiana University and a great friend from years gone by (and witness to some instances—in my case only—best forgotten). Dr. Davis provided the encouragement, plot suggestions, and copy reading par *excellence*. So errors of spelling, syntax, characterization, and plot are mine only. Also, many thanks go to Carolyn Robel Litwack for the cover concept and art. And to the iUniverse staff who were more than supportive . . . once I got my act together.

T hen he slipped away from us. And from the fury and the storm of our chaotic world. Quietly. Unobtrusively. As I think he had come to live in it.

He had barely reached his sixtieth year. So he never knew the grudging respect or the recognition that comes to many—to those of his class, education, and stature—when they pass into late middle age. But that sort of acknowledgment would not have mattered to him anyway.

He slipped away alone. No deathwatch. No renting of garments. His marriage broken long ago; the daughter never really known to him; our parents, our sister, gone.

The hastily organized memorial was lightly attended. The family of us Hamblins mostly. Some distant cousins.

There was only the priest's brief eulogy. And the mass.

None would identify as his colleagues or former colleagues. Except for a distinguished looking older gentleman, a Dr. Norman, I believe he wrote in signing the remembrance book—or it could have been "Noman." He also wrote "RIP O.S."

Perhaps in those years of demanding professional focus he had never created the bonds that more easily strengthen in later life when mutual memory provides the motive. Perhaps it was something else.

But his passing held for me, his only brother, an unexplainable and grating sadness. For the loss of scintillating, though infrequent, conversations while sipping single-malt whiskeys. As for me, a mystery and a nostalgia for something unknown nagged at me—a sort of emptiness in the story of his life.

To the surprise of no one, I was designated executor of his estate. And so I began the laborious process of sifting through the collectibles of nearly forty years. And I noticed that he'd made hardly a mark in a world wherein one's life is most often measured, at least in death, by the breadth of one's acquisition.

This is when I found this most remarkable collection: a sort of manuscript or diary in many parts plus letters stuffed haphazardly among his eclectic collection of literary and popular novels, obscure poetry, and historical tracts. Once I had gathered them together and tried unsuccessfully to determine their exact order, I was nevertheless caught in their astonishing sway for nights on end, even neglecting my duties as officer of the court. I will never know the true order of all these manuscript pages and even the composition books, though some of them were dated, and I added assumed months and even days to other entries. So I have taken liberties in presenting them, sometimes inserting pieces and paragraphs where they seem to belong.

I was at first astounded, and I am still overcome with an ineffable sadness that this courageous, ingenious man had a side that might have remained fully unknown to us.

It was at the peak of the cold war, with a hot war raging in Asia, that he was sent by our government to a far, obscure corner of the world—nearly another universe—in the service of our ideology . . . .

■ Prescript: The Bismal *(Muslim Prayer)*

"*B-ismi-llāhi r-rahmāni r-rahīmi. [In the name of God, the Most Gracious, the Most Merciful].* Then you must give them this story, a story with a bright and hopeful ending that will urge them to a pursuit. I swear to you that if you do not, they will then know an unfinished anger—forever—and make your life a misery—forever— Thus have I spoken."

****

A Letter Never Sent

July 1, 1969

Aaron,

Something dangerous is brewing, but I can't write about it since even the last letter to you was returned by the censors. Maybe all of my letters to you have been and will be rejected.

I may have been responsible for the disappearance of the lovely Amina or the telecom American, Joe—or worse. The Militia thinks I'm a spy; the rebels are pissed off at me. Big time! I'm not sure what I'll do next.

Harry

I missed Joe and Amina. Whom I saw as my charges, my responsibility. With that thought and with only the sounds of steps and strained breathing, the memories came flooding back. Every moment with every step—and how it began....

****

■ Gerard, Corps de la Guerre

September, 1967

He slammed into me just outside the hotel bar/coffee shop. As usual, I had my mind in the clouds—thinking about the next day's location assignments and not paying attention. Knocked me half way across the patio. I crashed into tables and chairs on my journey.

He was a bit short and prone to stocky in that Gallic way. At this moment, he had that hard look through piercing blue eyes, and I thought he must be plenty pissed at me. But then he came over to where I lay and apologized profusely while pulling me up and briefly clasping my shoulders. In a more than firm grip.

[Note from Aaron Hamblin: I'm not sure where in the chronology this belongs, so I'm inserting it here.] *This may have been when it all began. A meeting of coincidence? Or an intentional slam? A portent of the chaos to come?* [End of insert.]

I was assigned two weeks in Djemélia to get location assignments, and where I would learn to love tepid Douze Marches beer. I saw Gerard the Slam almost daily.

He took to me during the first week after my arrival; God knows why. I was billeted at the Grand Hotel, the only hotel in Djemélia. He was in civilian clothes—on leave or special mission—and perhaps he thought it would be interesting to get to know an American. Maybe any American of roughly the same age. Or maybe me. The next morning were both on the bar patio. He was drinking his breakfast beer.

"Are you with these Américains? The ones that arrived last week? Are you one of them?" [1]

"I am."

"So I am Gerard. Gerard Olivier Dubois. Welcome to *l'Afrique Centrale Francophone*. I'll have to buy you a drink to welcome you and celebrate this occasion. I am sorry if I hurt you with my clumsy slam. Soon I will bring you some joy." Oh my GOD. I doubt his French parents realized the implication—the English acronym formed by his initials—when they named him. Maybe that was the joy he meant.

"I am Harry. Harry Hamblin of the infamous Hamblin clan."

---

[1] Dear Reader: Yes, I'm giving a translation. It's all said in French, of course. Sometimes in Arabic. And several other dialects. Can I be trusted? But I will be faithful to the original. (As faithful as I'm wont to be.)

Indeed, he brought me some joy—like my first taste of Douze Marches. I was hooked.

A few nights later—he must have been on leave again—he showed me a bit of the underside of Djemélia. The red light district operating from the "swanky" Vietnamese restaurant, as I was soon to learn, the famous and infamous *Amis Sans Ennemi* or, in English, "Phren & Pho." Great Vietnamese menu. As close I hoped to ever get to Nam.

Off to one side, the ladies were all gathered. Gerard chose one for me— "Here is a pretty one. Can you protect yourself from hot piss? From gonorrhea?"—one to take back with me to the hotel.

"Yes, but with the beer I don't think…with this much beer, that I can perform," I protested.

Still, between the effects of Douze Marches and Gerard's insistence, I yielded to temptation.

As we were about to leave the bar, I noticed a huge hulk of a man slapping one of the other girls around. Hard. A giant, red-faced and angry. He caught me staring. "What's your problem, skinny little bastard?"

As I stupidly moved toward him, Gerard grabbed my arm, pulled me away, and uttered a few indistinguishable words to the hulk. The brute returned to a bar stool and his beer.

"Heinrich's from Alsace. He's a mean and angry brute. But he's a good fighter in battle. He'll watch out for you."

I'll bet.

"But never mind." And he led me to my hotel room and nocturnal pleasures.

She was reasonably compliant. And so I owed him.

***

The next morning, he knocked on my door, then threw it open. When the lady protested, he seized her by the arm and shoved her out the door. "Go away, whore!" And he threw her clothes and some money out after her. He turned his back on her, smiled at me, and added, "Come on. Put on your clothes. We'll get coffee."

"I'll buy you breakfast," I offered. But I was pretty bothered by what I had just seen.

"Agreed."

We settled in on the hotel patio café.

"What do you do here, 'arry?"

"I'll teach English at a CEG, a *collège secondaire.*"

"Excellent, 'arry. You're a teacher, a *professeur.* But it's a waste of time trying to teach those little bastards. And don't let any of them, students or adults, call you *Nasarah.* I would take that as a pejorative. Tell them you are Américain. *Point final.*

"Why don't you teach in the USA?" He was on his second coffee before I sipped my first. The coffee only increased his edginess. Made him a little bit jumpy. Like me and my hangover. Maybe I was also a bit wary of another patio slam. And his question took me off guard.

I scrambled to answer it. "I am with the *Corps de la Paix.*"

"And me, I am Sergeant Gerard Olivier Dubois with the *Corps de la Guerre.*" Eyebrows raised with a half smile. "I am a *parachutist* of the *Troisième Parachutiste, régiment des salauds.* I am in network and telecommunications." [Note from Aaron Hamblin: I'm not sure where in the chronology this belongs, so I'm inserting it here.] *Many months later it felt as if I had all this time been directly, and perhaps only, telecommunicating with him. Was that possibility what was bothering me even at that moment?* [End of insert.]

"Then what do you do here?" I was trying to turn the conversation. That is, do what would soon become my "other" job.

"We will keep the peace and respond to the so-called bandits, the terrorists north of Dar es Sabir. We will eventually kill them all. We will back up the Police militia and the National Army. In other words, we will do all the works these local forces seem not to be able to do."

First I'd heard about "bandits" and "terrorists." Up north. I think I'll put in for a southern *Collège d'Enseignement Général* (CEG) assignment.

"And what do *you* do?" I asked.

"I am chief of communications. We listen and make notes." He was pretty open about his job, so I let him continue on. "We listen to other communications."

"Ah," I pursued. "There aren't many telephones here."

"We listen to radio communication. From around the area. On various frequencies."

Whatever that meant. "Who do you listen to?"

"Ah, that I cannot divulge. It is secret. Let's just say friends and enemies, *Phren et Pho*." He grinned, to mark the joke but also as if sharing a secret—one I did not yet fathom.

I figured I'd better change this line of questioning.

"Where are you billeted?" I tried to drag out my best military vocabulary.

"Out of town. To the northwest—by the river. Not an obvious building. The old *Légionnaire* barracks. I'll take you there sometime. For the lunch."

I couldn't wait. "Are you on leave?" I couldn't help but ask. I hoped not. I hoped he would not be hanging around me and the other Americans as we got settled.

"I am leader of a team of four who are in town to get provisions. All three of the boys drove with me here, plus me. They will buy items and pick me up on their way back."

That's better. "So how long have you been here?"

"Six months. I am conscripted. My military service is two years, but I am paid more than other *militaires* for being a paratrooper."

"Have you parachuted anywhere?" Now I was getting into real information gathering mode.

"Only once. Two months ago."

"Where?"

"Up north where the desert begins. The Sahel. So now I am no longer a *bleu-bite*! You won't be for long either."

"Much fighting against bandits and terrorists?"

"Nothing. We shot off a few rounds at…nothing. We lost one man to a faulty parachute. *Une chandelle romaine.*"

"Sorry."

"He was a good boy. A Vietnamese. A leftover from the *Legion* days and the war in Vietnam. A great spy and interpreter in Vietnam."

"Our side could have used him in Southeast Asia as well," I noted.

"Ah, yes. The war *América* is destined to lose. As *we* did," he answered. Said with certainty.

"By the way, did I mention 'arry that with your dark curly hair you resemble some of those northerners. A little sun tan would help. Then you could be a spy for us," he added with what might have been a sarcastic smile. A spy for them.

We departed soon after. He, to catch his jeep back to base; me, to report to HQ, and to put in for a southern assignment.

Our chance meeting presaged more.

But at least I had some information to report. This spy stuff might be fun. And easy.

Or not.

■ Training

June-August, 1967

Before all this, that summer, we had trained in the USA like fighters, without respite, day and night.

Sort of.

First, volunteer training in Quebec. French immersion, language testing, physical trials, socialization skill observation. They wanted to make sure we still wanted in.

Then back to the college for more of the same. We did some serious socialization at the local pub. Even serious argumnts about current events. *En français* as required. Laughable. So we'd often slipped back into English to be sure we got our important points across. Especially me and Terry. And Joe, Terry's minion, when he got lubricated enough. Otherwise he was silent.

■ The Beginning

August 1967

The takeoff was rocky, the flight bumpy. I was alone for this first leg to New York.

I had left Terry there at the Cleveland airport—he was thoughtful enough to see me off. It was difficult for him. That we had trained together and were partnered at times, creating a bond fueled even more by plenty of beer. He hadn't done so well—couldn't fool those goofy psychologists hiding behind every tree, noting our every grunt and snort. I was coming to learn that Terry was truly a man with a cloud hanging over him.

Yet in all, I was in high anticipation of the unknown rushing toward me like Sahara sand in the desert wind. First Peary. Then Africa, Djemélia and, finally, the rain forest or flaming desert.

■ The Beginning before the Beginning: Serve Your Country

July, 1967

But before that beginning, this is how it all really started.

It was from the shadows that he approached me. Silently. Then a seemingly bodiless voice: "How would you like to serve your country?" It was dusk and the lights had not yet come on in the training building.

"I... I...." I was too startled.

"Let's move over here." He grabbed my arm to lead me farther into the shadows. Then "How would you like to serve your country?"

I got my voice back: "That's why I joined the Peace Corps. To serve my country."

"I mean *really* serve it. All you have to do is let us know what's going on—wherever you end up. That's all."

"That's all?"

"Yes, to be a kind of informant."

I moved around him to get more light on his face. To see if he was serious. I was not successful. This was too much like a movie. "This is like a movie!" I exclaimed.

"This is no movie, Harry. I need your answer now."

I thought this was some kind of test fashioned by the psychologists who were always checking us out. To watch my reaction. I searched my mind frantically on how best to answer. Which answer were they looking for?

"OK."

"OK. That's "yes." That's good. When you arrive in Africa, you will have a contact. He's Doctor Leonard Norman, the Corps on-site doctor." I thought he said "Noman." "He'll fill you in."

That they might already know exactly where I was headed. I needed to know. Invite him to go with me—to the bar. Time for a beer or something stronger.

"But…." But he was gone. Just like that. And I was troubled. Bothered again. I needed something stronger than beer to mull this over.

Training at Camp Peary for me alone then. Nothing really. I'd already passed the physical and language tests. Counter insurgency blah blah and how to lose a tail on city streets. Driving lessons. Should prove useful on the pathways through the jungle or among the dunes in the desert.

Also a compressed version of their famous interrogation course. Whoa, that wasn't part of the deal!

I'd learned a lot of stuff that wasn't part of the deal.

Truth is, they didn't know what to do with me most of the time. I certainly wasn't spy-officer material, and I wasn't foreign enough to be an agent. So I sneaked off base and headed out to Williamsburg for some serious refreshment whenever I could. Killed some time. Killed some mugs. They should have used the time to teach me to use the shortwaves.

■ Hair Shirt / Silk Shirt

September, 1967

When we arrived in Djemélia we were greeted by the Director. He must have been taken with my two-week growth of beard. Or perhaps what may have been my lingering, rancid breath from the Air France open bar and Heineken and other delicacies. Beard and beer. A wicked and unfortunate combination to these bureaucrats.

Was it choose your site—or have it chosen for you?

■ Whose Choice?

We were given a location choice according to our French language test scores. I scored fairly well, so I was given a choice ahead of many of the others assigned. I chose Albri, which was known as a "silk-shirt" option—all the comforts of home. At the base of a picturesque mountain with a Swiss Christian mission at the southern base of that mountain. I noticed that no one had chosen Dar es Sabir, definitely a "hair-shirt" location—none of the comforts at all. At the other side of that mountain.

Alice was assigned Albri. Ok, her scores were slightly better than mine. I was assigned Dar es Sabir. I assumed that the chief just didn't like me much. Maybe it was the beard—or the beer. Close enough to be homonyms and close enough for his displeasure.

I may later learn there are other reasons.

■ The "Other" Assignment

September, 1967

"For this leg?" I really didn't understand.

He was reciting a list of my duties during my first moments alone with him, Docteur Leonard Norman. Or was it *Noman?*

"Let me explain," he continued. "You were chosen because of your temperament and high test scores."

"If I tell you I cheated on the tests, will you reconsider?" I was definitely getting the jitters. It may have been the jet lag. Or common sense lag catching up to me.

"And reduce your pay by $150 a month, old boy? Besides, it'll get you out of the war draft!"

I thought for a moment. "So let's say I do this thing during this 'leg.' What *is* this thing?"

"So, Harry, we—and now you in your capacity as contractor-volunteer—are part of an operations group, a kind of political operations unit. We carry out activities like political, psychological, and economic stuff. Maybe we want to buy a strategically located airfield for our bigger planes as in this case. For example, to give us a rear guard action against Libya. Against Gaddafi. Or build an encampment. Problem is, we can't trust anyone here to be an agent. To be our eyes and ears. In part because we're short on resources, what with the Asian war."

"Meaning you haven't got the money to buy a reliable agent or send in an officer." I was a bit pissed. "Or all the other candidates are 'otherwise occupied,'" I added.

"We've tried."

"So you get the next best thing and cheap labor besides." I was a bit pissed.

"A little bit like that. But don't sell yourself short, O.S.—Old Sport. You've got the makings of a good officer." This time I noted the British—or Yankee—affectation.

"No thanks. I've heard about your Star Chamber," I answered with a tinge of righteous indignation.

"Well this assignment shouldn't be too dangerous. Just eyes and ears, old boy. And especially keep your eyes on that airport."

Just eyes and ears. And airport. Not too dangerous.

■ The Beginning After the Beginning: The Dar es Sabir *Sous-préfet*

September 1967

It was the filigreed *jalaba*h and its fine needle work that first caught my attention. I was so mesmerized that I failed to notice the high-pitched nasal, whining-like voice of the *sous-préfet* himself. Finally I took in the squat and childlike figure. Definitely not the picture of a helmsman at the wheel—in this forsaken boat on its sea of sand.

Nor could he speak to me directly, the *sous-préfet*, or look me in the eye. I instinctively clawed at my beard—searching for matter from our lunch or any other unpleasantness that he might have noticed and be attempting to avoid with his eyes. Then I realized he was cross-eyed as well.

He took in an attendant's advice and assigned me a cottage, what they called there a *case* (pronounced *kaz*). I played it with uncanny (for me) humility and gratitude; he might be in a position to help me one day. Or viceversa.

Still, he had to add "that will be good for this *Nasarah*."

"I am no *Nasarah*," I shot back reflexively. "I am Américain."

He stared at me a moment, this time over his Cokebottle glasses. "Américain then," he said, as he turned away from me. He was none too pleased.

Nice start!

■   Home, Sweet Home

September, 1967

I loved the view when, in the dawn, with shutters open, I could look south—sometimes through a fog of sand—at the mysterious Jumeaux, twin mountains like defiant fists that were swollen out of these sands. But no sand covered the mountains. Timeless.

I admit, I would often look at them with some longing though I'm not sure why. Only black rock from this view. Through the wind-swept fog of sand. No birds in sight. And that which bothered me—like the proverbial itch I cannot scratch—might have blossomed, or at least presented itself, that day.

And everywhere the sand. The burning sand that would sift through our fingers, slowly, then faster. Like time itself. Like the sands of time; islands of ever drifting sand—shifting dunes, shifting sands. Sand's ancient cycle—taking over more and more of this land. And the dunes behind my *kaz* stretching north to the encroaching desert, perhaps hiding the real, yet unfathomable secrets of this land.

Still the prickly cram-cram, like our crabgrass, managed to take hold here and there. Just enough to feed the wandering livestock, and just enough to insinuate into your sandals and remind you that even the ground you walk on will always be unfriendly to you.

But when the sun had fully risen its brightness was blinding. Such that all seemed the color of sand or khaki. Like a film in black and white, a land without color or any light at all. Sometimes blinding, sometimes disorienting. Sometimes black. I had the sunglasses, the clip-ons from my dad's army days. Poorly fitting over my horned rim glasses. Disorienting themselves.

There was the sometimes rapid firing. Soft, asynchronous, and distant, but nevertheless disconcerting. Hunters. Bringing down the antelope, the oyrx, of whom one or more would sometimes (accidentally) visit my *kaz* in their moment of terror. They would dance in the "drawing room," giving me brief company, then find the door, and continue on their terrified way through the dunes. I had found the scimitar-like antlers of some that failed to escape those hunters.

To accompany me day and night, I had a herd (or is it a "school?" Or maybe a "pride") of lizards, small and quick, and camouflaged to blend into the walls and floor. Some had given evidence, by their strewn skeletons, that they had failed to make up their minds at the critical moment, and were therefore flattened by my predecessors. Rapidly dessicated by the desert air. At first I walked gingerly for fear that I would flatten one as well, agile though they were. The effort became too much to make. They would have to decide their direction in a timely fashion. On their own. One chance only. Or suffer the worst.

As might be my fate. *Mon destin.*

■ Michel and Victor

The midget and the giant. My colleagues. Sent by our God to torture me. Or at least to make me terribly uncomfortable. They jabbered away, much faster than my rudimentary French could comprehend. Plus, they both had beautiful orthography as well, of which I bore great envy.

Victor would carry on about something or other. Michel would contradict. Victor would look to me for support. I would stare back, then nod and say "Oui" hoping I was on target. Sometimes I was; other times, not. At which time I would get a puzzled stare from them both. Then Victor would raise his voice and remonstrate: "Do you really believe that?" with frustration in his voice and Gallic body language.

Of course, I always said *"oui."* It was my default and backup response. Some of the discussions centered on Evian, my predecessor. [Note from Aaron Hamblin: I'm not sure where in the chronology this belongs, so I'm inserting it here.] *Only now have I learned that*

Evian was murdered and his privates stuffed in his mouth. No sight for the timid. That his penis had already begun to "wind off." Evian, around whom so much mystery and drama seemed to swirl. And who might have been informing for the Third Parachutist Division or the French spy outfit, the Direction Générale de la Sécurité Extérieure.(DGSE). [End of insert.]

So I studied and practiced the language with this powerful incentive. Like a madman, chattering away with who knows who about who knows what—chattering with my colleagues and others. Modou, my Indian colleague and a multilingual, would come to my rescue. *Directeur* Partenay would only look. Look a bit disgusted. As he did in every sober moment—which usually lasted from dawn till noon.

I also determined that my French was much more fluent with two Johnny Walkers or three Douze Marches beers. So I practiced the drinking of them, sometimes together, to great effect.

Plus, with them, the unknowable bothered me less—or not at all.

■ *Arabi* and *Shahadah*

November 1967

As a way to understand the Muslim culture, I asked for Arabic and religious lessons. The Toubou *Imam*, he of the black and filigreed *jalaba*, was very pleased and sent me one who resembled himself in maturity. Craggy face and husky build. His assistant, I guessed. We met in the town mosque, painted with beautiful calligraphy and decorated with touches of imported tiling.

This middle-aged, orthodox Muslim in a gray, filigreed *jalaba*—often called *al Hajj* by my neighbors, for he had made the pilgrimage to Mecca—would meet me once a week to instruct me to read Arabic and recite from the Koran. A gruff fellow who pounded the lessons into me with a kind of fierce remonstrance. And so I learned to recite (and practice) the Five Pillars of Islam.

Meanwhile, a lost one would beat his head, in the portico of the Mosque, in rhythm to the *Shahada*. Over and over. To its own rhythm. Or his.

I think the *Hajj* thought he had a convert within his grasp. Once he called a stranger who was praying and the head-beater over to us as I was learning the *Shahadah*, the statement of faith. With the strangers present, he asked me to recite the statement in classical Arabic. I fumbled it twice, and he left me that day in disgust, maybe even fury, from embarrassment.

I knew that a recitation of the *Shahada*, especially before two witnesses, would make me a convert. There would have been a conversion celebration. Nonalcoholic grenadine and soda all around. I chose to celebrate that evening with Scotch—to celebrate the bullet I had just dodged—to the everlasting irritation of the *Hajj*.

It may have been my finest victory among so many losses this season.

So I spent much of that school year learning the languages and cultural idiosyncrasies of this land and these people. Teaching English. And music. (My favorite was "À la claire fontaine" which, I am told, has been a favorite of all the *Nasarah* music *professeurs* everywhere as a kind of softening of the post colonial zeitgeist.) And trying to learn how to spy.

■ Alice

Alice was beautiful in that all-American way. She was tall, willowy, and blond. Graduate of Wellesley as well. Brains. And unlike the other Americans, she kept her complexion, even in these hot, windy, and sandy climes.

I thought I was in love with her throughout our training. Then, when she chose to room with me on the overnight in Europe, they paired us, two to a hotel room by gender, but one male and one female left over. Us. She said, "C'mon Harry, we'll make the numbers even out for them." So it began. Ecstasy.

■ Antoine

That's the thing about our constable, Antoine. The bright, perpetual smile, lit up by perfect ivory teeth, and lips turned up to his high, round cheekbones. Looking up at me from under his cap's bill. He was like a boy in his first uniform, reveling in its crispness, and his police cap swung to a rakish angle. Who can resist it?

(And it was rumored that he had a brother. Among the Wahid. Very strange, as all the rumors here tend to be. But a rumor from the most trusted source of rumors. Mama of Mama's Fine Restaurant, no less.)

Indeed, I soon learned that Antoine could be my best informant. "That's it, Monsieur 'amblin, they've done propaganda. Excellent propaganda. But they are bandits still." He gave a brisk nod of finality, no discussion brooked, and maintained the smile as he announced Docteur Lièvre's murder.

"They killed Lièvre?"

"Just so." Still, the boyish smile. As if, like a child, he can't comprehend this death. Only accept it. "Because this is what they do. Kill the *Nasarah*. This is their reason, their *raison d'être*, I think."

"Still, I am no *Nasarah*," I responded without hesitation.

"Whatever you may be, Monsieur. They will think you *Nasarah*. And look to kill you."

Said to put me on my guard? Ensure my alliance with his clan? With the Sara-Ngumbaye?

Or perhaps, in this backwater—or should I say "backsand?"— where death seems always so close—the Doctor's had no special significance for him. For them.

But for me, it was a kind of foreboding. Doctors have always been beyond death in my iconography. Immortals of the highest plane. While I knew the Doctor, had met the Doctor, I did not know him beyond a *"bonjour."* He and his wife, also a doctor, had not socialized much.

■ *Directeur* Partenay

But then a clank and clash yanked me from my thoughts.

"Hey, 'amblin, *les salauds*. They got Lièvre!" He was puffing like he'd been tearing across those few hundred yards on foot. His miniature, faded yellow Deux Chevaux was still clanking along over the miniature dunes, spitting carbon and coughing carburetion in competition with its master.

"Killed him on the road to Ain Saghir!" The machine grinded to a sliding halt, and he heaved his outsized carcass out nearly tumbling the "lorry." "Bird fuckers shot him in the back, the bastards! Oh, shit!"

One of the coquettishly veiled ladies slipped from the back of the wagon and caught his arm as he caressed her against the lorry. "Thank you, my dear. Lovely, this one, eh? Soft, milk-brown skin and the ass of a *vache normande*." He tried to grab her backside, but slipped back against the lorry again. *"Merde!"* He expelled a waft of rancid wine with the words "For what?"

The question hung a moment in the embarrassing silence. "Because this is what they do. Kill the *Nasarah*. This is their reason for being." I repeated Antoine's vapid justification. More to practice my French than to state a truism. And he, Antoine, gave Partenay a smart salute, holding his grin all the while. I detected there the hint of a smirk.

Partenay shoved another cigarette between his meaty lips. "It has become *merdique* here. These people have nothing, take everything." Not you, of course, Monsieur Antoine," he corrected in a delayed reaction to Antoine's salute. "You're of another race!" A nice and totally accurate, if irrelevant, distinction.

"*Here* we have given them everything! The world! And *here* are our thanks!" He gesticulated, encompassing the world as we know it with his outstretched arms in the shape of an arc. Then he lit that other cigarette and was seized with paroxysms of coughing. "But then, caraahh, you, Américain, would not, caraahhhh, cannot understand or appreciate!" He nearly doubled over with the coughing; tears flooded his eyes and the solicitous Arab girl bent with him, buttressing his mass with only that fine, soft hand riding lightly on his hairy arm. "*Merde!*"

"Come on, we'll have a drink for the good Doctor."

"Ah, you too, Monsieur Antoine?" I ventured.

"No, thank you, Monsieur, though your kindness is most kind. I have my rounds of the town of course."

"Of course." I offered my hand to Antoine. He accepted, then smartly saluted. "Until later, Monsieur 'amblin."

Again with Partenay. A half bow, weak salute for the maiden.

As Antoine wheeled around, Partenay gave me a look of disgust. Or he tried. The cigarette glued to and dangling from his lower lip contradicted that look. I went round to the free seat in the miniature lorry. The maiden, Fatima, helped Partenay in, then mounted in back. The lorry rocked with his weight, coughed, and revved.

He left her in the road not a hundred meters from his compound. She slid out the back, and I turned to watch her, through the swinging rear door, slip gracefully away.

Ahead, the long suffering Madame Partenay, hands wringing her apron, watched from the porch of their villa.

He waved me into his villa with a brisk, underhand motion as I trudged in front of him. The same, still beguiling ritual. "*Un apéritif*, Monsieur?" he'd ask, now the epitome of sobriety and good manners.

"Very much," I'd respond in tacit support. Madame will watch with hopeless resignation, her eyes red but tearless.

A *Pernod*, to Lièvre, and he was off again on a tirade. "You Américains can't understand this." He shaped the world again with his arms. "You see things unencumbered by history. Caraaahhh!"

I shrugged and nodded, knowing better than to dispute or even agree with such opinions. At any rate, he required no encouragement, the *Pernod* taking up where the morning wine had left off.

"You judge us ignorantly. Take Antoine, that clown of a policeman mimicking his betters. You cannot see it. You put yourselves above us. You who treat your blacks worse than we, ours.

"Ah, morality! Is that it, Monsieur?" he continued. "And when you bombed us in Normandy? To liberate us? Droping those bombs on peaceful farmhouses. Killing children. I remember well! My sister, running from the house after the first bomb hit. The tongues of flames from the next bomb lashing out to catch her as she fled, whipping around her dress, shooting up on all sides, licking through her hair. I hear those screams always. Yes, the Americans are coming! *Les* Américains, 'ooray! But my sister is dead before the liberation, her unborn children orphans, and her brother alone to explain it all to our aged mother. *Merde* to you! Always for the greater good, as you see it! My most stinking, bloody *merde* on you!"

An elegant tirade, most feelingly spoken. Not one paroxysm of coughing. Only the bloated, red-faced anger.

"Bernard!" Madame admonished, though barely above a whisper. "Bernard, hold your tongue to our young guest!"

"But not you, Monsieur," he continued, now subdued. "You, of course, may be different and of a different time."

Then "You are the blend of East and West. Just as we are the blend of the North and South. With the best of both!" He turned to watch her return to the kitchen, then winked mischievously and jerked his head toward where we left young Fatima on the Albri road. "Another, Monsieur?"

I thought he might be offering me a Fatima. But it was another glass of Pernod he meant. This afternoon will end with a long, dry-mouthed siesta.

Always the same, yet I relished these lunches. This elegant, sandless French *soupée* in these hot and gritty climes served as a happy retreat from the sandy meals I took in my little *kaz*. Despite the conversation. It was all his, of course. Madame, who prepared this excellent lunch, thereafter did not say a word but looked on sadly. She was withering away here, her last, sad days spent in desert fire, filth, and sand. Or as an image at the glassless window, red-eyed and awaiting her thoughtless mate.

"So what does an Américain come here for? To lose himself? To hide from this frenetic world? To observe us, even spy on us? To replace us? I've asked you these questions before, but you didn't understand." He stabbed the air before my face with his fork. "I remember when you first arrived, hardly a word of French. You had a stupid blank stare when I spoke to you. Absolutely infuriating. Infuriating! And now you even speak Arabic and Sara. Imagine that, Helène! Arabic and Sara! And his French is much improved as well."

A compliment coming from a French educator. Especially *this* one.

"I can even speak with the rebels and bandits." A foolish thing to say, to start him off. The Pernod must have loosened my tongue.

"Ah, yes! Bandits! Caaraaahhh! The ultimate ingrates. What is it your Shakespeare wrote? 'How sharper than a serpent's tooth....!' Those are no bandits, despite the propaganda from our administration and their leadership. No, they act like bandits, ravaging the countryside, killing Europeans like they did Lièvre and Santiago, where they can, destroying the homes of those they deem collaborators. We've seen it all before. They're revolutionaries! Marxists, no doubt! Supported by the Russians...like the one down the road." He stabbed the air with his fork, pointing toward Docteur Godin's cottage, or trying to. "Intent on liberating their compatriots from the yoke of colonialism by wreaking havoc! Destroy to gain. Not so unlike you brash Americans, eh? Destroy to liberate! Well wait until the *Third Para* get here. To take revenge for...for Lièvre's death, and that of Santiago, the veterinarian who was with the doctor. I have word that a response is being considered even now in the highest councils in Djemélia."

And on and on. Especially about the *Troisième Parachutistes*, reconstituted *Légionnaires*, Gerard's unit, *Régiment des Salauds*, and their prowess.

Then this lunch descended to a haze of babble as I attempted to parry the definition of "bandit" with his rhetoric of colonial paternalism.

■ Perhaps Another Night

January 1968

It was night, perhaps that very night, when my manservant, my "boy" Jean, roused me. "*Soupée*, Monsieur. It is almost ready."

He swayed above me, his face distorted and pockmarked, nose enlarged as if through a magnifying glass, his eyes glistening brightly, and his knotty grey hair spinning webs in the moonlight. A rhythmic beating competed with Jean's efforts to rouse me, the beat nearly lulling me back into my nap—the one who beat his head against the mosque wall.

"OK, Jean, OK, I'm awake. But don't let me drink my lunch with Partenay ever again."

"Then I have a surprise for you!"

"No cucumber salad?" Jean had to know I was joking.

"Oh, yes, I have made a cucumber salad of perfection. And your favorite, boiled and fried kidneys. But not too boiled." And, I hoped, no chickens running in circles with their heads cut off. As I ate. "But the surprise: Wahid is among us. And he may condescend to speak to us—to you. If *Inch Allah*, it is God's will, he may speak with you!'

"Just what I was counting on, Jean."

"I am so grateful for your gratitude. And I have even brought with me this one, Rashid, to serve and to bang his head like a fine drum in a rhythm known only to him. He has a sickness and he must be directed like a child. Yet he is a beloved cousin of Wahid...but does not speak...much. And one must be careful not to antagonize or provoke him—which can be dangerous."

"And I, grateful for the kidneys and cucumber salad." My mouth was thick and dry. But never show them your discomfort, I'd been told. Or the dying of thirst and a throbbing head. "When will he come?" I tried to ignore the somewhat muffled pounding of the beloved Rashid's head. Back of his head to back of my *kaz* wall. As if in an effort to break it down.

"If he comes, it will be in the deep night."

"The strange one, the seeming idiot Rashid?"

"*Ah, non*, Monsieur. Our Wahid. For he moves like the *guépard*, on catlike feet and in silence. His movements are a mystery, and it is only his courier that makes it known that he might come this way. To see the *Nasarah* who will be a good friend to his people."

This time I held my tongue—even when he characterized me as a "*Nasarah*."

"That is you, Monsieur! Rashid makes his home under the overhanging tiles of the house of justice which serves as our mosque. He is so trusted by his cousin that he will never blurt out or lead the enemy to the location of Wahid or the Wahidi."

"Me? Good friend to his people? What will I do? Who are his people?"

"Us all. We are all the people of Wahid, and Wahid is his name!" Jean usually sported that silly grin, a kind of knowing smirk that usually meant he knew nothing. But this time there was a certain tone of reverence, new to me.

And disturbing.

"You are of his people?"

"I am, Monsieur. I am Wahidi."

"And do you share in his booty?"

"Booty?" he asked.

"Yes, for they say that he is a great thief and, so, very rich."

"Rich? Is this a place of richness?" He encompassed our world with his arms in a circle—in the Partenay fashion. "None is rich here, Monsieur," he admonished.

He was certainly right about that. But Wahid was legendary, even as a thief. Some described him as a Robin Hood of the desert. For a few years now, the legend has grown that he steals from the rich.

Rich by the desert's standards. And gives to the poor. Perhaps a great common denominator among the poor in all societies, the legend of Robin Hood which never dies.

"Do you know the story of Robin Hood, Jean?"

Jean's eyes rolling in an expression of obvious condescension. "No, Monsieur, unless it is the story of a hero of old, evilly robbed of his birthright, taking to the forest where the wicked substitute Norman king forbids the hero's subdued tribe from hunting their own land. The hero takes the side of poachers and, through strength and guile, rescues the maiden kidnapped by the sheriff, the king's advisor, and shows up the wicked pair—substitute king and sheriff-advisor—to his true liege lord when that one has returned from the wars abroad."

He completes the précis short of breath. "If that is not the story, then could I know it?"

"That's the one." I was amazed by his powers of memory, drunken sot that he could be. "That's the one. Is that the story of your Wahid?'

"Very like. And Partenay and many other *Nasarah* are the Normans, are they not?" He's proud of his own analytical abilities.

"I should have guessed." It all made sense. As much sense as could be made of it.

Like many other nights, Jean served me up an especially fine set of boiled and fried kidneys, still tasting slightly of their former contents. And, as always, peppered with more than a bit of sand for extra spicing. The strange boy with the turkey-like nose, Rashid, ceased his head beating to help Jean serve me.

Then Jean brought me my traditional Johnny Walker. Scottish drink for this Gallic, Arab, and Sara Ngumbaye country.

"Will you be needing anything else, Monsieur?"

"Boiled water."

"Monsieur?"

"Did you boil the water that goes with this? Or do I suffer the dysentery?"

"Ah non, Monsieur, for it is always boiled. Indeed, Rashid has boiled it."

"So you're a consummate liar, as well!"

"Yes, Monsieur."

"Then I guess that's all. Aren't you and Rashid going to stick around for Wahid?" I was curious about the role he played in this developing drama.

"Well, it is not certain, and I have my woman to tend to."

"Your woman?" First I'd heard. My look probably showed doubt mixed with consternation.

"Yes, Monsieur, for she comes from Adouga in the East to be with me."

"How long has it been, then."

"Five years, I think, Monsieur."

"Then you have much enjoying to retrieve." I waved him off expansively. He would have taken his leave in any case.

"Good night, Monsieur."

"Good night, Jean. And may conjugal pleasures be great—and choirs of angels sing to you in your bed."

"Monsieur?"

"Good night."

He disappeared into the thick blackness beyond the gas lamp. Rashid, toward the "other" *arrondissement*[2] and his "home" in the mosque portico.

I nursed the first Scotch. Gulped the second. Ah, for a vodka. I listened intently for their singing, the Russians down the road. It was their night. The Doctor and his visitors. Often in the night, their wild Slavic passions would get the better of them after a couple of vodkas knocked back. Straight and lukewarm. This Scotch is their chaser. And then they'd belt out "Kalinka-Malinka" with "Moscow Nights" as an encore. I am not welcome when his handlers from Djemélia are making their monthly visit.

But this night was deathly quiet, a slight chill just beginning to descend from the Northwest, poised to combine with dormant

---

2 A quarter into which this town is divided.

diseases to affect this, the death month. And then, by August or September, the attack of the locusts. The plague of locusts to announce the coming of the Harmatan. And finally the purification wrought by the Harmatan winds. The Harmatan, which forces the rebirth of our topography, a resetting of the dunes—as dune follows dune—perhaps to their ancient, original shapes and locations. A purification by sand. As year follows year.

I poured another.

In the deep of the night, without moonlight, a strange, almost soundless vibration sweeps over the desert. Just the hint of sound. A sort of hum. And now and then the cackling of a hyena to break that wind-borne hum.

Neither *Radio Nationale* nor Voice of America would come through this night. I resisted the urge to fetch the harmonica and belt out "Moscow Nights" and wake those commies up. Instead, I poured another one.

By rights, I should be keeping up with my memoires. Get it all down for the million dollar killing and a spot on broadcast television, radio—or whatever. But for now, I'm sniffing into the pre-Harmatan breeze, that phantom hint of the devastation to come. With the diseases. With the locusts.

This night he did not come.

Perhaps another night.

Perhaps.

■ Earl and Hank

February 1968

They flew in twice a month. When the landing strip was clear of all other planes since there was room enough only to park this large one. Usually a version of a C-130, or maybe a C-141. (At Peary they only briefly mentioned plane identification.) They flew in but never on the same day or at an appointed hour. The tarmac could handle this large plane—courtesy of our French predecessors—the tarmac, not the plane.

I think the locals found the plane a bit intimidating although some also worshipped it as if it were a magnificent and magnanimous god. And their leaders, the plane cult's self-appointed leaders, often told their followers that the goods would be coming with the plane— but through the powers of ancestor spirits.

Earl wore his air force blouse with name tag. Maybe to not be accused of being a spy if things went south. Hank never wore pieces of a uniform or identification and I think he was a civilian contractor. Or maybe he could have worn a name tag—the one with "CIA" stamped on it.

Earl always did the talking. Hank nodded a cursory hello, but rarely offered anything else. He would sometimes kick off heavier cardboard boxes with C-ration cans, from the airplane hold's door. Items meant for the locals? Spam-like ham, not *hallal*, and so I never offered any to my Muslim friends. But to my animist and Christian friends and my Hindu friend and colleague. The rations kept me partially off the local diet—off the brains, pigeons, liver, kidneys, *esh*, and brackish, probably unboiled water—for a time. Now and then there was a bottle of Johnny Walker included—to cure me in times of my distress.

As always when they arrived, a grungy dog stood in the sand, then laid down on the tarmac, as close as he dared get to the parking plane. He was khaki-colored but caked with the detritus of his wild existence. I am told that he was once a trained and civil dog close to his master. Now I think he led his wild ways late in the night.

He would meet all the planes, large and small, that came in. Then he would watch with mournful eyes as the passengers disembarked. When it was obvious that there were no more passengers, he would whimper for his master, for Evian, who never came. A true *Hatchiko* out of the Japanese tale about the everlasting loyalty of an Akita dog.

All the tarmac workers tolerated him. They called him Monsieur

Chien, out of respect, I think. He walked mostly with his head down, forlorn and in perpetual grief.

Chien would track us all, from a distance, day and night, loping with a sad slouch. But he would eventually go hunting elsewhere when we ignored him.

The disciples of the magic cult, waiting for the treasure their anima told them would soon come by the white man's plane, waited in silence in the brush at the side of the airfield. They were perhaps the last remnants of the anima believers. At least of the whole-hearted ones.

Earl broke the silence—the silence, but for Chien's whimpering. "We got that couple back to Algers. The Berinskis. Well, the woman died of heat exhaustion on the way. We flew them in from Faya. Glad we could do it." Then he added, "You watch yourself when you think you might be hangin' around the hostage takers. Them Wahidis. We don't want to have to bring you in as well."

Then more from Earl: "Here, take this, Harry. Keep it hidden until the system is up and running. The transceivers. The microwave. We only need the relays up through the Jumeaux Mountains. We'll let you know. Then tell us what's happening with this Wahid, and other information. Like what the camel militia are up to. All of this for our assessments."

Somebody else's eyes and ears. For their "assessments." Does Docteur Norman know? Dare I tell one about the other?

Earl handed me a pretty heavy box. Through the cracks in the wood I could see only packing material. "I don't know how to use it."

"You'll figure it out. Instructions inside." Hank grimaced—or smirked.

"But do you know we have no electricity here? How will I make it work?" I was looking for arguments that would allow me to hand it back.

"There's a miniature generator in the package. There are instructions on how to work up current for a short time. You'll have to keep your messages quick and short." I think this was the first time

Hank spoke to me with so many words. The first time he spoke full sentences, at least.

That was when I saw Lièvre, or the remains of Lièvre, carried on a gurney borne by the male nurses, Alphonse and Giscard. Covered with a flimsy, bloody sheet. The sheet slipped off his face, revealing the half I recognized, the other half of which had been virtually shot off. The bearers, nurses from the clinic, replaced the sheet when they noticed. I snapped that image in my mind for all time. I knew it would trouble me, but it was too late to erase it. I helped the nurses and Hank lift the gurney to the bay door.

Then Earl: "Forgive the pungent odors. It's the heat. The other bodies are still in the hold. Two of our boys, air force boys, ambushed near Ayin Saghir. Undercover types dressed like natives. But some Janjaweed or someone figured it out. And executed them both. Maybe for the crime of being white. What they call *Nasarah*. Probably AFSOC (air force Special Operations Command). We'll deliver them to the embassy in Djémélia. In the dead of the night."

So, as I'd done before, I strapped a C ration box to the back of my borrowed mount's saddle. Then the radio. I left the other C ration boxes for a second trip. Then I figured out how to balance the radio between my leg and the bridle wrap as I rode sidesaddle. As I strained with the effort, Modou, my Indian colleague, had more words with these visitors. But the odor from the plane's interior hung with me. I was too distracted and distraught to wonder what was said.

"Eyes and ears." And now "mouth" as well. I put the device encased in its pungent packing, in my so-called closet, in a lockable space, and hoped never to use it.

■ Life and Times

February 1968

Meanwhile, my social life had coalesced. Doctor Ivan Godin, from Leningrad, USSR, the *juge* Yokura Jean-Paul, my Indian-Hindu colleague Modou Chatterjee, and Father Sean O'Sagarty, when he passed through our town, were my sources of serious intellectual stimulation and challenge in this place. And serious consumption of whatever beverage was available.

Modou for sipping Scotch (and other weird stuff like *billy-billy* that he somehow obtained), usually on Monday nights. When he would reveal the mysteries of Hinduism. Which, he explained, "does not worship any one prophet or any one god with any particular rite or act, does not even believe in any one philosophic concept in fact, does not satisfy any of the traditional features of a religion. It is a way of life, governed by concepts of *Karma* and *Dharma*, rather than a typical religion or creed. And we try to understand the cosmos through meditation and good works."

"How do you do that?" I asked.

"What?"

"Meditate and do good works."

"Well, I think the teaching we do qualifies as good works, Harold.[3] Then I also take long walks through the town to better understand the milieu of our students, how they live. I spend many hours meditating in the quiet. Among the dunes. With only the desert wind and sand to remind me of constant change."

It was a joy for me to contrast the androgynous four-armed warrior God, Shiva, and the art of meditation with the often vengeful and childish God of the Hebrews or the seemingly confused God of the holy, Roman, Catholic, and apostolic Mother church—comparing them with these Hindu beliefs as documented in the *Yoga Sutra* and other *Sutras*.

Which *Sutras* the good-natured Father O'Sagarty and I explored with Modou's guidance. (Father O'Sagarty had particular interest in the *Kama Sutra*.) As we would also do in plowing our way though

---

[3] I never told Modou that my name was really "Harrison" not Harold. Anyway, I never told any French speaker my first name either since it was a precariously close homonym (really a heterograph) to "hérisson" in French—meaning a lowly hedgehog.

the ever turgid writings of St. Augustine and St. Thomas Aquinas as they tried to convince us of the Christian God's holiness and glory.

So with the *juge* and Douze Marches beer on Tuesday night when he would attack, and I defend, what he termed the callous and wayward ways of the world's most powerful nation. [Note from Aaron Hamblin: I'm not sure where in the chronology this belongs, so I'm inserting it here.] *Where I would learn he yearned to visit as soon as he could afford to. To find what he called "the truth." For himself.* [End of insert.]

And with Ivan Godin for his *ruskii chai*, the "Russian tea," the vodka brought in by his handlers, for Wednesday night.

His Soviet handlers came at least one Wednesday every month. To check on Docteur Godin's well being. And get the latest news. Perhaps, as Dr. Norman insisted, to exchange the daily news, drop stuff off, and deliver instructions from the *Kah Djay Bay* as the French and locals say—the KGB. I would spend any remaining nights with Terry and Joe drinking Douze Marches or with Michel and Victor for Pernod or whiskey at *Père* Habert's famous bar. More about *Père* Habert later.

Then there were the Saturday night *soirées* at the Social Centre. The men all did a slow shuffle they called the samba. The girls, the "bar girls" of Dar es Sabir, all danced more vivaciously and, with impeccable timing, ululated at breaks in the Latin music. Exceptional. I joined the men.

■   Dr. Godin

Wednesday was often our vodka night when we would play chess at Godin's cottage, except when his countrymen were remaining overnight. When they came the first time, he mumbled *"ne udobno…* not convenient…." for me. Not good for us to be in their presence.

When we were invited, I would usually lose at chess, though the good Doctor would throw a game from time to time to make me feel better. When we were in that particular state of vodka-induced merriment, we would belt out Russian and American folk songs. Docteur Godin was a fine singer. And he would usually beat me at vodka too. Then we'd go to the Scotch chasers.

"You know 'arry, we are not all, as you say, *Kah Djay Bay*. We are some of us here only to help these colonies, *da?*" he offered once, in labored, ungrammatical French.

And, by the way, report on the naïve young American as well as the latest discoveries, *da?* Of oil and water? And uranium? But he wasn't going to tell me anything. *Nyet*.

"Then why are you visited so often? From Djemélia, I assume. From your embassy."

And recognizable, as they arrived in a black, late model Lada in black suits and fedoras. As uncomfortable as I could imagine with the one hundred ten-degree heat. No wonder they always seemed so gruff. And they usually made the trip and return all in two days with an overnight in Godin's *kaz*, when the road was passable. Less likely to come in the rainy season. In those times we had to husband the vodka. The Scotch was never a problem.

"They concern. For my wellness. And they bring nourish and wodka."

"It's a mighty long trip from Djemélia to deliver food and vodka. Hell, they could fly it in. Including the caviar."

"Also I am grateful that they come to give me Russian language time also. I can talk freely for them. They are *Tovarishches* and they want to be sure I am not in *krompromat*. With you or others. Ha! Yes, I joke. And we joke, my countrymen, as well. For example, we will tell these Lada jokes from the homeland."

"Such as…?"

"I will try to tell in translate. What you call Lada at top of hill?" He gestured to make sure I got it. Then went to his French-Russian dictionary.

"I give up. What?

"Some miracle!" He laughs; I smile.

"Ok, 'arry. One more. What you call several Ladas at top of hill?"

"Several miracles?"

"Good try. You call it *scrapheap*." Thank goodness for the dictionary. Or we might be short a punch line or two.

"And sometimes they will fly it." Yeah, well that would go in my report.

"Your plane or this government's?"

"Of both." A tidbit to add to the report. This guy was spoiled. Air lifts and personal visits from the embassy. Jeesh. Probably caviar with the wodka. Maybe it will give my Corps folk ideas. I doubt it.

"This is the best one. Man goes into car shop and says to owner, 'Can I have one hub cap for my Lada?'"

"Owner thinks for moment and then answers, 'OK, it seems like fair trade.' Ha-ha! Hubcap for Lada! Fair trade! You get it, 'arry?"

"Yeah, I do. Pretty funny." It was ok. Maybe it was the translation, but they all sounded like Corvair jokes from home.

"So why do your superiors drive Ladas on these roads—if the cars are so bad?"

"To show CCCP making of autos so much better than Western making."

"Of course," I agreed.

Of course.

■   **With Godin and Prokaza (?)**

March 1968

I had little idea how Godin spent his days. And nights. Other than Wednesday evenings. I would find out soon enough.

In fact, it was one of those Russian parties on Wednesday night when, after we had but one shot of vodka, a courier came. He bowed to Godin in a funny way, then spoke of *maladie*. Godin said "There is a sickness in the village. I am called to the village of the *Prokaza* sufferers. I must go to see." Then he uttered a string of what may have been Russian curses—a string of consonances which sounded as if they were shouted (even when spoken quietly) in random order—from which I picked out *"ne udobno,"* "not convenient." Maybe since we were just getting warmed up.

I had no idea what he was talking about. "Could I come with you?"

That was when I received the note handed to me by Rashid, which I shoved unread into my pocket. Rashid made a clicking noise with his tongue and disappeared into the night.

"Da. Of course." I think he was happy for the company. I would soon know how he spent his nights. Up close!

So we mounted his Land Rover. And, of course, I couldn't resist. "How come you choose the Land Rover instead of a Lada?"

"Lada no good in sand but perfect in snow."

"And Lada jokes?" I reminded him.

He gave me a look that said, *"Tovarishch,* I just told you why. 'Lada no good in sand.'"

"And anyway, I thought Lada's were made to ride well in snow."

"Yes, *tovarishch,* but not sand. Da?"

He had enough of the prying *Amerikanski.* I figured I'd better let it go. *Da?*

We bumped over very rutted pathways until we hit the Sahara sand—going at first on the northern road, then turning off. We weren't harassed and challenged. I think they were lurking behind the dunes but left us alone—perhaps out of respect for the Doctor. Near a copse, Godin made a U to aim the Rover toward the road back to Dar es Sabir. I guessed in case we needed to make a quick exit. I asked why. Godin only put a forefinger to his lips to shush me.

"Yatu? Qui est?"

"Docteur."

"Kuoiyis. Bon." Then there was more exchange between that voice and another. Passwords.

No sooner had we gotten out of the Rover than a dwarflike little man with an elf-like gait came to greet us. "I am Abdel-Hamid. I am chief of this village. My father was of Dar es Sabir. He was once a chief…" I couldn't grasp the rest of his recitation. The patrimony. We were in an open area. I was following carefully behind Ivan, trying to stay as close behind him as possible. But away from the voice of the waddling Abdel-Hamid. He ushered us to a circle surrounded by large stones that served as our seats. We sat, and he offered us tea. The Doctor took a glass. He took the glass and then whispered to me, "No *ogon* for tea. No fire. They are perhaps expecting troubles." He indicated that I must take a glass as well. The tea was tepid and I did not feel it had been boiled. To protect myself, I knocked it back like a shot of whiskey.

All around our circle were shadows. Not even a fire evident for heating the tea, though I smelled hot charcoal that must have been doused as we arrived. A few inhabitants came out of the shadows, and it seemed in that blackness that every one of them was in some way afflicted. We were then ushered into a one-room hovel where someone lay on a pallet. I assumed this was the sick one.

Ivan moved toward the pallet; I hugged the nearest wall and felt obligated to sip the refill of the lukewarm tea.

Ivan bent over the afflicted one and checked the usual Doctor things. He mumbled to himself, strangely, in French and Russian. "Of course, this terrible *Prokaza*." Then he rummaged around in his doctor's bag and pulled out a small, vial-like bottle. "One of suppository capsules one day until finish. He will soon be better if he follows this. One by anal for one day!" he said to the entire gathering. I guess he hoped someone would listen. And understand.

Abdel-Hamid did. "Yes, one capsule each day. Into bunghole. But what is the malady, Doctor?" Then the two, Ivan and Abdel-Hamid, conferred in a corner, away from me and all the others. I couldn't grasp the content though, no doubt, both spoke in broken French. I thought I picked out several mentions of *"carabines."*

The Doctor then came over to me and announced *"La grippe."* Flu. They seemed pretty isolated and insulated here. I wondered how one of them would contract that. "One each one day." He shouted it this time as if Abdel-Hamid or the sick one were deaf. Then he made for a quick exit, and we were on our way back.

"How could he have contracted the flu in this little village?" I asked.

"He left village for somewhere. Maybe among whites who carry this flu from Europe.

Or maybe manifestation of *Prokaza*." Or arms trade.

"Will the pills cure him?"

"*Nema*. Nothing. Only in mind."

"Don't they risk spreading the disease to others?"

"Already done. You even sound like doctor, 'arry."

"Then what is *Prokaza*?"

"For you and me, as I don't know exact French for it, I will look up later. In doctor speech is caused by *pauci-bacillary et multi-bacillary* in medical French."

"Thanks."

"Always at the service, *Prokaza* and me." Maybe his sense of humor was better than the Lada jokes suggested.

■ Judgment

March 1968

As for the *juge*, our time was often passed with philosophical and political discussions. He was the judicial representative of the state, often in competition with the Muslim *imam* and (or) *Ulema*. For the *ulema* is thought to have the capability, through learning and wisdom, of judging those who transgress. And forgiving them. And giving them penance. For many, the *juge's* rulings did not count. So the *juge* had time on his hands to study other things. And to prepare himself for the Judicial Ministry to which it was rumored he would be appointed.

The *juge* usually slammed (and I defended) America and the presence of Americans in this country. Or our arrogance. A continuation, in substance, of the discussions often taking place between us.

"So you will bring to the heathen your great democracy, the democracy where a good portion of those people who bear African color cannot vote. Where Caucasian cowards make mischief in pointy white hats—and cover their faces."

"And you, your French patrons who taught you what they themselves believe. That we are crass materialists, yet religious fanatics. Except for me, Monsieur," I added, mocking Partenay.

"And yes," he went on, "where even those of the tribe that cannot vote are split into tribes, sous-tribes: one for those who would make a change but always follow the nonviolence and passivity and another for those who would use force to wrest their rights from the anglo-whites. And even the whites are in two sous-tribes: one to grant the vote to those of color, and one to use violence to deny those of African descent these rights. This is your panacea?"

Pretty good summary.

Or, for my riposte: "That we are all conformists—or wild cowboys. That all Americans are money-grubbing; yet full of their democracy. Except for me, Monsieur." (Grin to underline the sarcasm.) "That we brought back venereal diseases to Europe and, so, to Africa. Yes, and that, like the Jews of their imagination, we are all master capitalists, yet arch-socialists. That we were all short. Except for me, Monsieur. That, as that buffoon George de Buffon LeClerc asserted, all humans and animals were puny there because of the damp, dank New World climate; yes, and that dogs in America could not bark."

And:

The *juge* was ready: "Buffon was highly respected in his time and thought, by some, to be the father of evolution. Besides, what are you offering to sell us? You and your lectures about all men being equal. Your democracy? *Mon dieu!*" This is roughly what he said to me.

Or my response: "These are all these beliefs carried from Europe to Africa. This is your *héritage francais*! This is what you took away from your colonialists! Our President Lincoln once said 'A lie is halfway around the world while the truth is still putting on its pants.' *Mon dieu.*"

Then he said, seemingly out of character, "Still, I must someday come to see this Ooo Es Ah. If only I had the way to pay it."

With that tirade we exhausted ourselves. But there would be more as the Tuesdays rolled by. More back and forth and *"If only I had the way to pay it."* Almost as if he was asking me to pay for it.

Back and forth.

■ Like Torture before the End

April 1968

It may have been the illness—the desperation to sleep to mask the pain. And the constant treks to the back yard though I was barely able to squat. Or the contents of that syringe. It may have made me sleep, the sleep of—of the dead.

But then, it felt at first that I may have only been dreaming it. Movement and fluttering at the foot of my bed. Whispers and soft grunts swirling in the shadows. Accented by a flickering bright light and the constant creaking of a door.

And the quiet, rhythmic knocking of Rashid's head against our mud-dried wall. Then a silence.

The closet near the foot of my bed had a secret space, under padlock, where the colonials kept their valuables. Where I kept mine—and the radio.

I felt I was slipping in and out of this dream punctuated by the grunts that grew louder. As if a task was not succeeding. As if something could not be moved. I dreamt then of Alice, and my dog at home. And snow in a blizzard. But snow hot like the desert sands. Then I slept without the dreams until dawn.

I woke, looked around, and all seemed well. Rashid was pounding his head. I rose to go to the closet, but my legs would not hold me, and buckled under me. I hoped I could hold it in by fighting the pain. I didn't succeed, and I shit in the hallway. At the front door threshold.

I struggled to get back into bed by crawling inch by inch. With the help of the last tastes of my dreams to encourage me. And once more, among the bed clothes, I tried to sleep and waited for the medicals.

They finally came. Finally. Two of them. (The same who had carried Lièvre. Whose mangled face would always be with me.) Alphonse, the very thin, small one, the head nurse, pulled out the syringe.

"I am trying to rise." I gasped.

"Remain there, Monsieur."

"But I must use the toilet. Help me to the toilet." At first he made a sign as if to refuse saying "You have already soiled your sheets." Then he must have thought better of it. But my legs refused to carry me. Alphonse, small as he was, put my arm around his shoulder. The other nurse, called Giscard, went to the other side, and they carried me as I hobbled.

The pain was like torture—exacerbated, torturous pain. How it must be before death. Of course, the indoor commode itself was no longer functional, and it was now full of cockroaches. Mostly dead. Maybe killed by our human shit. So the nurses led me to the huge hole in back of the cottage where I was compelled to squat.

As he held me, Alphonse seemed to be watching my privates with fascination. Alphonse had it on with Evian? Or was Evian, alone, the only abuser of boys?

Then I felt the great urge and continued to squat as best I could. More came out, though I had eaten nothing since yesterday morning—and then only small bites. The pains returned. The toilet hole seemed to be filling up—without a working flush. I might have to dig another in our back yard.

Meanwhile, I caught a glimpse of the neighbor boy watching it all from a distance. And the rhythmic, quiet pounding of Rashid's head against our adobe wall.

"Is that yours?" Alphonse asked, pointing to the mess on the floor where I had left it.

"Or it belongs to a *djinnii*, a ghost with remarkably human characteristics," I answered.

"Then I must take some of the ghost's leavings to test for the disease." He had his assistant, Giscard, scoop some into a letter envelope. State-of-the-art testing facilities. Reinforcing my confidence in their medical diagnoses and cures.

"You can keep my sample!" I offered generously. But I could tell that neither Alphonse nor Giscard appreciated the attempt at humor. He led me back then and let me drop on the bed. He once again pulled out the syringe and checked its load.

"Is the needle sterilized? Did you wash and sterilize your hands" I forced myself to ask; yesterday I was too weak to do so.

"How is that, Monsieur?" Just as I suspected.

Then I changed the tack: "What is that, then?" I pointed to the syringe's load.

"Strychnine, Monsieur."

"Strychnine?. . . . I'll have no more!"

"But Monsieur, this will cure you. This will kill your germ." Alphonse seemed certain and serious.

"And do me in as well! This is what you have been shooting into me?"

"Yes, Monsieur."

"From yesterday?"

"Yes, Monsieur. Three doses yesterday. We were told it is the *Nasarah's* cure." Alphonse was getting nervous as this conversation continued. Giscard fidgeted by the doorway.

"Well I am no *Nasarah*, and yesterday's doses may be enough to cure me." I tried to speak and to look certain of myself. "Whose idea was this? To shoot me full of this." I was as angry as I could work myself up to be.

"Why, the Docteur Godin. And the directeur, Monsieur Partenay agreed as well...."

"Ah, Partenay, the medical doctor. And the Soviet. I countermand them. I do not need these shots!" I was on a tear by now.

So Alphonse packed his medicine bag, and then he and the quiet one withdrew. Leaving me to my pains and misery.

I faded off again but was awakened by Michel and Victor, my thoughtful colleagues. Mutt and Jeff. Michel, short and smart; Victor, huge and dim.

Also Chien, who hung back at the front door threshold—licking up the remaining product of my innards. The scientific term is "feculence." The polite term is "excrement." Via "defecation." Our everyday word is "shit." Whatever, Chien cleaned the threshold with his tongue.

"My, you're a lazy one." Michel quipped.

"It's the dysentery." I don't know why I felt obligated to make excuses.

"Yeah, yeah. Don't eat so much and you won't shit so much!" Michel advised. Victor smirked in agreement. I think they both really believed that.

"Here, try the French cure. It will go away much faster. Don't take their shots." He thrust a bottle under my nose.

"You tell me that now?"

"Five doses will kill you. It did so to Evian last year."

"That is not how…" Victor began but Michel cut him off.

"I've taken two."

"We've saved you. Now drink this!" It was the remains of a bottle of *Pernod*, somewhat watered down, I think, because it was a bit cloudy. I sipped it. I was not cured, but I was at *"relax."*

"And play with this." From behind his back, Michel brought out the tiniest puppy, black and white, of unidentifiable breed.

"Where did you find this one?" I asked.

"In the back of our *kaz*. Alone and no mother in sight. Someone left him to us. He is yours," Michel answered.

At that point, the puppy made a bark that sounded more like a chirping bird. I took him into my sickbed, whereupon he proceeded to urinate across the bed clothes. Then he burrowed into my own bed clothing. Thus were we bonded.

"I'll call him Kalb. From the Arabic for dog. Thank you again."

"Phew, this place stinks. What a mess it is…especially the floor here and this closet" was Victor's discerning and thoughtful observation.

"Not of my doing," I said. "Not the closet at least."

But Victor's gigantic torso blocked the inside of the closet from my view.

"Whose then?"

"Phantoms in the night. The *Djinnii* of the dark."

"They may look good in khaki. For I think it's your fine khaki suit, the one you wear on holidays, they've taken."

I experienced great relief. It appeared they came for only the wardrobe.

"And this," Victor added with a hint of victory in his voice. "This shelf is open. Where Evian kept the rifle. It's not there."

"One thinks Evian shot himself with it, you dunce." Michel again, irritated that Victor could not grasp the need for secrecy. "The police, Antoine, took it away for forensic study."

"Ah…"

I dared not ask if anything else was up there. They did not offer to tell me. "Here," Victor said and threw me my wallet. My life's savings was all there. They did not come for my money, nor the suit, I surmised.

"We hope you'll enjoy the dog," referring to the almost newborn black and white puppy.

"Wonderful! Very cute! And I'm very thankful." I was.

"We must go back to work…to cover for your absence. Keep drinking our cure." They left me the bottle and the puppy. And that fine reminder and remonstrance.

"Thanks for coming to cheer me up," and I forced a smile.

"Rest. And play with your dog." Michel went on. "For now, let him shit in your bed. Along with you. He will sniff it all. The mixing of the shit smells is a wonderful mode for attaching you two. Train him later. When you are cured. You will be cured of it in time."

"Only that it might return to you afterwards. Again and again." Victor interjected.

Always a catch, eh Victor? [Note from Aaron Hamblin: I'm not sure where in the chronology this belongs, so I'm inserting it here.] *But for years on, I will be forever cursed with the image of walking with a pants-load of diarrhea (an indignity which I imagined at each expulsion of gas, each miserable fart) and which became yet another symbol of my time there.* [End of insert.]

And meanwhile, Kalb had again relieved himself in my bed. Chien, who had sat quietly at the door, whimpered as Mutt and Jeff departed. Then he picked up where he left off, helpfully clearing the threshold where I had left a part of my inner contents, my excrement. Though he checked on me—on my attention to him—from time to time. I turned my back to the open door. I thought I heard him lick his chops, whimper once again, then depart.

I hoped that Chien would not befriend or influence my Kalb. But to my chagrin, it would probably turn out that Kalb would sometimes wait at the airfield with him.

Then I could see the closet, now that the giant, Victor, was no longer standing in front of it. The suit was gone. The loss of the wireless would be to the detriment of everything I was meant to do.

The wireless was gone.

■ Almost Yet Another Loss

April 1968

So I was contemplating this loss. As I negotiated the dunes behind my *kaz*. Lost in thought. Not unlike at the moment preceding the good-morning body-slam from Gerard. From GOD. When I wasn't paying attention. But this time more threatening and frightening. I must try to pay more attention!

For a carbine was pointed at my heart and, for me, no place to go. "Antoine! What are you doing?" I shouted to the *soi-disant* friend that seemed to be threatening me. For he was surely Antoine. The look on his face suggested that he was serious. Serious about doing me harm. And angry.

Just then, before I could even gulp, much less prostrate myself in fear, a replica of that one, of that Antoine, arrived and quickly jumped between us. A perfect replica, even unto the aviator sunglasses.

The first one shouted "What is this *Nasarah*? Why is such a *Nasarah*. . . ?. . . .Who are you to be so familiar with me?" he shouted at me, waving the carbine angrily and dancing around the replica.

"Alain, what's the matter with you? *Ça va pas la tête pour toi?*" A turn of phrase unique to this country. Translating roughly to "*Your head's not working right?*" "Do not harm this Américain," the replica shouted.

So I had been rescued. By the replica. The twin. Ah, by the true Antoine. Who had been called by the neighbor boy who saw it all. (And likely knew it all.) That is how Antoine had appeared. That is how the rumor of these twins was confirmed to me.

"Please explain this to me, Antoine," I demanded, still shaking. "I'm not provoking him!" And looking from one to the other of them, since I still had not identified each of these identical twins. Individually. I needed them to talk for me to determine their identity for certain.

"He provokes!" he cried, pointing to me. "I don't provoke!" Definitely not Antoine. Definitely his twin, and yet somehow different. So I sensed. And it was Alain who had nearly assassinated me. Antoine had determined that he, Alain, had misconstrued Wahid's instruction to "take care of that *Nasarah*" to mean eliminate me. Wahid had probably meant that he should take care to remove the bodies of Dr. Lièvre and Santiago before they are discovered half-eaten and dessicated in the desert.

Perhaps.

Alain, Antoine's identical twin brother, is a Wahid. It is "so we have family on each side, one for the Government, the other for the rebels," Antoine explained. Brother against brother, I thought. That phrase sounded familiar to me. "Whichever side wins takes care of the other one."

"Good God!" I exclaimed.

"Ah, that is good that you believe in God, Monsieur!"

"The one to whom I just prayed? Who rarely answers the prayers? Yes, that one," I said. It could be Gerard Olivier Dubois of the infamous acronym, I thought.

April 24, 1968

Aaron,

The last letter I sent you got returned to me too. By the censors. I must have written something sensitive, something not approved by the censors. Probably the Wahidi *(pronounced Wa-hee'dee as the "i's" are pronounced the French way like "ee") stuff. Or maybe it's the suspicious recipient!!!*

Is everyone all right? Janie? Mom and dad? I just went through a bout of dysentery but I'm ok now.

The kids are fun and seem to actually be learning English. Some are very adept and I'm beginning to meet their families too. Not all the parents are Bedouins or dirt-poor farmers. Some seem to be very well educated and one family consists of royalty—escapees, I am told, from some foreign troubles.

So, ok, it turns out that this Wahid *I mentioned before is something more than, or different than, a Robin Hood. It turns out that he comes from royalty, dethroned by the current, post-independence regime and not real happy about it. I'm a little bit disabused of the notion of heroism I attributed to him. On the other hand, knowing him will be a trip in itself! Besides, his enemy, the Militia and their colonel are some real sh**heads as* *are some of the French guys drilling for oil around here. To whom I have not been formally introduced.*

Oh yeah. I have a puppy given to me by my French colleagues. He's as cute as can be with his soprano, cough-like bark that sounds like the chirping of a bird.

I hope this letter doesn't get read by the powers that be. Otherwise…

Until the next one.

Your brother,
Harry

■ Terry

May 1968

That was a surprise. Even a bit of a shock. Terry leaning against the Land Rover, a half smile to welcome me, a pipe hanging smartly from his closed bite. It gave off a mellow scent. "Hey, *pardner.*"

Even that bothered me. "You the guy?"

"I'm the guy. How you doin'?"

Yes, I knew him well. "Well, thanks. Great to see you again. And so soon!" In fact, it was almost eight months since I last saw him. At the airport that day. To see me off. "Glad you made it to the land of your dreams."

"You mean after the washout? Might 'uv been a case of lost nerves…" But he didn't seem as distraught as he did when he was first told he'd washed out of training.

"Might'uv been. How'd you get through the roadblocks?"

"Friends in low places. So it's Joe who's hangin' out near the cop shed. You remember Joe?" Joe was another one of our washouts. He functioned best as Terry's minion. He liked his drink. He liked to play the stupid one. "We gonna run those towers across the desert."

"For?"

"Make the future come here to the livin' past. Microwave. line-of-sight. I'll give you a ride and look-see." He seemed excited by this venture. So we mounted his Land Rover and headed out of town, past the miniature mosque, through the town's crumbling walls and gates, onto the northern road that turned from brown clay and asphalt to sand after the first paved half kilometer. We passed the turnoff to the airfield.

"See there?" Pointing to a lonely pole in the ground. And to a mass of wire and pie-shaped devices beside it. "Joe got the pole and *wares* out here on the truck. We hired some local guys to help us out. We keep the satellite receivers and other valuables, all them doo-dads 'n stuff, locked up in a shed behind the police station. But the injuns have been takin' pot-shots at the pole, even without anything on 'em—might be a problem when we get to mounting it or after we get that stuff mounted."

"Sounds like a challenge. I guess you're taking this job seriously."

"You bet."

"What about the other one? The *other* job?"

"Glad you asked. Ah got some papers for you, just in from Djamé." But he didn't hand me anything. "Back in the shed."

"Takin' a chance?"

"You mean on their security? We're OK. We got my new good friend, Sheriff and Chief of Police, Antoine, watchin' things for us." Actually, Antoine the cop. Antoine the cop trained in France as a traffic patrolman. But there was not much traffic to patrol around here. Good thing, given his poor eyesight. So he used his initiative and took on other roles. Like "*Sherif.*" Which Terry, with his poor French, misheard. For he was no *Chef.* Of police or otherwise. Nor would he ever make us a feast.

I said "Good choice." No use disabusing Terry of the mirage-like, shifting-sand reality of this place and these things—all at once. He would just now be learning to taste the sand.

A shaggy, beige dog barked at us from an embankment along the roadway. It was Chien, warning us.

"Whoops! Injuns!" He did a fast U to avoid a straight-on

encounter with, I think, the *Tauregs*—and maybe some *Toubou* mixed in—camel- or horse-mounted and rifle-ready. They didn't give chase nor fire their weapons.

These are the guys who wear veils that give them a fierce look—that's probably the point—what the eyes say. I said, "Those guys used to police and guard the trade routes across the desert. No more need. So no more *baksheesh*, tolls and bribery money. Haven't gotten over it. They're called the blue people, you know, like those blue people of Hazard, Kentucky. But not inherited; rather because the indigo dye from their robes and especially their veils wears off on them. By the way, *Taureg* means 'abandoned by God' though they call themselves 'the free men.' Maybe the blue dye pisses them off too. Whatever, we want to keep out of their way."

"Maybe they'll want to keep out of *ar* way." Still, I guessed it would be a while before I saw a line of microwave poles installed out there. In fact, I bet this would be the first of Terry's several attempts to do work outside the northern gate.

"Saw 'em on the job yesterday afternoon. They took a shot at us; we took a shot at them. Wild West."

So Terry and Joe seemed to have gotten here at least yesterday, but only announced themselves to me today. And Jean, who knows everything going on in this town, didn't betray the "secret." Made me wonder. What other business they might have had. Already.

Terry sped back to the city, through the gate, around the deteriorating announcing stone carved "LeClercville," but with its letters scratched nearly clean by the desert sands and wind. Memorial to the great general. Fallen into ruins.

■ Mama's Fine Restaurant

"Let's have a quick one at Mama's," Terry suggested. Beer, fiery sauce, and sweltering heat. Good combination. Good idea. And how'd Terry know about Mama's?

"Ok, but I've got to ask—where'd you get the weed? There sure isn't any around here."

"Brought it from Texas. San Antonio way. From the best dealer. Ol' Judd."

"You mean there's more than that?"

"You bet. Want one? Keeps ya from smokin' cigarettes."

"I'll smoke cigarettes. Where's the rest?"

"Wrapped up in the police shed. With the other stuff." Good place to store it. With the cops.

Then we came to Mama's, deep in the northeastern *arrondissement* of the town. A stone-arch entry, then a mud hut with a tiny courtyard and benches. Two tables. Local fare and some remnants of another era. Of course, *Directeur* Partenay was there before us.

He greeted us with his usual panache. "Ah, now two Américain*s*. *Formida-a-able*! What have you brought us, Américain? What have you brought us this time?" But he never let me answer. "Why aren't you in the school, 'arry?" he went on.

"Day off."

"Ah, 'arry, you've brought yet another guest." It was Mama, the owner and chief cook, interrupting Partenay. In past times, chief chef in the only restaurant in town, now defunct. Strong, hefty, and never shy. Honored as a *grandmère* among her people. "Welcome again," she said to Terry in the local dialect. After a "What'd she say?" he bowed gracefully. Then she turned back to the "kitchen" and the *esh bou eké*.

"Of course." Partenay groused. "Cigarette?" I passed. Terry took one and slid the toke pipe into his shirt pocket.

"What'd she say? What's he sayin'?" Terry asked.

"She said welcome for another go, and this time she's not going to charge you extra for the exotic view," I translated. Loosely. He didn't react to the "another go." Nor did I.

"He's also sayin' why am I not in school. He's the principal, the *directeur*. I told him it's my day off."

"Good answer. Why isn't *he* in school?" A quick giggle. I think Terry had already had a toke or two.

"On his lunch break. Early lunch break; and it'll last the whole afternoon. He'll gather up his girls when he's drunk enough. Eventually go back to the wife who's prepared him dinner." It seems now that I was getting sloppy and anxious—doing the translation and answering the questions from both sides.

"What? Man after my own heart. What's a 'arry?'" He went on.

"Me. Harry. Most of these guys don't do h's. At least not the French guys. Unless they sigh, cough, or sneeze."

"He doesn't like us much."

"Old story. He'll tell us why when he gets drunk enough." He would.

"What a place!" Terry made that gesture with his head.

"True." Then I ordered, "Beer for everyone." Everyone being Partenay, Terry, and me. Big spender. So Jean, the house "boy," magically appeared at that moment to hand me the marketing change. Good timing. He gave Terry a cursory look, then quickly looked away.

"Ah, Jean. Have you met my compatriot, Terry?"

"Enchanté, Monsieur." Well played. He may have lied. Now I was developing just a little concern, just a little paranoia.

The service was performed by the most beautiful woman I had ever seen. Skin smooth as silk—the color of milk chocolate. Large, round eyes, comforting but not really inviting. I had never seen anyone like this. We were all served. I was momentarily mesmerized. These things happen. I think it had never happened to me before.

Partenay started in on his diatribe. Eyes rolled. We were on our first liter. He was probably on his third. On the Americans. How they destroyed his Normandy village and farm, killed his sister, during the 1944 invasion. During the invasion to loosen the grip of the occupying Nazis. A bomb gone awry. Or not, he speculated.

"...And then the gas blew up in the kitchen where she was making our soupée—the older one. Older sister—not kitchen."

"Where were you?"

"In the cellar. Plenty of time to get in the cellar. But she was intent on making the soupée, the lunch—showing off her capabilities to make the meal in place of our mum who was in Sabreville. She wouldn't come or answer our calls. Stubborn girl."

"Good move on the cellar!"

"I read books there for three days. Without sleep. As I trembled. It made my life—to become an educator, a *professeur* of French and history. My own life." He was slurring it now. "...not saving hers..." Hard to follow his train of thought, his slide into *patois*. "I should have..." He spewed on, "This is our last place. We can go no further. This is where they have put us. Our last place. As punishment. Carragh...!"

"Who is *they?*"

"The others. The ones who hate us most. Perhaps the Nazis. Perhaps the Jews. Perhaps the Nazis and the Jews. Perhaps the berbers, the Rifs."

He would go on: "Jews who manage our country's wealth. And direct who shall have it. A Riffian Berber....no written language but with a powerful will to fight. To protect what? Carragh...! No culture, no painting, no written language, no literature, no learning."

Terry leaned over to me and whispered in English: "Small man in big body who suffered great fear-inducing trauma when a child—will now punish all the world for it." Astute.

And at that moment we were saved from the rest of his diatribe by the appearance of the *Légionnaire Capitaine*.

"*Messieurs et Dames.*" He gave us a smart salute. "Ah, but there are no ladies here. What a pity." Same joke, different day. The *guépard*, his cheetah—or panther—that was always at his side—sat. Subservient to him but threatening to the rest of us.

"There's Mama! There's the...the beautiful one... (named Amina)," I offered—or thought.

He gave me that look, then extended his left arm. An awkward moment for Terry and me. We took our signal from Partenay and extended our right ones in salutation. It was said that he'd left his own right arm in Algeria.

For France.

His ever-faithful *guépard*, his cheetah, always loped at his side. It seemed to me that he was ever ready to pounce. We exaggerated our friendliness to the *Capitaine* for the *guépard*'s sake. Ok, for our own sakes. In our effort to make the *guépard* as comfortable with our presence, and our interaction with his master, as we could.

"He has well chosen," Antoine once told me. "For among my people, the *guépard* is the wandering soul of the ancestors searching for rest that would be brought by an accounting of deeds. The *Capitaine* is wise to have one accompany him wherever he goes. It will keep him safe from all the tribes."

The *capitaine*'s story came to us in dribs: how he had been a *Légionnaire* originally from the German-patois side of Alsace; had fought for the French since Dien Bien Phu; had perfected his French to give him the credibility of command, Alsacien-accented though his speech might be.

"A beer, sir?" I offered in what I intended to be a gracious tone. And hoping that his companion would deem it so.

"I truly would like one." The *guépard* sat and squinted. Menacingly.

We shared pleasantries and news of the day.

After the first liter and a call for the second, the *juge* stepped in and took a place in our circle. "Good day to everyone, and I hope you're all behaving." The *juge* always spoke with a gleam in his eye, though I had been told he was hell on miscreants and those who displeased him.

The *capitaine*, though, gave him a look that could be interpreted as disgust.

"I was just telling our new visitor how it was with the Americans in Normandy."

"Ah, yes. Normandy. And now you're *here* to bring us your shiny democracy" the *juge* added, turning to me.

"That's it." Terry said after my translation.

"That's it," I offered.

"While meanwhile you assassinate your leaders at your own

home, one by tragic one" the *juge* added, holding up a recent edition of *Le Monde*.

"It's not necessary to respond" the *capitaine* said to me. Or did he simply mouth it?

"Yes. I mean no, we do not assassinate all our leaders. Recent events just show that some of these crazies are more fanatical than others." I had no idea what I meant.

The *juge* pondered my weak response and carried on. "So you will bring to the heathen your great democracy, the democracy where a good portion of those people once from Africa, the black-brown color, cannot vote. And are not sure what to do about that…"

And I was too full of myself to know when and how to keep quiet. "And you, your French patrons taught you that we are crass materialists, but also religious fanatics. Except for me, Monsieur" I added, mocking Partenay. "That we brought over venereal diseases to Europe. That we were all short. Except for me, Monsieur. *Mon dieu!*"

With that tirade I had exhausted myself and perhaps he had as well.

"*Touché,*" Terry would say after each of my pronouncements, even though he understood only some of what I said. "*Touché.*" Thanks Terry.

"To our ancestors," the *juge* offered as he lifted his drink and, as was the Sara-Ngumbaye custom, poured some drops on the ground.

To the ancestors.

The beautiful one no longer came out to serve us. I guessed I wouldn't ask her on a date after all.

Not that day.

April 16, 1968

Aaron,

Yeah, I know. It's been awhile. Since my last letter got returned to me. Something in it offended the censors or whoever reads this stuff. Who knows if their translator gets the English right anyway. At least it hadn't been redacted and forwarded on to you—unreadable. Well, you know me. I'll still persist.

I hope everyone's doing well. How's school going for you? Still acing all your courses? Jeesh, you're embarrassing me! You may be an embarrassment to the whole family! Keep up the good work, brother!

Thanks for the birthday card. It got through the censors. This very day! I won't mention how old I am, hoping you and everyone else might then forget it.

I live in this cottage, called a "case" in French (pronounced "kaz" by the locals) at one end of the parade ground where once the French colonials had lived. Not far from twin black mountains that loom to the south. The place is pretty well infested with a variety of lizards and chameleons, none of them threatening. A cute little hedgehog, what the natives call a hérissons, to give me more intimate company. Once in a while, I see a svelte gazelle roaming the environs. There's an annoying ostrich that hangs around here and comes running at me at times, and I hear the cough-laugh of a hyena in the dunes nearby in the late night.

As for the people, they're a mix of Northerners, Bedouin and Maghrebi Arabs, Bantu Southerners up from the rainforest, and what I call Sahelians, a veritable melting pot (sort of) of Northerners and Southerners, Arabs and Sara-Ngumbai Southern Bantu. An interesting mix with tribal loyalties, competitions and jealousies.

I'm settled in, begun new school year classes, made acquaintances—a lot of them. I'll be mentioning some of them in my letters.

One stands out for me. This Wahid *character, leader of a group of bandits. Or maybe rebels. His given name is Hassan Ibn Jema'a. Jema'a bespeaks "royalty." I've been trying to get a meeting with him. His arch-enemy is the National Militia Capitaine Martin Ngokuru, a perfect a**h*le.*

Also, there's this beautiful princess—she could be a princess. Her given name is Amina bint Mohammed al Albri. She's a rare beauty with huge black eyes, silken hair, complexion brown like crème de café. I could go on, but I'm not waxing particularly eloquent nor can I do her justice. I see her now and then as she goes to the medical clinic in her tiny blue Deux Chevaux (she must have a chronic health problem to go there so often), driven by a male relative, or on a donkey also led by a male, no doubt from her family. Veiled (though her veils are of suggestively transparent cloth) and, yes, I often watch her descend from the donkey or car—the abaya, in some places sheer, fits her figure nicely.

Yet always with smiling eyes.

I better not go on much more or the censors will deem this letter too salacious to be sent.

Yeah, there are many characters that I know in this little town, but these letters will be enough of a reference if you ever see the notes I am keeping. So I hear these Nasarah *(there I go—just like the rest) letters get read by censors before going out to the world. By the way, the locals as well as the other foreigners refer to me in different ways—étranger,* Emricani, Américain, Nasarah, *even Français from time to time—and don't know what to make of me.*

In future, I'll watch my language. But I'll stick any returned-by-censors letters in with my diary notes so

you can see what you were not permitted to read—as
soon as I return.

[NOTE: Aaron here--I never saw this letter
until now.]

Your brother,
Harry

■ Epiphany

It was then that it came to me. Thanks to a healthy dose of
Douze Marches. That the theft of the radio could be fortuitous. That
the thieves could tune the stolen one to our microwave, our 3,400
Hz frequency for voice, and listen to our communications. (Gerard
Olivier Dubois's job?). And that we then could devise whatever it was
that we wanted them to hear. But how to ensure that they have the
correct codes?

Next flight in, I asked Hank.

"You mean the one you let get away?" He had to dig the knife in.

"Yes. Were the codes the same as the one you delivered to me
afterward?"

"Of course not. Each one is coded to read the other, and the
encryption is different for each one."

"Then can the second one you delivered to me be encoded to be
readable to the stolen one as well as to our HQ?"

"If we use what we call the 'open' one. If we had the open code
of the one stolen. Or knew their algorithm for decoding." He was
dancing around the issue. "But that won't be necessary. Just keep this
one on its current setting."

"At that setting would they be able to understand us?"

"Yes."

"Then what if I didn't want them to understand?"

He saw where I was going. "Then flip the switch and you're in secret Morse mode. That's all." He said I could send and receive without the codes, since they would be ciphered and deciphered automatically by the devices. Each device had two ciphers and deciphers. Hank probably concluded that giving me a copy of the codes would be an unnecessary risk. Or he might have been pulling my leg about the tech things.

"How can we get that one set up?"

"It would have to be delivered to you by us. Or by Doctor Norman." Ah, "Doctor Norman." A sign of respect or a mere automatic honorific?

"But you're not due again for what, a month? And there's no plan for Leonard to come up. Beside which, I hear the road from Djamé to Albri is periodically cut off. I'd need it soon." The rumor was that the Wahidi had cut off the roads near Albri as well. "And finally there would also be the impassable summertime road floods."

Hank may have also been pulling my leg about the codes. Then he just shrugged like a Frenchman and gave me that look—the look emphasizing the hopelessness that he must have attributed to me.

■ School Days

June 1968

Partenay was in close and animated conversation with the *Capitaine* Ngokuru of the National militia in front of his *bureau*. When he saw me, he quickly cut off that conversation and came trudging up just as I was stepping into the school room.

"Good morning, Monsieur *le Directeur*."

"Good morning, Monsieur 'arry. You are bright and early for once. "Why are you so early?".

"I have these comp books to review and grade."

"The *Capitaine* tells me the Wahidi are on the run. It is as *Radio Nationale* says. They should be of no more trouble for us. No more bother with this 'situation.'" As if this would answer my questions about his *tête-a-tête* with Ngokuru and quell any doubts I may have about the current "situation."

"Ah-ha. And where is your Deux Chevaux?" I asked.

"*En panne,* the piece of shit." And then he added. "Carraagh," to clear yesterday's tobacco.

"Ah. Sorry to hear that." I decided not to ask about the health and whereabouts of young Fatima. So with an expression of sympathy, for whatever, I slipped into the classroom, the *Quatrième,* sat at the teacher's desk, cleared my eyes of the sand, and began to read the latest composition entries, heartbreaking as they were.

The assignment was to write a short essay in English. The topic was "My Plans for the Future."

Here's one:

> *I plan go to Université de Djemélia to make my road to Sorbonne and become the physician. Then I will examine peoples merde under des microscopes to find their malady. Like the sand sickness. I will then cure people with the strychnine shots and other medicines. This is how I would serve this state and my people. But not the Moundang.*

Short, clear, to the point, and hopeless.

Another more hopeful one:

> *I want to become soldier to live in the discipline and become a officer. I want to be trained by Légion with we must form allies. Together, us and the Nasarah Légion, to beat the merde out of the Toubou and Taureg Wahidi.*

A reasonable one:

> *I will become a soldier to fill up my national duty. Then I will take the quit money and buy a farmland. I will work this farmland and grow millet, gum Arabic, and cram-cram.*

One more:

> *I will be a priest. If that is too merdique, I will become a revolutionary. They are the same thing. I am Hassan of the Toubou.*

Likely he will have his hopes fulfilled.

I noticed that many of these essays had given attention to *merde.* I guess I have to teach them "bowel movement."

Or "excrement."

Or "shit."

■ Moussa

July 4, 1968

It was this day that Jean led a limping horse into our "back forty." It was covered with sand and even mud, and looked like it was on a starvation diet. It had a severe limp. It may have been a roan. With all the filth, it was hard to tell. It was certainly a gelding.

"What have you brought, Jean?"

"A horse, Monsieur."

"Yes, I can see that. Why have you brought it here?"

"It was being sold for its meat. Only 1,300CFA[4] because it is so thin. I bought it with the shopping money you gave me." I must have

---

[4] CFA stands for *Communauté Financière d'Afrique*, the monetary unit used throught this part of Africa, where 250CFA = 1 $USD.

flushed and assumed that scowl of irritation that was so transparent with me, for he added: "It was being sold for its meat, since it could no longer work. I thought you might wish it for your *soupée*—this one and some to come."

Of course, this took me completely off guard. "I...I don't eat horse meat."

"Ah, you are certainly not like the other *Nasarah*. The other *Nisarah take* great appetite for this horse meat. I should have asked you. But it was about to be slaughtered by someone anyway."

"I don't like horse meat and don't want to see a horse slaughtered."

"Of course not, Monsieur." Jean could certainly play at being the obsequious one.

I was not much of a horseman, but grew up where the families of many of my friends owned horses. For their leisure and exercise. "Then for now, we'll put him in that out-shed where you often sleep. I'll show you and Rashid how to groom him. We'll inspect that leg and hoof."

"Yes, Monsieur. I was about to suggest that we install him thusly and fix his leg. Thank you, Monsieur." Jean's simulated obsequiousness could be infuriating. Still this was when he learned to ask first before making unusual purchases. Of course, I was served a vegetarian dinner of cucumber salad and boiled carrots. And a ballet of headless chickens running around in cacaphonic, random circles in front of me.

As I ate, I calmed down and offered, "Never fear, Jean. I am grateful for your thoughtfulness. If you groom this one, I will pay you more."

"I am grateful for your gratitude. How much more?"

I took a whack at it: "1,000CFA. Per month." The equivalent of about USD4.00.

"For *that* I would clean this animal?"

"And feed it."

"Monsieur?"

"Ok. 1,000CFA plus $2US."

"Done." (I was grateful. Jean was grateful that I was so.) And so it was done.

"We'll call him Moussa, named after a vibrant, curious, religious, and studious student."

"The people will be pleased to hear that. The *Imam* will be pleased as well." And I was sure that Jean would ensure that they heard.

I tried to remember the grooming lessons and techniques for hoof and leg repair that I had gotten as a teenager. I thought I would have to rely on my own first aid kit since the veterinarian had been killed. But then I broke into his cottage office and helped myself to the medicines and bandages there. His first aid supply was better than what the Corps had provided me; and as good as the town clinic's. Then, in the market, Jean found what would pass for a curry comb.

"Do it thusly, in a circular motion," I told him and showed him how. At first he insisted on combing down and up the legs. "No, no. Do the legs and head with a soft cloth. I'll give you one of my bath towels. Watch me again."

I used a screwdriver as a hoof pick to remove the sand and rock from Moussa's wounded hoof, and then I cleaned the area thoroughly. Next I applied an iodine salve solution to the right hoof where it bled and wrapped it in bandages. The veterinarian had some thrush antibiotic as well. Then I wrapped the lower left leg, although there was no evidence of cut or breakage. Only this, and Moussa was on his way to good health.

Moussa was silent and stoic throughout the treatment.

"Jean, apply this iodine and antibiotic salve once every day to the wounded hoof, and it will heal. We'll unwrap the leg bandage in a week." So Jean, Rashid, and Moussa became fast friends. Especially Rashid. They took walks together. They often slept together in the out-shed. Moussa seemed not to mind Rashid's head pounding.

And, after a week of combing and hoof salve, Moussa was healing well and looking bright. His coat shone like brown cured leather with flecks of white throughout. Then I rode him—but slowly at first.

With only a blanket until I could procure a proper saddle. And I would ride him daily, at a casual trot plus a few sprints, once he was fully healed.

I quickly learned to keep Moussa away from other horses, since he would bite, kick, and snort in their proximity. At times, he would become furious, and uncontrollable.

But with little Kalb he was different. Kalb was excited about this newcomer and let him know it by yapping incessantly as he danced around him. Kalb decided he would be in charge of chasing off the chickens that invaded Moussa's space. And he yapped at the monster ostrich that rummaged through our leavings during the day and at the hyenas that foraged at night—enough for them to keep their distance. Kalb would follow or lead Moussa—or both. But mostly Kalb ran around and between Moussa's legs, as if they were playing— being just missed by a hoof now and then. Moussa seemed not to mind. Rashid smiled only at these times. Chien, however, watched but kept his distance.

Moussa seemed to take to all of us, Jean and me as well as Rashid and Kalb, whinnying when he saw us coming and nuzzling us often, as if he knew we had saved him from the meat grinder.

■ Amina

July 1968

I finally arranged a date with Amina, the beautiful one from Mama's Fine Restaurant... Amina who served us beer and *esh* at mama's.

Though she served the beer, she still practiced her faith as her people knew it, picking and choosing among the Koranic *ayats* and commentaries. For this one, to justify the animal's use as more than as a beast of burden, they seem to have borrowed a twist on the *ayat* that *"when you hear the braying of donkeys, seek Refuge with Allah from Satan for (their braying indicates that) they have seen a devil."* The donkey for protection? I always thought the braying meant "I live here so you other males back off!" A sort of first dibs on the females. I guess I had it wrong.

All by way of explaining why females in this country rode the donkey—as a kind of superstitious protection. The human male gets to walk alongside. Or ride on horseback. Or there was the blue Deux Chevaux parked in front of her wall. But that last didn't at first register with me.

Yes, taking this ride with Amina was certainly a totally "different" experience. So that, when I rode up on Moussa, and offered that she ride before or behind me, she refused. "*Hamar*" she said. "I must ride on the *Hamar*." "Not you" she added to reassure me. But when I looked at her quizzically she repeated "*Hamar, Hamar.*" With that lovely laugh. I knew she meant a live donkey, but it occurred to me that she might also be calling me one. A *double entendre?*

And I signaled with my forefinger, turned on my heels, mounted Moussa, and urged him on in the half-mile run to the cottage, praying that Jean and his donkey were there. Moussa was now well fed, well groomed, and well muscled. He could sprint like the wind. And did. I dodged pedestrians, and there were many who were certainly impressed by Moussa's speed and agility. I left him at my door so, if I found a donkey, I could ride it back.

"Jean," I said breathlessly.

"Monsieur?"

"I must borrow your *Hamar*."

"Of. course, Monsieur. Here he is. I have named him Omar." Omar the *Hamar*. The more I learned about Jean...

I left Moussa at my door. "Sorry, buddy, this one's for me." He made that fluttering sound, as if in consent. As if to say "Go get her, buddy."

I grabbed Omar's bridle, said the appropriate "Thank you. May the ancestors bless you," and headed back to the residence of Amina. But Omar had his own pace and sense of time; I was forced to adopt it.

So I arrived more tardy than "appropriate." Amina had taken to her mat in the courtyard again and resumed her exchange of rumors and gossip with an elderly woman. But she remained costumed in her exotic garb festooned with multicolored filigree and many golden bracelets. And a touch of henna.

"Madame Amina," I breathed out. "Here is the *Hamar.*"

"So kind of you." In her sing-song. Again, my heart took an extra skip.

She mounted (no help from me accepted) and we made our way—I, on foot, leading the *Hamar.*

Amina talked the town gossip, such as Hamid's infidelity with Miriam, dishonoring his first wife, Fatima, and I had no idea what the stories were about. Until I think she said "My cousin, Hassan Ibn Jema'a …called A Wahid…"

"You know this one?" I was astounded and caught off guard.

"Yes, he is my cousin."

"Many fear him." I stammered.

"He rides with ferocious bandits and, sometimes, the Janjawid."

"They say he too is a bandit," I pressed on.

"Only to take back what is rightly his. For all this land was ruled by our family until the arrival of the *Nasarah.*"

"Then you are of the royal family?"

"Yes, of *Derdre.* The first of all the families. The *Alwahla.*"

I wanted to ask why then she waited tables, but first I had a more important question: "You know him?"

"As I said, he is my cousin, of the same family. All one. And I was once his betrothed."

I wasn't prepared for this one and surely showed my astonishment. Then, as if to underscore our newfound solidarity, she drew a fine cotton handkerchief from her sleeve. "Here, you may hold this part of the handkerchief as a sign of my esteem." Or am I making the *"estime"* part up? From my dreams?

[Note from Aaron Hamblin: I'm not sure where in the chronology this belongs, so I'm inserting it here.] *Now I understand that women of her stature and faith would not hold the hand of a male friend, especially*

a "lover." The handkerchief was their sign of affection. Or so I was later
told. For the moment, this remained a mystery. I eventually surmised,
as it so signaled, that I would not share her bed. Nor her mine. Until
marriage, so I was led to believe. Hard luck. Worse than the girls at St.
Julienne. [End of insert.]

So, for the moment, I walked beside Amina, who was mounted
on Moussa's donkey, Omar. To go out beyond the town wall and on
to the southern trail that led toward Albri. Where I hoped to go later.

It was just no more than two kilometers from the town walls that
we spotted the *Taureg* or *Toubou*. Or both. Lining up as if to form a
road block, mounted and seemingly in the same robes and clothing
as yesterday—yesterday when we, Terry and I, attempted to drive
beyond the gates to inspect the microwave structures.

This time I blinked hard into the shimmering, almost visible
heat. Then I squinted as I was taught to do. You blink, then squeeze
your eyes shut. You hope, when opening your eyes, that it is indeed
a mirage you are seeing.

It was not.

I instinctively began a U-turn to head back to the town walls. The
poor excuse for town guards had come back from their afternoon-
long lunch and were at the ready, if you can call it that, behind the
walls. The guards would challenge us, but a few words from Amina
and we would be motioned through. But not so easy with the *Taureg*.
Or *Toubou*.

Meanwhile, when Omar, seeing the rough-looking contingent,
halted, not wishing to challenge them, she would whisper in his ear.
I can only imagine what it might sound and feel like. Only wish it
for myself. After each whisper, Omar would move again, towards the
ruffians, at least another fifty meters.

But "It's all right," she said to me. All right for her! "Those ones
ride with the Wahid and know me well."

"But they don't know *me*."

"You are well dressed for this encounter. Though your colors are
some bright." Did I mention that I was wearing my fancy red-brown

jalabah? The bachelor color? "Here, wear this blue cap," she offered. "It is not the *tarboosh*, but will fit you well. Speak only salutation."

"Why are they here?"

"Perhaps to keep their eye on me. My cousin is protecting me."

She insisted we go forward, each of us holding one end of the handkerchief. This gesture would be conveyed to Wahid—to no good end, I think. Amina remained on the donkey and I walked beside, feeling foolish and a bit fearful as well. It was then, before we reached the ragged group, that I dared ask her, "Can you set up a meeting with me and Abu Wahid?" I felt I needed her extra push. "I will be alone. Only me."

She looked at me quizzically for a long moment and then turned to face the horsemen. "*Salaam alékum, rafi'igim.*"

"*Salaam, Amina bint Mohammed al Albri.*" They were a motley bunch, dressed mostly in grey *jalabas* with a few in dapper pale blue. Each wore a wrap-around turban, mostly white and some red-checked like an Italian-restaurant table cloth. One wore a Kansas City Athletics baseball cap on top of his turban-like head wrap. For me, nostalgic memory of home.

Yeah, right. I was a Cleveland fan in those days.

"*Kif halékum?*" How are you—and so on. Salutations are an exhausting protocol in this culture, always ending in "*alhamdulillā,*" a sort of "Praise be to God," I think. Always with right hand over heart, like the Pledge of Allegiance—only personalized.

They seemed only to glance at me and not to take too much notice. I did likewise. Trying to blend into the background was tricky.

I thought she had not heard me, but then, amidst all the palaver and exchange of gossip—"How's Hamid and his new wife?" or "Is Astar recovered from the difficult birth?" or "Daoud has lost his urges" (I was interested to hear more about Daoud's urges)—she responded to the questions. I was only half listening to the to-and-fro when I think I heard her ask of them, "When could we meet Wahid himself? This man has said Abu Wahid is his hero, and he would like to salute him."

"This one very much looks like a *Nasarah*."

"Half of Emricani, half of our people. His mother was Saali of the Djewadi family."

There was an instance of silence and, for the first time, they looked at me squarely and up and down. It seemed that they where examining me for signs of that illness—*Nasarah*. I kept my head well down. And thanked the lord for my suntan.

I would trip over the *Shahadah*, "the testimony"— the Islamic creed declaring belief in the oneness of God and that Muhammad is God's prophet—in Arabic, if asked. Instead, I was asked to recite my patrimony. Harry ibn Guillaum, grandson ibn Ethan of the Johnson tribe of the Hamblin family. And they seemed satisfied.

"He is only just returned from Emrica, but he has learned our language well."

"He looks familiar, like the school teacher. Is he in nature with you? Or is that another one?" Or something to that effect. A most indiscrete question from the one with the baseball cap—almost an accusation, I thought.

That comment set her off. "I am Amina bint Mohammed al Albri, of the Alwahla, cousin to Abu Wahid! Do not suspect my honor!"

"Forgive me, then, O Amina bint Mohammed al Albri." The big mouth looked like he was going to shit his pants—or pantaloons. "I meant no disrespect," he quickly added.

He was the one who wore the Kansas City Athletics cap which added to my irritation with him.

No disrespect. Yeah, sure.

"I will be at this meeting between this one and my cousin, Lord Wahid. I guarantee that all will go well." Or something to that effect.

The gang seemed satisfied and the big mouth, shamefaced, had already turned his horse, preparing to make his escape. I think he was praying that she would not mention his indiscretion to Wahid.

The salutations were repeated ending with "*Alhamdulillah*." As they turned into the sun, I noticed how young members of this gang were barely bearded. They completed their about-face and rode off at a fast trot, soon lost in the dust and sand.

I easily managed to U-turn Omar and lead him, and Amina atop him, back to the town gates.

To make conversation, I asked her why she never married Abu Wahid. I was rewarded with a flushed face and angry pout. But she answered, "He would always be rebellious. I could not live this life, a life on the run, and certainly not with the other wives who would resent me as their chief wife. Also there are the Janjaweed, his sometime allies. Besides, my father and mother had, before they were killed in the Ain Saghir and Albri raid (executed by the Janjaweed, or a rogue offshoot so it is said), refused the *mahr* (the dowry) from such ill-gotten gains, to be brought to the marriage."

"Did your parents tell you this, may they be in blessed heaven? Did Wahid?" I dared ask.

At that point, she pulled the handkerchief out of my grasp and stuffed it into her blouse sleeve. I then knew I had gone too far.

"Abu Wahid said nothing."

I fell silent—the only thing I knew to do. I wondered if Wahid, pissed off by the rejection of the *mahr*, was implicated in her parents' murder. I assumed I would have to wait a time to restart our friendship.

A long time.

■ **More Dates with Amina**

August 1968

But not that long.

I was asked to take tea with her not a week later. Where I was introduced to her confusing cadre of aunts, uncles, cousins, sisters, and brothers, who then offered me a seat with the males. There was a lot of silence. Perhaps the men, unlike the loquacious women, were too shy. Perhaps they didn't like this "half *Nasarah*." Perhaps they were afraid of offending Wahid.

But they were generous with the sugar.

I waited until they all finally left. All but the uncle who would remain her guardian until I left. Lots of *alḥamdulillās* on their way out. I went out, but lingered at the front gate to see who would take the blue Deux Chevaux.

No one did.

[Note from Aaron Hamblin: I'm not sure where in the chronology this belongs, so I'm inserting it here.] *There were several "dates"—minus the shared handkerchief. Leading me nowhere.*

Except with the one other promenade. The near to last one, where I told her of our plans. I did not offer her a reservation on the plane or on our trek over the mountain. I waited for her to ask for one. She did not. For this outing, we shared the handkerchief once again.

It was when she asked if "you, Nasarah, also take four wives?"

"I am no Nasarah" I answered with some hesitation but added that, in my Emricani *world, we were only allowed one wife. "The more to offer four times the romance to the chosen one" than a quarter of a romance to each of the four of them.*

"Oh?" she sometime later asked, without a moment's thought, "then do you not have the one in the lovely Miriam?" I was never able to respond to that one.

Also she once stated that "All of you, all you Nasarah, are spies. I believe you are Say Ee Ah and Godin is Kah Jay Bay. It is most funny, for poor us to be the object of so many spies." She laughed in her lovely way. "Know too that there are spies within the Militia and government and no doubt others among the Wahidi. Who knows, perhaps I, too, am a sort of spy since I collect the information off the tongues of those I wait tables for. And pass it to Mama, chief of the National Party for Dar es Sabir."

And then she shared this gem: "If it weren't for these spies, we wouldn't need more spies."

"How would you think I am a spy?" I protested. "I who am but a school teacher."

She laughed, then added "And probably the French teachers as well. Perhaps the Docteur was one." Of course, she began to tear up at the mention of the Docteur and thereafter returned to her happier gossip. But I never found out if Daoud recovered his urges. Or how he lost them in the first place.

Another memorable moment when she asked "Where do the noses go?"

"For what?" I replied, not understanding what she was getting at.

"When you Nasarah kiss. We don't do that thing here. How do you do it? How do you place the noses?"

"With great passion," I answered. I was too taken aback to say any more. However, I think I asked her if she would like to try it.

At this point, she demurred and instead, without another word, shoved the scented handkerchief at me. As a sort of grudging gift. I still keep it in my front shirt pocket, a wistful reminder.

Even so, the remainder of our outings always included hints of her underlying displeasure. Or maybe disdain.

That's it. Disdain. [End of insert.]

■ Judgment

August 14, 1968

It was one of those Wednesdays, with Godin MIA, so we gathered at my *kaz* on what passed for the courtyard behind—inches from the wild undergrowth, dirt and the beginnings of the miniature sand dunes. The chief of police, a jolly fellow, joined us.

And the *juge* fell into one of his argumentative moods. First he argued with my newfound friend, the *imam* in his black *jalaba*, about some point of law that contradicted *Sharia*. Then, when he must have tired of that, he turned to me. "I'm still challenging you, 'arry." He was referring to the peace overtures that I mentioned to him, but that I hadn't really made yet.

"Yes, I tried . . ."

"You did indeed . . . but it was destined to happen anyway, sooner or later, eh? That would be your answer, *non?*"

"Yes." It was. To so answer will help me to shed some of my guilt. For not yet making the effort. Yet.

"We don't need your help, your do-gooder shiny toys and Hollywood culture, to make our way. That's the problem with both sides. Soon you will be looking down upon us, in yet another way, spying on us from your spaceships in the sky. Or from the moon itself. This will happen soon! Perhaps it already happens!" Now he was working himself up. A slight change of subject carried him on. "I have studied your country and especially your Constitution and the war between the states fought a little more than a hundred years ago."

"That's great." I was trying to smooth over the potential for another "cock-up" discussion, to move on to the weather or dinner or another more placid topic. He would have none of it.

So as we sat and cooled in the evening breeze, he went on. "In your Constitution, for the ten-year census, your Africans count only as three fifths of a man. That is us.

"For example, there was the Senator from South Carolina inciting to civil war with his comments about race. In fact, I was noting it from my world history book, Part 4, USA, in English to show you. We could not keep the books, but I copied pieces of it out.

"So here is what he said in a 'great' speech before your USA Senate:"

He opened his diary and took out a frayed page:

> *Never before* (before living as slaves in America, the *juge* pointed out) *has the black race of Central Africa, from the dawn of history to the present day, attained a condition so civilized and so improved, not only physically, but morally and intellectually.*

> Calhoun said "*They came among us* (as slaves of course) *in a low, degraded, and savage condition and*

in a few generations they grew up under the 'fostering care of our institutions to a civilized state."

"*Milles mercis!* Many thanks!

"Yes, the tender, loving care of four hundred years. And that is about us, here in Africa, as well! We are still in the low, degraded, and savage condition. Furthermore the current movement for voting rights in USA, and you have what? How many are dying to prove that point? The point that we are each more than three-fifths of a man.

"Not a place to copy, not a lesson to derive. Would such a lesson make us more *evolué*, more civilized?"

"Yes, but a belief, that 'all men are created equal,' a belief in that and an effort to live up to that...!" But I knew that I shouldn't have stepped into this donkey pie!

"To be made fools of by your own failures? Who is it said 'we are all cuckholded by our own history?'" he asked. Whatever that meant.

"Yes and you as well have your sla..."

■ Saved by the Gunfire

It was the first time I ever felt a moment of relief under fire—only a moment—immediately followed, I admit, by moments of terror. A gazelle hunter's shots in the paltry moonlight? Antoine was away in a flash, pistol drawn. Stumbling over clumps of sand. Going to direct the traffic? (Robert, the deputy, once told me that Antoine could not hit an elephant standing still in front of a sand dune, at 20 meters, with his revolver. With or without his glasses. Very encouraging.) The Chief and *juge* were away as well. Each showing pistols and each in a different direction. Good thinking.

The rest of us sat like targets in back of the *kaz*, not in control and not knowing where to place ourselves. I think I lay flat, hoping they could not and would not see me.

Whoever "they" were.

Another firing. No grunts or screams. I think some bullets flew in our direction. The *imam* was down among the nearby shadows. I knew because the moonlight shined on the filigree of his *jalaba*. Perhaps he had brought these intruders. A spiteful accusation, an undeserved thought. So I thought of half faceless Lièvre instead.

We waited.

It seemed a long time that there was no further firing. Then the *juge* and Antoine returned, one by one, each smiling.

"A Wahidi at the gate," Antoine said. "I believe I wounded him as he fled. He may have been in a truck. In the morning we'll search by the northern gate from where he came," he said with utmost certainty, in that way of his. (Perhaps because he knew it had been Alain. Looking to assassinate someone? Reputed to be as bad a shot as Antoine. Perhaps. But he "doesn't provoke.") ' [Note from Aaron Hamblin: I'm not sure where in the chronology this belongs, so I'm inserting it here.] *Antoine later told me that he believed it was Alain sent to assassinate someone that night. (Perhaps the Police Chief.) But he would never mention his theory to others since then they would kill Alain. Who, up to now, was allowed to move freely among us.* [End of insert.]

"The bullets we saw were from Antoine," the *Imam* whispered.

"Truck backfire," the *juge* countered. By then we were brushing off the evidence of our terror.

"Only truck backfire!" the *juge* declared. Then, "See how we are in fear? In fear of the Wahidi?" he added.

Indeed we were. And the Police Chief did not return to us that evening.

■ When It So Dawns

August 15, 1968

I never see these things. I never see these things coming. Like the slam from Gerard Olivier Dubois. Or the attack by Alain. It was there, right before my eyes. When he slipped into his blue Deux Cheveaux at her side of town. When her cousin led her, in her very finest, on his donkey to the Doctor's side of town. Or to pass by the *Clinique*. Or to stop there. In her finest. Some spy, me!

Antoine underscored the rumor with the bringing together of both his outstretched forefingers in a parallel motion as a sign for the coming together of lovers. It was difficult to be discreet in this town, especially with these local (supposed) morés. And *de mortuis nil nisi bonum*, I reminded myself. Never speak ill of the dead.

While his wife, the other Docteur Lièvre, waited for him those long, lonely nights. Or cried herself to sleep. Hoping no one knew. But she surely knew some did.

And there were the lurid stories and rumors about Amina that I had chosen to ignore.

So it was true. Or Antoine, my better nose for these things, said it was true. Docteur Lièvre, *femme*, could have done the killing of her husband herself. Or hired the roadway assassin. Or it could have been by one who could get close enough to the docteur—such as Antoine's brother, Alain, posing as Antoine. In replica uniform. Capable of the same obsequious pose. Imitating the same twist of the neck.

For Alain was Wahid's *Almlak Alaswd*—Wahid's Dark Angel.

"Perhaps it was a Wahid. Even the spiteful Saghir. Maybe even posing as me, or as Alain attempting to pose as me." It took great effort and courage for Antoine to suggest it could have been his brother. His twin.

I suggested to Antoine that he send a message with this theory to police HQ in Djémélia.

"I must send it only to the *sous-préfet*. Through the new *pneumatique*. He must stamp it. Thus he will decide whether to send it."

If he is in the stamping frame of mind. "But you can carry this information to the telex machine yourself," I suggested. A bit forcefully. The telex machine was not twenty yards from Antoine's office in police headquarters. The *pneumatique* was a suction or vacuum pipe between the offices. Using "state-of-the-art," (but virtually useless in this case) technology.

"Ah, *non.* Such informations must follow the sending process. I cannot bypass the *pneumatique.*"

About the assassination and Wahid's *Almlak Alaswd*—Wahid's Dark Angel?

Of that, I dared not ask Antoine.

■   My Turn

1968

She first came in the night—unsolicited. Devastatingly beautiful high cheek bones. Under her robe, she wore only a diaphanous white wrap, one that accented her fine figure.

She slipped into my bed without my knowing it, and cuddled up to me until I finally awoke to this pleasant and unexpected surprise. I was mystified, but soon ready. She only said *"Nasarah"* before we made love.

I had seen her several times before. In the marketplace, at the banks of the tributary branching out from the Chari River which began at the grand lake south of Djemélia, selling cheap, handmade trinkets. Which I bought for Amina.

She was called Miriam. She gave me an inviting smile. And whispered *"Nasarah"* and some other words of invitation. No mistaking those eyes—those invitations. But I was at first too obsessed with Amina to notice. I had been told that she was taken with *Nasarah*s and that Evian was her former lover. A veritable switch-hitter, that Evian. I inherited his cottage, his students, and perhaps his dog; why not his woman as well?

This might well be what Ivan would call my *kompromat.*

And so it came to be. The diaphanous white wrap came off. She was beautiful and as black as the night. There was no need for a garment to give her breasts lift, and none for other things.

We made love that first night as if it was the natural thing to do. She screamed in a perfectly timed orgasm, though I would later learn that it was probably an act she had learned from another white man—since she had likely been female-circumcised when she came of age, and so her sex feelings were dulled. Or nonexistent. Still, the laying with *Nasarahs*—I took no pains that night to tell her that I was otherwise—had kept her in fine silken things and silver rings.

She wore rings on every finger, fingers and rings that made a sensual scratching on my back when we made love, and she wrapped me with the silken robe like the one she wore that first night. And like Amina, she wore bracelets of varied colors and metal on both forearms. The bracelets made a pleasant and exciting jingle announcing her arrival.

So she became my regular lover. I never asked why. Why should I? (But I knew I should have.) I gave her money now and then—money that she used to feed her mother, son, and brother in the mud-baked hovel where she lived. In the northeast corner of the town—the area most open to raids from the Janjaweed and thieves and bandits of all stripes. She gave me trinkets. And Sahel love.

"Come live with me in my nice cottage," I offered.

"I cannot."

"Why not? You live there most of the nights."

"I have my mother and brother . . . and son."

"Then bring them, as well," I urged.

"That is the home our grandfather built, and we cannot abandon it."

"You won't. It will still be yours to keep and, perhaps, to rent." I knew I was asking for it, but I couldn't resist.

I could see she was mulling over the possibility. But in the end, she refused.

So I became familiar with her family, and her neighbors became familiar with me. This may have helped me with the Wahidi. Or, given our illicit acts of love, maybe not.

Her mother, toothless to the point where I rarely understood her patter. Her brother Ali, a *cinquième* student of mine, which made things all the more awkward when I visited her place. And, yes, her son, the little *metisse* Youssef, who may have been Evian's, and who was often still clinging to the skirts of his mother.

I never asked her what brought her to me in the first place. One more item waiting to be added to the cock-up list.

One more—waiting to happen.

■   First Visit

September 1968

So, lost in reverie, I automatically reached to pour a glass. Jean had long gone, and Rashid had moved into the shadows and ceased his soft and rhythmic head pounding. My eyes glanced up involuntarily. To see him sitting across from me, watching me intently, squatting in the desert way, veiled, and his hands wrapped around the stock and barrel of his carbine. As calm as you please. I admit I was in a bit of a panic. My instinct to rise yielded to the numbing effect of the alcohol.

I assumed it was him, sitting across from me, watching me intently. He only continued to stare with that stern malevolence the races of the desert have mastered so well.

He toyed with his veil, broke the silence after bowing his head. "Salaam, sidi."

So what do you say to a killer, an anti-*Nasarah* bandit? For that's what he's reputed to be. "Salaam, sidi," I responded with rapidly acquired sobriety.

Then again I saluted, "Salaam, sidi."

"You have wanted to see me? Thus you see." He spread his arms to present himself. Then he mercifully lowered his veil to show his sallow, blue-tinted face—and what I would characterize as that "lean and hungry" look.

"I . . ." My eyes may have darted in search of Evian's carbine. (It had been residing in the so-called closet, protecting the disappeared radio, but then acquired by Antoine for journeys between places of "forensics." So I think it was safely re-ensconced with the police. No doubt for the best.)

"My Arabic is faulty. My tongue is weak."

"I am told that your Arabic is pure. But your tongue is numbed by the *Nasarah*'s drink. I am Abu Ibn Jema'a, of the family of the tribe of Asouyé Kerem Alwahla."

"Yes."

"I have come upon your repeated requests." He switched from French to English, and his English was more than passable.

"My father was a great chief and military leader, a *derde*, during the Sahara wars that you Europeans call World War II. He was the chosen *derde*, chieftain, of the Tomagra clan of the tribe of Asouyé Kerem. He led that division, called the Wahid*i* division, in battles such as Murzuk, Kufra, Sebha. and Mizdah, and even the second Al-Alamein. They fought the European way but kept our swords handy for close combat. So shall we."

"A great thing of which you must be immensely proud," I offered. I knew we wouldn't get down to more substantive conversation until he had recited his complete patrimony.

"So my grandfather fought the Libyans and others." The "others" included the encroaching French legions at the beginning of the twentieth century. He was being diplomatic not to mention their nationality. "It is with great pride that I am called 'Wahid.' 'Wahid' means the first one, or the only one, in our dialect.

"I am also sometimes called Lord of the Desert, '*Rabb alssahra*.' And still again 'Djinnii *alsahra*,' 'Ghost of the Desert.' This from the Holy Koran, the seventy-second *sura* and other places. It is my pride to carry such names, for I am the prince of the Asouyé Kerem and Baya lands, lands taken away from the great prince, my father, and from me by this illegal government."

He then left another uncomfortable silence. Squatting in the desert fashion. Hands on the carbine, which was resting on his thighs.

It seemed as if we were both frozen in an embarrassing silence that I dared not break.

"I come to you so that you might have your questions answered, and perhaps cease pestering your only manservant, Jean Abdel-Melek, with your questions about me."

Jean must have complained.

"Your tongue must be numbed by your *Nasarah's* drink." I braced for a harangue, but then he smiled. "Do you not offer such to a poor pilgrim."

I could see Amina and a fine stallion behind him, away from the petrol lamp, in the shadows. Miriam had not come that night, although I thought I heard the tinkling of her bracelets coming from the opposite side earlier. A momentary shifting of the winds? Perhaps she had slipped away to watch from afar after seeing the company I was hosting.

"Forgivenesses, sidi," I stammered as I tried again to rise to fetch a glass. His hand reached reflexively for the stock of the rifle that he had been rolling on his thighs, then relaxed. The hard sternness, then wide smile, took turns flickering across his face. With some effort, I rose to find him a tall glass. I noted that now he was again veiled as I would expect a *Taureg* male over the age of twenty-five to be.

"Pour it thus." His finger touched the tall glass halfway.

"Yes, Excellency."

"Thank you, Excellency," he answered. He raised the glass in a toast, in the Western way. He poured a good portion of the valuable Scotch on the ground. Perhaps to ancestors. Then unwrapped his veil and barely sipped the leavings.

Finally I got up the courage to ask, "How is it that you, a practicing Muslim—you are so are you not?—can allow this whiskey to touch your lips?"

"The fault of my years in the West. Where I realized that the drink soon turns to water—and water is surely not forbidden by our belief." He offered a slight smile. Wit or . . .?

Yet I was bothered by this. That somehow he didn't meet my

expectations. Fully. A lingering disappointment. And I may have shown it. He took note. Of something. And not in a pleasant way.

"And to what good fortune do I owe this visit?" I was pushing it with my formal language.

"To my curiosity. For I, like you, am curious. To the intervention of Jean Abdel-Melek and our friends, and to the kindnesses you have shown to Amina."

The last startled me. So he knew. And knowing, he could that moment condemn me. I was completely at his mercy. "I am undeserving, yet honored."

"Most of all I am curious. Why does this *Nasarah* want to look upon such a poor one as me? Why does he ask about me—though we have never met—with such persistence?" He stopped for a moment.

"A measure of how exciting things are here," I thought but didn't say. "Anyway, I am not a *Nasarah*!" I stepped one foot into this camel pie to avoid the other questions. He raised his eyebrows over the rim of the glass. "I am Américain!" I stepped in with the other foot, soon feeling boorish and naive. Not exactly what I had meant. I tried a slight correction: "I am not from Europe," I had waded in stubbornly, body and soul.

"Still, you *are Nasarah*. But yes, Emricani as well."

So I had recently been told, by Modou, my encyclopedia, that the word derives from "Nazarene," from Middle-Eastern Arabic, and means any follower of Jesus of Nazareth. There are too many camel pies I am already sunk in or awaiting me that prevented me from taking refuge in my agnosticism (shuffling with my atheism). I tried to slog out of it. "Do you know the story of the rebel, Robin Hood?"

"It is Jean who has told me of this *Nasarah* who revolted against the evil tyranny wrought upon his father and restored the people to power," he answered. "What has that to do with us?"

Was this the legend I had deftly told to Jean? To try to lure this bandit, through praise? "He robbed from the rich to give to the poor." A good summary and was, yes, intended to imply a comparison.

"Perhaps that is the way they tell it in the land of *Nasarah*!" He was a bit contemptuous now and his features gathered to a swift and frightening storm. Perhaps from jealousy? "This is the way they tell it to prevent the other lesson from taking hold!"

Even in the half-light of the petrol lamp I could see his burning eyes. Eyes that confirmed the volatility I sensed. He rolled the stock of his carbine on his thighs ever more persistently. For all that, it was but a benign habit, for me it was a bit menacing. Perhaps more than a bit.

"He succored the poor," I forged on, scraping the depths of my most classic Arabic.

"Perhaps. But, yes, his struggle is for the people. His theft, to finance their quest for the power stolen from them. For me, it is another lesson: that to strip away a man's land is to steal his identity. And that so it is better to die standing than to live on one's knees." He stopped.

"I am astonished by your knowledge of the stories of the English." I attempted to nudge the subject onto more neutral ground.

"It is the history of us all, so says Abdel-Hamid." He quoted the one I soon learned was his sometimes oracle. The dwarflike chief of the Prokaza village.

"You see yourself in those terms, then?" I asked.

"I am myself also for the people. Yes." And he took on a look of certainty and self-satisfaction.

"You're also called a thief and a killer," I wanted to retort. For once, I held my tongue—unlike the overanxious teenager that I could be. Or always the smart ass, as she once said.

A long and thoughtful silence followed, broken only by the sipping, slurping sound as he worked at his drip of remaining Scotch. Then "I have come to see. To see this *Nasarah*, this Emricani, who persists in asking for me. And to see what I can bring you—and what you might bring me. Us. The assistance of Emrica. I will come yet another time if this seeing should make for the doing." Then, as a storm again formed on his face, he added, "I will leave you alone with your whiskey and come again at a more auspicious time. By the way, this half *Taureg* you claimed, and your ridiculous maternal line, is pure donkey shit. Your mother, a Saali of the Djewadee family. There's an old story about all the fools of the Djewadee. I'll bet Amina made this one up. Ha-ha!" He really grunted rather than laughed. Then quickly replaced his veil.

And he was gone. Amina and his stallion with him.

So I sensed that this meeting had not gone so well. Perhaps I should get an interpreter for the next time. Also, I vowed to be sober and emit fewer slurs should he come again.

Miriam joined me soon thereafter. Without a word.

But oh the foreplay....

■ Radio Lesson

September 1968

Since they were putting up the microwave devices, I asked them for help. That's when I learned that while Terry was usually the strategist, Joe was the brains. At least when he was sober. Opposite of what I had always assumed. Joe just needed Terry's lead to spur him to action.

So Joe came over. And I poured him a beer to get him started. "Ok, let's get some power," he began.

"Uh, Joe, you know I don't have any electric power. It's like the black mamba snake serum they gave me. 'KEEP REFRIGERATED AT ALL TIMES.' 'Cepting I don't have a refrigerator." Nor was I ever destined to.

A big sigh. "Alright then. Come on to my place. As you know, I've got a generator." He seemed to be proud of that. "Bring the radio. We'll figure something out."

My donkey mount (I named him Evian), the one I used when I could not borrow Omar, was a bit obstreperous—maybe horny. But I finally convinced him to carry the device wrapped in my blanket. I walked beside him.

Their generator was running on kerosene and made enough racket to piss off jealous neighbors. We hooked up the radio and I got my lesson....

"Plug in. Power on using this switch. Once powered, leave it running. The internal battery should charge sufficiently for several uses. For at least two hours of communication. When the battery is drained, come back to me for a recharge," Joe added.

"And when you leave here?" I donned my most pessimistic look.

"Perhaps you will be leaving too. If not, you will inherit our generator. Now, this is the dial for setting the band. And this is the dial for type of modulation or bandwidth selection. Turn to here. But then this is the switch to use Morse Code. You can use the Code, eh?"

"Can I write all this down?" I'd brought pen and paper to reinforce my feeble memory.

"Sure. Antenna up and stretched its full length. Micro-speaker here, receiver there. Or these earphones. This modulation is such that only a like receiver can understand it. So far there are none of these in country. Outside the embassy. Except the one stolen from you." He just *had* to remind me. "But now I'm given to understand that's OK. And also, of course, understood at our HQ."

"How do you know there are no other compatible radios?" All I needed was Captain Ngokuru of the militia or the *Third Para* to track down the source. Hello Yekbar.[5]

"We've already run several tests. Plus we use a technique called single-sideband frequency to carry your data or voice. With their current AM listening devices, all they will hear is a quack-quack like a duck when you speak."

"What if I quack like a duck when sending?" Always the smartass. That's why I'm so loved.

"Yeah. Funny. So we call it the Green Hornet method. A hangover

---

[5] Yekbar is the notorious national prison in the middle of the Sahara. The prison for traitors, murderers, and a litany of malfeasance and malevolence. And for capital crimes like treason—and spying. To be Yekbared, *être Yekbaré*, is to be so imprisoned.

from World War Two. It can be cracked by someone who knows what they're doing. Like the Germans. But not these folks. Yet." Joe was soon in full instructor mode.

"That's encouraging."

"But we also have a little surprise for the listener who makes it that far. In addition to this modulation, we reverse Green Hornet at the sending-to-receiving end for double encryption."

"Cool!" I supposed.

"Well that's not exactly how it works, but close enough for you. So you need to have your antenna up and the device turned to the five on this knob for good value. To start a call, say (if you're in voice mode) or code, 'Whiskey Tango Foxtrot.'

"Keep repeating. Actually, '**WTF**' does it. You know what that means, eh?" he smiled at me conspiratorially. "To signal 'over,' turn three to two and back again. Then another three to two. That means 'over.' If you're receiving, it's two to three twice after you hear the double clicking. That means 'receiving.' That's the most important part. Also close with signature, HH or dotdotdotdotdotdotdotdot in your case."

"What if they don't receive?"

"You will send it all over again. Same if you don't receive a response. Signal with seven."

"As for voice....?" I asked.

"Yes, you have the voice option. Right here." He pointed to the toggle switch. "But you probably want to minimize its use, since you'll have to shout to make yourself heard, and you'll wake up all your neighbors. Maybe even the whole town."

"Well, the most important thing is that the surreptitious listener gets the message." I noted.

"Ah. He will. He has the machine. Right?" He rubbed it in again.

"Its receiver is programmed to decrypt this stuff. Of course, he won't signal back that he got it. So you'll have to hope it works. He probably won't understand WTF at first, but he'll catch on. Everyone does. Who is he, the one that's listening in?"

"*Third Para*. The *Third Parachutist* Division. Army of France. Nice guys." Except for Heinrich.

"How's their table wine at mess?"

"Excellent, even at the noncom mess. The food is good too. Even better than our C rations. You ought to try it some time."

"I hope to get an invitation. So far the one-armed captain has only given us a cursory, left-handed salute," Joe opined.

"He's got a lot to handle." Pun intended. "And little to do it all with." Another one intended. "Plus he has to get used to you. Anyway, their mess is in their barracks in Djamé."

"We've set the signal at low frequency which carries to a maximum of one klick. The antennas on the poles are the relays. They have to be in sight, each one to the next, like a relay. That's your radio relay. The carrier is called microwave. It picks up the signal in Albri where it's relayed to Djamé. So we've had to go over the mountains. See that one?" He pointed to the pole and antennas a little less than a kilometer away. "Putting poles in. Hard work. They can't be more than one kilometer away from each other, line-of-sight. But we couldn't go around the mountains, the other way. Terry's tried it several times, but they warned him away. With weapons. They had it pretty well blocked. Poor guy. Couldn't go north, Couldn't go south. Nor east, nor west."

"If the poles aren't yet in, how do I send?" I asked, proud of my ability to ask a "technical" question.

"Good question. You will have to send your message at a specific time. When you are pointing at the satellite. It is…" he consulted a small, thin pocket notebook. "It is 0300 That's 3:00 a.m. In the early morning. Only. That's when the satellite is in range. For about fifteen minutes."

"Why *then*?" I was not relishing this early, early morning rise. Besides, Miriam and I might be just finishing up.

"That is the only time everything is properly positioned."

"Ah-hah," I muttered, trying to sound like I understood

everything he was saying. It was a little garbled for me. Everything except the 3:00 a.m.

"You might ask, why bother with the microwave later when you already have a delivery method. Why not just use the satellite? At 3:00 a.m.?"

"Yeah, that's it," I lied. "That's what I would have asked." I was back to where I had been—out of my depth. "Or change the satellite time to a more civilized passover time."

"Good question." That *I* hadn't asked. "We rent space on that thing. Too expensive over time. Besides, this new system is more permanent and will be used by the nationals. Then it will be virtually free for us! For our air messaging. And we won't have to get up at 3:00 a.m. to send messages."

"Good reason." I was already not relishing getting up at 3:00 a.m. When I'm thoroughly exhausted, hung over, and apt to make grievous errors.

"And by the way, we'll send you a message if the time changes."

"That will be most welcome."

"OK. That's it. Be sure to wrap this up again, against the sand."

I did. This time my donkey mount was a better sport about carrying it back to the *kaz*.

I secreted it. This time, better than in the closet—in its box behind the useless toilet—and hoped to never have to use it. But I had one less excuse now.

■ The Caves of Jumeaux

September 1968

Modou was the Indian colleague I wrote about earlier. With a penchant for languages and a take-charge attitude. At least I think that's what it was. To master so many languages required a take-charge attitude. Yes? "There are more than one hundred languages and dialects in this country, Harold. Yes, I know some. And I speak

Hindi and Farsi as well. The Ngumbaye and Arabic are useful to discipline the students. In their own dialect."

But, still, Modou seemed often to be both angry and depressed. (Maybe those emotions go together.) Except when well juiced. With at least three glasses of Johnny.

He taught science and the maths at the upper levels. He loved archeology and prowled around looking for Neolithic artifacts. In caves on the Jumeaux, for example. He kept his homosexuality under control given the Evian drama. It was rumored that Alphonse the nurse was his paramour. Only rumored. And he drank Scotch. So of course we got closer (and more often plastered) as the school year went on.

Chien despised him and would growl fiercely when Modou approached, if he, Chien, was in the vicinity. I thought that it might be Chien's assumption that Modou had something to do with the disappearance or removal of his master, Evian.

Maybe.

■ First Climb

September 23, 1968

Modou convinced me to climb with him. Jumeaux's cleavage—between the twin mountains. The cleavage of Kahina's great breasts. Maybe a foreshadowing of some kind. Our search for caves that may have, at one time, housed the ancestors of these very races. And explain certain current behavior and idiosyncrasies of the present-day demographics.

For the Sara, the twin peaks were the firm, life-nourishing breasts of Kahina, the great anti-Arab warrior and Berber, perhaps ancestor to the modern-day *Rif* or *Riffians*. For them, these mountains are their succor and will save their country, their southland, from the Arabs and the all-encroaching sand. And they represent Kahina's fertility. And so, *their* fertility as well.

"You see, Harold, the story of Kahina" he began as I was still catching my breath, "pivots on the pronouncement that 'Ifriqiyah [Africa] divides the hearts of its inhabitants'—referring to the great number of disparate tribes and groups here—'which causes them to be disobedient and unmanageable.'

"And more, Harold. 'Our cities,' she said, 'and the gold and silver which they contain, perpetually attract the Arabs. These vile metals are not the objects of our ambition; we content ourselves with the simple productions of the earth. So let us destroy these cities, let us bury in their ruins…those pernicious treasures. And when the avarice of our foes shall be destitute of temptation, perhaps they will cease to disturb our tranquility.' The Sahel version, given that they are so arabized—that she was a destroyer, a city burner who, having defeated the Arabs in their Hajira in North Africa around 700 AD, carried out this scorched earth policy."

"Certainly the land has become destitute. Maybe there are riches still buried in the sand. And history may be repeating itself," Modou stated.

Often. I was certain of that. History was repeating itself, like the sand dunes that disappear with the wind, come back together, reform and recompose themselves—as, I think, they must.

"And Harold," he often repeated, "my greatest desire will be to explore all the great monuments of the desert, such as the towers of Ennedi and the cliff paintings in Borkou."

"And someday we will," I assured him. "As for me, I long to see the great camel valley, the *Guelta d'Archei*, and the ancient crocodile. Together, when this so-called rebellion is over and the desert is again tamed and quiet."

"Perhaps together. You know the rock art found in the Ennedi region has been dated to before the seventh millennium BC," he went on.

"Yes." But I could see he was full of doubt and losing faith in our emergency escape plan.

"And then on to Timbuktu," he reminded me.

Though that was in another direction. Still, I said "Yes." That, indeed, someday we might.

We climbed for seven hours, with the acacias and rocks tearing at our hands and our clothing. We reached a cool wadi where the breasts came together and a few caves appeared.

Not much of a mountain really, but the highest point in these parts with even a bit of vegetation to hold down the coal-like rock and black gravel. We trekked in those low spots that Modou called the mountain's cleavage, the cleavage between the two "breasts." On paths carved out by the telecom workers.

■ The Cave

One cave in particular seemed to be deep. And dark. The first thirty feet of the cave were open to the sun at sunset and afforded a good view despite the sunset glare from the west. Not so blinding from the west as the morning sun from the east (I want to say the "blinding east") and even afternoon sun.

"So you see, Harold," Modou added. "This is the only place for an escape. The camel soldiers will fall back and will only be able to follow on foot. I think even their allies, the Jinjaweed, won't bother. No loot. Not enough anyway.

"We have water. And come, look into this." He led me to a cave-like entrance, where I had to stoop low to gaze into its green-black shadows. "We can sleep in its silence."

We explored the several Jumeaux caves. There weren't many. Modou was small and thin and was able to pass through incredibly narrow openings where he left me behind.

At the summit of the cleavage, and in what we thought would be our last cave, Modou slipped away through a narrow fissure—his perseverance overcoming the very narrow break in the cave wall. I could hear him slip about the wetness and slime on the other side.

And then a good thirty minutes of silence followed by an alien howl that echoed back to where I stood, silent and superstitious.

I could hear the echoes of the howl and his footsteps as he slipped and slid on the rocky-slick cave floor in what must have been a terrible hurry. Then the flapping of bats as they burst through the fissure, followed by Modou.

"So you see! Look at this, Harold." He ignored the bat tangled in his hair and struggling to escape. "Stuck in a crevice beneath a stony outcrop!" he exclaimed excitedly. "That protected it from the humidity, slime, and bats. All these years!"

He held up the morsel of…whatever…close in front of me. It was pieces of parchment folded inside a wallet-like piece of moist leather. At first I could only focus on the bat that finally freed itself and flew off. Then I looked more closely at the object he held up to me.

"And this tells the tale. Look where it is from…" He thrust the piece of parchment toward me, then pulled it back.

What a surprise! Given my recently acquired suspicious nature, I would forever wonder if Modou planted it. Yes, how convenient! When the discovery of this parchment was made known, the recognition—the applause for him and his find—would be deafening. So why would anyone else plant such an artifact? "What is it? Where is it from?"

"Why, from *Bet al Hikma*. The House of Wisdom, I believe. Two pieces. One in a very strange, maybe Berber, dialect and the other in Ajami, *Teckmesh* Ajami, language of the Sahel at that time. I can read words and pieces of that one. But the other, probably a transliteration of a Berber dialect. I believe that buried in this one is the story of the rocks that, when mixed, would make heat, eventually burn, and render what I believe here it says a terrible sickness.

"Perhaps these were belonging to a scholar intent on hiding his precious books. We aren't the only ones who attempted to hide this dangerous information from the general public!"

That statement got my attention. I'll never be sure what he meant.

"I read somewhere that these mountains were often used by the intellectuals and professors after Timbuktu fell. I read that it is thought that this is one of the places they came to, to seek shelter. But there's been no confirmation….Until now. And, if it is so, there must be more of these documents. And even more and older scribbles and paintings on the walls."

He announced in a near-whisper that carried all his awe and my foreboding. "You see—this, a piece of history, from the Caliphate times, the times of the search for a successor. To Mohammed, Harold. Perhaps the Abbasid times!"

"And the twentieth century times," I added pointing to the discarded bottles of Douze Marches. "And it has survived all these years?"

Modou didn't acknowledge my sarcasm, though I thought I glimpsed a brief smile. "Maybe a thousand years! And there may be more. I was just so lucky to have stumbled onto this piece!" He virtually danced with joy over his discovery. But carefully, so as not to injure the parchment. "Probably from…yes, what does it say? This written in the sixth century after the *Hajira*, that would make it from our thirteenth century AD. In Ajami, the scholarly language of the time. What a find!"

Yes, even I understood that this was from the Golden Age of Islam. A source of nostalgia and envy. And of his joy, though momentary, after so much personal sadness.

"How was it that this old artifact, this parchment, has lasted here and intact so long?" I finally asked.

"I don't know why intact, or for so long, but Jumeaux is where many scholars of the time hid out in the caves reputed to be between the two breasts, the two *tetons* mountains. Other pilgrims have hidden in these caves as well."

"For sure it is a mystery. Still we must report this to the *Département national de l'histoire et de culture (des anciennes découvertes)*." I remarked. "Where they will not understand its significance and it will be placed in some dark corner." I was already feeling regret for this.

"Yes, and forever lost to mankind." Now Modou was emotional to the point of tears.

"Can you read it?" I urged.

"It seems to be script and drawings from a history." Modou refocused. "My Ajami is pretty shaky. It's definitely about Kahina, Dihya, the Berber queen, whose pastime was to study ornithology. See, this fragment of parchment is with a painting of a bird on it. She was a great general and warrior. But why only these pieces? I must go back and search for more."

He did. For over an hour. But made no more discoveries.

"I guess we'll have to make another trek."

"Yes, another time, for a more thorough exploration." Then he astonished me. "I must ask you to carry this piece back to the USA with you; that is, if anything should happen to me. It will fit nicely into your copy of Shakespeare or the Bible. Like a bookmark. No customs official will think to search through that. Then it will be properly handled. I'll bring you other pieces if I should find them. Of course, I'll give you the name of a good and trustworthy archeology contact on the USA side."

"How can I qualify for such a thing, I who have screwed up plenty in this short period of time?" I said in all modesty.

"I have a premonition. I have dishonored my parents and the lady chosen for me. For this and other reasons and because I have not acted well in India, I can never go back to my home. Or to the USA. For I have not acted well and according to custom. I have spent the dowry meant for our marriage on university, on curiosities, and on exotic travel. Now I am doomed to wander the back and downtrodden roads of this world. I know it sounds nineteenth-century romantic, but these are the facts."

"What is your premonition?"

"That the time will soon come," he said mysteriously.

"Yes, the time will come for you to go to the USA with me," I offered, hoping this was the meaning of his morbid announcement.

"Destined to wander the world except to India and the USA where the lady's father is being well ensconced for protection from the many of India who wish to kill him; and has many Indians there in the USA who owe to him. He is a sort of godfather. He had paid us the dowry. A fine sum which I have spent traveling the world. A stupid thing to do. But she was ugly and talked incessantly. And...."

"And...?"

"And you know what I am, Harry, and I might never make children."

Yes, I knew. Plus I had heard of these godfather types, like the Sicilian mafia, vicious, who never knew remorse, but only *omerta*. The Al Capones of the world. Thank goodness we had none here. At least none known to me.

It was then he turned to relieve himself. Left of the mouth of the cave. He began to weave and I seized his shirt for fear he would topple over. Over a very steep drop.

"Go there." And I pushed him right, where a friendly path angled slightly down. "You really scared the shit out of me!"

"You have saved my life."

"From a nasty fall?"

"You see, Harold, I truly feel as though you have saved me from a most deadly fall," Modou insisted. "In fact, this is rumored to be where they tossed the body of Evian. Wrapped only in linen, in the Moslem way. Yes, I'm sure of it. But with the fog down there, it is impossible to see the very bottom of the valley."

In modesty and confusion, I tried to change the subject. Besides, I wasn't so sure about his intentions for this "fall."

■ The Interpreter

Late September 1968

My colleague Modou, steeped in these Sahel ways and culture, had said, "Now you see Harold, there are over one hundred dialects and languages spoken here. I speak about ten that are the most related and similar. Including this strange mélange of Sara-Ngumbaye and desert Arabic. What you are mastering, Harold, perhaps in spite of yourself!"

"Then you could be my interpreter," I suggested.

"Ah, no, Harry. In this political climate, I would be very suspect as an outsider. Suspect because I know the language and yet I'm not one of them," he said in his typically self-deprecating way. "Besides, I am seen frequently with my friend, the nurse, little Alphonse. Who also helps my *Sara-Ngumbaye* and *Zaghawa*, by the way. It is better to use another."

So without Modou and despite the training and diligence that refined my French and gave me more than rudimentary Arabic, I knew I would need an interpreter for some of the dialects, especially in the oases and plateaus where commercial, vernacular Arabic only was spoken, and even then mixed with the other, indigenous languages. That's when Jean found Mohammed bin Akhween.

Akhween, with a back-of-throat, roof-of-mouth *kh!*

Mohammed later told me that he preferred being called Akhween to distinguish him from all the other Mohammeds in our town. At introduction, I said "Pleased to meet you, Mohammed bin Akhween."

"*Akh-khween*," he said. "You must pronounce the *kh* in the back roof of the mouth." He would remind me, and others of that, repeatedly.

"I will. Of course I will." And here I thought I had a pretty good *kh*. I think they call it a *palato-alveolar consonant*. Hey! Hey! I might've learned something in linguistics classes after all.

Listening to Partenay's cough and clear had given me pointers too.

■   A Bargain Well Made?

I introduced Akhween to the *légionnaire capitaine*. "He might be able to help you as well—to translate from the French for the less gifted in French of your militiamen recruits." As usual with those newly introduced to the *capitaine*, he and Akhween fumbled their handshake.

"At your service, Monsieur Akhween." The *capitaine* said as he saluted.

"*Akh-khween*," my interpreter replied. "*kh!* You must pronounce the *kh* in the back roof of the mouth."

"Yes, Monsieur A*kh-kh-kh*ween. I might find your skills useful. I know there is at least one militiaman-recruit who understands very few of my commands. And there are no doubt others."

"Are they Naringar?" Akhween was quick to ask.

"I have no idea."

The *capitaine* and I bargained and shook hands (mine the right, his the left) on an agreement to share Akhween's services—roughly half and half. We hadn't yet resolved what it was half of, however. And Akhween did not participate in closing the bargain either. This might later become a problem.

It appeared that Mohammed Akhween was pleased to have two jobs. And plenty of unexpected encounters to correct the pronunciation of his name.

It would be Akhween—*khkhkh*.

And so on.

■   Younis 1

October 1968

It was a late afternoon, well into my second year, that I finally, truly met him. He was listlessly wandering the acreage next to my *kaz*, chewing on a whittled acacia stalk that, someone once told me, served as a toothbrush. He must have been eleven or twelve with a happy countenance, but ragged clothing. He appeared to be looking for something.

He eyed me shyly but did not speak.

"*Salaam alékum,*" I ventured. "How are you?" I remembered how he had saved my life by calling for Antoine when Alain threatened me and also how he had looked when he had wandered near the outdoor "facilities" (ok, the "shit hole") during my illness, my amoebic dysentery.

"*Alékum as salaam.* I am well, thank you, Master."

"Who are you?" I asked.

"I am the servant of the master of this land, Master," he replied, but backed away as I tried to approach him. "I am called Younis."

"Who is the master of this land?"

"His honor, Master Yacob Mikune." He twisted about uncomfortably.

"Then I am not the master of this land. So you can address me by my name. I am Monsieur Harrisson."

"Ha, ha. *Hérisson? Vraiment?*" Yeah, I know. The cute little hedgehog. My attempt to put him more at ease.

"OK, call me Harry!"

"Yes, Monsieur Harry. Thank you, Master." So much for putting him at ease.

"Are you in the school?"

"No, Monsieur Harry Master. I am working from dawn to midday. And then again in the evening until darkest night."

"But you are not working now," I remarked. Brilliant observation.

"I am only on a short rest to clean my teeth. And other things."

"Why can't you go to the school where I teach?"

"I must work, Monsieur Harry Master."

I left it at that, feeling that I was already sufficiently intimidating poor Younis.

■ November 18, 1968

Aaron,

Tell Mom, Dad, and Sis that I'm fine and living the life of Livingston—or Conrad—or Kurtz—or any other of the European figures of this heart of darkness. So how are you? Still certain not to follow your older sibling? Good choice!

The last letter came back. Maybe it was the mention of Ngokuru and "a**h*le" in the same sentence that ticked off our censor.

There is a bitterness here between the Southerners, especially the Sara-Ngumbai, and the Arab people of the North. Also with the Tuareg, who don't like the Arabs much either. The people I work among in the Sahel (I call them Sahelians; they are Muslims and somewhat Arabized) are caught in the middle of this, racially and linguistically, just as the Sahel separates the rain forest and the Sahara. The Sahelians are careful with both groups and walk a fine line.

Did I mention in my last letter (which you never got anyway) that I've recently made the acquaintance of a most formidable character—the leader of a group rebelling against the government here. He is constantly on the run but I was able to get an interview with him. His nom de guerre is "Wahid" which means "The One" or "The Only One" or "The First," in their language. His merry band, called Wahidi (pronounced Wa-hee'dee), roams this Sahel and the Sahara, stealing from the rich, giving to the poor (really!), harassing the government militia, and wreaking general havoc. He seems to be able to unite all except the Southerners into his band. I think he's a true Robin Hood, and I may be the only

Caucasian in this land to have actually met with him. He seems to have been educated in Europe. He wants things from America, and I might be able to help in that regard. The channel to providing American aid. Maybe in exchange for an end to hostilities. I'm very excited about this and may extend my service in the Sahel even though I earlier mentioned my hope to extend it and transfer South—which is at peace—I think.

As for Amina, the woman of my dreams, I believe she is a true Smiyet sidiya as they would say here— indeed, truly saintly.

Your brother
Harry

Note from Aaron: Likewise, I never saw this one!

■ Holy Beneficence: MIA

October 1968

And sometimes Father Sean O'Sagarty joined us for merriment at Ivan's place. A motley group which included a Hindu, a Catholic, a Soviet Communist, and an American atheist. You could call it fantastic, ironic asymmetry.

But he was there rarely. When the Father was there, he and I talked into the night about God, the one I called the "missing" God, MIA. And drank the holy water, the Scotch or sometimes Irish whiskey, which we could be sure was purer than the water of Dar es Sabir.

One morning, after a night of tumblers and our usual argument about the mysteries of his God, I could no longer resist: "Then come with me, Father Sean."

"Harry, I . . ."

"Just come on. I want you to see what I see everyday."

"I'm worn from taking confessions and from this heavenly water that we've imbibed."

"Never mind. So am I. This won't take long." But I also grabbed his hand and tugged mightily.

Then we marched like two hung-over fools, and holding hands in the *Sara-Nagamaye* fashion. My grip was still firm and strong.

We began from the front portal of my *kaz*. Not one hundred yards away lay a woman, obviously in distress, but with a basket held out asking for alms. She smelled as if she had eaten a can of beans, beans gone off, the night before.

"Here's the detritus of your loving God."

"But Harry, we don't know anything about her."

"Oh, you mean she might be a great sinner. What could she have done? We feed our convicts and murderers better than this!" I dropped a few centimes in her basket and led him on.

Another hundred yards and we encountered yet another woman, under a tree, a young boy of about six lying beside her, his hair turned reddish and stomach distended—signs of acute malnutrition and hunger. She was too weak to even hold out a basket. "Look at this one. What sin did this little boy commit? I hope she survives him, if only to soothe and prepare him in his last moments—to prepare him for his passage to your heavenly reward. And bury him. That would be all the mercy he could expect." I dropped a few *centimes* in her hand. This time Father Sean did as well.

"Harry, I . . ."

"Wait, there's more. And I'm only half way to the schoolhouse!"

"But . . ." Father looked truly distressed.

"Ok. Just one more," as we came upon an old man. At least he looked old. He was missing one leg, with jagged, flesh covered bone protruding at its knee, as he sat leaning against a tree and stretched the other leg towards the roadway. "*Mutilé de guerre*, wounded warrior," I said.

"Whose side?" Father Sean blurted.

"God's side, I'm sure he thought," I said.

"This is what I see everyday, Father. This mercy of your loving God and His Son and beloved Intercessor. This is what I see every day. Imagine how many lost and dying souls there must be throughout just this town. Imagine the whole world so. Your heaven must be terribly overcrowded. What do you say to that?"

"I say . . . I can say only that God works in mysterious ways."

"Yes, mysterious ways. Mystery, miracles, and authority—that is what we get from the one holy, Roman, Catholic, and apostolic church—*Sanctam catholica et apostolicam ecclesiam . . .*"

"Ah, Harry you always amaze me. But yes, we are a faith, Harry. And all this, this mystery, must be taken on faith."

"And then a cure to any one of these three would be a true miracle. And what does the Authority say about those who remain uncured?"

"Perhaps a confession would smooth their path. Perhaps . . ."

"Then you explain that to that dying little boy. I cannot."

Indeed Father O'Sagarty went back to the boy and his mother and spoke to them in their dialect as he smoothed the boy's forehead.

"Perhaps that he'd been born a Muslim. Unlike us Christians, he is predestined for hell."

He gave me that disapproving look. Then he said "Okay. Enough, Harry! We cannot agree on this. I cannot win you over."

"But I will bequeath to you my Missal."

"Do you have another? If not, as a result you'll have none?"

"One of your acolytes will profit more from it, Father, than will I."

"So I believe, Harry."

"Then let's go back to my place, play chess, trip around Aquinas, and sip the nectar of the Celtic gods," I suggested. "And *Illegitimi non carborundum.*" (*Really, fake Latin for* "*Don't let the bastards grind you down.*")

"Aye. Well said!"

Indeed, well said.

■ Second Visit

November 1968

On his next visit, Wahid did not ask for an invaluable shot, and I did not offer one. He came to try to understand this Emricani. We exchanged salutations. He moved slowly. "Think of what I asked you last time." Then, suddenly, he tore himself from a sort of lethargy. He'd chewed and spit (figuratively speaking) and made a decision, I realized.

"There is something I wish to show you, *Nasarah*, Américain, to assist you to understand that I am for the people."

"All right."

"But it must be done now. I must do it now. And then you must tell them about me. Write about me. After the great battle." He rose and slung the carbine over his shoulder.

"Now?"

"Yes. We must go this very instant. You must bring an unopened bottle of fine whiskey."

Fear made me attentive—and sober. The dry mouth and head on the verge of a migraine had become chronic these past few months and put me in no mood for a midnight foray. Still, I had sought this meeting, and I was committed to carrying it through. Besides, Leonard would have my ass in the proverbial sling if I backed out at this point.

"Do you have a jeep?" I hoped.

"Jeep? Where we go no jeep is needed! This way is better. Come!"

I retrieved an unopened bottle of Pere Habert's finest. Then, we went back round my cottage, where a small copse of bushes and dwarf oaks planted by some overly zealous, green-thumbed colonial, obscured the beginnings of the desert beyond. He moved swiftly, though he was stooped in the effort to shield his gangling body behind the dwarf trees. There was a new, almost hidden breach in the shard-topped wall that separated the property we're on from my neighbor's. The place where the watchful boy, Younis, lived.

"Where are we going? On foot?"

"We must be silent," he ordered. "Follow but do not speak."

The dunes were unimpressive little humps at this point, hardly worthy of the name. This panorama had always struck me as a poor imitation of the "real" desert beyond. Still, I was amazed to find how well they can hide man and beast in their ever-changing shadows.

"Here!" He had unslung his carbine and now signaled me to stop. He made a low grunting growl in perfect imitation of the hyenas that forage on the outskirts of this very place. A growl returned from beyond the dunes. "Ya, Hassan," he called in a stage whisper.

"Ya, Wahid!"

"I come with another. A *Nasarah*, an Emricani."

Two figures emerged from behind the dune not twenty feet away, rifles pointed at me, eyes fierce in the blackness. One beckoned, eyes darting, "*Ta'alee.*"

As we moved, I spied the young boy, Younis, watching us from the ersatz window of his poorly constructed hovel.

I followed the Wahid. The barrel of someone's rifle followed me as we moved around behind the dunes. There assembled, the most ragtag group of brigands I have seen, even in this wild, untamed country. Twelve or fifteen armed men, all dressed in filthy gray or white *jalaba*s, most under coarse, camel-hair vests, hunching in a tight circle, hands gripped tightly to the stocks and barrels of their carbines—all staring ferociously at the newcomer.

I recognized the one who misspoke at the meeting with Amina. He hung his head in an attempt to avoid being recognized. In fact, he was the one wearing the baseball cap, the short one they called Saghir. From his demeanor, I sensed that he did not approve of my presence and perhaps would like to become my sworn enemy.

Farther out I could see the white turbans of the others guarding the perimeter. I thought that they've got to do something about those white *jalaba*s and turbans. Yeah, a good laundering. But which will make them to even more efficiently reflect the moonlight and expose them. Wash and color-dye, then, I'm thinking. Or, as I sometimes do, go for brown, the batchelor color, which will serve to hide the dirt and filth.

The nonsense that takes possession of your thoughts—when you're scared shitless.

Several of those bandits closest to us broke into broad grins when Wahid moved up behind me; and they whispered in unison "Ya, Wahid!" as he stepped around me. They rushed to touch and grasp his hands, then the right one over their hearts, as if he had been long lost. I heard snippets of conversation about a "goal" or "mission," and I cursed my creaky, desert Arabic.

"Here is the *Nasarah*," as if offering up a gift for a feast as he stepped away from the gang of greeters, the better to expose me.

They all stopped their chatter, and, above their veils, eyes stared fiercely and seemingly without mercy.

"Welcome him!" Wahid ordered.

One by one they filed by me, first staring me straight in the eyes for a long, embarrassing moment. Lowering their veils, smiling, offering *salaams* and *ahamdileelahs*, and shaking my hand vigorously. Finally nodding as if to stamp the welcome with sincerity.

"Bring us three camels!" Wahid commanded.

Camels materialized from behind a nearby dune. They're hissing, filthy creatures, and my morale sank even further.

"Mount, *Nasarah*. Now we go. Ali!" He called to the tallest in the gang. "Now, *Nasarah*, we go!"

"But... I don't ride!" This is much more than I had bargained for.

"Ha! You ride!"

Nothing inspires greater fear than mounting a camel. I was on, grasping wildly at the smelly blanket and the seemingly lethal, knife-sharp, forked saddle pommel. The one called Ali stood beside, urging the beast to mayhem. Or at least to rise. "Yaa, *jemele! Gume!* Yaa-eep!" He whacked its tough, smelly hide with a stick akin to a birch rod.

The beast undulated, rising a bit from the forelegs, then fully from the rear, protesting in hisses, and spitting all the while. I was wrestling wildly with the soggy, putrid blanket, then grabbing at the razor-like pommel with my shirttail, nearly oblivious to the cutting pain.

"Ya, *Nasarah*, more slowly. Cross your legs. You fight it like a woman," whispered Wahid.

He had a great laugh, as did Ali and the gawking brigands. I fought to regain my dignity and bearing. "Keeya!" Ali struck with the rod and the beast hurtled into the blackness ahead.

"Hut, hut, *Nasarah*! Sing to him!"

I mustered enough voice to deliver my anger. "Hut, hut, you bastard!"

Wahid was then beside me, fiercely grinning under his veil, I imagined, and firing off meaningless expletives. "This way. Heeya!"

Whipped-up sand burned my eyes. I'd lost my way. We'd covered a distance over sand and come to another copse. I nearly crashed into the branches before I realized what they were. The camel slowed to munch, perversely snacking on the dry and thorny growth.

"This way," Wahid whispered now. The band followed behind, dropping away one by one, no doubt to cover our way to the destination and guard this trail.

I had to dig my heels in and strike at the beast to tear him from his prickly, thorny delights. "Heeya!"

"Silence! Now you must go in silence!" Wahid whispered to me and Ali.

I reigned in behind him as best I could. The strange vegetation grew more dense, and the smell, thicker with corruption.

There was the whisper of life here, but I could make out Wahid only by the white points of his *jalaba*, and the glint in his eyes. Even my own mount was invisible to me. I held a hand in front of my eyes to fend off the invisible branches and barbs. They whipped around me. I was riding blind.

"Ya," Wahid whispered.

There was only the brushing noise of our beasts, and the frightening occasional crack of dry, dead underbrush.

Soon I felt pressure and a tug as my mount came to a halt.

Then I heard "The hyenas are plentiful tonight."

"It is the night of the second moon."

"Abdel-Hamid!" Wahid stage-whispered.

"Wahid."

"I have brought the *Nasarah*. Of which we last spoke."

"Then he is as welcome as you are." The voice was hoarse, the speech thick like a drunkard's.

Another tug and the beast knelt. Quietly and without protest— first the forelegs and then the rump. As if recognizing, at last, a force greater than his own. "Descend."

■ ## Prokaza and Promises

November 1968

I dismounted quickly. Ali and the others hung back to guard the entrance. I could barely see the outline of the figure before me. Then a pointed object was thrust at my chest. "I am Abdel-Hamid!"

"He is 'amblin, who has lost his tongue." Wahid stated in seeming consternation.

"Peace unto you. And welcome to our home, our humble village of Zenig Etnin."

"Peace unto you." I repeated. "I am Hamblin." I croaked hoarsely. "I bring you this," I added, holding out the bottle of whiskey.

"*Alhamdileelah.*" The pointed object reached under my arm and tugged me forward. "Come." But the voice was now bodiless, and the object and dense underbrush were all I could feel.

"The peace of Allah on your house," Wahid broke in.

"And on the guests of my house," responded Abdel-Hamid.

In the near distance I could make out a tiny flame, then the opening, through which the flame flickered and revealed a mud and straw front to a squalid hut. A spare movement, then the figure that prodded me from the side. I remembered this place from the visit with Docteur Godin. We could have taken a jeep. But Wahid did not have one, and I suspect that pride wouldn't let him admit it. And there may have been other reasons.

There were others now, perhaps there all along, who moved alongside us, barely disturbing the underbrush. Their eyes flashed wildly, like hundreds of pearls or shooting stars rushing back and forth across a black backdrop.

Then hair and the rough outline of facial features and broken bodies.

"You are the poor and homeless of which this great *Nasarah, ah,* Emricani, speaks! He whose Emricanim can succor the poor. And bring us wished-upon gifts if we are so deserving," Wahid began. Drawing from my brief discourse on the poor and homeless—in class at the *collège?* Something else I might have said in a moment of sentimentality and inattention? Probably an offering, via Jean, to tempt Wahid to come to me, done in my comatose inebriation. Or with one of my monumental hangovers.

I was already losing the thread of this conversation. "What?"

"Look about you, *Nasarah,*" he went on.

"Where are we?" I asked.

"A poor village." Something was different. I noticed it last time, of course. These were not the usual nomadic tents and lean-tos that we see across the desert, nor the mud hut clusters that pass for towns in the Sahel. This gathering was hidden deep in a forest-like copse, a copse in the middle of the desert, dense bushes and acacias like a low canopy of eternal night.

I found my voice. "I am honored that you receive me." Again I held out the bottle to him. This time he grabbed it and tucked it under his longer arm.

"It is we who are honored." It was the same Abdel-Hamid. Standing so close that I smelled his fetid, thick breath, saw the points of his wild and unruly hair and thick, white beard, noted the stump of an arm, that pointed object, which he continued to thrust at me. "We have seen you with the great Docteur of *Russkiye*. He is a blessing to us. We thought we had lost our docteur when the *Français* was killed."

"And how is the sick one?" I had to try to show concern.

"*Mort, mat*…gone. The disease was too much for him. We put him just there behind that outbuilding, in our rapidly overcrowded cemetery."

Then his face came into focus, and my mind again searched frantically back and forth among English, French, and Arabic for the accusing word. It escaped me for that brief moment as it had done the last time. Ah, Russian—*Prokaza!*

The image leered at me. Nearly noseless and pocked face. Squinting eye. One stump of an arm, another almost fingerless fist. My eyes darted to the others, now standing close, eyes fixed to measure my reaction. I noticed the lack of naked, dancing children ubiquitous in the villages in these parts.

"Is there tea, then?" Wahid broke in mercifully. Then to me in English. "You must promise gifts from America—American aid. For all!"

(It seemed that everyone wanted something from us.)

Abdel-Hamid held the stare a moment more, then conceded. "Yes, tea. Miriam! Tea!"

■ Second Epiphany

I was prodded by the stump toward the hovel. "And cigarettes for the *Nasarah!*" There were others. One who crawled on his stumps, another who stared from a featureless face, a woman, gnarled and twisted. *Prokaza!* . . . *Ah* . . . *per!* Such was my epiphany. It finally came to me amid a strange complaisance—and no fear. I will drink tea from their glass. I had already done so. I prayed that no amoebas lurked here—this time. It was good that the tea was still bubbling and so boiling in the glass. *Ogon . . .* This time.

I was prodded through the hut's opening, into the mud dwelling, heavy with charcoal smoke. The tiny flame shot up with our coming and revealed a wild and despairing scene.

Their hovel was packed with neighbors and their adopted family. Noseless, earless, faceless, toothless, lacking a variety of appendages, squeezing in close and staring as fiercely as their desert brothers. These, the very ones I hung back from when I was with Godin.

"Chai, *Nasarah*." She handed me a hot glass of tea and a huge lump of sugar. I, ecstatic that this time the tea was still boiling in the glass.

"Thank you, madam." I first looked her in the eye and then took in the rest. She was topless and breastless, her chest a topography of scars and lesions.

"To you and your guest, Wahid." Abdel-Hamid raised his tea-glass in a mock Western toast. "But, oh, that this were whiskey," he whispered. He gave me what he may have wished was a wink, but succeeded only in fashioning a smirking smile. He poured a bit of whiskey in my tea, then in his. "After all, this will soon turn into water. Within us. And water is nowhere forbidden." Then he attempted what I think was a wink.

"Of course," I agreed. I winked back. "Of course."

They were all watching me with fascination as I raised my glass to silently return the toast. By gesture only, I hoped. I trusted to the flickering firelight to disguise my now trembling hand. I told myself that the trembling was from the combination of whiskeys past and the frenetic camel ride.

They were watching intently, the huddled masses, creeping on their haunches toward the firelight, crowding to watch the *Nasarah* as he was put to the test. I first put the sugar in my mouth, then quickly sipped the boiling tea as if it were a nectar. Or an aged Scotch. I ran my lips along the rim of the glass licking at bits of sugar.

No applause.

All the while, Abdel-Hamid and Wahid were having a very quiet discussion and directing others on how best to unload the camels. It was then that I realized that there were also well-packed donkeys that had soundlessly followed the camel riders. I hadn't noticed, focused on my own camel as I was. The loads were then piled with heavy thumping and clicking sounds as they were loaded into the hovel of the recently departed.

Then "To you, *Nasarah*, who have been brought among us by the merciful Allah." Abdel-Hamid raised his glass. The others still stared, but any fierceness was gone. My hand trembled only a little. I savored the sugar and sipped the tea again. And hoped it would not bring on the dysentery. Again.

"This is the one of whom many have spoken." It was Wahid. I was tempted to think he was maudlin, perhaps from whiskey in his tea. "This is the *Nasarah* who was promised to us. To complete our mission."

Still they squatted on their haunches in front of me, and stared. A ghostly moan came from another place. Those before me only stared, mouths unmoving, stares implacable.

"This is the *Nasarah* of whom I have much spoken, and I have predicted; he will help liberate us from the tyranny and poverty that oppresses us all!" First I heard. News to me. Wahid may be pushing it, our newfound friendship. I was cornered and thought it best to remain silent. He carried on, as if I were not there, or uncomprehending—or a silent, brooding god in this fabricated, mythical cosmology. "This is the one, and you must yield your trust to him! He will bring us a lake of sweets in silver trays. And we may put our liberation in his hands . . . !"

Then there was a humming undercurrent, a low moan of assent.

Wahid*i* urged me with his elbow. Then whispered "They are in dire need."

So I declared, "If my Emricani brothers so will it, they will send many gifts to make your life better."

"*Houri?*" ("Grapes" or, in this dialect, "prostitutes?")

"Virgins," I replied stupidly.

"Services of silver?"

"And that. At least aluminum." They stared at me in wonder. Maybe wondering how a man could lie so.

Abdel-Hamid peered at me through cloudy eyes. Another spoke up. "Yes. I remember this one. He came with the Docteur, the *Ruskiye.*"

Wahid watched and listened from the distance. "Perhaps he was deciding if we are worthy of these things," he interjected.

It was Abdel-Hamid who then interceded, and saved me from myself. Saved me from some other foolish uttering. "It is indeed the same one," he shouted.

Another grunt of assent. As if they all remembered. I felt that I was in a strange dream or nightmare, carried along by the tide of my own fears. I had no answer because I had only the slightest inkling of what they really wanted from me. The very slightest. What these and all the others expected. And so I had a terrible urge to contact Leonard—and I realized that I was truly alone. Aside from Wahid.

"Then let us take *esh, esh b'weke,* and *boule,* to celebrate." It was Abdel-Hamid, village leader, who had interceded, doing so again to save me yet again. "Miriam!" He was merry and jubilant now, hardly aware that he had cut Wahid off in mid-harangue. Just as well. His bright merriment overcame his disfigurement and, in the flickering shadows made by the firelight, he seemed to be dancing like a mad, merry Father Christmas. This was Wahid's wise—but "afflicted"—oracle.

Miriam magically appeared at the instant with the *esh* and *boule* and cigarettes. Great heaping plates and bowls.

"Eat! All eat!" Abdel-Hamid cried, hopping to a spot before one of the bowls (perhaps set there in deference to this guest alone, was one spoon), squatting ceremoniously, and reaching with his almost fingerless fist to scoop up the thick, warm liquid.

"Eat!" came a command in unison from the staring hoard. One urged me with the stump of his arm. Others moved in to squat over the bowls in a pecking order known only to them. I was urged to be first. "Eat, *Nasarah!*"

"I will eat." This, then, was the real test. They were all reaching, with what appendages remained to them, toward the communal plates and bowls, all reaching into the fiery, wiggling millet mold—and shoving gobs toward their crooked, broken mouths. Chunks broke off and fell to the dirt. I could hear the rustling as the second tier scrambled like dogs to retrieve the fallen morsels.

"Good, eh, *Nasarah?*" Abdel-Hamid nodded vigorously in answer to his own question. His eyes were laughing and sparkling. Gobs of hot, wet, jello-like millet fell from his lips, and red, hot sauce dripped through his beard to his neck as he talked. "Miriam makes fine *boule* . . . and also *esh!* Made from the canned tomato sauce from Emrica and the peppers that she grows here!" He was reveling in his self-characterization as the gracious host.

"Very fine. The best I have ever had." Again, the watching as I brought a gob of millet, scooped (yes, by hand) with fiery sauce and microscopic bits of chicken, to my lips. "Miriam is a fine cook," I added. Miriam stood proudly at the back, fanning an invisible blush.

"Well, said, *Nasarah!* And she is my best sister!" It was as if the food and hosting had made Abdel-Hamid drunk. Or maybe the large shot of whiskey in his tea. He weaved back and forth on his haunches as he shoved the hot, rubbery substance to his mouth with rapid and regular motion. A murmur rose all about us.

My mouth was on fire. I dreamt of frothy beer to quench this thirst. Then Abdel-Hamid made leering faces at me, jerking his head wildly in Miriam's direction, crinkling up the right side of his face. At first, I imagined this pantomime was an uncontrollable malaise that attacks these *prokaza* sufferers from time to time. But he continued the jerking twists and contortions, no doubt hoping to guarantee my rapt attention. "My best sister!" he repeated more loudly.

This was one test I could not pass.

Then he jumped up wildly and reached for Miriam who wriggled free and slid away along the wall of a hut. She giggled. He hopped after her, grasping wildly.

"Sidi Abdel-Hamid!"

◼ The Militia Intrudes

"Who goes?" Abdel-Hamid cried as he stopped dead in mid-cavort. The murmuring undertone ceased. Wahid raised his carbine, cocked it, aimed at the sound.

"The hyenas are plentiful tonight!"

"It is the night of the second moon." The same passwords in return as before.

"*Ay-ee-wa!* I am Louis."

"Come, then," Abdel-Hamid beckoned to the intruder. To Wahid: "It is Louis, our lookout. That is our password." To Louis: "What is it?"

"Pardons. The Camel militia are coming."

The gathering lurched into activity. The plates were cleared; the fire, doused. There was a hushed scampering as our audience fled. Flaps of woven branches dropped over the entrances of the huts. Floorboards in what appeared to be the storage hovel creaked and dropped with a clap.

"Here, *Nasarah*, you must wrap in these." Wahid held up soiled, putrid rags. The wardrobe of a recently departed, no doubt. Another test?

"But. . . ."

"The militia are looking for *us!* You must!" Wahid began to don similar rags. "And lie against the furthermost wall, as if you are dying. Face to the wall." He shoved me. To the others, he whispered harshly, "The rifles! Above all, the rifles!"

There was more clamor, grunting and the shoving of heavy objects across the dirt and roots at the back of a hovel. I was nudged again and slumped into a dark and moldy corner. In my putrid garments.

"Eshkoon! Ya eshkoon!" A shout some yards in front of the hovel. They'd found the village. A carbine was cocked.

"Wahid, I . . . ."

"Shhh!"

"Yatoo heenak! Who is here?"

"These are the unclean!"

Another voice from further away. "Unclean. Unclean ones! Out!"

"We are only little villagers." I recognized the voice of Abdel-Hamid.

"Come out, little villager!" the militia-man commanded.

"I am coming out." Abdel-Hamid was busy stuffing gobs of dropped millet from the ground onto a dish.

There was a rustling and sliding. Then, "Eeeyaa! This one is ugly! Stand where you are!"

"Sidi, lord, can we offer you food and drink?" He held up the plate he had just prepared, offering it to the militiaman who stood in front.

"Not from this place! What is this village? It is not on the *Nasarah's* map!"

"The village of death," a subaltern shouted.

"We are *Zenig Etnin* Sidi," Abdel-Hamid offered.

"Ayeewa! We have followed bandits by the camel tracks we have found. Someone tried to erase them, but our trackers see. They end at the edge of this oasis. Are there bandits here?"

"None. But of course you may look. You will take not even tea?" Abdel-Hamid offered.

"Nothing. Only the bandits! If you are hiding them . . . ." This is the voice of the one in command.

"What would we have with bandits? We are only sellers of charcoal, suffering from our curse and the nightmare of our end."

"Yehh, you stink, old man! Lieutenant Vincent, search there and there." To Abdel-Hamid: "Where are the camels that made those tracks?"

"Gone to sell charcoal to the *Taureg* encampment. They have left for the north dunes. For that I am sorry. Forgive me, just lord."

"Just watch your tongue!" the commander shouted.

"I shall, for it may be the next to leave me!" Abdel-Hamid. I'm chuckling in my new wardrobe. Chuckling in silence.

"Leave you?"

"As my hand did."

"Do not hold that stump to me!"

"Or my fingers!" Now he was pushing it.

"Yehh, you have few fingers! I may take another! Or an ear!"

"Yes, lord, some fingers left me a year ago. May yours remain a bit longer as a part of you!"

"Do not sass me, villain! I know you are sassing us. *Alors*, Lieutenant Vincent, what have you found?"

"Only darkness, *Capitaine* Ngokuru."

"Then make fire to give us light!" Exasperated by the lack of bandits, the *Capitaine* had an ever more menacing tone.

"Fire, *Capitaine?*"

"You will know how. As we did in the Zaghawa village."

I could hear Wahid crawling toward the front of our hovel. I imagined seeing the glint of his rifle barrel. Someone shuffled up behind him. "No, Abu Wahid. They will only come with more. Unlike Zaghawa villagers, we can hide nowhere! Please, Abu Wahid!" There was whispering and shuffling back towards my place.

Meanwhile, the militia *capitaine* was staring at me through the darkness. Even in this dim light, I could see his lip curl to the right and his right eye twitch uncontrollably. Still, he tried to squint and appeared to focus on me. I quickly turned my head again to the wall.

After what seemed like many minutes, Abdel-Hamid again attracted his attention. "Yeeahh, *Capitaine*, I beg you!" Now he was kneeling and begging. "Take what you wish! All the charcoal we have! But please do not burn that house!"

"Which house?"

"That one to the right of you! Where your man now stands!

Please do not burn that one, for it holds all of our poor possessions! All of our charcoal!"

"You beg well!" A muffled blow.

"Yaaee! Yes, I beg you, *Capitaine*! You may rain your blows upon me, but please do not burn that house! That is our palace and the center of our village!"

"Do you have fire, Lieutenant Vincent?"

"Yes, *Capitaine*!"

"Then have your soldiers burn that house!"

"Oh, no!" More muffled blows. "Please do not!" Abdel-Hamid was clearly in agony now.

"Yaha! And prepare to fire when the bandits come out!"

"There is no one!" Abdel-Hamid was overwrought, truly terrified—or a consummate actor.

Next the crackling and rumbling gusts that signaled that the fire had taken.

"Stand, Lieutenant Vincent, and have your men prepare to shoot!"

"I see them, *Capitaine*!" There was a round of popping from his automatic. Then from others. Wahid shuffled his feet impatiently.

There was a magnificent groan from Abdel-Hamid. Then more firing. Abdel-Hamid still groaning histrionically.

"There! One is there!" The *capitaine* himself began firing. The entire militia fired for what seemed like several minutes. Then silence. The only sound was the crackling of the dry wood as it burned.

Moments passed. Then "There is no movement, *Capitaine*! They are all killed!"

"Yes, Lieutenant Vincent. The General will be pleased with us."

There was more quiet. I could hear their boots grind on the dirt and sand. "Maa-ee! There are no bodies!"

"Then they are in the fire!"

"Yes, *capitaine*! But it is so hot!" Nevertheless, the lieutenant began to walk through the burning cinders. And ordered his men to do so as well.

"Walk into it, Lieutenant Vincent!"

"But it is so hot!" a subaltern echoed.

"If we cannot prove bodies, the general will not hear of it! We must take ears that he must see to prove this success. Well, then, some of these will have to do." He pointed into the crowd of the afflicted.

"Yes, *capitaine*. Yet we have none."

"Yes, we do." He plunged into the gathered crowed, seized two denizens by their collars, shoved them at Lieutenant Vincent. "Take these ears. Ha, they should pull off easily enough."

There were mild screams from those who know such pain every day.

I could still hear the gusting roar of the fire and the crack of straw matting as it curled and tumbled.

"Bones, Lieutenant *et Capitaine*! Here are bones!" a subaltern shouted.

Abdel-Hamid emitted a deep groan. "Our palace! There were no bandits. Only the village goat. For milk."

Next we heard running boots and another muffled thud.

"Only goat, my lord!" Another thud.

"Still we have done well, Lieutenant Vincent. We have given them notice. We can bring back ears to our general. Let us gather the others and leave this putrid place. We or others will return tomorrow to prevent the bandits' return. A reminder, hider of bandits!" Another thud for good measure.

Then, at that moment, with brilliant timing, the lepers' (the Wahidis') camels, groaning as if cursing, were ridden in to prove the truth of Abdel-Hamid's story.

Wahid had slid to my place and held my arm. His breathing was fierce and irregular.

"Are you sure you will take no food?" Abdel-Hamid offered. It has been dusted with our magic charcoal that makes men strong and virile."

"It makes men more virile?" the *capitaine* asked. Without waiting for an answer, he ordered the lieutenant to take the dish. "Then eat of it, Lieutenant, and let me know if it wreaks its magic. Tell me when it does so. Eat! Then pass it to the others. Eat of it!" he ordered.

The lieutenant grimaced. Abdel-Hamid retrieved the dish and scooped in some more millet. And charcoal dust. The lieutenant took a tiny morsel in his hand, soaked it in sauce, and ate still holding his grimace. Then gagged. The other militiamen followed suit.

"You will see," Abdel-Hamid declared. "Warn your women, for you will be very mighty."

"If this works," said the *Capitaine*, "we will be back for more!"

"Then for this moment, go with Allah," Abdel-Hamid called.

The militia men mounted and quickly rode off, no doubt fearing the *capitaine* would have them eat of the *esh* as well. The groans of the militia camels quickly grew distant.

■ A Great Laugh

"Come, *Nasarah*. I am sorry for this unexpected intrusion." Wahid rushed out, carbine still at the ready. He bent over the two unfortunates, ripped off pieces of his leper's *jalaba* and wrapped them as bandages around their bloody, earless heads.

Then he strode to Abdel-Hamid. They conferred in whispers. All was quiet for a moment, then wild laughter.

I rushed out to confront them, angry and bewildered. The two of them were sitting in the soft earth and sand, laughing wildly.

"Feh, Abdel-Hamid, you are a camel's ass!" I saw a new, rollicking side to this fierce bandit.

"And you are like the wind, like the fart that thrusts through and out our donkey, grinding the arsehole!"

"You call me what? 'Yes, *Capitaine*. Oh pity us! Do not, oh *Capitaine*, do not burn that edifice, our palace, the center of our village!' Ah, hah, hah, hah!"

"I will roast in eternal damnation! Ah, but I was magnificent, was I not, Abu Wahid! That building could only protect the charcoal from the rain. And truly we have no need of it since, as year follows year, there are no rains. And now we have even more charcoal to sell! And a goat to make *meshoui!*"

"You were! Magnificent! You should be in the national theatre!" Wahid affirmed.

"Would that there was such a one! The play could be one about, and by, the already dead."

"Would that there was! If ever I am in power, I will create one. For you." Then they recommenced guffawing, rolling on the ground like five-year-olds and slapping each other wildly. "I will steal you another goat."

"Ah, hah! Oh, come here, *Nasarah*, and share our mirth!" He was beckoning to me.

I stood helplessly, amazed at their capacity to taunt their enemy. And I sympathized, not knowing how to show it, with the earless two who endured such pain. Then Abdel-Hamid shook his head, looked toward me, and nodded toward these two with missing ears. "They are the brave ones."

"Indeed they are."

Then they recommenced the hilarity. The tall, lean one, muscular in those torn, fetid rags, and the short, paunchy one, a disfigured Father Christmas. Both now sitting in the sand and dirt and doubled over in rollicking hilarity. Even now, even with that demeanor, Wahid looked fierce and foreboding. "Ha, ha! What is it, *Nasarah?* Have you ever seen such masterful acting?"

"Never. Aside from the English actor, Lawrence Olivier, or, rather, the Three Stooges of America."

"This one is a *waha*, a true master!" Wahid pointed to Abdel-Hamid.

"I am!" He rose, still shaking with laughter and evidently pleased with himself. "Miriam!"

"Ah, we must go, Abdel-Hamid. Ahhyai, we must. Abdel-Hamid, forgivenesses, but I must ask this one to call in the *Ruskiye* Docteur for your injured ones and return himself to his sleep!"

"And I must gather my people to move the merchandise. Blessings, Wahid. But you must return in one day for our *meshoui*. Bring this one as well."

The villagers appeared as if on cue, from the shadows of the woods. Converging, like the living dead, on our cluster. "Pack up the things! We must move them tonight!" And the near-dead shed their paralytic fear and rushed to the task. "Mohammed, go bring over here the camels of our guests."

"These militiamen, these police, what were they looking for?" I asked Wahid.

"For me, of course. They always try to track me. Or other Wahidi." He seemed very pleased with himself. With that, we mounted those very same camels that we rode in on.

"How did they know to search for you here, and not in our town?" I asked.

"I cannot say. But they have good trackers."

"Can't they track us from this village to my *kaz*, then?" I wasn't sure I liked this.

"They can," he answered. Then I was sure I wasn't sure I liked this.

Alarms sounded in my head as the rushing, pre-dawn, pre-Harmatan winds cut through us in the desert.

"And if they come to ask me?"

"Don't be such a woman, *Nasarah*. Ah, Emricani. They would never suspect you. We are murderers of *Nasarah*! Of all whites! And our friends will cover our tracks from their village to the third dune. But don't go on telling them you are not *Nasarah* as you do!"

"How is it that the police did not know of the village until now?"

"The French have contributed to increasing the camel police, the militia. They have new people, from the Ngumbaye and Narangar tribes, and they are infiltrating throughout the desert."

"They seem very brutal."

"They are not well trained as police. And they hate the *Taureg*, *Toubou*, and *Ajima*."

"A feud?"

"Yes. The story is that the Narangar were once slaves bought and sold by the *Taureg* to the Arabs, in what was called *razzia* or *rezzou*. Who then sold them to the Europeans. Now they have an opportunity to turn history on its head."

"So do we all."

"Aye, so do we all. And you are the great *Nasarah*, the Emricani (at least he was making an effort), who will lead us out of this cauldron. You had better think how so, little *Nasarah*." The diminutive was surprising. Then he took his rod to his camel and pulled ahead of me.

It was a rough and sandy way back to my *kaz*. Wahid was pensive. My mind was in a chaotic search to isolate a commanding theme, to orient my report to Leonard.

The long night and incipient hangover finally caught up to me. I relaxed my grasp of the pommel and rocked to the ship-like rhythm of my mount. The brooding wind, black night, and slow, clumsy rhythm lolled me into a half sleep.

I only heard the word "*Nasarah!*" simultaneous to the thump that met my tail bone. There was a guffaw in the distance. My camel was spitting between roars as if to imitate that guffaw. I was not too surprised to find myself on the ground.

"A good landing, *Nasarah*." Wahid was standing over me, elbows akimbo. "You must be a veteran of the *parachutist*s!" Finally, grudgingly it seemed, he offered me his hand.

An explanation would have been useless.

"I take my leave of you, *Nasarah*. Emricani. 'arry, I think they call you. I'll take your miserable beast as well. Now you are in good hands."

"Thank you, Wahid," I grumbled groggily.

Jean was suddenly beside me. "Come, Monsieur 'arry."

"Jean, you rogue, you saw it all! And I thought you were with your woman."

"Monsieur? I have brought her with me." Pretense of naiveté? Enough for one night. I was too tired to challenge this.

Still, I rushed to Godin's *kaz*, woke him, and told him that Jean had brought me news of great injury at the *Prokaza* village.

"You will go with?" he asked.

"I cannot. I must prepare tomorrow's lessons." It was near 3:00 a.m. I had to send a message.

Godin rushed to his Land Rover, old fashioned doctor's bag in hand. Rushed to minister to them, the afflicted ones—without further word to me.

"Take the spare bed, Jean," I offered, "for your conjugal reuniting."

WTF: LEPERSATZINIGETNIN.COPSEAT4KM.MAYHVGU NCACHE.STOP

Maybe I shouldn't have mentioned guns at all.

■ Younis Again 2

November 1968

The next time, before dusk, Younis was stooped in his yard as if digging for something. I had brought lesson books to get us started. I tried to engage his eyes and avoid peering at the hole made in the sand that he was scooping out.

"*Salaam*, young man. How was your day?"

"*Salaam*, Mas . . . Monsieur Harry. My day was of too much work."

"I'm sorry to hear that. Must you work every day like this?"

"Every day, unless the family of Master Yacob Mikune make a *voyage*. But then I often have to watch his two little children."

"Does the master pay well?"

"I am not paid. My father has been paid. Paid by the master for me—for my work."

"Where is your father?"

He seemed to be holding back tears. I thought I might be digging a little too deeply for the poor boy. "My father is at Bakuru. He is a grower of sheep."

"Ah, a shepherd. Do you have brothers and sisters?"

"Many. But our mother is dead in the last birth, and my father has been doing all. That is why he must sell me. He has sold my sisters for the *mahr* and the brothers as well into servitude. Some to the Toubou and others far away."

And now the tables were turned. For centuries the Arabs and some Sahelians, like the Zagarhia and Toubou, had been capturing and enslaving the Sara-Ngumbaye. Now it was the other way around. The vengeance of history, as Wahid called it. Or the cuckolding by history, as some have said.

"So how have you ended up here?"

"I was sold as a young child and made to do the bidding of my Arab masters—who also used me for pleasure. That is how I was gived to the Master Evian—a slave to serve always his body needs."

His story caught me off guard. I understood that he had been "lent" to Evian by his master. I dropped my questions—at least while I searched to position them more, should I say, "gently."

Younis turned to enter an outbuilding, a hovel it seemed, behind the main house. I did not feel I could approach to make my teaching offer at this point.

■ Younis 3

November 1968

"But how can I understand that?" He was at the height of excitement that very evening.

"By first reading this." I handed him a heavily illustrated set of books and comics that I had brought from home.

"But I cannot read these . . . ." Tears began to flow.

"Then I will teach you. I've seen you begin to pick out sounds and words!"

I went to talk to Yacob al Bashar about giving Younis some study time. He was a mid--level bureaucrat working for the *Ministre de l'Energie*. The oil and gas man. I bet I would later learn that he had been hedging his bets, neatly cozying up to all the rebellious groups while working for this government. He was skeptical. "Why would you do this *Professeur?* He is but a servant. What need has he to learn? Especially English."

"You and I know, Monsieur Bashar, that he is very bright and eager to learn."

"I can think of no good reason to educate a sla . . . servant."

"I can. To help you with your bills and correspondence, and other requirements of your very demanding job." I might as well appeal to his ego. Kiss his ass.

"I and my wife have done this well." He was looking for reasons to discourage Younis's education.

"Shouldn't your wife be tending to the children? And having more? More 'things?'" Nice appeal to his manhood. This was getting painful.

But then I hit upon it. "There will be many requirements to communicate with English-speaking counterparts throughout Africa and Europe and even the USA, once oil and perhaps gas discovery occurs and production is underway. Even the telecom people speak only English. Are you proficient in English?"

His look told me he hadn't thought of that. The wheels began to turn.

"I would only need two hours per day of his time since he is such a fast learner." I was pushing it here. "And it would be at no cost to you."

"Except in Younis's lost time." Still on point, though I could tell he was softening up. But then I'd learned never to take Ngumbaye social behaavior as ceding an argument.

"You will be more than remunerated when he has mastered the language," I assured him.

"One hour per day and we'll try it for a maximum of three months."

"One and a half. Ninety minutes," I countered.

"If he is struggling, we will cancel the lessons," he countered. Hard bargain. That discussion was closed. "And Américain, watch your back. Once the telecom is in, they believe they may not have further use for you or, especially, your compatriots." But I thought I could tell he reveled in such rumor mongering.

As for the "no further use" warning—rumors, I think. Did he frequent Mama's?

I determined to use the weekends for these lessons as well. And insert a bit of math where I could, e. g. how many in Robin Hood's Merry Men? How many if one is killed? Then triple the number killed. How many additional men should Robin then recruit? . . . X – 3Y, etc.

I related this story of recruiting via radio message, noting that a youngster was my new informant. A great addition, since he would relate all dinner gossip to me.

Once in a while, there would be a useful nugget.

■ Second Try—Injuns

November 1968

Terry and Joe were mounted in their Land Rover. Heading for the outback to raise the microwave poles, I guessed. Across the parade ground. Terry was driving. They stopped for salutations.

"Where all y'all goin'?" I asked in my best Texan.

"Start to set up our MCW poles," Terry grinned.

"Start to set up our MCW poles," Joe grinned.

"Bright 'n early," I offered.

"Catch the worm," Terry shot back.

"All y'all be careful out there."

"Finally soundn' good, yer accent," Terry grinned again.

"Workin' on it." I was. Studying Zane Grey and Larry McMurtry's books like *Horseman Pass By* and others. Really.

Then they tore off the parade ground and onto the road. The road north. The very same road we took on what I might have assumed was Terry's first day. I don't think I'll ever know if it was. His first day, that is.

I was on my way to school to catch up on my students' entries in the comp books when the two of them came tearing back through the gate. Even made the sleepy guards jump. Terry saw me and sped over the parade ground to where I was, at the door to the school, classroom *cinquième*.

"That was really quick work!" I observed.

"Same as th' other day. Tooregs mounted and waitin' fer us, I think. That's two outta two tries to go north. We're gonna need some protection."

"We'll go to the *sous-préfet*. With Antoine. Get you some guards. I'll try to get my waterman, Ibrahim. He can fight off the whole gang of them. But not until I'm off duty, say around 13:00. Let's meet at Mama's."

"That's twice." Terry repeated. I don't know if he meant twice chased by "injuns" or twice at Mama's.

But the *sous-préfet's* assistant was our first obstacle. He was irritated that we had roused him from his siesta. He told us that the *sous-préfet* was not in town, and that we could not see him for at least a week. He bore a perpetual smirk that raised my blood pressure.

"Yep. Welcome to Dar es Sabir," I said to Terry. "We'll try later."

We did—that very afternoon. In fact, the *sous-préfet* returned to his office a week earlier than expected. To our chagrin, since the request for assistance produced nothing. Only a half-hearted offer that he might speak to the *Capitaine* Ngokuru. To give Terry and Joe an escort. So much for Terry and Joe's second try.

Interestingly, when the *sous-préfet's* assistant opened the door, I caught a glimpse of a woman not likely to be his wife. In fact, she was the alluring Fatima, previously of Partenay's pre-lunch, Deux Chevaux lorry fame. In a state of incomplete dress. That must be where he planned to spend his week, our *sous-préfet!* Save this for later use, I thought.

If necessary.

■ Père Habert

His sobriquet, *"Père,"* was a term of respect like the "abu" in Arabic. (Not the honorific for a priest.) He was the son of a bartender and barmaid; but now a relic of Leclerc's desert war. Or he was one of its casualties. He was quick to show us the scars where a machine gun had caught him in the legs.

Thirty years ago, *Père* Habert was kicking around French Equatorial Africa, mostly in Djémélia (Djémélia before the name changed from Ft. Ferfina, as "our" town was Leclercville before Dar es Sabir). "I yearned to join, but I was told, being neither foreign nor officer material, that I could be neither foreign subaltern nor French officer," referring to the Foreign Legion recruiting rules.

When the Germans invaded and set up the Vichy government, Habert answered the call. From General Leclerc and the *Force Françaises Libre*, the Free French. Where he could be a noncom.

And there he found his calling. Logistics and supply; but, he did not hesitate to tell us, supporting the infantry on foot, day by day.

He followed Leclerc from Chad to Libya, back and forth, north and south across the desert and eventually to the Sudan. He took the oath, the renowned *Serment de Koufra*, that he would fight on until the French flag flew over Strasbourg Cathedral.

"C'était pénible." It was tough duty.

And so Habert fought until he was wounded. "I was so wounded that I would not walk for nearly six months. And then I was placed in the care of the Troisième Medicale nurses of Leclercville, now Dar es Sabir.[6]

I was lucky to be cured and lucky to meet the lovely Belita, whom I married. There it is."

---

[6] Meaning "house or door to or of patience"

And there it was. The bartender and barmaid's son knew the trade. He received his discharge and began to service the various divisions stationed at this desert outpost. Which he dubbed Harry's Bar. For the romance of Hemingway's Venitian bar. (And an honor to me as well—anticipating my coming? Right?

Right.)

And, of more interest, he was commissioned by the *Service de Documentation Extérieure et de Contre-Espionnage (SDECE)*, to watch the movements of all the populations. He made his life here and thought of me as a man of quality, a gentleman. I must be, given that I carried his bar's name.

Actually, since independence, he was also commissioned by the SDECE to keep an eye on everyone. The *Taureg* and Wahidi. Also the Russians . . . the Americans . . . and others, too numerous to list. Like my Miriam, his Belita was a font of information that she picked up through gossip from her sources around the town. Though I was never sure how much of Miriam's was true, and how much made up (and often from those same sources). The gossip gave local color to my reports, which no doubt paralleled his. So that the wireless listeners, the *Third Para*, would get similar reports from two sources, making mine all that much more believable and confirmable. I needed to stay in good stead with this man.

This last vestige of colonial hegemony.

■ The Course of Our History

November 1968

The course of our history is often spiced with coincidences. So it was on that day that I took a different route to school and ran into the *légionnaire capitaine* on his way to militia drill. As, always, he proffered his left hand, expecting my right one. As always, I hesitated from confusion before offering my right hand. He looked straight on at me as I flushed.

His faithful *guépard*, his (really kind of scaled down) cheetah called Féroce, at his side, also looked straight on at me. So that one moved slowly, almost cagily, when meeting the *capitaine*. It was said that the *capitaine* saved this cheetah's life. Or that the *guépard* saved the *capitaine's* life; and so was responsible for his soul. One or the other.

So the *légionnaire capitaine* had Féroce well trained. Although this *guépard*, had the wild ways he showed off to us. Still, he responded to his given name, Féroce. Even as he marched alongside upon command, he continued the menacing growl and sneaked a quick and forboding look at the closest human. He smelled of his raw meat dinner that the *légionnaire capitaine* managed to procure for him. How and where was a mystery to me since we were at least a hundred kilometers from the nearest cattle ranch, if you can call it that. Jean, and especially Rashid, seemed to get along well with the beast.

Salutations done, he added, "This is the one you must have for your escape."

Or he may have said "escapade."

"I'm on my way to teach them some discipline as I have done morning after morning. I fear they will never be to form! Perhaps they cannot understand."

"Then I hope that you will not know conflict until you have succeeded in the military drilling," I said. "How does it go with your interpreter?"

He ignored the question (a sign that things were not going "great" with Akhween) and went back to the warning thought. "Well, there isn't much time. Not much time before we see the Wahidi and perhaps, with their allies, attempt to overwhelm this town."

"Soon?" I asked.

"Yes. You haven't heard? Killing the doctor and the veterinarian was the first salvo. They will come."

"And how do you know this thing?"

"Ah, we have the best of intelligence, we the Third Para. We know what is known by the very best." If he only knew.

"Also, it is said that Wahid wants to make Dar es Sabir the capital of his newly acquired province."

Thus it was that I was certain who had stolen my first radio. Who was listening to our conversations. The *Troisième Parachutists*, the Third Paratrooper Division. I mentioned the Dar capital in one of my messages. From a hint from Wahid, but with no certainty. Anyway, thanks for the compliment, I thought.

I then shook his hand and waited until he was out of sight before turning on my heels and heading back to my *kaz*, back to report this enlightening conversation.

But the message I composed in my mind was not sent. The parties were not further notified about the assumed Wahid*i* plans, at least not yet. For it was then that I realized I could not send this information by radio, even encoded, without risking tipping our hand about the double twist (the one I hadn't completely figured out) as well. Or should I? But that we had to find another way to inform HQ and, perhaps, settle on a date to make our escape (or "escapade") from the impending havoc and possible death. Confusing.

After all, I planned to tell the Wahid*i* not to attempt to overwhelm the town at this time, when the militia will be present in great numbers; or tell the militia that the Wahid*i* are planning to attack before militia reinforcements come. I thought this would encourage some wisdom of thought, some second guessing, by the two leaders.

But instead, it could provoke the very attacks I was hoping to avoid and, like our nemisis, "I don't provoke."

Really.

■   Younis 4

Mid-November 1968

The next time I saw him he seemed to be digging at the same place in the back forty of his honor, Master Yacob Mikune. I approached just a bit closer but not too close, so as not to spook him. He was burying something. It looked like a red, spherical candy box.

"*Salaam*, Younis Sidi. What are you burying?"

"*Salaam*, Monsieur. It is my *gris-gris*, Monsieur Harry. It will protect me. I have digged it up to place this medicine in with Koran."

"Do you have the entire Koran in that little box?" I tried to approach for a better look at the open box. He moved around, back to me, so that I could not see.

"No, Monsieur. But a small piece of it with a saying about Mohammed on the container, *Mohammed, the messenger of Allah, the one and most merciful.*"

"Ah, a *gris-gris*. I thought you wore them."

"I have another that I wear. It is from my father and wrapped in fine leather. This one is for special prayers and my passage to *Yondo.*" For his rite of passage, his attainment of adulthood.

This I understood. "And does it work well for you?"

"I do not have diseases, Monsieur, so it is working well."

For reasons I cannot explain, I was hesitant and nervous about broaching my suggestion. I may have feared a rejection and a slap at my powers of persuasion. I may have feared not being able to reach this one and, so, all the others at the collège as well. One day, it would finally spill out: "I can teach you things."

"Of what things, Monsieur? What more could I learn that I do not get from Master?" He might shoot back with a note of skepticism in his look and in his voice.

"School things. Reading and the maths. As we do in the *Collège.*" I would fumble for a good answer. After all, these are not tools for a working slave. "But for when you are free of this indentured servitude."

"When will I be free? I believe I have been sold forever."

"There will come a time. When you will be freed of this. It is known that such slavery will be banished from the entire world."

"From the whole world. But not this part of it. So why would I want to know these school things?"

Foolishly, I stammered out, "And then you will use these tools you learned to make your way—like a wise prince among men."

"Like Wahid, who went to university?"

"Exactly! Like Wahid, who may free you all." I said this with as much certainty as my skeptical mind would allow.

"Yes, Monsieur. My father has told me of such things. Of how the Wahidi will free us all. But now I must go."

"I have even spoken with Master Bukuru who agrees. He has given us ninety minutes each day. A true gift." I shouted as he receded.

"So that the next time I see you, I will also tell you a story from my world. A story not unlike the one you have heard about Wahid and the Wahidi."

He turned, then smiled as he put his hand over his heart and gave me a slight bow in salutation.

And thus it began, with many turns and twists, and the usual frustrations and, sometimes, anger. And we did English first, in the theory that once Younis mastered the Roman alphabet and learned to use a dictionary, both languages, French which he knew to speak, and English, would become his.

I vowed that they would.

■ Leonard

Late November 1968

The sticky, stringy haze seemed glued to my eyes.

"Come on, Hamblin, Old Sport."

"Away, rogue!" I mumbled.

"You know I can't understand that dialect shit!"

"Who?"

"Me, sport."

And there he was. Sporty himself in his pressed khaki shorts and bleached white knee socks. The plaid shirt matched nicely. All neat and crisp and topped off with that winning, boorish, all-American smile.

"Leonard, my nemesis."

"I guess you've been through a bit. It's 10:00. I told the director you'd be late for work."

"I'll bet he chewed my ass. . . ."

"Says we Americans have stinking work habits. 'Not you, Monsieur,' he says to me. 'You are different, having come all this way and not a piece of your clothing out of place.' Breeding, I tell him."

"Yes, breeding. I'm sure even he grasped that implication." I doubted whether Leonard grasped my sarcasm.

"No doubt. But what can we do?"

"Where's that hyena, Jean? Jean!" I emphasized the command on the last syllable (OK, the only syllable) an ultimate *ne* that I add for emphasis. As always, he appeared from nowhere, still bearing his roguish grin, and bowed like a practiced Oriental to our guest.

"Jean, coffee."

"Yes, Monsieur."

"And goat's milk to sweeten it." Jean grinned vaguely at Leonard.

"What did you ask him for?" Leonard asked.

I was not so convinced he didn't understand. "Coffee."

"Something a bit stronger for me, please. It's the middle of the day, Hamblin, isn't it?" he added with that Northeastern tone of half apology that some must find engaging. "And five o'clock somewhere. Besides, your milk is not pasteurized." He understood all right.

"Not pasteurized," I repeated and then "And whiskey for our guest. Well pasteurized!"

"Well pasteurized, Monsieur?"

"Never mind, Jean."

"Your wish is my command, Monsieur." Jean was on his best, most obsequious, behavior. But the hint of a grin seemed to recall my tumble the night before last. Or perhaps he was in collusion with Leonard—as he may have been with Terry and Joe.

Leonard, always careful, waited until Jean had disappeared into the detached kitchen. "Did he really say what I thought he said?"

"He really said that. It must be in the training, yes Leonard?"

He stared at me a moment, then recovered. "So, Hamblin, how is this business coming?"

"Wait till I have my first cuppa."

"Of course. So how will our weather be?" he joked.

"I think it will be sunny and warm, today."

"You're always pretty accurate in these things, Old Sport. From this moment, I'll call you O.S." I wished he wouldn't show me that British affectation of his. Maybe it's only a well-bred Yankee accent. A reminder that this one isn't from the same species. As us.

I stood reminded.

"I'm a good guesser," I added.

"A good kisser too, I hear, O.S." Him too. Somebody must have written an article about us. I'm glad Miriam is off to Abouchard or another place this week and not in my bed—with Leonard here. As for Amina . . .

"We get pretty desperate out here, but you're not my type." I reminded him.

"I gathered that. Ah, thank you Jean. *Merci.*" Jean bowed again to him and added his unique phrasing, "I am grateful for your gratitude—most kind one."

Leonard seemed to like what he perceived as Jean's obsequiousness. "Well trained, that one, O.S." It was obvious to me that Jean was having him on.

"Trained him myself," I lied. "From experience." I lied some more.

"I didn't realize you'd had servants before. I mean before coming here."

I slurped my coffee noisily to cover his grating good humor. Jean brought me a pack of cigarettes right on cue. I couldn't resist adding "Leonard, there's really a lot you don't know about me." Or about what I've read.

"Well, I'm sure. Now tell me how you've been doing," he added, quickly mustering to the point.

"Very well." I lit a cigarette to stall and watch him wriggle in unbearable suspense.

"You know what I mean," he says with some remonstrance in his tone.

"What exactly *do* you mean?" I stalled in replying.

"Your work."

Let's see how he likes this one: "The kids are cute. Disruptive sometimes, but cute. I've got that American openness that they're not used to. 'You give them a finger, they take an arm.' That's what my colleagues tell me. Not as a compliment. Then again, I'm beginning to take on the traits of the colonialists here. Not good."

"That's all very interesting, but I'm not doing that part of the job evaluation." Raised eyebrows.

"You really should come by and observe a class." I was half joking.

"For your director, what is it, Partoi? He insists on it. I'll have to, for show." He sounded sorry.

"Partenay. Then we had better go. I've got *quatrième* at 11. Last class today."

"We can do it tomorrow," he said.

"So you're staying the night?" I felt some disappointment.

"At least two nights. Or until a plane comes in. Maybe the air force. To rescue me."

"How nice. We'll have to do a proper dinner. And, by the way, who will rescue *me*?" I was sure Jean would never be up to this. The dinner, I mean. Spiced with a typical dollop of sand. I'd show Leonard how delightful life can be here. Rub his nose in it. Or C rations all around.

"Yes. Three hundred miles of this country, I'm in no mood to turn around and do it again. Also, I should stick around for Thanksgiving. Happy almost Thanksgiving."

"And to you. I see you brought the turkey. I thought you'd come by plane," I said. "The air force had been coming in about once every two weeks lately. And taken time for a little chat. Nice to keep my C ration inventory up, but not great for subtlety. They were asking lots of questions." I'm glad he missed the "turkey" innuendo.

"Actually, I came in a Rover. Hired a driver in Djemélia. Delightful chap. Fought with LeClerc and knows all the bandits. Got us through the bandits' roadblocks. He seemed to know those guys. Got us right through using the doctor ploy. Always carry my great Great White Doctor black bag." He pointed to the old-fashioned black bag on the table. "Driver claims to know Wahid, though he won't have anything to do with him, he says. Says he knows this Habert, the expatriate. Good guy, he says. Do you know him?"

"You'll have to introduce me to your driver who knows Wahid. As for Habert, I sometimes drink at his bar. He says he's named it Harry's Bar. Not after me. After the Hemingway one."

"Yes, perhaps my driver can help you make contact. Do you need help in making contact?" I was impressed that he'd taken so long to get around to it.

"Actually not." Meaning actually I don't need his help finding Wahid.

"Then you've made contact!" He seemed overjoyed. And a bit surprised, I think.

"You could say that."

"Finally." He slumped in his chair, suggesting great, long-awaited relief. "And which reminds me, here are the codes you asked for. They come with directions on how to load them. It's in a cryptology they will easily break. The better to allow them to think your messages are secret. Hell of a trip to bring you this small package." He handed me a manila envelope. Hell of a trip to bring me this stuff.

"Well, contact of a sort."

"Of a sort?" He slumps even further in his chair. "What does *that* mean?"

I couldn't help but tweak his nose. I was sort of stringing him on. Getting him back for the kisser stuff. "Just what you might think it means . . . old boy."

"Don't smart-ass me, Hamblin. We haven't had a transmit from you in nearly a month. Believe it or not, we were worried about you!" He was back-up-straight in his chair now.

"How touching!"

"Why haven't you maintained contact?"

"I thought it best not to—without the breakable, unbreakable code. You might also say I'm being watched." I was trying out my most conspiratorial posture.

"By?"

"I'm not sure. Well, I think Jean might be on to me. The closet keys in this place are not very functional. He might have been prowling around while I was gone. Anyway, my best suit is missing. I thought I had put it in the closet with the transmitter."

"Is the transmitter still there?" He seemed genuinely concerned now.

"Haven't you heard? Gone within seventy-two hours of receiving it. When I was asleep with the debilitating shits. Earl and Hank brought me another. That's when I noticed my khaki suit missing. Now *that* was heartbreaking. They were shooting me full of strychnine at the time. I might have been suffering some kind of delirium. The visions came and went."

"Of the suit?" he asked.

"Of the thieves. The radio thieves."

"Ah, when did you report what sounds like amoebiasis—if not via radio, to Hank and Earl?" A doctor's mind must go directly to diagnosis.

"Immediately. Yes. But I forgot to save you a shit sample. And report the theft. And the strychnine shots from our local urgent care unit."

"Jesus. You should never take their shots! Strychnine! Jesus!" Still, that was but a concern only of the instant. "Well?"

"Not like there were lots of medical choices. As for the thievery, Jean would wait for the highest bidder. He might go to the Russians, but never to Wahid. No *baksheesh* in that."

"Yes, I suppose you're right. But have you actually met this Wahid?" he plowed on.

"And if I have?"

"Quit playing with me, Hamblin!"

"Sorry, Leonard. There might be bugs around here. Can't be too careful."

I let an awkward silence play out. I'm really enjoying his discomfort. I want him to feel as bad as I do, hangover and sore butt included. "Leonard, I cannot tell a lie. I have met the enemy and he is mine."

"Very histrionic of you. What is he like?"

"Sharp like a *kabira* knife," I stated firmly.

"Did he threaten you?"

"The contrary. Took me up-country to meet some of his favorite 'people'." I enjoyed his building consternation.

"Dropped that Marxist-Leninist bullshit on you, eh?" he assumed. With a bit of a smirk to go with it.

"Not really. I think he's hoping for some aid from us. From the USA. So he just let me look. Rolled his carbine on his thighs. I saw some other interesting stuff."

"Like?" He was all the way forward on the chair. All ears.

"First of all, he had his cousin Rashid lead me round behind police headquarters. To a forlorn old shed about thirty yards behind. The stench intensified within the first twenty yards. Overwhelming. Rashid covered his nose with a bandana, fiddled with a lock (God knows why a lock) and swung open the door. Then showed me in. I nearly lost it. Thankfully, I had shoved a scented (Amina's) handkerchief in the pocket of these very pants. I brought it to my nose.

"Well, there before me were stacks of Campbell Soup cans, a few perforated and others bloated and spoiled. Piles of them. Mostly tomato soup. Nourishing. 'No vegetable soup?' I asked. 'For the virility,' I added. Rashid looked at me as if I were insane. But then, he always looks at me that way. While he's the one missing a full deck.

There were also rolled up posters, inside-out so I could make out only the outline of that famous portrait of John Kennedy. The same that hangs in many homes here. I signed to Rashid that he close the door, and we quickly returned to my *kaz* where Wahid waited among the shadows.

'And now you have seen the generosity of your government,' Wahid said, as if taking me to task. 'Posters of an American hero to decorate mud walls, and soup to be heated in this hot clime. But not to last too long.'"

"And?" Leonard said.

"And there it was. I think he expects more this time. And, well, here, Leonard, take my hand."

He looked uncertain, very uncomfortable. He tried to make a joke out of it. "I thought you weren't interested that way."

"Just take my hand for a minute."

He reached out with hesitation but did as requested. I held his hand firmly for a long moment, then announced, "I got pretty close to those people Sidi Wahid introduced me to. Very close. One of them even offered me his sister. I wore another one's unwashed clothing. They were all, everyone, man, woman, and children . . . lepers."

He yanked his hand away as if from a fiery flame. "Very funny, Hamblin!"

"Good reflexes, Leonard sport."

"Cute. Very cute." He was royally pissed.

"Want to have a wash?" I continued to play with him.

"Yes. But what was the point of that little excursion?"

"I'm not sure. Show me the underside? The point of the revolution? Get free gifts? Free wardrobe?" I really wasn't sure myself.

"There's probably no revolution," he insisted.

"You'd better ask Wahid about that."

"You just remember that we're here to help the government. Helping them eradicate the countryside of those bandits and Communists so that their peasant farmers can get on with raising their gum, cotton, millet, and other crops in peace. That's the one reason why we're here."

"I know." I searched for the tritest phrasing I could muster. "To build up their 'capability'."

"To make these people free to pursue development," he stated with a tone of certainty; and with a bit of solemnity as well.

"Well said. But not here." I did the Partenay embracing-the-world motion.

"By the way, what did the air force guys ask about?" He tried to sound matter-of-fact but I sensed tension—and anticipation—in his question.

"Not much. They mentioned the landing-strips idea." I thought all these guys were on the same page. What was I missing? Who was missing what? "They warned me to watch out I don't go more native. Underline the *more* part, I guess," I added.

And he deftly changed the subject. "Also, I've been meaning to talk to you about something, Old Sport."

"I've been meaning to . . . ." always got my attention. "Old Sport" may have meant this was serious. What happened to O.S.? "I'm flattered."

"Yes, well, it's about that report we got. Just a rumor that floated through the Center. About you and a woman you'd taken up with rather seriously, so they say."

"They?" So he even had me watched. And I was ripe for the paranoid suggestions that this nugget implied.

"We ran our usual check on this Amina."

"How thoughtful." I was glad he didn't go on about Miriam.

"It seems she was once betrothed—you know how they arrange things here—to a very wealthy young man of relatively high birth, as things go here. His name was . . . is, Abu Hassan Ibn al Jema'a."

I could see he was soaking this for all the drama he could muster. I was not going to betray my curiosity. "I'm not surprised. She always claimed to be a princess or a sort of duchess. As for Hassan Ibn al Jema'a, he is the very Wahid we've been discussing"

"Yes, I know." But I'm not sure he did—or understood.

"She was the very one who led me to meet with Wahid," I noted. I thought this was important. And would win her points. And me as well.

"Before the new regime . . . ." I began.

He interrupted me, again deftly, and continued on—ignoring my point. "Some of the people no doubt still honor her as one. Her great uncle was apparently a beneficent ruler. This entire province was his domain. All the way to Faya province. Dar es Sabir-LeClercville was this province's capital and a thriving city. He himself was the son of a very successful slave trader, so I'm told."

"You have terrific sources, Leonard."

"He was a *Derde*, a Toubou chief. The French allowed this fiefdom to continue. It was their way of pacifying the population, and he didn't seem to mind. He even raised a militia to support the colonials. They joined LeClerc and fought valiantly for the Free French in the World War II desert wars. He attained the rank of *capitaine* in the A-Wahidi division." Just a slight lift of his eyebrows.

"Interesting coincidence," I noted.

"No coincidence. He returned a hero, but when colonialism ended, the new regime saw him as a threat. Too much the cult of personality, they might have termed it. The French helped the new regime. They say he was assassinated by the new President's own guard. Expendable. Troublesome."

"Kings and princesses and assassinations. It all sounds Renaissance Italian," I added.

"I rather prefer Byzantine Arab. Anyway, it all made our files. We have to keep these embassy boys busy doing something. They're getting dried out, those files. It's a good job I took a look at them when I did."

"Thank God!" I exclaimed. I tried to look appreciative at the same time.

"The fact is, Hamblin, Abu Ibn Jema'a is your *Derde*, your Wahid."

"*Alhamdulilah.*"

"Is that all you have to say." He really didn't get it.

"Someone's been cuckolded," I added. Marxist-Leninist indeed.

"Is that how you feel?"

"No pop psychology, Leonard. Please."

"Of course not. Can your Jean bring me another."

"I'll see." I rose to find Jean, or just to get away from this stifling conversation. I always found it funny that when there were no Americans to talk to, I might feel overwhelmingly lonely. Even with Terry and Joe down the road. Then one of them comes, and I can't wait to get rid of him. Aside from Alice.

"Jean! Another whiskey for Monsieur!"

"*Bien sur*, Monsieur. *vos désirs sont des ordres.*" [7] Well done, Jean! Of course he will, Jean's smile indicated. Jean has a crude, but effective gift of sarcasm.

When I returned, Leonard didn't miss a beat. "There's more."

"I had no doubt of it. Your Scotch is on its way."

"Monsieur Hassan Ibn Jema'a is the son of our *capitaine* of the Wahidi division and himself of princely, or even royal lineage. He was chief of the *Toubou Daza*. Some call them the 'rock people'—for their toughness, I suppose."

"Was?" The Toubou are a fierce desert tribe not known for their fickleness in affairs of state.

"He is no longer a chief," and then he added "or so I'm told."

"That's strange." I just had to add. "I guess the Toubou are not known for their fickleness when it comes to affairs of state. Also, it's rumored that he renounced the so-called throne; and that there is a *goroga*, blood money, owed as well. For Amina's parents and many others, as I understand it."

"You're a mine of surprising information, Hamblin."

"Of course, I haven't caught Wahid observing any of these customs. But it could account for the rather ragged associates

---

[7] Approximately "Your wish is my command!"

constantly at his side. They may be Toubou, of the rock people. And of his tribe. By the way, in the old days, in the event of war, Toubou spears were dowsed with their chief's leavings. Lethal." I thought he'd like to know.

"I wonder if they can do the same with M-1s or their bullets." Nice. "And where's that Scotch?"

I leapt up again at that excuse to leave Leonard's company and rushed around back to find Jean. He was considerably tasting and testing a fresh, newly-opened bottle himself before serving our guest.

When I returned, I stopped at the corner around the side. Partenay was there haranguing Leonard. "Shit, I say. One can take on the trait of these people, if one is not careful. It is so easy!" He was obviously talking about me. Implying that I'm too sympathetic to the students and inhabitants or have a penchant for goldbricking. "Ah, we can so easily become like them—make the women work, sit around the boiling tea. Ah, yes, just to pass the time waiting for the wheel barrow to be invented and watch the world go by." He began to prance in a mincing style, all the more ridiculous given his girth. "Waiting for the twentieth century world to be invented."

Leonard was laughing at the slapstick. Encouraging the drunken sot. Whose prominent nose was again swelling and turning scarlet.

"Ah, yes," he repeated in falsetto, the burnt out cigarette hanging from his lips. "Did you know it was the Europeans that brought them the wheelbarrow? Imagine that. They hadn't even invented the wheel!"

It looked like Leonard was going to have a fit. The more the fat man pranced, the more comical Leonard found it. Encouraging him. It was embarrassing.

"Ah, there is our sick man." He pointed an accusing fist at me as I came around the corner.

"I *am* feeling better."

"So happy to hear. I feared your imminent demise." He'd regained his professional demeanor.

"I see you've met my friend." I nodded toward Leonard.

"Yes, very charming. None the worse for wear, given the long voyage here."

"None the worse," I agreed.

"And your intentions?" He turned to me, attempting to put me on the spot.

"I think I can pick up the next class. Quatrième, isn't it."

"So it seems, Monsieur." He returned to his most elegant behavior for Leonard. Leonard was taking it all in.

"Just an historical note," I had to add. "The Baguirmi Kingdom of this land used mounted cavalry, equipped with etched armor worn over leather and chainmail. As you've no doubt seen, ceremonial use of these armored horses persists today and the armor is brightly colored and often spectacular."

"I . . . I" he tried to interject. "Caragh..."

"No, wait! There's more. This land was known as a center of learning, of wisdom, the *bet hakima* of the Middle Ages." I was pushing it here.

"And furthermore, the rock paintings of Ennedi are dated to the seventh millenium and rival only those found in France."

I turned on my heels, starting to go to gather my books and materials.

Partenay peered over his relit cigarette with what appeared to be amusement. "Never mind, Monsieur. I dismissed all the classes. David Moussa, one of your students in *quatrième*, died early this morning. Or it may have been late last night."

He stood stiffly, measuring my response. I went for my books nevertheless.

"He was in class yesterday!" Irrelevant really. I was trying to collect my thoughts and my response to this.

"Ah, yesterday. . . ." He made a flowery, supposedly elegant motion with his hand, a wave indicating, perhaps, portentous destiny.

As he did so, I recalled with some effort the stocky, muscular boy, with the looks of a Sara Southerner. Truly Sara-Ngumbye. After each class period or in the afternoon, he would come to me to ask me about how it was in the Ooh Es Ah. "How are the streets paved? Are they for cars only? Are there walkways for those on foot then? Are all the cars the large ones I have heard about and like this picture?" Whereupon he showed me a picture of a Buick LeSabre torn out of a magazine. "Do the buildings reach beyond the clouds?"

"Where are you from? Who is your employer?" Perhaps Evian's seeming idiosynchrasies as a spy made Moussa David a bit wary— suspicious. Of English teachers.

I made him ask all these questions in English, which was a challenge for both of us. For me, grinding out his words, phrases, and sentences with him. For him . . . well, you know. But he always came back in the next day or two. With a smile, he'd dive in again. Sometimes asking the same questions. Each time better prepared than the last.

'Why are you in this country? What are you *really* doing here?" Curious, or himself an adept spy? Nevertheless, a good-humored, robust, and healthy young man, though he seemed to be losing weight lately. "Could you take me back with you to the Ooh Es Ah?"

"So the funeral is today?" I continued. The custom here was to bury the dead within the first twenty-four hours after death.

"Yes, Monsieur." Partenay wondered why I might be asking this. He was reaching into his pocket, which reminded me of the note I had stuffed unceremoniously into my own pocket the night before:

> "*Teacher, please come to meet me at our mosque. Please*
> *bring bagnole (automobile) pictures. Please hurry. Your*
> *student, Moussa David*

He feared trouble and sought help. Perhaps my intervention. Or only my presence to frighten away his likely assailants. Surely not for the automobile pictures that late at night. So I knew then that I should have made an appearance last night. I should have responded to his note.

And, as if in confirmation, a terrible keening arose on the wind.

■ The Funeral of Moussa David

Late November 1968

There was a moment of respectful silence before I turned and headed for the burial ground, the books still clutched under my arm. Maybe I thought I could offer the funeral attendees an English lesson.

Jean was running behind me. "Monsieur, Monsieur, you must not!

"Must not?"

"You must not attend."

"Why not? David Moussa was my student." Now I remembered his face even more clearly. Serious but welcoming. A strong, stocky lad, slow but intense. An intended farmer as his brief essay told. Not the kind to be carried off by amoebiasis or cholera. Or other diseases. And seeming to be fit and healthy, though thinner, in class the previous day.

The keening carried unbroken on the wind. I could hear Rashid's drumbeat at the rear of my *kaz*, in rhythm with the keening, even as I moved away toward the burial grounds.

In the distance I could spy black cloaked figures, hovering crow-like, moving aimlessly in a weird, unrecognizable choreography.

"Monsieur, you must not."

"Why not, Jean?"

"It is forbidden, Monsieur."

"Nonsense."

"The *imam* of the town has put out a, how do you say, *fatwa* that this is the *Nasarah*'s doing. The doing of Evian."

"But Evian is dead and no longer a threat."

"Likely his djinnii, his ghost then . . . . Besides, you are thought to be an infidel, a *kafir*. It is dangerous for you."

There's that Evian again: "I must do this for David Moussa, Jean. Besides, as you know, I have begun the conversion." He might think I was putting the conversion off only so that I might continue to drink alcohol.

This, Jean understood and respected.

I was still struggling to conjure up the image, a clearer image of this poor youth. I was sure it was the one who wished to join the Army after schooling. Then receive a farm subsidy for the military service rendered. But I couldn't concentrate as the eerie keening undulated on the wind.

"Then I will go with you, Monsieur."

"Thank you, Jean. I am most grateful."

"I am grateful for your gratitude. Still, it is my duty."

I moved closer to the group. Now I saw them more clearly. Black-clad women directly before me, urchins running under their robes, men behind them, hovering in seeming bewilderment over a lump of white cloth.

There was a moment of silence.

Then the women on the hill took up the keening again, an anguished cry mixed with fierce warlike ululating—all caught on the wild, pre-Harmatan winds.

I had never heard a more terrifying sound.

Suddenly it stopped. They all turned to stare. And a man in a grey *jalaba* and embroidered skullcap forced his way through the swaying women, shoved them a bit roughly aside, and faced me. He stared fiercely as if to will me away. Or worse.

He shouted something in a dialect I couldn't grasp. Jean answered him gruffly. He shouted on, gesticulating wildly, turning to the crowd for support.

I understood "This one! This one!" and then *"Nasarah!"* The women drew up to an imaginary line, gesticulating angrily, flicking their fingers off the thumb of their left hands in a gesture so foul that Jean moved up to the man leading them all, arms raised, palms outward, in an effort to reason.

"Ke?" he demanded. "What is it?"

The fierce man, none other than my *Hajj* ex-tutor, sensed Jean's authority. He delivered the next in proper Arabic. "He should not be here. I am an *imam*, who will speak this young one's blessing. But that one is of those who pay the camel soldiers. They are the ones who have done this!" He gestured toward the lump of cloth. He raised his arm. At that, other men raised their *kabira* knives menacingly. I spied several of my students among the crowd.

I was thankful I no longer had the dysentery. Because with this extra trigger, I would have shit my pants there and then.

"No, he is not of them," Jean insisted.

"He is *Nasarah*." The women took up this chant: "Death to *Nasarah!*"

Jean let them gesticulate fiercely, demanding my death. They sent up a vengeful keening, wailing in misery, but all the while facing me. I stepped, no, jumped back, as if I had been pushed. Jean waited until the din had subsided, raised his arms again, and spoke very softly. "Brothers and sisters."

The black lumps moved closer to hear him. "Brothers and sisters, hear me."

Even the bearers at the back moved forward to hear him, abandoning their swathed burden.

"This one is not *Nasarah!*"

There was a low murmur.

"You know me, Jean Abdel-Melek, that I am this one's manservant."

"Aye, that you were manservant to the filthy *Nasarah!*" a huge man cried, raising his *kabira* knife as he shouted.

"No, brother. It is I who abandoned the work for the *Nasarah*, the one who loved boys, and I who declared the curse of my tribe upon him. It is I who protected those such as David Moussa from that one who fornicated the bungholes of our young men as if they were women. You remember me for that!"

This time the murmur was with him.

"And I would never . . ." he spit, "never be the manservant to such a *Nasarah* again. This one," he indicated me with his right hand, "this one, I tell you, is not of them." Another murmur, and a giant at the back lowered his knife.

"This one is a *professeur*, a teacher of children, children who will be our future. He is becoming one of us—he is learning to recite the *Shahadah* and the five *Salawat* and pray with us. He comes here out of duty—against my counsel—out of duty to his student, our brother, Moussa David."

Jean then yielded to an older man in his black *jalaba* decorated with calligraphic designs, who stepped out beside Jean, turned to the crowd, and intoned "*B-ismi-llāhi r-raḥmāni r-raḥīmi*. I am an *imam* and the *ulema* of this city. I speak from the knowledge and wisdom of more than one thousand three hundred years—the wisdom of all of them. And I say that it is written: all who come to us, to pray with us, with sincerity in their heart, shall participate in our mourning for our brother, Moussa Daoud, and for his burial. Thus have I spoken. Allahu akbar."

"*Alhamdulillah*" Someone cried.

From another one, "Let him mourn among us."

"So be it!" the *imam* pronounced.

The others turned back to the swathed corpse. The women started their keening again.

Jean gestured for me to join him. He gave me a cap to make me more like the rest.

"Thank you, Jean."

"Yes, I am grateful for your gratitude. You are not of us. I know that. Drop to your knees before Allah, Monsieur, as we pray."

"But will there be no viewing of the body?" I knew I was pushing it, but I was taken with a morbid curiosity—and the lessons of spycraft—to confirm by sight.

"Ah, *non*, Monsieur. Though it has been washed, this body is not proper for viewing."

"Not proper?"

"Not to be seen but by those who perform the *ghusal*, the ritual for washing of the dead."

The lump wrapped in sheet was laid on a sort of pallet and lowered into the sandy grave. The men then laid out their prayer mats, faced east, and bowed in prayer led by the *imam*, the one in grey *jalaba*, who at first would have barred me. Or worse. Finally, the women were silent. All the men said the *Janasah* in unison, praying for the deceased's soul and asking God to pardon them for their sins, and took a final moment to finger their *gris-gris* as Catholics might their rosaries.

After the prayers, I found the family, mother, and brother, of David (Daoud) Moussa and offered my sympathy. They were politely receptive. I gave them our English text book, Moussa's I told them, with pictures of American cars between the pages, and 2,000CFA as well. Not much; a gesture.

Then the one in the black *jalaba* came to me where I stood and whispered, "*Asmah rafigi*, 'Hear me friend.' The Evian who preceded you was a teacher of English. And a PD (pay-day) of his students. A *pederast* of the boys. And some in the town are suspicious of you since you take his place. Afraid that you are the same. And others think that the stories of these obscenities apply to you. The rumors fly, but in this case they are last year's rumors. So that you may better understand, I have spoken." Then he bowed to me, hand on heart, and suggested that we may see each other another time.

Thus it was that David Moussa was laid to rest.

■ Prejudice and Pride

"Well, how was it, O.S?" Leonard was flushed as he looked away from Partenay.

"A bit frightening, actually."

"That was unfortunate, that you should go among them," Partenay pronounced in obvious disgust.

"Yes, sir."

"You should leave them to their mourning."

"Who is the one who loves boys?" I should have left it, but I'd had enough of his backhanded insults. Jean froze as he looked on.

Partenay coughed uncontrollably. And spit. He bent to the extent that his ample middle would let him, turned bright scarlet, and yielded to an apoplectic-like seizure. "Keeyaw, carragh, keeyaw, carragh!"

Jean stared in stoic silence, only anger in his eyes to betray his true feelings.

"Then it's true," I said.

"Carragh! It is of no importance."

"They think so!" I jerked my thumb in the direction of the hill and the cemetery. "It seems to hold a lot of importance to them."

"They speak of Evian. The Corsican. It gives them a burnished rumor—something to talk about."

"No, Monsieur, I know it for truth," Jean, out of character, interrupted.

"Keeyaw! What do you say? What ingratitude! Who are you to contradict us? After all that we have done for you, *garçon!*" He spit out the last word and choked again.

"But he wished to make me his procurer. A procurer of young boys. He preferred fair skinned and Moundang." Jean spoke this in a monotone, but with unmistakable anger.

Partenay began pacing madly. Pulling wildly on his cigarette. Even more scarlet. Nearly apoplectic. "Moussa David was killed by Wahidi! You are ungrateful and no longer deserve our benefice!"

Jean turned on his heels and strode to the back of the cottage.

"There, you see how it is! For you it is just an exotic adventure." Partenay was addressing me now. "For us, it is the life and preservation of our culture. And theirs. Caragh!"

"The gift of your culture—the one who loves boys?" I was out of control.

"You are not in control, Monsieur!"

"Hey, Hamblin, calm down," Leonard urged in English. "Let's all have a drink. Eh? Jean! And you too. *Et vous aussi.*"

Jean had returned—with a sardonic grin.

"Me, I will not drink with them. Keeyaach." He was still nearly apoplectic, but I had no sympathy.

"Come on, Monsieur Partay." Leonard tried out his most gracious manner.

"I must go, Monsieur. Until we meet again. I trust you will infuse this one with an understanding that we both have. *Au revoir.*" Partenay stormed off.

"Good riddance," I said to his receding back. In English. And *au revoir* to those refined, sandless, and delicious lunches.

"Damn it, Hamblin! You are supposed to get along with the locals!"

"He's not a local. Jean's a local." I realized that even Jean is not, as I spoke.

"Don't nitpick. You know what I mean."

"Yes, Leonard."

"And don't *yes* me. Can't you walk the fine line? That's your job." He was sounding like a petulant teacher.

"Yes, Leonard." I could tell him that I'd done quite well until his arrival. It was not worth the effort. Jean brought our drinks.

We sipped in silence. I could tell that Leonard was getting more infuriated with every sip, and I, about to become more condescending. He was seething that I might have exposed a sordid truth. I refused to be the first to break the silence.

"All right, Hamblin. Why the need for histrionics?"

"That being?"

"Attending the funeral. Flying in the face of good advice. Defying Partay."

"Partenay."

"Jesus Christ!" Leonard was a hue of deep red.

"I did not defy *Him*." A slight gesture toward the heavens.

"Not funny, Hamblin. Not even close."

I can see he was revving up for a diatribe full of consternation, spiced with vitriol.

■ A (Thanksgiving) Invitation

A roundish figure in a straw hat that half shaded his sun-burned face appeared at the front gate at just this opportune moment. "*Hôla! Messieurs les américains.* May I?"

"Of course, Monsieur." I called Jean to serve the refreshments. "Jean!" Then turned to our visitor. "Please seat yourself."

Leonard gave me that don't-screw-up look.

"I am Boudin from the SHG, the *Societe de Huile et de Gaz*, the exploration company." He fanned himself with his straw hat, increasing his resemblance to a plantation patron from our deep south. Hatless, with a markedly receding hairline, a sun-line where the rim of the hat marked the protection from or exposure to the sun. He was middle-aged. Like Partenay.

"We're very happy to meet you," Leonard intoned in halting French.

"Whiskey, Monsieur?" I offered.

"Thank you. We will be in the environs for a while, exploring for . . . minerals."

"Uranium?" I blurted. Leonard shot me a poisoned arrow of a look.

"*Ah, non*, Monsieur. Nothing so exotic."

"*Ah, non*," my foot. I'd hold my tongue for Leonard's sake. Poor boy, God knows I may be acquiring some sympathy for the bugger. It was the heat and alcohol that have this deleterious effect. "To your health, dear sir."

I might as well make a hash of the remaining day.

"Well, we're having a bit of a *m'ishwi* this evening and thought you Americans might like to join us." That accounted for the squealing of pigs at the slaughter that I thought I heard. It had harmonized with the keening. In fact, I thought it was the keening women, or a woman with a remarkably screechy voice.

Leonard looked a bit lost.

"He's having a *m'ishwi* and wondered if we'd like to join him!" I repeated in English, over loudly as if I were addressing the hard of hearing.

"What's *that?*"

"A lamb roast. But in this case, I think it will be a pig roast."

"Very nice. Tell him of course we would."

The red, round face was contorted as he held his eyebrows uplifted in feigned expectation.

"Very nice. Of course we would!" I repeated, but in French.

"Excellent! Skoll, then. Cheers!" He took his whiskey in one gulp. Then he got up to go. "Bloody hot, eh?"

"Thank God for those cooling winds," I joked.

That seemed to go right by him. "Well, I'll take Abidjan anytime."

"You were in Abidjan?"

"Two months actually. Now *there's* civilization." He sat back down. "There, the women are truly, eh, accommodating. Not these Moslem tramps." He distorted his mouth and spit "these Moslem tramps."

"What's he mean by 'accommodating?'" Leonard cannot resist interjecting when he latches on to a phrase.

"I'll ask. Monsieur would like to know what you mean by 'accommodating.'"

Boudin stared hard, probably trying to fathom the depths of our stupidity. Or searching for a synonym. "Why, accommodating, that's all. Willing."

"Willing, Leonard. Another round, Jean." Jean reported front and center, never modifying his half grin. Fire still in his eyes from the previous conversation.

"Monsieur, when you were in Abidjan, did you ever encounter, that is, run across an American woman by the name of Janice Hixby?"

"Ah, Janice Hixby. I don't recall such a one. What was she like?" Leonard shot me another arrow.

"Very nice, Monsieur." I retreated from using "accommodating." But the thought of her and my three days' liberty brought me a certain warmth.

"Aha," Boudin expelled.

"Old flame, O.S.?" Leonard asked.

"Special operative."

Boudin looked at us both blankly, but Leonard let me know I'd erred nonetheless. "She works for the Peace Corps," I fumbled, in an attempted save. Boudin only maintained a blank stare.

"And what were you doing in Abidjan?" Leonard leapt in with his attempt at conversation.

"On vacation, Monsieur. From our work in Niger." But his mind was on other things. What's the equivalent of *asshole* in French? I asked myself. It was my instinct. Boudin lurched up, at the same time shoving his hat back down on his head with abrupt decisiveness. "Until this evening, *messieurs*."

We forced ourselves to our feet and shook hands all around. "Until this evening, then."

Leonard fell back wearily, sipped his Scotch, and retrieved and put on his sunglasses, after viciously rubbing his heavy eyelids.

"Siesta, Leonard?"

"No, thanks."

"We want to be sharp for this dinner. I think the Russian will be there," I added.

He perked up a bit and stared off toward an acacia grove. I followed his stare and, as if on cue, the black Lada passed laboriously behind the small grove on its way to Djemélia from the Russian's *kaz*. "There they are, O.S."

■ *Docteur* Godin, Kah Jay Bay?

He still hadn't bought the story. That the Russian, Doctor Godin, is offering his medical expertise to a hospital, a clinic really, that had lost its only physician, Docteur Lièvre. In fact, Docteur Godin was Lièvre's understudy. Leonard still wouldn't accept that the man is a doctor of medicine and an intellectual who would have been offended by the insinuation that he is KGB.

"He's KGB," Leonard insisted, as if reading my thoughts.

"I'm not so sure."

"He's been enlisted. That Lada comes up from Djemélia every month, doesn't it? Even through the Wahidi and *Taureg* lines. Like clockwork, as they say. Doesn't it?

"Or at least enlisted to do their intelligence work. And they're watching you, O.S. Believe me," he assured me.

"That'll keep them busy."

"Not if this is a typical day in your life. Over a year here, and still you have nothing to report on them?" There he went again.

"Not quite accurate. I've given you motive. Anyway, I guess I'm decadent. And I'm going to take a nap. Jean will see to your needs, sir."

"Sleep tight, smartass." And then he yawned.

"I intend to." After all, he needed the time alone to go through my things. I suddenly regretted the little smartass notes that I'd peppered the house with. In French and Arabic. If he can make them out, he's going to take the colic, "O.S."

Smartass note examples:

> l-arḍa walā yaʾūduhu ḥifẓuhumā wa huwa l-ʿaliyyu l-aẓīm. *He knoweth that which is in front of them and that which is behind them.*
>
> Islamic Declaration of Faith

> *"Don't lies eventually lead to the truth? And don't all my stories, true or false, tend toward the same conclusion? Don't they all have the same meaning? So what does it matter whether they are true or false if, in both cases, they are significant of what I have been and what I am? Sometimes it is easier to see clearly into the liar than into the man who tells the truth. Truth, like light, blinds.*

Falsehood, on the contrary, is a beautiful twilight that enhances every object."

— Albert Camus, The Fall

Like in an avalanche, if one is buried in sand, deeply buried, and begins shoveling himself out—not knowing which direction is up—he could dig the wrong way and thus dig to his own demise.

H.H.

Time is like a handful of sand coursing out the fist.

H.H.

Even if you give a donkey a thousand CFA to fart, he will not. Not without the urging of a beautiful damsel.

Pashtun Proverb

My favorite:

There is nothing noble in being superior to your fellow men. True nobility lies in being superior to your former self.

— Ernest Hemingway

My second most favorite:

Dans toutes les professions chacun affecte une mine et un extérieur pour paraître ce qu'il veut qu'on le croie. Ainsi on peut dire que le monde n'est composé que de mines.

In all professions we affect a part and an appearance to seem what we wish to be. Thus the world is merely composed of actors.

--François de La Rochefoucauld

... And so on.

■ Ibrahim

Still late November 1968

I arose from my short nap to find Leonard sprawled in his chair, sunglasses slid well down his nose, mouth open in invitation to the dusk-borne fauna. Those various notes would have to wait their turn.

"Up and at 'em, O.S. Time to primp for dinner."

"Shit!" Leonard intoned. "How about a bath?"

"And rat turds. Jean!" I called.

Jean had been squatting, with what I call "Ngumbaye patience," just around the east corner of the *kaz*. "Monsieur?"

"Hot water for the Monsieur, please."

He grinned as if on the verge of total paroxysms. It must have been a secret, and no doubt unpleasant, joke.

Leonard came around the corner. "I must have dozed off."

"Jean will prepare you a bath," I said.

"I trust I will have some privacy." Leonard may have been implying sarcasm. I was inferring sincerity.

"The road is yours alone." I indicated the sandy path in front of my *kaz*. He didn't take it well.

"Around the back, then. Jean will prepare the bath around the back, near the baobab tree."

"Jean, Monsieur would prefer a bath in privacy."

"Of course, Monsieur." He stared at me as if in sympathy for Leonard's low intelligence—or mine.

Jean swiftly stripped the beds and hung the sheets on rope clothes lines around what passed for a tub. Ibrahim appeared over the rise, a giant against the late afternoon sun, carrying the seventy-liter drum as if it were empty.

"Ya, Ibrahim."

"Ya, Jean."

"The *fakir*, the chief of my Emricani master, wishes to bathe in your heated water. He will sit in his own filth and sing to us," Jean intoned.

"Ya, Jean, so it shall be. My water is heated in the barrel by the midday sun. The filth shall burn off him. Ha, ha, ha." Ibrahim was a giant out of a fairy tale. Or an ogre. He towered over everyone, a heap of muscle topped by a jovial, distorted, but grinning face that belied his reputed ferocity. "Tell the master that his chief shall be thus purged of his own filth."

Ibrahim swung the huge barrel onto a platform over the iron tub that Jean had dragged to the back of the shed, the one serving in his kitchen. The steamy water at first poured onto the ground, thick and brown with the rust from the barrel. Ibrahim swung the barrel with the remaining water back over his shoulder and marched on to the overhanging cistern. The cistern hung from the baobab in my back forty, and only Ibrahim could hoist the barrel to fill it.

Leonard was impressed. "Who is he?"

"That's Ibrahim, my guardian."

"Good God, Hamblin! I've never seen such strength!"

"Definitely Olympic material."

"How did you get him?" Leonard pressed on.

"They had a drawing." I couldn't resist.

"You won the drawing?"

"I lost." I lost Leonard too. "A joke. He's a prisoner. He was assigned to me by the *Sous-préfet*."

"Assigned, eh?"

"Maybe he's anti-American!" I noted.

"Ibrahim?"

"The *sous-préfet*."

"Is he from this area?" Leonard was truly intrigued.

"The *sous-préfet's* from the south."

"I mean him." I could see the wheels turning, but I wasn't sure in which direction. But then, Leonard had only one-track curiosity. Likely he was searching for a diagnosis for gigantism.

I thought, then said, "Up north, I think."

"Faya?"

"Why the curiosity?" I asked, now curious about his curiosity.

"Curiosity? I could win the war with an army of these. Are there many like that."

"No idea. May we should go and explore that region." With that, I thought he'd let go. But no . . . .

What did he do?" Leonard pressed.

What war, I was wondering. "He was a shepherd. Now he is our waterman by day and chained at the prison at night."

"I mean, to become a prisoner."

"Killed six men." I couldn't wait for Leonard's response.

"Six? That's awful."

"That's what the dead guys must have been thinking. As he killed them." I was playing it for all it was worth. "Ibrahim says he was attacked. He fought off the attackers. Using one of their *kabira* knives . . . . Six, he says. They were trying to steal his sheep."

Ibrahim came up to us. Leonard nearly bolted in panic as the giant hovered over him. But Ibrahim's awkward smile disarmed even Leonard.

"Peace unto you, Ibrahim sir," I intoned.

"And unto you master. Is this *Nasarah* your brother?"

"As a manner of speaking. And he is my chief. Emricani. He does not speak Arabic."

"Ah, poor *Nasarah*. He has not been blessed, then." He threw back his head and laughed in great, unforced heaves. "Ha, ha! Allah has deprived him."

■ Younis 5

Late November 1968

While Leonard was bathing, I saw the neighbor boy, Younis, again. Again with the acacia stalk in his mouth. I surmised that he may be using the teeth-brushing as an excuse to escape his duties in the big house. To go out, if only for a moment.

Again, digging at the burial hole, perhaps to place another *gris-gris* in the spherical box.

"Can you stay for a while Younis?"

"Only a moment, Monsieur. Then I must return to my duties."

And so I took advantage of what little time we had. He was my perfect student. Despite his handicap, his late start, and his demanding daily work, Younis absorbed the lessons as if the study would mean his release from this slavery and the promise of better times.

And it would.

"Let me begin my story. It is the story of a young and valiant freeholder, the son of an owner of land like Yacob Mikune, whose father is stripped of his lands by an evil sheriff."

"Ah, *sherif*. I know of them." His eyes lit up as he made the connection and relation to his own place and time.

"Then the son is made an outlaw for hunting in the woods. For killing a deer on what was once his father's own land."

"Just as the Wahid has done." He was into it now.

So it is just then that he is called in by his mistress. "Younis. Where are you. You must come!"

"I must go. Please tell me the name of this valiant one," he begged.

"It is Robin. Robin Hood." Robin Hood from my world. No doubt there was such a one from his world as well. Perhaps it was Wahid, after all. Whatever I might think.

"I will dream of him in my sleep," Younis shouted. And with that he was gone.

Out of curiosity, I dug around where the red box was buried.

Just to satisfy my curiosity.

To have a look.

■ M'ichwi: Thanksgiving Dinner

November 28 1968

The m'ichwi was an evening affair, so soiled clothes would not be noticed. My good luck since I no longer had my well-kept evening suit. Gone with the radio. And other treasures.

Monsieur Boudin introduced us to his four cohorts, all looking like they'd just come off a pirate ship. There was heavy drinking and light, very French, hors d'oeuvres. Then we partook of the main course, the unfortunate hog who squinted at us in the twilight. With scorn for us all and remonstrance toward the faithful of Islam.

The barbecued part was served in the traditional fashion—a line formed that moved clockwise around the spiced and roasted carcass which hung on an iron spit. Since there was insufficient cutlery, we ate in the traditional way—by tearing off pieces of pork and carrying them, on a plate, to a seat.

"*On ne connait pas les mains*" intoned an *invité* in the line. Roughly "We don't know whose hands (implying 'whose germs') have touched this." It was Alphonse, my strychnine nurse. Probably the one fiddling with Modou. Having fiddled with Evian, so I'd been told. Via Mama's rumor channels. He was suddenly concerned about hygiene! Still, it was a good line.

I could barely hear the *sous-préfet*, deep in conversation with Boudin. Intense, as he fixed his crossed eyes beyond Boudin, but mostly garbled. I managed to suss out only "Yes, we will both need the American telecommunications. We must let them finish it first. And teach us ...."

The SHG workers were a rough-looking bunch. They looked like rejects from the Foreign Legion, or like mutinous pirates from a ship run aground.

One of the pirates may have taken a shine to me. He had served me my drink and, later, came to sit by me as we wrestled with the stringy pork.

"How is it, Américain."

"Very good."

"All in the sauce. And you are Américain, are you not?"

"I am."

"What do you do here?"

"I am a *professeur*. Of English. Also, sometimes of art and music."

"Ah, a difficult but worthy profession. Perhaps I'll come see you and drink with you later. After this job, and when I have *du fric* (some dough). A lot of *fric*! Maybe then. More wine?"

"Please. Thank you." He went to fetch a bottle.

When he returned, I couldn't help but ask, "Why will you then have lots of dough?"

"When this job is done, we will be surely rich. There is the oil here, perhaps some beneath our feet. And other rich ore as well. I think you should come work for us, Américain. I hear that all Américains love the oil.

"But" he added, "we will first have to clear this town, at least part of it, since the oil lies beneath it."

"Clear?"

"Yes. Clear out. By fire or other means. We have done this before. In Niger and elsewhere. People in a certain part of the town will move or be removed. Though only Monsieur Boudin knows the exact plans, it is said the militia will be there to guard us." Sounds like eminent domain without the legal niceties.

"Excuse me. What is your name?"

"I am Jacques."

"Excuse me. But I see my boss over there, Jacques." I felt compelled to tell Leonard, Right away.

"Nice to have met you, Américain. You are 'arry, yes?"

"Yes. And nice to have met you as well, Jacques."

I pulled Leonard aside and repeated Jacques' tale. "What do you think?"

"And the militia is helping and protecting them?"

"So he says."

"Then it would be almost impossible to stop them. Perhaps we should have a word with the *sous-préfet*."

Like that would do some good. "I don't think that will do any good."

"But we must do it as protocol. And perhaps, to verify the story. "But Harry," he added, "please be at your most diplomatic!"

My most diplomatic.

■ Younis 6

Late November 1968

"But how can I do that?" He was at the height of excitement that very evening.

"By reading this." I handed him a heavily illustrated set of books and comics that I had brought from my USA home.

"But I cannot read these . . . ." I thought tears would begin to flow.

"Then I will teach you. I've seen you begin to pick out sounds and words!"

And so, more of the many turns and twists, and the usual frustrations and, sometimes, anger.

After the lessons, when Younis had returned to his duties, I dug for the *gris-gris*. The one that Younis had buried.

Just for a look. A little look.

■ Akhween with a *kh*

Early December 1968

I finally had a chance to see him in action with the *légionnaire capitaine*. The militia recruits were in formation, all eyes on the *capitaine*. As well as on the *guépard* that seemed to threaten them and thereby kept them in good order. The *capitaine* would speak and then illustrate the meaning himself. For example, "You must hold the carbine like this."

The *capitaine* would pronounce this sentence, and Akhween would follow with a translation into Sara-Ngumbaye. The language was tonal but interspersed with French words. Still, all the words were pronounced in the lilting Sara sing-song. Followed by the act itself.

In this repetition by the recruits, only two carbines were dropped. Only one fired. The *capitaine* was on his belly in two seconds. The *guépard* too. Me too, even though I stood well out of the line of fire.

Akhween ran toward the line and virtually attacked the recruit who "misfired"—or *missed*. And I heard him yell a garbled "*pas. . . tirer. . . tenant*"—Akhween to the recruit who had "accidentally" fired on the *capitaine* and the *guépard* (I wasn't sure if Akhween was shouting "Don't shoot him yet"), both of whom had fallen prone in the dirt and sand.

When the *capitaine* realized it was a suspected "misfire," he quickly stood up and brushed himself off. His *guépard* rose and growled. Both were impressed by Akhween's quick action. The *capitaine* assumed Akhween had taken the recruit to task for his clumsiness.

With that look of disgust that was the *capitaine*'s trademark— that he had learned well from his French colleagues—he then turned the moment into a lesson. What to do when there is incoming gunfire.

I could see that Akhween was barely keeping up when one of the recruits interrupted him. He sang in hesitant Sara and repeatedly spoke the words "Moundang and Zaghawa" which were others of the tribal languages. Of those who scarify their cheeks, in the *Yondo* or manhood ceremony, scars on each side. Like the Sara-Ngumbaye. For the Moundang and Zaghawa speakers, one of them seemed to be delegated to do the translation from Akhween's Sara. A good opportunity to confuse everything! Even the moment of "misfiring."

Then the one questioning stepped out of formation, much to the *capitaine*'s chagrin. And continued to speak, but not the music of Sara.

Altogether a different sound. And he seemed different. For one, he had only two *Yondo* scars on each cheek. The Sara had three.

Akhween shook his head dramatically, and the recruit questioned with a little more insistence each time. Akhween repeated the "Akhween" and *kh* requirement each time as well.

The recruit scrunched up his nose as if to spit, tried to repeat the *kh*, then shouted some other words, and fell back into formation.

Nor was I ever privy to this exchange. Nor was the *capitaine*. So he went on with the lesson about survival. It was then that I began to suspect that Akhween might not be as multilingual as he claimed.

■ Something Different, Something Strange

Early December 1968

There was another instance. Walking across the parade ground, we chanced by a recruit who stopped Akhween with a plaintive look and launched into a recitation and monologue in very broken French. He stared directly at Akhween, which was not a Southerner's way.

His voice climbed to higher pitches of excitement. It seemed that he was complaining about the *capitaine*'s explanations and descriptions. "*Trop vite! Trop rapide!*" Too fast! Also, as near as I could tell, using words and phrases unknown to me. And to Akhween as well, I suspected.

Akhween tried to put him off, or walk far enough away that I wouldn't overhear the substance of their conversation. I had heard enough.

When I engaged him, I should have asked Akhween if he knew Goundo, or Moundang, or even Karanga, or Zaghawa-Beria. Or some of the myriad others the militia were recruited from, in this multiethnic country. They were right off the farm, those recruits, undereducated as regards their neighbors' languages. I should have asked. But I hadn't.

So Akhween stumbled along with the *capitaine*, satisfying the *capitaine* and the very few Sara-Ngumbaye recruits, and slipping by the others with the help of the other recruit. The complaining recruit, who was called Adin Azuku Vincent, stumbled along as well, repeating movements made by the others, but often staring blankly. The *capitaine* assumed they all were mentally deficient—deficient of a few grey cells. There may have been that as well.

As for me, I had most of my dealings with the bureaucracy, mostly Sara-Ngumbaye Southerners who spoke Sara but also French. Akhween was useful in those few instances where Sara-Ngumbaye would prove useful. Also, in disciplining the Ngumbaye students, especially in the *sixième* class where they were just beginning French and English. Ngumbaye were the majority of students because their culture held education, especially *Nasarah* education, to be more useful than did the Arabs and the Arabized. Most of the Muslims gave priority to learning the Koran and its commentaries.

So, though deficient, Akhween with a *kh* was useful to both of us. And we kept him in pocket money.

■ Younis 7

Mid-December 1968

It was two weeks before I saw him again. Same place and salutations. Then "I must hear more of this story of Robin Hood, Monsieur. I have dreamt of him since last I saw you."

"Well, Younis, Robin would not accept that his father's land was stolen and that he was an outlaw. So he organized a band of like-minded men: A poet and singer, one called "Little John" though he was a giant, one often dressed in red whom they called Will Scarlett, a priest called a friar—a kind of *imam*—and others. All were generous and courteous. All fine archers. They hunted to feed themselves, even though it was against the sheriff's law. They listened to the singer and feasted at night. They were known as the Merry Men.

"What would my name be, Monsieur Harry. If I was of the Merry Men."

"Why they would call you Younis *le bon coeur*, Younis the Good Heart. But the most important thing was that Robin and his Merry Men waylaid the rich who travelled in the forest."

"Forest?"

"A large gathering of trees. Like many acacias and baobabs in one place."

"Ah, we have those, though small," he piped up.

"Yes. So there was only one road through this huge forest. All the rich and powerful allies of the wicked sheriff had to pass that way. And that was when Robin and his band, his Merry Men, would stop them and demand all their money and jewels. And sometimes play a joke on these rich ones."

"A thief?" He was wide-eyed, but also looked a bit troubled.

"Yes, but don't be upset. For they would then give the money and jewels that they robbed to the farmers and sheep-herders who had fallen on hard times. The ones who lost their land to the sheriff and his friends.

"What kind of jokes?"

"For example," I said, desperately searching in my mind for an example since there were none in my book. "They would come down from the tree branches on ropes and quickly tie the rich man's feet. They would then pull the rope up and, so, hang the rich one upside down. Thus, all the gold and silver coins would fall out of the rich one's pockets and money-hiding places. Money he would not otherwise give up."

"Ahh . . . .'

"And thus Robin became a legend among the poor and desperate. It was said he robbed from the rich and gave to the poor."

"Like Wahid and the Wahidi." Now Younis was truly on board and excited.

"So they say. It was said that Robin was an excellent archer and swordsman . . ."

"Archer?"

"A good shot with a bow and arrows. A weapon for hunting and fighting your enemies. It's what they used in those times."

"Come now, Younis!" The call of his mistress.

"I must leave you!"

"Ah, we're getting to an exciting part. I will make a bow and arrows for you so you may become an archer." I could come to regret this promise—as I had many others in my past. So I was even more determined to keep this one.

"I will come to see you again soon. Then we will begin the lessons every day. Thank you for telling me of the Robin. I shall dream of him every night until I see you again, Monsieur Harry."

I think I had finally roped him in. *"Au revoir*, Younis."

Now for some digging. While his attention was averted.

■ The Kindnesses of Refugees

Mid-December 1968

It was another student, Mohammed Idris as Senussi, who asked me to come with him to visit his dwelling—and his family. A most apt student. But at first, I declined, thinking that such a visit would show favoritism as regards the other students. Then, finally, when I accepted—really to stop his repeated but diplomatic insistence—I was bidden to follow him home on an afternoon after our class.

Mohammed Idris lived in a modest arrangement of typically connected, adobe-like, mud-walled huts, surrounded by a wall topped with broken glass to keep out the thieves. And the huts were around a courtyard, which itself was under a tent. The tent was cooling for reasons I couldn't fathom, since it sat and baked beneath the burning sun for most of the day.

I was introduced to the three elders of the clan, his uncles, who addressed me mostly in a curiously accented Arabic. So I did not grasp their names until later. Each was introduced as *al Hajj*. I bowed to each elder and wished them each well. In my mind, I named them Tom *Hajj*, Dick *Hajj*, and Harry *Hajj*.

Uncle Tom *Hajj* then bid Mohammed Idris to fire up a device that created soda from still water. They then produced a bottle of Johnny Walker (Black) and invited me to pour myself a drink of Scotch and soda—an absolutely civilized Western custom at a local's home in the heart of the Sahel! Especially strange, I would later learn, in the house of Senussi Muslim believers.

Mohammed brought me the soda and the bottle of Johnny. I felt obligated to play the grateful guest by mixing a (very weak) drink. The others had Grenadine mixed with the soda water, which I would have preferred, and we toasted to the monarchy, Idris, his long life and return to Libya.

They then explained to this Westerner that they were cousins of King Idris, themselves an adjunct to the royal family, and thus refugees who fled over Libya's southern border with a bit of money and the clothes on their backs. And the soda-making machine.

"Mohammed is our youngest of three nephews, all brothers. Abdel Idris al Tripoli and Ali Idris al Tripoli, both older than Mohammed, are occupied fighting a rebel war just on the other side of the border." Their parents had been killed by the tyrant.

It was then that it came to me—they were victims of the Gaddafi coup d'état and kind of revolutionaries themselves. "We are kind of revolutionaries since, before Idriss went to Turkey, he governed what you call a constitutional monarchy. He was a most enlightened king and a believer in all things in moderation. Then came the Gaddafi coup d'état. Idris was deposed. We believe he should be restored. For now, we are poor refugees."

"Ah," was all I could offer. These were truly revelations for me.

"This colonel of the coup d'état, this Gaddafi, wants to form an all-Arab collective, a *Tajammu al-Arabi*, which would exclude the Idris royal family but include this land and those to the north. But we want Mohammed to be educated in the French, and he has done well. He is an apt and adept student, is he not?"

"Absolutely" I responded. I sipped the Johnny slowly to control its effects in this heat of the day.

"And we want him to be adept at English as well. For that we are grateful to you. With French and English, as well as Arabic, he will be well prepared to serve as the royalty's UN diplomat when we have been restored."

"That you may soon be restored," as I raised my glass in toast. They did likewise, and there were smiles all around. Mohammed Idris whispered something to one of his uncles.

Then the Uncle said, "May Allah reward you for the kindness you showed the family of Moussa David." We drank. It was a good thing, as my arm was on its last leg for the holding of my glass in toast.

"We only ask one thing," Tom *Hajj* continued.

Here it comes, I thought.

From Uncle Dick *Hajj*— "That you promise that, if you must abandon Dar Es Sabir when it comes under siege, that you will take Mohammed Idris with you to be educated in America."

There it is. And "in return, we will lend you body guards to help you and those you choose to make your way to Djemélia and, if necessary, beyond. We ask only that."

It must have been the Johnny Walker—and my belief in their belief in my outstanding teaching qualities—that led me to respond so quickly, "I so promise. I will take you all!"

And so the die was cast.

"So, Monsieur 'arry, *professeur*, we wish to show our gratitude in some way and have had fashioned this beautiful *tarboosh* for you to wear." It was Harry *Hajj*, perhaps a haberdasher himself like his sort-of namesake, Harry Truman.

Uncle Harry *Hajj* brought it out. It was indeed a work of art. Filigreed with tiny beads that may have been gold and silver, and carefully woven, multicolored threading. "Truly fine needlework." I said as I held up the beautiful hat. "I am very full with gratitude so it is with great sorrow that I cannot accept your wonderful gift. For it would . . ."

"You must accept it!" cried Uncle Harry *Hajj*.

"And someday I will. Please understand that I cannot accept such a gift from the family of one of my students without irritating and seemingly insulting all the others—and it *will* become known."

"But it was worn by *El Sayyid Prince Muhammad Idris bin Muhammad al-Mahdi as-Senussi* himself," Uncle Dick *Hajj* insisted.

I held firm—as I must. "Then I will trust it to Mohammed's keeping until such time as I can take it from your generous hands." And a thank you to the Johnny Walker for that inspiration.

They held council, and then Uncle Tom *Hajj* said, "It is a good resolution and you are a most honest *Professeur* and gentleman. I believe that the other *Nasarah*, the Evian, would have accepted it without thought."

"Uncle," Mohammed interjected for the first time. "This *professeur* is not like the others. He is Emricani and not *Nasarah* as such." A+, 20/20, 100% for Mohammed Idris es Senussi.

"Inch Allah," they sang out in chorus. Meaning, in this case, "Maybe. We hope."

"Then remember, Emricani, teach Mohammed well, and we will do other things for you. We know how it is, the desperation of refugees."

[Note from Aaron Hamblin: I'm not sure where in the chronology this belongs, so I'm inserting it here.] *How well they did know. It was only later that I fully understood his comment—and also knew.* [End of insert.]

■ A Bit Unusual

Mid-December 1968

The next morning, I rose at dawn as I often did. To admire the sunrise as it lingered halfway up the dunes, the dunes beside the black Jumeaux—to their southeast. Before the full morning sun would blind me. To peer through the early morning swirling sand—dense almost like a fog. I happened to look across the parade ground and up the path where my beggars lay. The sickly woman and the mother and child were not yet there. Perhaps still too early for customers.

The *mutilé de guerre*, the wounded warrior, however, was there, under his customary tree, and may have spent the night hoping there for a passersby. Those who were stumbling back from *Père* Habert's Harry's Bar and in a half-inebriated state—so therefore more generous than usual.

When out of the sandy fog came the *capitaine*. All spit and polish. Odd time to take a stroll. In uniform. His one arm swinging to an imagined beat. He halted at full attention before the wounded one. Saluted sharply. I could almost hear his heels click as he saluted. I could see the *mutilé* salute back though he did not try to stand.

Then the *légionnaire capitaine* kneeled and spoke to the *mutilé*. There was an exchange of words, after which an exchange of something that looked remarkably like paper bills, CFA, neatly folded.

The *légionnaire capitaine* rose as quickly, saluted, performed an about-face, and marched towards his billet.

A mysterious encounter. For which I could think of no explanation.

None at all.

■ Third Visit

Mid-December 1968

As usual, he came in the night. That very night. And, as usual, he was a fearsome, foreboding sight. I was stone-cold sober and faced him straight on. He did not flinch. Nor did he ask for the *Nasarah*'s drink. He sat pensively for a moment. "Come to my encampment and see my force. You will tell about it, write about it, someday soon."

I rode with him, zigging and zagging through the acacia plants and baobab, tracing a route on the edge of the wild sands. This time

I was mounted on Moussa, who showed off his speed. Such that the sand burned my eyes and turned to mud as it caked my tongue.

I was amazed that he did not blindfold me for this part of the journey. Amazed that he trusted me so. I took careful note of the roadmarks—deteriorating tank, several jeep-like vehicles, various thrown-away arms, large and small. All providing road signs that one could later find and follow. I took careful note.

Only fifteen kilometers from Dar es Sabir, I guessed. I thought it would have been further.

He trusted me so.

■ Their Encampment

We arrived at his encampment. Dry and desolate, but organized. I recognized some of the dirty dozen I had met that day with Amina. There were many others, all around his lodging, in tents, like his own. That is, his tent was as simple as the others, there among the others, and in that way, cleverly hidden.

I left Moussa at a baobab outside the camp where he could do no harm to Wahidi or their horses. One of the Wahidi showed me the way.

Then I told Wahid of SHG's plans and my predicament. I also suggested a counter-trap. It would be good to capture that Ngokuru and force him to order the hostages released. Or to take two hostages in reprisal. Actually, they weren't exactly hostages. Amina was commanded to remain in her dwelling. No trips to work in Mama's Fine Restaurant (so no possibility of listening and spying). Alice was told not to come to Dar es Sabir (which she had no intention of doing anyway).

He seemed to already know these things.

"You are not surprised?' I was a bit surprised that he was not surprised.

"We have our ways of knowing," he responded mysteriously.

"Then?"

"Tell them, tell him, this is the place. Where there is an oasis. East of the Faya Road. The Wadi Abuyad, the White Valley. Tell me via Rashid and the red gris-gris when you have told him, so we will then make ready."

"And if they come under a white flag?"

"We will have our Janjaweed brothers with us." He pointed to the other, larger encampment a kilometer further on—soon to house another, greater force. "They know no white flag."

"Now the Janjaweed are your brothers? They are rapists and murderers." Of this, I was certain.

"They believe in our cause."

"They believe in killing and looting. They are scum and should be your enemy. They use Islam as their cover." I was pretty worked up by now.

"You know, 'arry, that the enemy of my enemy must be my friend. Or at least my ally. Then, in the end, you know we will win."

I didn't feel good about this. But I wanted her—*them*—kept free.

■ Truth in the Night

Mid-December 1968

Last night, after our particularly pleasurable, and energetic session, she asked me, "Will you go away from here?"

I tried to change the subject—to something more romantic. "Let's go to sleep."

"Will you? Are you going this time?"

"I'm only going to Djemélia. But someday I must go to Emrica. Would you come with me?"

"You know I cannot. I have my mother and brother to look after. My people are here. My life is here. The souls of my ancestors are here."

"As mine are there."

She might have expected me to offer them lifetime accommodations as well. In the USA. Maybe just a summer home. Like the Florida snowbirds. That would be a gas. However, my plans on return were rather "flexible."

■ Fate Calls . . . upon my "Diplomacy"

Mid-December 1968

Not the bearer of goods news, our Antoine. And he was accosting me daily these days. With bad, I mean scary, news. He was showing mood changes himself. Alain had an identical sky-blue police uniform and wore replica glasses (with plain glass only) of the type worn by Antoine, so I was not always certain who was accosting me. And whether his "latest" news was "accurate." I was starting to shy away from this person, or change direction when I saw him coming my way.

This time I missed escaping him. He had been literally running after me. And caught up.

"Monsieur," he began with a smart salute while panting—though ever smiling and tilting his head upwards as if he were looking up at me. To see if I would lie? But perhaps only to focus his glasses. "Monsieur le *Professeur*." He used the polite and formal salutation. I knew this was Antoine. And not the other.

"Monsieur le *gendarme*," I replied with as much enthusiasm as I could muster. "What good news do you have for us today?"

"It was reported over the telex at police headquarters that there has been another kidnapping for ransom."

"*Nasarah* folks, I suppose."

"*Nasarah* folks," he answered with a seriously and perhaps deeply felt look of sorrow. As if these *Nasarah*, all *Nasarah*, were my kin and therefore close to me.

"Are they still alive?" I inquired with equally serious and sorrowful concern.

"For ransom. They are the Taylors and Gaugins."

"Shit." I *did* know these people. They had passed through in a Land Rover not two weeks ago. A French couple and a British couple intent on greening the globe. Or as much of it as they could. Bad start to my day. Bad start to theirs. "Who has done this thing?" I asked, though it couldn't have mattered.

"Wahid*i*, we think. And Janjawid, we think."

Too much thinking, I thought. Without confirmation. Perhaps a rogue gang. Perhaps directed by Wahid.

They were a strange mix, the two hostage couples, proof there can be Gallic and British harmony. "How much do they want?"

"Fifty thousand US dollars. Twelve million, five hundred thousand CFA *Africains*."

"Jesus."

"Or three hundred carbines. Or rifles—newer than Bertier or Enfield. Perhaps M-1s or Karibiner 98. But this time they want the ammunitions in great quantities. The last ransom did not have those. Perhaps because they forgot to ask for them."

"Perhaps." My mind was working overtime on this one. "Who is negotiating for us?"

"It was to be the police chief, but he has mysteriously disappeared."

"Perhaps he is enjoying early morning delights with his mistress," I suggested.

"We visited there as well. He has not been there. She is also absent." Frightening portents.

"Of the English and French speakers, we have only a recent militia recruit. Named Adin Azuku Vincent." Whose English is virtually nonexistent. Whose French is questionable.

"I know who he is." Shithead with the bad attitude. Dropped his carbine in mid-drill. (Maybe an assassin.) "And for them?"

"Abdel-Hamid. From the afflicted village."

"How do we know the captives are still alive?"

"Ah, yes, Monsieur. And you know them and can recognize them. So you should go under the white flag to bring us proof."

I hedged. "That was not my thought." Definitely not my thought.

"You are safer. Any *Nasarah* would do, but you know them. If there are other captives, ones that you do not know, we can bargain for them as well. We will send Akuru with you as protection."

My internals started acting up. The accompaniment of Akuru, the possible spy, did not mollify me in the least. "I know them, so it is me that must go? You know them as well."

"Sorry, but with my poor eyes, I do not always tell these *Nasarah* well apart. You would do better."

"I will ask the other *Nasarah*." Only Partenay had met the French couple, and I wouldn't impose on his playtime. Otherwise, only I, among Caucasians, had met all four. So I was stalling, waiting for an epiphany.

That would not come.

■ Trade Mission Prep

Late December, before Christmas, 1968

I talked with *Père* Habert, procurer of all things. "I can get these weapons, but we will need a large means of transport," he offered. "Plus, I know the lepers have many. Maybe two hundred."

"But they will not be so eager to part with them. They may be saving them for the coming battles," he added.

That did not sit too well with me. But then I thought and said, "They will end up in the same hands at the end, and we can later replenish those of the lepers."

"Good point. Who will ask them?"

"I will. Their leader will be our guide to the hostages."

I sent the message in daylight, hoping it would be picked up by a satellite:

WTF:NEEDC1302DELIVERITMS:HABERTPURCHSE2RA
NSOM4TOURIST:STOP

WTF:GO2VOIX:STOP

I did.

Nice going, satellite.

■ Who Pays?

In crackly voice-mode: "Leonard? Ok. Listen: Ransom four tourists for fifty thousand US dollars, which is twelve million five hundred thousand CFA *Africains* or, alternatively, three hundred carbines or rifles—newer than Bertiers. Perhaps even M-1s or Karibiner 98. Habert can procure the rifles, which are valued as a lot cheaper than the dollar amount. He will need transport, however, and, given that the roads risk being blocked, I suggest using the air force plane for one hundred. Then two hundred from the lepers."

"Whose nationals?"

"French and British."

"Well then, let them …"

"There may also be the Berinskis, Americans who disappeared in these parts a few months ago."

"Ah. OK, but we'll have to have the French and British pay …"

"Yeah, ok," I said. Like the hostages gave a shit who paid. I knew the Berinskis had been picked up—actually the survivor, one of two— and flown to Algeria. But Leonard didn't know.

"Harry, back to you at 19:00 via text."

"Roger." I guessed I might as well sound professional, especially when I didn't know what the hell I was doing. Exactly.

And all this time I was rising to send messages at 3 a.m. Perhaps the time was just a ruse (by my compatriots) to insure our secrecy.

■ Trade Mission Things Got Rushed

Late December, the Week before Christmas, 1968

I got Partenay's permission to take leave time, gathered provisions, and fed and watered Moussa. Abdel-Hamid would meet us at the fourth dune north—or thereabouts.

He was there as planned, at a healthy distance and in dune shadows, greeting with signs and smiles (it seemed), well armed, and ready for the rough ride. I'm not sure he recognized me. Rather, he circled behind us, checking whether we had been followed. Then he immediately skirted round us, to point, turned his back to us, then back to his place in the shadows, without the usual greetings and recitation of patrimony.

We rode hard, he on his donkey who moved at some speed, but with great effort. We rode at least thirty kilometers with not a word. I counted the dunes and the footprints would keep in the sand for my return. Also, I noted the two battle-marred and discarded Land Rovers at two locations along our way. Abdel-Hamid kept his back to me, perhaps attempting to prevent revealing his affliction to us.

"Abdel-Hamid, we must speak," I finally shouted out.

"Ah, it is you, the Emricani, who rides with us." He knew this very well, and reluctantly came out to me from the dune shadows.

After *salaams*, etc., I explained our situation. "Can you give us the rifles you have cached?"

"We are saving them for the coming battles."

"If there are such battles," I said, hoping the contrary.

"There will be."

"But if these fellows get them, will they not go to the Wahidi anyway?"

"Yes."

"Then . . . ." I pressed.

"We have made a big circle on this."

"Big, perfect circles are the work of Allah," I noted sanctimoniously. I handed him one of the half-litre Scotch bottles I had brought.

We approached an encampment before he cried out, "We have two hundred!" I assume to me. Then "Ya-eee, the *Nasarah* to see for your bargain. Aha!" I rushed to show the white flag, attaching it to my saddle. He then rode off to a small copse, where he waited in the shadows. I think he was waiting to lead me back to Dar es Sabir. This was my fervent hope, since I was not very sure of the return route and our tracks might be eradicated by our departure time. A good thing to worry about while negotiating.

The band of kidnappers included some of the youth who had met Amina and me on our first "date." A ragged crew. The one with the New York Yankees cap. Where do they get these things? Another of them, one I knew well, came forward to talk.

It was Antoine's replica, even wearing the sky-blue *gendarme's* jacket.

"Ah, *Professeur*. You are so chosen. I am chosen because I had some schooling and learned French and English." He seemed proud of this accomplishment.

"I am the *professeur* of English. The one you almost murdered."

"It is known. Are you, like Monsieur Evian, a lover of young boys?" By his tone, I determined that an affirmative would have gotten us off on the wrong foot.

"Not at all. I am not like that Evian." Even though I had his *kaz*, his woman, even his dog. I waited while this one thought out my response.

"Even though you have his *kaz*?"

"It was assigned to me by the *sous-préfet*."

"Even though you have his woman?" He was well informed.

"She came to me, not I to her."

"Even though you have his dog?"

"The dog comes only for my dinner bones and leavings. I have my own little dog as my pet."

"But you do not do this other evil thing."

"No."

"Then dismount, *Nasarah*, you and your assistant, and sit with our band." The reference to Akuru as "my assistant" no doubt was starting on the wrong foot as far as Akuru was concerned.

Not the merry band of Sherwood Forest, these ones, as each

one immediately pulled up his veil, covered chin, mouth and nose, to emphasize his fierce and angry eyes.

■ Haggling

Akuru began his well-rehearsed soliloquy. "Lords, Sidis, I am Adin Azuku Vincent, a brother to you, whose father . . ."

But he was immediately cut off by the arrogant Alain who seemed to be running this show. That's right, Alain, the assassin, of the loose trigger finger and hopeless eyesight, who said, "Yee-ah, we don't care who you are, but what have you brought with you?"

Akuru was flustered for a moment, during which the assassin again asked "What have you brought to trade?" I even felt a bit sorry for Akuru.

But things could get worse. So I dared intervene with "Nothing. We came to see the prisoners."

"They are not prisoners," he snapped. "They are guests of the Al Hadjer Tuareg clan who ride with the Janjawid.

"You don't look so Tuareg to me," I dared suggest. He was definitely not. Definitely Sara-Ngumbaye or other Southerner. (Which seemed not to matter in this case.)

"We are all of the same cause."

"Plunder and murder," I nearly suggested.

He ignored my previous insolence and went to the heart of the matter. "Since I see that you do not have the rifles, you must have brought the money."

"Neither. Before we deliver the arms, we want to ascertain the health of the *Nasarah* guests and bargain their true value." Even I was surprised at my own daring. "We want to determine their true worth." Said and intoned with a meaning these types would understand.

Another gang-banger reached over to throw open the canvas of a sort of leanto. Against a baobab. It must have been hot as hell in there.

The four guests were deeply ensconced to the rear of this

makeshift leanto, so that they could barely be seen. Probably forced back by a long rifle. And gasping out the back for "cooler" air.

"Harry, old boy!" Clive shouted out. "What the hell are you doing out here? Wherever 'here' is."

"Lets keep our chat at a minimum or they'll suspect something untoward, whatever that could be," I suggested.

"He means shut up, Clive," Grace clarified. "Clive fancies himself a Johnny Appleseed." [Note from Aaron Hamblin: I'm not sure where in the chronology this belongs, so I'm inserting it here.] *In fact, Clive was an agronomist (as was Jean-Jacques) with ideas about how to halt desertification. How to make the desert flower again.* [End of insert.]

"Right-o, Harry. I got it. That's all right dear." Clive was always a very good-natured sort. Grace ran things.

"Do you have enough water?" I asked.

Grace held up an army-issue canteen. Etched "Lièvre" near the spout.

"Food?"

Clive held up a US military C-ration can. Where the hell did these bandit scrubs get that? At least they weren't cans of spoiled soup.

"This is the shits, Harry," Grace shouted. In her lovely English working-class accent.

"Help is on the way."

"Two things." Jean-Jacques said, barely above a whisper. "We need more water, and we need a breeze,"

"Where is your Land Rover?" Jean-Jacques pointed to a blooming acacia about eighty meters east. "We'll need it to take you back." I hoped that gave them a glimmer of hope. I was surprised twerp didn't insist on keeping the Land Rover as well. Maybe he would at our next visit.

"How about you, Marie?"

"OK," in her soft, mellifluous voice. But she did not look well.

I turned back to Alain with a command and a bargain. "You will bring down that leanto and allow your 'guests' the shade of this baobab. We expect them to be better nourished and hydrated when we return. For that, we will bring you two hundred rifles, probably of M-1 design."

"Only two hundred? We are expecting three hundred for these four. These four 'guests.'"

"And you might have gotten them but for the poor treatment of your 'guests' that I have seen. One is not well and may die on the trip to Dar es Sabir." I was on a roll now.

"Now you provoke. Perhaps you are watching us always!" Alain, of course.

Akuru nudged me and suggested that I be careful for fear of getting only three hostages in this bargaining, if I kept pushing him. Good point!

"Two hundred seventy-five" Alain haggled.

"Two hundred fifty for all four, if they have been well treated from this time forth. That is our final offer!"

"This *Nasarah* does the *musawama* (the bargaining) well. We have no time for this haggling. Bring the two hundred fifty tomorrow or we will kill these *Nasarah* 'guests,' and you will have to take back their bones if the hyenas leave you any. *Fehemt?* Understood?"

"I cannot promise tomorrow. But it will be soon. Meanwhile, you may keep this one (Adin Azuku Vincent) as a sign of my good faith."

"Monsieur, you cannot do this. I am a soldier!" Azuku protested. With great vehemence, I should add.

"You are a lot of things," I noted, looking him straight in the eyes. I think he knew that I knew (about his double duty, his spying) and he backed off. "For these days you will do a soldier's duty and help these good folk. And help these Tuareg behave like good hosts."

He only hung his head. I felt sorry for him. A bit. I took a swig from my water bag and handed it to him as my sign of good faith. I hoped I wouldn't need it for the ride back. Then I mounted and wheeled Moussa. I hoped he knew our way back. Or that we would find our tracks from our inbound journey.

He did. Between the memory of Moussa and the two wreckages,

we made it back in short order. *Père* Habert was thrilled that we had haggled the number down. More than half would be delivered by the US Air Force today, and the rest tomorrow from the lepers. Perfect. We organized the donkey carriers and awaited the flight. Praying that the heat-seekers would not be deployed.

They weren't. Everything was gathered and counted. I must have thanked *Père* Habert a dozen times. "I'm sure you will return the favor, H'arry. In time. Plus, I will reprovision these ones with their proper payment."

"I will repay much of it in purchases of whiskey and wine. Whiskey and wine that I will need to manage my temperament. Then with other things at your command."

"I hate arming the enemy like this, but I must do it for my countrymen. You say the French woman is not well?"

"Marie, she is not well."

"Then I'll have to ask that Russian doctor-spy to be standing by."

"And I'll go back to them by horseback. Moussa can lead the way for the trucks."

The deed was done as agreed as planned. The "guests" were freed and taken back to Dar es Sabir. In their Land Rover. Marie recovered once she got Ivan's care and attention.

I guess I was feeling exceptionally proud of myself despite having helped to arm the Wahidi. Even more proud that I had maneuvered the lepers into trading for the rifles, which were bound for the Wahidi anyway. I held onto that moment.

Exceptionally proud.

■ Younis 8

The Day before R&R Departure

I should have learned by now to temper my promises. I had not. So I had spent the last week or more searching out acacia branches both bendable and sufficiently strong. I found an acacia branch that had fallen. It was dead but not yet breaking, and it was almost Younis's height. I found the bow's natural curve and then carved off the thorns in its belly and made notches for the string ends. I thanked the Great Spirit that I had been a Boy Scout and had done this before.

Then I searched and found standard twine in my hoard of mostly useless things. It was twine that had wrapped "care" packages from Aaron, from "home." And I bent and carefully strung the bow, until I got a reasonable facsimile of one (after having broken several trial bows).

I made arrows of random sticks that I found around the hovels in town—leftover pieces and branches, perhaps dropped as the women carried loads of wood for their cooking fires. I carved points on them and would have glued on feathers if there had been birds in this place.

But it was yet another week before I saw Younis again. In the meantime, the string would loosen, and I would have to repeatedly restring the bow.

When he came, we exchanged salutations. Then I asked, "Where have you been, Younis? I have missed you this long time."

"I have worked, Monsieur Harry, but thought only of Robin of Hood and archers."

"I've made you a bow and arrows. Here." Then I demonstrated how to use them. Sometimes the arrows went well. Sometimes with little effect. But he got the idea. I gave him an illustrated archer's manual that I had done up in English. Good learning tool. At least for the English learning exercises.

"I will become a great archer like Robin of Hood!" A broad smile. He was excited about his new gift.

"Yes, you will become a great archer. And the best in this land."

"Oh, but I think there are no others in this land, Monsieur!"

Caught me on that one. But then I had a sort of epiphany. "But you can teach many more to be archers like you, though you will be the best of them all."

First some English grammar. But he gave rapid and correct answers to all my drills in a rush to get to the story of Robin. "And what happened to Robin of Hood and his Merry Men?" he asked, the minute I closed the lesson book.

"Well the sheriff tries to arrest and perhaps kill Robin and his men for their robbing. Besides, he wants to marry a highborn lady, lady Miriam, who Robin loves. And she loves Robin. But the sheriff locks the lady as a prisoner in a cell-like room, a dungeon, in his palace."

"Like Wahid and Amina," Younis exclaimed.

"Ah, is that the way with Wahid and Amina?"

He was called back to servant duty before he could answer. He left his bow and arrows with me.

I gave his *gris-gris* to Rashid with my updates inside. I explained to Rashid that he must carry the *gris-gris* to Wahid. But leave my messages hidden among the Islamic texts to fool the guards inspecting all the incoming and outgoing packages. Rashid would then bring back the responses, also in the *gris-gris*. Thus was born our courier and his courier "sachel."

■ The Fair and the Race

Late December, just before Christmas, 1968

And so it was that the idea of a futball tournament was rejected. By both sides. But a fair with a wrestling match, a shooting contest (whoops, not a good idea, that one! I called for canceling that for obvious reasons and replacing it with hoop shooting). But a horse race, where bets could be placed, was more attractive to both sides. Winner take all (the bet money, selected horses, and the town). There would be second- and third-place winners of prizes as well.

Yes, both sides were suspicious but yielded, perhaps not to their better judgment, because of the bets, the money, involved. Besides, it sounded like fun! Wahid needed the money for rice, millet, and arms. He'd love to take possession of the town without a fight. Then the Wahidi would show how well they could govern. Control of the town without the bloodshed of a fight was too much of an opportunity to pass up.

Besides, as I heard one remark, probably in his cups, "We'll let the Américain run it. Then he can take all the blame, deal with the Wahidi, and pay the bills when it doesn't work."

I thought I had played this one well. That I was getting good at this. Or lucky.

Probably lucky.

■ Fourth Visit (Not Counting the Short Briefing Regarding the Fair)

Late December, before Christmas, 1968

The next evening plus one and he was back. Rolling his carbine on his thighs, more rapidly than the night before. "We have the best rider, the little one called Saghir, but no good horse for him to ride."

"With all the horses you have? Not one?"

"They are stolen work horses. So they are all strong horses good for long voyages. Not a one for short races. You have the best fed and groomed. The fastest. We saw when you rode him from Amina's to your home."

Jeesh. I shouldn't have pushed my Moussa that time. The price of love.

We looked at each other with manufactured blank stares. Then he added, "So you have Moussa."

"Moussa is not a race horse. He is no Barb, no Berber horse. He is merely a work horse, a *metisse* Dongola. He likes to work and carry riders alone because he has a bad temper with other horses. Maybe too competitive."

More staring. Then it was Wahid who said, "Competitive is good. Also, if we are to have a bond and an understanding, 'arry, then we must each give and trust. I have given the rider."

I offered the child, Younis, as rider. For his light weight.

"Yes," Wahid quickly answered. "But he is not tried and does not know the tricks of a competing rider." I think he meant the roughnecking and cheating that jockeys would do.

And so it was settled.

■ The Price of Our Bond

Late December, just before Christmas, 1968

The next day, Saghir came to claim Moussa. He threw off my saddle, while I wished Moussa well and placed my cheek to his. Then we walked my horse to the nearby field and tied him to a lone baobab.

There Saghir examined Moussa's back and, without so much as an explanation to me, he drew his *kabira* knife and proceeded to make slashes on Moussa's back. I had heard of this custom. For bareback riders. The slashes would clot and heal to eventually form a giant roughened area of scar tissue. Saghir intended to ride on these slashes. With only a blanket on them. And with only a few days to heal.

He must have assumed the horse was now his. But I held the reins.

Moussa flinched, but endured the cutting without a sound and hardly a movement. Brave boy. I embraced his head one last time. Then I let go the reins.

Yes, I will write about this.

Anyway, I will bet against Moussa. For old time's sake.

When I returned to the *kaz* without Moussa, Kalb cocked his head in that way puppies do when they are questioning. I had no answer for him. He lay down on his belly and stared at me with mournful eyes.

For me, I was making this contribution to this fair—a contribution for peace.

Such was our bond, between Wahid and me.

■ The Fair: The Day of the Races

Late December, just before Christmas, 1968

I was fair project manager by default. No one else wanted that job. And I worked my ass off.

It was fair day too soon, and both parties came in their Sunday (or, since there were many Muslims, should I say "Friday"?) best. The militia riders, in their finest *jalabas* covering their olive-green uniforms and some Wahidi—I think they were—in robes of white and azure. And brown for the bachelors. Not all the Wahidi were so dressed, since that would certainly be a giveaway to the militia and others.

So it was difficult to tell the Wahidi from the civilian denizens, which must have been what their leaders had anticipated. Anyway, I could not see Wahid. He may have opted out on the assumption that someone would recognize him and, intentionally or inadvertently, signal the militia.

Antoine sidled up to me. Wearing his sky-blue dress *tenue*. The usual captivating smile. The usual neck bend so he could look up at me. Perhaps to give his spectacles a better focus. Or to determine whether I'm telling the truth. Or perhaps his way of mimicking an obsequious pose. "I see no Wahid, Monsieur 'arry. Perhaps he fears recognition and that someone would signal the militia. Or the police."

"Yes, I think it might be so. But as the new chief of police, you may arrest him."

"But I am ordered to refrain from arresting him. Indeed the town council and militia have given them (the Wahidi) free passage— assuming they do not descend to their reputedly dishonest ways." He'd left the "they" reference ambiguous, so that I wondered whether Alain would show up to confuse things.

There were sausage vendors with their slices of *merguez* marinated in fiery sauce and a significant amount of Douze Marches or billi-billi to wash them down. Even some grenadine for the non-alcohol drinkers among them.

There were series of wrestling matches where the winner took on the next challenger until an ultimate winner would be declared. And bets won. The tall, muscular stranger did not take off his turban or *jalaba* nor lower his veil, but donned the traditional animal hides and covered himself with dust and ashes for strength. The prisoner did likewise. Both wrestled in a flurry of feints and contacts, as well as some astonishing feats of strength. The stranger miraculously maintained his veil up, which handicapped him throughout the match. So after a valiant showing, the stranger was tossed down, pinned, and lost to the one in prison garb—our Ibrahim whom the militia set free for these wrestling matches. The Yekbar warden received the reward of a brass-made statue— "on behalf of the prison."

Meanwhile, the hoop-shoot was played. No layups. Just free shots from the indicated line. To a metal hoop without netting. The militia guy won with a perfect twenty. I wondered where he had been practicing.

Then Antoine sidled back to the banker, who was Partenay, and stood by him while he grandly spread his arms in his way (the way that our students imitate so well when his back is turned) and announced the bets on the race with yet another flourish. "For the Wahidi winner, 16,372CFA. For the militia winner 19,232CFA. After the first round. Plus a donation of 100,000CFA from our Libyan cousins." For the first-place winner then. Overall betting of 135,604CFA. There was a murmur of approval. They had chosen the *juge* to manage the prizes, since he was deemed incorruptible.

The two winners would be determined by the first round and receive first round prizes. One militia and one civilian (Wahidi?). "These winners of the first round will then compete one-on-one, and that winner takes all." Much of the action was in the side bets. My guess was that more money was bet on the Wahidi horses because it was assumed that the Wahidi so often had to race their horses to escape the militia. And were always successful.

Capitaine Nbokuru was there in all his splendor. He brought his eye-tick and lip-curl. So was Saghir who had mutilated my Moussa. So was Moussa.

For me, this was not merely a race.

Antoine had previously relieved everyone of guns and swords. He gave the owners colored matching ribbons so as to later identify their weapons. He secreted them well away from the festivities.

There were twenty-seven riders in the first round, all jostling for an "advantageous" position at the starting point, which was etched in the sand. There was tape at the finish line. I guessed the distance between start and finish at nine hundred meters. The winner would be the one who broke the tape. First Wahidi or first militia rider. A single shot would start the race.

Someone had the bright idea to line the riders up so every other "jockey" was a militiaman. That made for some yelling, angry retorts, palm-up gestures. What? Rules? Rather, "organization" as known in this world.

Meanwhile, there was much pointing among the observers, pointing and arguing about which horse, and rider, would win. And much more side-betting occurred.

The starter got tired of yelling. When horse or rider misbehaved, he had been shouting his reprimands by calling out the horse, since the rider uniforms and *jalabas* were so much alike. The onlookers, and they were many, were starting to get restless. They had gathered at the finish line.

"You there, on the brown Dongola, dress your horse!" He said it in French. Using French must mean he was really pissed. It was Moussa he was calling to. Moussa showing his temper with the nearest horses around him. Creating advantage with his leg kicks and swats. Brave boy.

The shot was sudden and caught me off-guard. Mostly we saw a cloud of sand, dust, and seemingly spastic mounts. The riders looked fierce beneath their bandanas.

The race was done in a flash. The winner broke the tape by a head and took 5,000 CFA francs from me.

I was astounded. It was Moussa.

Moussa, full of heart and soul. At least I hope he had a soul, for he collapsed at the finish line and was declared *mort . . . mat*, by many including a momentarily jubilant and, then, a rapidly, fiercely angry, Saghir—who now saw his potential new livelihood already having slipped away.

I approached Moussa gingerly. Moussa, lying there completely collapsed and eyes wide open, but unseeing. As I came closer, I could see the wounds made on his back by Saghir, and the riding blanket caked with Moussa's now-drying blood. I was glad I had not brought Kalb to see this.

I knelt and cradled his head, closed his eyelids frozen in death. Then I sat, rocked his head, nuzzled him, and angrily berated him for his temper and his heart. "Silly Moussa. You ran in your anger and your pain. Perhaps you were running to me. Don't you know, I was to precede you in death? Then you to be buried with me. That is the way of things here. But you leave me like your namesake did. Good-by, my friend . . . ."

Maudlin, I know. Still it was at that moment that I knew how much I would miss him. Perhaps he would have been better off as a feast ground up for the French *Nasarah* after all.

Ngokuru may have been wondering why I was nestling a Wahidi horse. More evidence of my collusion with them.

But then the two groups started really mixing it up all around me. Spoiled the whole point of the races. Antoine and his cohorts waded into the melee with their batons swinging. Into a cloud of dust and sand. I thought I spied Alain in civilian *jalaba* and pounding away at the cops. My eyes deceived me? Or Alain was among us. Beating up on his brother. That was probably the case. I guess Alain chose to leave his police uniform at the encampment.

Antoine and the other police officers were outnumbered and

soon overwhelmed. There was not a centimeter showing of Antoine's bright blue *tenue*.

He had wisely hidden the weapons. Thanks be to Allah. Although some small knives did appear, menacingly.

But no throats were cut.

They finally got some order restored, and Partenay declared the winner of each team. More shouting and vilifying. Some insisted that Moussa was dead and therefore could not be declared the winner. Alphonse appeared, doctor bag in hand. He loaded a syringe and was about to give Moussa a shot.

"What is in that, Alphonse? What are you giving our Moussa?" I said through my tears.

"It is to revive him."

"To revive him from his death? What is it?"

"It is strychnine, Monsieur." I slapped him, and he ran off without his nurse's bag.

I was urged by the less sentimental ones to help move Moussa away from the finish line. I then shed tears as I sat with him under an Acacia tree—hardly hearing the starting shot for the final round and not interested in the winner. I was at too much of a loss to pay attention to the results.

■ I Should Have Paid Attention

Maybe I should have paid attention. Or tried to organize a peace conference right there. Finally, after arguing with Ngokuru and his lip-curl tick about who had won the first round, they went forward with their one-on-one, civilian (Wahidi) against militia. Saghir was given the Wahidi horse that came in second after Moussa.

But this time the militia won. No Moussa to defend the Wahidi honor. The Wahidi would have to abandon Dar es Sabir. Not that there were any admitted Wahidi in the town. Horses would be exchanged. Money changed hands. Even the Wahidi took some private betting.

Then a hue and cry went up, for all the public betting proceeds had disappeared. No doubt under cover of the melee. The missing public betting proceeds, the 135,604CFA, were not to be found.

They carted Moussa away. Probably to grind him up while the meat was still fresh. I did not claim the bridle.

Accusations all around. But when the uniforms were bared under *jalabas*, the civilians stopped their shouting. No one wanted to be identified as Wahidi.

The militia immediately came to attention as Ngokuru and the *juge* instructed that each nonmilitia person be subject to body and horse search. Ngokuru immediately ordered a perimeter to be formed around the fair site. As each individual passed the search, he was nudged through the perimeter. Horses as well. (Even Moussa was searched, I'm told. An ultimate indignity.) Each "suspect's" weapon was then retrieved from Antoine.

It was almost dark before I received a full body search and was sent on my way. I heard later that each militiaman was himself subject to search by a comrade up to and including Ngokuru. The treasure had disappeared.

It was later, in the *kaz*, that we began the mourning period. I poured my usual libation. Kalb cocked his head. But, then, he somehow understood and was already beginning to mourn his friend. He went to Moussa's shed where he whimpered for his beloved Moussa for several days. And he ate very little. Only with Chien's urgings did he eat at all. I had to be grateful to Chien for that, despite his bad taste in masters.

Rashid understood as well since his head pounding became more rapid, one would say even more fierce.

But otherwise, Kalb sat and waited. Sat and waited for the friend who would never return. So did we—all of us.

■ The Visit to David Moussa

Late December, just before Christmas, 1968

It took me awhile to find the headstone among so many on that hill, the "Death by *Nasarah*" hill, mostly broken pieces of shale-like flat stones. Some still up and some fallen down. All in a frightening crowd, so close together that I was obliged to stumble onto, and walk onto, their graves.

And my memory of the funeral didn't serve me well with regard to location. Perhaps I was too frightened that day to take note. So, as it turned out, I should have been looking to decipher the Arabic of "Moussa Daoud," but I was searching for "David Moussa." I wanted to offer a Christmas prayer.

When I finally found it (it read **Moussa David Daoud | 18: Death by the hand of Nasarah**), I had not a clue of what to do next. So I knelt and laid the wildflower bouquet I had picked against the headstone. As in every cemetery where I've been, the wind picked up, imitating a soft wail and blowing the sand and broken stones along with various detritus around me and, as it seemed, through me.

I knew my fragmentary Latin would not solace his soul. *De profundis clamavi ad te, Réquiem ætérnam dona eis, Dómine; et lux perpétua lúceat eis* . . . .Then it petered out. I did then say *B-ismi-llāhi r-raḥmāni r-raḥīmi* to bring some solace to these dead. That I knew the *Shahadah* better than my own catechism. Then I only spoke to him as my one-time student.

> "Moussa David, I am Harry Hamblin, your teacher
> of English in *Quatrième*. I hope you are well in your
> new abode. I hope you are in Paradise where you
> belong. God does not care about the sins of the sex
> that you were made to suffer.
> "By the way, we named my horse after you.
> Moussa. He was a bit feisty but sprinted well and

was kind to his grooms, Jean and Rashid. He was also kind to me and carried my burdens. Finally, he was kind to my dog, Kalb, and treated him well. They were fast friends. I lost this horse Moussa as well. As with you." I began to tear up.

"Next time I will bring you pictures of large American cars to add to your picture collection."

But I may break that promise, for I may never bring the pictures of American cars to his grave.

"Help me remember you as kind. As you were. And forgive me that I was not there to save you. Amen."

At that moment, I felt a tap on my shoulder. It was the black, filigreed *jalaba*, and I stood up quickly to render him proper honor. "*Imam*, you surprise me."

"And you, me. I am touched that you come visit the grave of our brother and I thank you."

I don't know what impulse moved me to say the next, "I am sorry I was unable to say a proper good-bye at his burial, but I understand his privates had been stuffed in his mouth."

"You are misinformed. He died of a terrible wasting disease. One that we think was passed to him by Evian. A disease wasting the privates parts. But also, he was covered with this disease and in no condition to be viewed except by those who perform the *ghusal*, the body washers."

Communicable disease? Perhaps from Evian to Miriam to me? A moment of uncontrollable panic. I thought of this for the moment, and then, in a low mumble, asked "Would you say some words?"

"I will." Then, with a sweep of his arm, a motion that seemed to encompass this entire world of sand dunes and dry brush, he uttered:

"*B-ismi-llāhi r-rahmāni r-rahīmi.* You, Moussa Daoud, had your life cut short by the strangers, and it is true for all of us that surround you: Arabs, Baggara, Haddad, and Kanembu, Bilala, Sara-Ngumbaye, Toubou, and Hadjerai. And the many dozens of others. They could have left us to our dreams. I do not know how much was ended. When I look back now from this hill, I see the women and children dragging their burdens along the crooked pathways. And I can see that something else died there in the bloodied sand, and was buried by the fierce winds of the Harmatan and by the dunes of sand. A people's dream died there. The sacred world is dead. It was a beautiful world in a beautiful dream (his voice broke for a moment), but now the people's hope is broken and shattered. Allah is our only recourse, Mohammed our only savior. Thus have I spoken. *Allahu akbar.*"

Thus had he surrendered the animism of his forefathers to the Muslim God and Prophet. And preached it in this cemetery. To the sand, tombstones, and me.

I did not realize the extent of this spiritual confusion and sense of loss. The spirituality and loss of these animist-Muslims, and their confusion—until I heard him weep as he prayed in the midst of the ever-swirling sand and ever-changing dunes.

The *ulema*, the *imam*, overcome by the mysteries of constant change.

For their old gods and wandering souls were no longer doing their job.

■ The Last Flight to Djemélia

Late December, before Christmas, 1968

The Corps was generous enough to buy me a one-way air ticket to Djemélia. Perhaps to ensure that I not be turned back by the militia or the Wahidi. To ensure that I arrive to bear testimony to the events in Dar es Sabir? Leonard, Old Sport, had already gone by unscheduled air force lift the week before. I stayed for the fair and race, then flew out by regular transport—discounting the threats of a Wahidi plane hijacking. And I still had a superstition about hanging around in Djamé.

I had one about flying back as well—on time and in one piece.

So I went later by a DC3 knockoff. Encouraged by the Made-In-USA look of it.

Dr. Godin also took that flight back. I had already taken a window seat over the starboard wing when he sat down beside me. "*Droboe Utro,*" I said in my astonishment. "I didn't know you were going to Djamé."

"Djamé? I do not know this thing."

"Djemélia."

"Ah. Made short." A quick study, our Godin.

We took off without incident. The plane was a DC3 look-alike but Russian made, I figured. Maybe because the "Fasten Seat Belt" signs were in Cyrillic. Quick study, me. And not too clean, the plane, having carried too many chickens and goats. No hostess service.

"Made in CCCP" Godin offered. "Ivchenko. Fine machine."

We were an hour into the flight when, staring at the scenery from five thousand meters, as the pilot announced, I noticed smoke from the starboard engine. I stared at it for a few minutes to assure myself that this was no mirage.

It was no mirage.

I climbed over Godin, and I bolted to the cockpit.

"Smoke on the right engine. Is that normal?" Quick study, me.

The pilot kept his eyes forward. Searching. "Yes, we know. We're looking for a place to land. Please be seated."

I guess I'd been told.

We swept down in a half glide to a barren and flat expanse. I looked at Godin and he looked at me. Fine machine, I thought. But I kept silent. The landing was a bit rough, but manageable.

We suffered some rocking and shaking, some puking given the sounds behind me, and the usual screams. When we'd stopped completely, the pilot got on the intercom. "Well, ladies and gentlemen, sorry for the rough landing. We have a crack in the cylinder head, and we had to shut off the starboard engine—the one on your right."

No hijacking. Maybe repair sabotage. It was unlikely we would ever know.

"We've sent for a repair crew and parts from Djemélia. I suggest you debark since the plane will soon heat up. We have a little water, which we'll ration out. Children first. Then women. Then the rest of you." Very Western of him.

I assumed he meant us men by the "rest of you." Anyway, there was some male muttering. We sat under the wing, some on their haunches, sweating, waiting for the repair crew and parts, with African patience.

We were a United Nations mix. French flight crew, Ngumbaye and Sahelian, American and Russian paying customers.

I imagined trekking towards Djemélia with them. Then a death march in this sand or buried in the re-forming and shifting dunes. Nourishing the local fauna. What little there was of it. With my UN comrades. And the eventual guilt-tripping at HQ. In my view, it might be worth it—their guilt—for having sent me to Dar es Sabir in the first place.

We'd been aloft for an hour, which meant we were about forty minutes flight time from Djemélia. The best option was for the plane to limp into Djemélia with the repair crew.

Adoum Justin was also on board, though I only noticed when we gathered under the port wing. He was Sara-Ngumbaye, so our salutations were of the French variety. "It goes well with you, Monsieur Justin?"

"Very well. And you?"

"Yes, but for this delay."

"You must learn the Ngumbaye patience," he admonished.

"Yes, I must." Like Alain, I thought. "And what brought you from Dar es Sabir to Djemélia?" Assuming we get there.

"It was a stop-off. A connecting flight. I started in Faya. The annual inspection."

It figures that they would do a school inspection the last day before the "winter" break.

Monsieur Adoum had been a colleague of ours in the early days. He taught history (European with an emphasis on France, and maths, which Partenay and Modou now taught since Adoum Justin had been promoted to assistant superintendent at *le Ministre d'education* in Djemélia. We had even partied together, he and I. And had often held hands in the Sara-Ngumbaye way.

Now we could only have the politest of conversations. Polite until he said "'arry, what happened to your eyebrow, the left one?" The one I injured falling in one of my inebriated accidents.

"Car accident."

"Or working your moonlighting job?" He smiled conspiratorially.

"A little of both, I suppose." We were in full sparring mode now.

Then his clincher. "So tell me, is it true, what I've heard? Are you Say Ee Ah (CIA)? Should I rather ask 'are you *still* Say Ee Ah?'" He may have been suffering from a dose of heat exhaustion, I thought.

Anyway, I'd had enough of this. I told him I was and forever would be.

"Then I will have to arrange for your dismissal." He gave me a wry smile. Maybe he wasn't kidding.

HQ will love that. Please send me south. By the way, Godin was standing beside me, attentive, but didn't seem to have a clue what the last exchange meant. I think.

The repair crew arrived and replaced the cylinder head.

We completed our journey to our destination.

Without incident.

[Note from Aaron Hamblin: I'm not sure where in the chronology this belongs, so I'm inserting it here.] *I have heard that there had indeed been someone messing with the cylinder head, and no accident that it had been cracked, as if beaten with a hammer. An amateurish or half-hearted effort—or we would have truly eaten our fill of sand that day.* [End of insert.]

■ Another Christmas, Another Brutality

December 24, 1968

Of course, while in Djamé with Leonard, I verified our story to embassy personnel and took advantage of the respite to contact Gerard. I needed the R&R but had a superstition about hanging around Djamé. After all, that was where I was assigned to Dar es Sabir for having a beard—or too many beers.

The Johnny Walker helped to calm my anxieties. And we, Gerard and I and others, did some serious drinking the night after the embassy meeting. Christmas in Djemélia—I should write that song. For Djemélia was not particularly holiday-festive then—no wreathes and little green branches set off against the khaki, sand and mud. But there were all the pretty lights—twinkling as the town's electrical power went on and off. It was relatively cool, cool even there, as the Gregorian New Year approached . . .Year of our Lord—Anno Domini 1969, etc.

I rode in the back of the truck to catch the evening breeze. And because there was no room in the truck's cabin.

It was then that we lurched to a stop, giving my eyebrow injury another good blow on one of the truck's iron overheads.

There in front of us was a miserable scene. That ex-légionnaire and all-around Alsacien brute, Heinrich, having it on with a short, slight Sahelian. We jumped out to help.

"That's enough," Gerard said.

"Never enough!" Heinrich insisted. He had stopped to answer, then began pummeling the poor guy again. Ever so slightly touched by the Johnny Walker, I attempted to intervene. And for my bravery,

I took one or two more forehead blows meant for the boy. Whom I recognized as one of my students. Hassan Habré. Hassan, whose hovel, I'm told, is festooned with academic medals. I pushed Hassan away from Heinrich's reach, really aggravating Heinrich. That's when Gerard stepped in to reason with Heinrich—parachutist à parachutist.

I pushed Hassan further away, and held him by the arms for a moment. We were both bleeding at that point. I had the original head injury, another from the truck's sudden stop, and a third from Heinrich. Hassan was bleeding from the nose and mouth. And I was hard put to tell from where and from whom the blood that dripped into the sand was coming. After all, it seemed to mix nicely, our blood, and without distinguishing marks. And would be swallowed completely into the mud and sand by morning.

"What is it Hassan? What's going on?"

"That monster attacked me!" He was ready to rejoin the fray.

"Why?"

"He said that, at this hour, 'the streets belonged to the para.'

"I said, 'No, at any hour the streets belong to my country, my people.' Is that not true Monsieur 'amblin?" You don't hear this kind of patriotism very often in this country. So I was not hard put to answer.

"Yes. Let's move to this side, to the shadows, where he may be more likely to forget us. Note that he is also plenty drunk!" The last thing I needed was to report these events and these injuries at this time, on this street, in my current condition. Meanwhile, Heinrich was still in a temper. "Look at the lovers! You're both PD (pay-day—pederast)," he shouted at us as Gerard pulled him away. I took his intended insult with some grace as we moved further into the shadows.

"I do not understand th . . . this brute. Why does he do this thing?" Hassan was halfway between tears and fierce anger.

"Well you must calm down. The drunken sot is not worth your

anger!" I was not very good at these things. He may have seen in me just another *Nasarah* making excuses.

So concerned was I for his thoughts on this matter that I failed to see him drawing his *kabira* knife from under his torn *jalaba*. He pulled away from me and rushed toward Heinrich, whose back was now to him. He plunged the knife in at least twice and then disappeared down one of the dark alleys. I turned to give chase but was frozen by the bloody sight. Gerard bent over Heinrich, removed the knife and administered aid. At the same time he turned his head towards me and asked, "What did you say to the little bastard?" I was immobilized for a moment, then took that implied guilt back to my billet. Out of sight of the others.

Perhaps Hassan would come back to school after the break. In the last quarter, he had written in the composition about his future hopes:

> ... And when I grow, I will be trained by the *Nasarah*
> and then become a revolutionist and kill these French
> parachutists and Camel Militiamen ....

[Note from Aaron Hamblin: I'm not sure where in the chronology this belongs, so I'm inserting it here.] *Hassan became a great revolutionist.* [End of insert.]

Peace on Earth; Good Will Towards Men

■ Bulgarians

Early January 1969

Happy New Year!

There's where I first ran into them. Literally. At the Djamé café, the Vietnamese "Phren and Pho," in the early dusk. At the place where, in this country, I first began to sin. Where all the Europeans hung out.

I often seemed to encounter bad luck when I went to Djamé, so I was wary. They were at the next table; and by my second Douze Marches, my auditory senses were honed. It wasn't a local dialect, nor Arabic, but sounded Middle Eastern to me. That *kh* sound, among other things. Akhween would be proud.

So then I arose on wobbly legs to go to what passed for a toilet. And, in my inimitable way, I tripped over one of their chairs, tipping the table and, so, their drinks.

Their reflexes were outstanding. One had a caring hand on me in two seconds. It wasn't out of concern for my injuries but to hold me down. He very rapidly patted me down, decided that I was of no danger, and then helped me to my feet.

"My deepest pardons," I exclaimed. "Did I injure anyone?"

"No problem," one answered in English. "No injured."

I brushed myself off and offered to buy them a round. They turned me down.

"But you must!" I protested. I made my way to the bar where the proprietor, one Cao Ahn Diem, was there to be greeted by me. "*Xin Chao, chao bac,*" I offered.

He hadn't gotten to the kitchen fast enough to escape and hide from me. He gave me his typically inscrutable look. "*Chao em,*" he replied. He'd gotten used to my flubbed Vietnamese. He realized that my vocabulary was limited and didn't try to overwhelm me—although he had had his fun the last time. Mixing genders and age groups to keep me off balance. As he had done with great glee that time. Too bad he had no one to share these jokes with.

Nevertheless, I soldiered on. So then we had a long conversation in French riddled with my sympathetic declarations about the travails of his country. We didn't take sides.

This time, I gathered up the three Douze Marches and saluted him briskly "*Hen gap lai, nhe,*" thereby nearly exhausting my Vietnamese vocabulary.

He gave me another look, inscrutability spiced with sympathy.

"*Oui . . . bien,*" he responded, as if this was very boring, and he'd had quite enough.

Since I was buying, I gave myself permission to sit with them. "I couldn't help but overhear you; but I don't recognize the language."

"We're Romanian," the dark one said.

"Romanian businessmen sent here by our government," the blond one followed up. Almost instantly.

I doubted it but had to play along. "What sort of business is the Romanian government interested in?"

"Various."

"Oil? Uranium? Silica?"

"Can't say. Who do you work for?"

"I'm American."

"We guessed so."

"I work for Leonard Norman at the Peace Corps." I don't know what possessed me to give them Leonard's name.

"Ah, No'man." He didn't pronounce the "r." "Yes, we know of him. You working here in Djemélia?" He pronounced the city's whole name.

"I'm up in Dar es Sabir."

That's when they looked at each other, definitely surprised. Good work, Douze Marches.

"I'm going up there myself." It was the blond one.

"No kidding. Whatever for?"

"Business. And to get a look at the microwaves."

"Outstanding. But the microwave is not yet finished. And I gotta tell you what you were talking sure didn't sound Romanian."

"OK, well, it wasn't."

I waited, hoping they would volunteer what it was. They didn't. So I sort of guessed. "So I get to play a guessing game?"

"Yes. Go ahead." But the blond one didn't seem too happy with this.

"I'll say Bulgarian."

"OK." But with no conviction.

"Greek?"

"What's the matter? You don't like Bulgarian?"

"No, I don't." Then Douze Marches did its work. "Ah. Hebrew then!"

"You get free Douze Marches."

"So you are Is. . . ." I blurted.

"Shhhh. Quiet please."

Yes, quiet.

■ Alexandru and Ionatan

The blond one was called Alexandru; the dark one, Ionatan.

"Very appropriate," I said.

"We thought such. Alexandru will go to Dar es Sabir to look at workings of SHG oil consortium. And American microwave installation. Then perhaps other things. I stay here to do other things. I doing marketing.

"Maybe you can help with introduction at SHG and also the Russian doctor." Alexandru was direct, forthright. No more bullshit.

"I can do that. Do you speak French or Russian?"

"French and Russian and a dialect of Arabic."

"Perfect. Doctor Godin has no English and very broken French."

"I can pass for Russian. In part, that's reason for me to go. Remember, I am Alexandru."

"Yes. Do you have transportation?"

"I have lorry. Land Rover."

"Could I ride with you then? I was going to take the bus but, with the check points from both sides—the militia and Wahid—and overflowing streams, it might be unreliable. I'll pay you a fare."

"Of course you can ride with me. No fare, but you can buy wine or beer. And you speak the local language, yes? My Arabic is good, but Palestinian Arabic. They don't understand me here. Nor I don't understand them."

"Yes. I can help with interpretation if necessary. But at the checkpoint they will speak French to white men."

"*Donc, trés bien.* Meet me 06:30 in Wednesday morning at Hotel le Grand." (On the patio where it all began.) "We'll get good starts, though with roads in their rain condition, we may have to spend nights in Rover."

Ionatan asked me for a meeting with Doctor "No'man." It was Tuesday. We set the meeting for Wednesday at 19:00 at the Hotel le Grand, when the patio bar was most crowded. I suggested that Ionatan wear military camouflage to blend in with the mostly French officers there.

I suggested to Leonard that the air force be invited as well. He did not react too warmly to that. I would learn that I was not invited to this meeting either. No matter, I would be on the road to Dar es Sabir, *Inch Allah.*

Inch Allah.

■ The Ride

Early January 1969

I would have liked the ride to be uneventful. But it was an initial worrisome sign when Alexandru handed me an M1-type carbine with a bullet chambered. Then it began raining cats and . . . by noon. Then, not too far from the road to Dar, we hit a militia checkpoint. A guard halted us.

"*Papiers, Messieurs.*" It was not an officer but a lone guard. But there was an officer who looked at us from the guard shed and then over the guard's shoulder. I had shoved the carbine under the floor mat. It just fit and was well hidden if I kept my foot on the stock.

I gave the guard my *Carte de sejour* and *Permit de travail*, permitting me to live and work in the country. Alexandru handed him his short-term visa. The guard looked at both documents, not sure which one to examine first. Plus he was looking at them upside down. So much for this country's education system. I made a mental note to check my students. Check to insure that they were reading their lessons right side up. Maybe my lessons worked well both ways.

By the way, the guard was the same who asked Akhween to translate the *Capitaine*'s instructions into *Moundang*. Or something. These guys move around.

The officer had come strutting out of the guard hut behind the guard. He looked none too happy as his snappy uniform took on the water and mud.

The officer ripped the documents out of the guard's hands in exasperation. He spoke to the guard in a Sara dialect. Then "And Monsieur Alexandru, why are you making this trip?"

"For the meeting I have with the SHG in Dar es Sabir. It is for tomorrow." His French was fluid and grammatically correct.

"And then you will leave Dar es Sabir by this very road?"

"I will."

"Did you know there are bandits further up on the road?" A lip-curl and eye-twitch began.

"I did not."

"You might want to detour on the right fork to go through Albri. Less commotion on the road. Stay there until things calm down." The *capitaine* seems to have calmed. The tick slowed down. A bit.

"Thanks for your advice. So we are in a bit of a hurry." Alexandru played the game well.

Then, unconcerned with Alexandru's answer, the officer looked at me. "So we meet again." The eye-twitch and lip-curl sped up.

Then he turned again to Alexandru. "But fear not, for you are with Monsieur 'amblin of the American Peace Corps, who is friends with the Wahidi and, as I hear, with Wahid himself." Here we go again.

My turn. "You'll frighten my friend with such stories as these. Who has told you that?"

"It is well known and I shall prove you are consorting with bandits and traitors."

"Impossible." I tried to look my most offended.

"And I now believe it was you, Monsieur 'amblin, who was dressed in leper rags that night that we burned the storage building in the unclean village.You in filthy leper rags to hide from us. Taking a big chance in such plague-infested, filthy garments. And I would wager that Wahid himself was among you." Indeed it was my favorite *Capitaine* Ngokuru of the mouth-eye twitch.

"How much would you so wager?" Well, I couldn't leave it alone. After a moment of silence: "Why do you believe this thing?"

"Ah. We have had a talk since that night with Osman Adir, an elder of that leper clan. It is he who told us so."

"What? Under your tender, loving inducement, I suppose. Don't you know that people will say anything to stop the torture?"

"We would not do such, nor touch the leper. But Osman Adir is a lover of horses, and we tested him by letting him handle a wild one with bridle. He failed the test and lost a half finger in the process. I should make you *Yekbared* now but, as you say, the leper is not a trustworthy witness. And as so afflicted, he would be difficult to bring in front of judges." As if the *capitaine* would care for such legal niceties. Or the concerns of judges. Was this a threat or a promise?

Or could it be that Osman Adir, the one-eyed leper elder, gave up my name under "duress" to avoid giving information on the whereabouts of Wahid. Brave man.

Capitaine Ngokuru held my stare for a long moment, and then waved us through. "You are blocking others." There was only one peasant and his donkey behind us. But if we sat here and jabbered long enough, the Wahidi might catch up to us.

"There are Wahidi you should be fearful of. Up the road, Monsieur" he said to Alexandru. Then he turned to me. All lip-curl and eye-twitch. In harmony. "But not you Monsieur 'amblin. Perhaps the Wahidi will shoot before they know it is you. And do our work for us. Take the road via Albri. *Bonne chance, messieurs.*"

We rode the rough, muddy road for at least a hundred kilometers of no man's land without incident. And without much conversation, as

Alexandru maneuvered the Land Rover around newly-formed gullies and ditches. Twice I got out to push. Alexandru put the Rover in first gear to grind over the deep, mud-made perforations. One time, he put the Rover in neutral and got out himself to help me push. Then, suddenly, the road got smoother. We were in the sandy Sahel, less rain, fewer ditches and gullies, and the Wahidi were there to receive us even on the road to Albri—not entirely as Ngokuru predicted, but maybe as he intended.

They looked a bit fierce, as always. No document checks here. But several of them had seen me with Amina. Amina bint Abdel Albri.

Also, there was something familiar about one of them. It was on my way back to PC headquarters in Djamé, a bit tipsy. I took him for the one who had kicked up a ruckus with Akhween about the latter's translation during one of the *capitaine's* lessons. "*Trop vite! Trop vite!*" Now he was in a *jalaba* and pantaloons. Munitions strap across his shoulder peering out from under his *jalaba*. This one must change sides with facility.

He saw me see him. In Djamé, it was a contest of stares only, he and I. Sloppy spycraft, Ali Azri Edouard. And he drew way too much attention to himself. Maybe I did too.

This was the "less commotion" route. This time the road-blockers looked in at driver more than passenger, then had a brief discussion among themselves. One of them seemed a bit overwrought. The one with the Kansas City Athletics cap. Ah yes! It was the big mouth insulting Amina from our encounter with the Wahidi riders outside the town gate. The one who had killed Moussa. Roadblocking must be punishment for that indiscretion. Then, after another look at the Rover and its contents, they waved us through. "To Dar es Sabir," the overwrought one called after us. "Soon to be ours."

That sounded like a clue to their plans.

Alexandru asked what they had said. Actually, he asked if they had said, "Soon to be ours? Is that a clue as to their intentions?"

"Exactly that."

"Then only question of when," Alexandru stated.

For the next half hour we were alone with these thoughts.

Yes. When.

■ A Stop With Alice—in Albri

She was in Albri, and I often arranged the bus and, in the early days, plane rides to deposit me there for a short time. A little love, a little spoken English, perhaps a hair and beard trim, and it would keep me for another three months or so. This time, with Alexandru, I had to be more careful. No hints.

"You look like shit, Harry." Good salutation.

"And *Alhamduleelah* to you too. I don't have a mirror in the wilds of the Dar."

"So let me, at least, trim your hair."

Her cottage offered her relative comfort in a relatively comfortable town, and she had enough "front yard" to seat me, and let the cuttings blow away. And the right tools, no doubt to keep her blond tresses under control.

"At least. Though I don't want to be any trouble," I said after introducing her to Alexandru. There was a bit of flirtation between them during our stop. Blond to blond.

"Of course not." And so she trimmed it all off, as she did my beard. Now I would be incognito in Dar es Sabir, at least for a time.

Most visits, I was so exhausted from the two-day bus ride—or even the two hour plane ride—that, with a single Douze Marches, I would crash on her bed, no invitation given, and sleep away the time till the next bus. So much for our conjugal visits.

I often discussed teaching with her. She was an excellent teacher, and her students excelled on the last end-of-term English tests.

So there were times before the end of the first year, during one of my first visits, that I began to harp on the rebellion and my fears for her.

"Nothing like that down here," she'd say, blowing it off. But during the last several of my visits, she would add, "Besides, there are the Swiss missionaries up the mountainside where I could stay if the situation becomes dicey." And to change the subject, this last time, she added "Oh, and did I mention that we climbed Jumeaux? Nearly to the summit. In one long day. Quite an effort. We slept over that night, in a partial cave full of leavings and deep crevices. We came back the next day."

Good to know.

■ Alexandru at Dar es Sabir

Early January 1969

It was a bit awkward introducing Alexandru to Dar es Sabir. We started with the *sous-préfet,* he of the Coke-bottle lenses and filigreed *boubou* robes. "Who the hell is this? Who is this *Nasarah?*" he asked. He peered at me—at least I think it was at me—until one of his staff whispered in his ear and he realized, though much shorn, it was still me. "Ah. Monsieur 'amblin! Without most of your hair! Without your beard! You are a different man perhaps. Without the beard, how can you be a *professeur?*" He laughed at his joke. Then he turned to the guest.

"*Bienvenu,* Monsieur. *Bienvenu,*" He began in his childlike voice. "You made it through the bandit roadblock? Congratulations and welcome!" He didn't really seem too excited to see us though.

"Oh, were they bandits? They seemed to be government officials." Alexandru, composed and straight-faced. This one passed right over the *sous-préfet's* head.

It was evident he was not expecting us, so at first he looked around for his advisors. None present. So the question of living quarters dangled in the air.

Then "Perhaps Monsieur 'amblin can put you up for your stay with us."

Alexandru was quick on the uptake. "Ah, then, the hotel is fully occupied." Another one that passed by the *sous-préfet*.

So it was settled. We arranged for Alexandru to sleep in what passed for my living room. I offered my bedroom to him—hoping he would refuse it. He did. So we arranged for the wicker chairs to serve as a sort of couch-bed. He had come prepared with a sleeping bag to lay across the chairs.

"Now I must see what is here." He was ready to move.

"Yes, we'll have a drink Then I'll make you a guided tour." Hey, what was his hurry? After all, he'd had plenty of time to flirt with Alice!

■ School Days

Early January 1969

Then we passed school inspection for this quarter. Perhaps with Adoum's recommendation for my dismissal. The guillotine might just as well fall from here as from there.

So school and class reconvened after the "winter break." With English grammar drills. But without Moussa David. Without Hassan Habré.

Perhaps Hassan was now undergoing drills as well—military-guerilla drills. Of course, given his recent take up of residency in the Muslim cemetery, Moussa could no longer participate. But we at the school carried on with our English grammar substitution drills. Maybe with the same cadence as Hassan was experiencing.

> Progressive tenses:
> I go—>now = (Ans) <u>I am going</u>
> He goes—>now = (Ans) <u>he is going</u>
> They went—>yesterday = (Ans) <u>they were going</u>

And so on.

■ The Capitaine's First Warning

January 1969

The next time I met the *légionnaire capitaine*, I planned the encounter. Across the parade ground on my way to school.

Less awkwardness and less sloppy salutation than usual. Aside from the fury of the morning sun. Which always seemed to throw me into darkness when I met the *légionnaire capitaine*. "What news?"

"I am to be released back to the army. But to liaison with the militia for the time being. Nothing's really changed until I can get my ass out of here. I suspect that they will want me here, especially with this bunch, these undisciplined ones, should there be full-fledged battles."

Full-fledged battles.

■ More "Diplomacy"

January 1969

Ngokuru definitely got around. He was back in Dar es Sabir not long after our arrival.

"All right. I'll tell you if you let them free," I said.

For Nbokuru had had them taken. Rather, put them under house arrest for now. But with guards. Wasting militia manpower.

"I'll let them go, if the information you give me turns out to be accurate, and if we defeat them." He had just splashed a bit of Douze Marches to his ancestors. We were actually sharing a quiet beer moment, the colonel and I. I held on to my information about the Wahidi spy.

"I'll share all the information with you, if you let Alice go first. And give her safe passage to the missionaries up on the hill just outside Albri." Was it the Douze Marches talking here?

"What other information could you possibly have that would

make me give up my leverage with you and them? Besides, if I come to know you are withholding important information from me, I may make you and her both *Yekbaré*." Of course, by this point, his twitch had picked up in speed and ferocity.

"Just kidding, of course." Not about the spy, though. I kept that as my final ace.

"I do not know his encampment." I showed him my amateurishly drawn map leading to Wadi Abuyad. "This is where you and they will gather. Keep your accompanying force small and show a white flag. He will respect the rules of truce."

"I have my doubts." But he looked like an actor working himself into this audition of anger, the lip-curled, and the eye-twitch picked up even greater speed.

■ The Proposal to Wahid

January 1969

"*Capitaine* Ngokuru."
"Ayeewa, him. You are callow and naïve, Emricain."
"Does that mean yes?"
"I will consult with my council." As if he had one.
"God is great. *Alhamdulillah*. God be with you and with all of us." I was getting the hang of it.
"Ayewah *Nasarah*. Ayewah Emricani."

■ Courtesy of the United States of America

January 1969

The woman was by the side of the pathway, in her usual place on the pathway to my *kaz*, wrapped in a rug against the drop in temperature. (Nothing to us, the *Nasarah*, but a sort of "cold" to them.) She was all alone.

But then she turned over, and the child rolled out from underneath her, wet with her sweat, but totally lifeless. She held him up to me, insisting in a dialect I didn't understand. She wanted me to have him. To cure him by some miracle. . . . Or to bury him.

She thrust him toward me. I think she meant for me to give him to our doctor.

Or to our Father. I took him just as she passed out. Or worse.

I took him back to my *kaz*. There I worked fast, hoping I would finish before Younis could see us. So I tried to ply the poor infant with the powdered milk I mixed. No movement. I tried a kind of modified CPR. It was no use. Too late. Nothing left.

So I found my way to the soup-and-poster, fetid and rank-smelling shed where the lock was undone. I quickly wrapped the corpse in John Fitzgerald Kennedy posters. I placed him carefully on a plank on top of unopened boxes in the rear corner, next to tomato and chicken noodle soup cans. A corner where the cast-off refuse was not yet leaking. Perhaps an appropriate crypt for him. With the soup boxes marked "Gift of the United States of America."

The smell of his decomposition would blend in well with the stink of the rotting soup. In a sense, another gift from the United States of America. I said a brief mix of the *Shahadah* and a Hail Mary.

Then I left quickly, Amina's handkerchief held to my nose.

■ Menagerie

January 1969

Alexandru and I were getting used to each other. My colleague, Modou, who knew Russian as well, could often be seen imbibing with us at my *kaz*. They made an interesting pair. Both speaking the same language but learned in entirely different latitudes and longitudes.

And Modou did a perfect imitation of Russian loss and nostalgia for it. Convincing. As if he meant it. Perhaps his songs as well.

So Alexandru, Modou, and I were sometimes seen gathered at Godin's *kaz*, where we all made a wild party full of Russian merriment and sadness. When Godin wasn't called out in the night, as he often was. It was not that all these folks took ill only at night. But they did not want their fellow tribesmen to see them using a *Nasarah* doctor—rather than their own healers. Their own spiritualists would likely advise the recitation of the *basmala* ("*Bismillah al-Rahman al-Rahim*") seven hundred eighty-six times (the value of the Arabic letters in this recitation) in sequence over a cup of water which would then, having received spiritual empowerment, be ingested as medicine. Beats strychnine. Slower acting.

It turned out that Alexandru had a wonderful voice, perfect for all the old Russian folk songs. Modou and I accompanied Ivan and Alexandru at various levels of flatness. Rashid sometimes joined in, nearly shouting, and thus adding to our raucous, keyless attempt at singing. There was much clinking of glasses and, later in the night, the more and more rapid sloshing of spilled vodka. Then Scotch chasers. We excused the spills by repeating "To our ancestors."

We kept the alcohol away from Rashid, citing religious restrictions to him.

Good job too, as once he showed me the two grenades hanging from a belt under his *jalaba*. He removed one to show it off. He demonstrated to me how to pull its pin—and how one might pull both pins at once. So he then detached both grenades from his belt.

"You must not, Rashid. You must not. . . . Who gave you these things?"

"My master, Wahid. He says I will be able to explode them both. When the 'time is right.'" He grinned like a clown would. "He has shown me how to explode them. Pow! And big noise. Without removing them from my body at all."

Were Rashid's grenades loaded? Probably not. I was never trained by the Say Ee Ah or anyone else to determine a loaded grenade's weight by its heft.

I tried to take them away to a safe place, but he wouldn't let go. And I was afraid he'd pull the pins out in our struggle. So I insisted that he reattach his two grenades to his belt. He did so only grudgingly. While insisting "The master-cousin has given me these as my very own. They are mine for when the time is right."

For when the time is right.

From time to time, Father O'Sagarty would pass through, on no particular schedule. I did not have to modify my intake with him, but I drank with him on the moderate side, the better to explore the mysteries of our Holy Roman Church. And I often excused myself to the others in order to sit with him alone.

Apostolic that we were.

■ Younis 9

January 1969

The next time we read *The Legend of Robin Hood*, I posed the question that had occupied my thoughts. "Ah, is that the way with Wahid and Amina? Are they like Robin and the lady called Marion?"

He fiddled with his bow and shot some arrows. Then, "So I have heard from Master Yacob Mikune. I hear him as I serve the *soupée*, and he talks to his wife. There is a question of the *mahr*. Lord Wahid did not have it, since the land and all on it was taken from him and his father."

"Ah, he needs money, *mahr*, to give to her family?

"Yes, Monsieur. To her uncle and others."

So this rebellion is to recover land taken, but also to collect money for the bride payment. My head was spinning. I did not know how to read this or what to believe—was this his true motive for the rebellion?

"Is the sheriff like the scary Nbokuru? Who wishes to marry Amina as well?" Younis asked.

"Well eventually, you know, it must come to a fight between Robin and the sheriff," I answered. "So these things make for great adventure."

"Must there be a fight then?" Younis was really fascinated by the prospect. He picked up the bow and shot several more arrows toward his hovel. He made the arrows sing despite the makeshift nature of their carving and of the bowstring.

"There must be a fight," I said. "Robin must rescue the lady and put a stop to harassment by the sheriff. So Robin must attack the sheriff's palace.

"In fact, the sheriff has organized festivities to celebrate his upcoming marriage to poor Marion. The festivities include an archery contest and a horse race. On the day of the festivities, people come from all over the province. Robin and his Merry Men may be there, but in disguise." This is what had just transpired, in a way, at the fair that had taken Moussa's life. It was then, that I knew what to do to make a truce between them. Between Wahid and Ngokuru, as no one could for Robin. For Younis.

Callow and naïve as I was.

Younis bent over to retrieve the buried candy box and *gris-gris* inside it. Just as I had feared—that he would notice that the *gris-gris* had been disturbed.

"What does this mean, Monsieur Harry?" But before I could explain, he was again called by his mistress—just at this critical moment. He quickly reburied the red box.

"Imagine that all of them, Robin and the Merry Men, are dressed in a different way over their natural clothes. And their faces hidden by hoods. You can not always trust what at first you see," I shouted after him.

But he was gone.

I resolved to access the *gris-gris* only after our lesson.

After.

■ New-Made Friends

The New Years Parade, January 1969

It took me a while to catch on to it. I should have been quicker. After all, it was my "job."

Sort of.

OK. Let's back up a bit to clarify—a bit. Ahem:

The national president, Mugibai, is represented here in Dar es Sabir, Faya Province, by the civilian *préfets* and *sous-préfets*. Who are afraid of the rebellious Wahidi, but also of the militia, whom he ostensibly commands. But he has no forces to rein in General Héman, the militia general, who has his own agenda and ambitions (to enjoy the anticipated oil wealth, etc.).

The army is led by General Rochedure-Na'ar and rivals the militia—where such rivalry is viable, like for arms. The French *Troisième Parachutiste* Division is allied with the National Army and government of President Mugibai. Yes? Byzantine.

So the National Army had universal echelons and the national flag patches on their upper sleeves. The militia had only the crossed swords in front of a camel on the patches over their hearts. Ranking on their sleeves. Yes, the uniforms were otherwise the same. Including camos. Probably castoffs from the French paratrooper or infantry divisions. (Their uniforms showed tears where previous patches had been ripped off.) The rifles certainly were alike—Karabiner 98 castoffs found or captured from the German losers by the French and Russian winners. Yes, from World War II. Later given to the colonial armies and their collaborators. That they should not go to waste.

The militia occupied themselves with suppressing internal uprisings. And there may currently have been others—besides the Wahidi. The army was responsible to engage state enemies coming from across the borders. Or *coups d'états*. The Janjawid fit neatly into both categories. So there was a back-and-forth between the army and militia to hand the responsibility for the Janjawid, one to the other.

I only just caught on. The day of the fête, Independence Day, when the soldiers came to town to march in the parade. And we were honored with the appearance of an army general, Rochedure-Na'ar, festooned in rich flag colors and bright gold echelons. And lots of medals (for a country that has had no wars) for a soldier to be so honored. Perhaps he was rewarding himself for all the past battles fought as a *collaborateur* with the colonials, the French. It is not spoken of.

For this parade, the militia formed one contingent, the army, another. All spit and polish, or whatever they say. Still, it must have been tough trying to get the road apples (the horseshit) and camel pies off those shined-up boots.

There were horses dancing smartly in their ancient and colorful Baguirmi Kingdom armor, armor dating back to the battles of the nineteenth century and before. Just as I had cited to Partenay. The camels wore colorful saddles and other decorations.

But as they gathered, the two uniformed groups jostled for the front position. At first just to march in front, then for seats at the observer seating. Jostling and pushing. Then striking with the rifles, fortunately unloaded. Nevertheless, they pointed the parade rifles at each other in a threatening manner. And began to fix bayonets.

At this point, the First *directrice* of the National Party, Dar es Sabir branch, stepped into the melee, and flung her arms out to calm both sides. She was rewarded with ugly bayonet slices, one from each service, in a neat X across her breast.

Then the yelling and finger pointing began. Observers started screaming "Mama," for the injured one was indeed Mama of Mama's Fine Restaurant fame.

Fortunately, someone was also yelling, *"Infirmier! Clinique!"* The cry went up in an uneven mixture of French, Sara-Ngumbaye, Arabic, the mélange, and a host of other indigenous languages.

Docteur Godin had taken this holiday to join his fellow Soviets in Djémélia. But Alphonse materialized, totally unarmed—medically speaking—to minister to Mama. He took a quick look at his ER patient, pronounced it "Not mortal," and ordered her to be carried .... But then he realized that he knew not where, since there were no available beds at the clinic, the one bed being occupied by an important enough *functionnaire*. He stared at the ground, in grave concentration.

In the chaos that followed, no one offered to help. So, in desperation, (maybe to prevent the loss of the fine restaurant's wonderful *boule* and fiery sauce), I offered my *kaz* and bedroom. Alphonse staunched the wound as best he could, using my fête-day shirt (he did not offer his), and gathered several others including Jean, to carry her to my *kaz*. I told Jean to have Mama put on my bed for further treatment. They retrieved a gurney already caked with dried blood. I recognized it as the very gurney that had carried Doctor Lièvre upon leaving Dar es Sabir. Resources being tight in these parts, Hank and Earl must have been requested to return that gurney once Lièvre's remains had been delivered to the Djemélia mortuary.

After Mama was carried off, the crowd settled down. The militia captaine, Ngokuru, and the army general, Rochedure-Na'ar, conferred, and it was agreed that the militia would march in the forward position with a camel rider contingent of seven, and the army marching behind them with their horse contingent, also of seven, bringing up the army marchers' rear. Then the students. But, for the speeches, the army would be given parade-route seating, and the militia would stand guard at the perimeter. Good compromise. That this were always so.

This settled, the parade restarted, and the soldiers were rewarded with juicy, fresh camel pies to march in. The students, who were the youthful future of the country, marched behind all of them, hopping skillfully around the camel pies and road apples, as those previously raked had been replaced by fresh ones during the melee. Perhaps symbolizing, for the students, their not altogether unexpected future.

There was much fine ululating by the females, and one *tendi*, a Taureg drum, beating to four-four time. Here, Rashid kept his head well away from solid objects. And the joy of this fête was dampened only by the injury to Mama.

I came back from helping arrange Mama in my *kaz*, in time for General Rochedure-Na'ar's windy speech and his presentation (in place of militia general Héman, who was invited to these festivities, but to the ones in Djemélia as well. He chose the latter, where Mugibai would be.) So General Rochedure-Na'ar was asked to present the ranking of colonel to *Capitaine* Ngokuru. (Even skipped a rank or two.) More oral wind, including a reminder that this elevation was reward in part for the *capitaine*'s valiant attack on, and capture of Zenig Etnin (the Prokaza/leper village) without loss of militia life.

As the parade and speeches ended, I returned to my cottage to find Mama in my bed, lying in some pain but in still more comfort than she would have had on her hovel pallet, on the ground—even though blessed in her hovel with the portrait of JFK on the wall above that pallet. She called me over and showered me with *shukrawns* and *mercis*, with many thanks, while she held my hand tightly.

She did not mention free meals, beer, or privileges with her waitress. But she pulled me closer to add hoarsely, "I will warn you *Nasarah*, if the Wahidi are coming or the army is in rebellion, and when it is time for you to go! Please warn me of impending disasters caused by the petrol company or militia."

What could that possibly be? What could she possibly mean? And the army in rebellion? I had never thought of that!

I came away, hands and face covered with red-brown henna.

■ **Other New Friends?**

Did I note that when Mama was injured, the Army officers soon congregated at my house to wish Mama well and offer apologies? No sign of the militia. Even General Rochedure-Na'ar came, a great, commanding hulk. And so the soldiers already there came to swift attention.

That was when Colonel Ngokuru, with an attitude of friendship I had never experienced from him (perhaps stimulated by the thrill of his recent "promotion"), came to me and whispered, "Keep the general occupied just long enough for us to accomplish our mission, and you will be duly rewarded." But he was gone again without explaining their "mission."

Then, after paying his respects to Mama, the army general called me over.

"So you are the Américain who is so friendly with the Wahidi, our enemy."

He was imposing, and I couldn't force out a vague denial. So I stared in silence.

"Look, Américain, Monsieur Habert speaks well of you, and so I will ignore your dalliance with the rebels whom you might find romantic. Also, to love his cousin, it is not necessary to love or even to sympathize with Hassan Ibn Jema'a."

I found his initial omission of "Wahid," and instead using his given name without the term of respect, interesting. For he avoided pronouncing "Wahid" or the honorific "Abu." "I'm not a romantic. I'm only curious as a stranger in this strange land."

"Strange land, eh?" He seemed a bit perturbed by this attribution. "Not so for us!" Maybe a bit *more* than a bit perturbed.

I looked to wriggle my way out of the direction this conversation was taking. "Strange to me, I mean. Can I get you anything, General?"

He didn't hesitate a moment: "Whiskey for my officers, Douze Marches for my enlisted men." He was obviously used to command. "I expect neither to be cooled in this electricity-deficient town."

I guess this was payback for the bit, or more than a bit, of perturbation. Or my acquaintance with Wahid. "Jean!"

Jean was cowering behind Moussa's shed. Cavorting in place with Kalb and Alexandru. Neither was a friend to the military. "Monsieur?"

"We will need five Johnny whiskeys and twenty Douze Marches."

"Are we to be made to feel guilty for the injury to Mama? Are we celebrating it?"

"Very astute, Jean. At any rate, we will have to obey these orders." I gave Jean the rest of my paltry savings. "Ask *Père* Habert to put any remainder owed on my floating tab." Thus, I became the host of this gathering. And of this general.

And broke.

■ *Général Rochedure-Na'ar*

The soldiers and lower-ranking officers began to filter, I should say stagger, away. Before leaving with his remaining officers, and after drinking most of my supply of Johnny and *Douze*, army General Rochedure-Na'ar called me over to continue our chat. I had been wise enough to minimize my intake. He hadn't. He poured my expensive Scotch to his ancestors more than once. I looked for a *guépard*, a wandering soul of Sara myth, even maybe a staggering one—but saw none.

But through the verbal haze punctuated by burps, I managed to determine (and therefore attempt to reproduce) his meaning. I think.

"You listen now, Américain. This country needs *professeurs* like you. But not to mix in our affairs. One kind of affair or another. Grps! And don't let them whisper around about *my* affairs." Yes, the word was already out about the general's prowess. For hard drink and other things.

"I won't." I wouldn't dare.

"Good. Then heed me. Grps! This is dangerous country to mix in with the bandits and those claiming to be rebels. Dangerous country. Grps! Besides, the militia is also dangerous. They can use the threat of Yekbar. Grps! Not to mention the Russian who is Kah Jay Bay (KGB). And the *juge*, who would rather send you to prison Grps! to make an example of arrogant Américain white men like you. And even the French ones who are jealous of your presence Grps! in what they think of as their country." A momentary gasp before he continued on. "And the loss of Evian. And the beautiful ladies. All of them! They will tell on you. All dangerous."

He topped it all off with a canon-shot finale burp. "**Grps!**"

"What about Miriam? And Jean? And Modou? And the Bulgarian?" I almost let Alexandru's nationality slip out.

"Aw, they're OK, I think. That's what you say in American isn't it? OK? Modou is difficult to know or understand. He is like the Harmatan that has moments of great strength followed by . . . nothing. Or he may be just a big cry baby." Another heaving breath . . . "Come to think of it, Miriam is quite taken with you—which means she can't be trusted either. Especially if you intend to leave this country without her! . . . And the Bulgarian also seems suspicious to me."

That about covered it. My entire universe. I couldn't think of anyone else he could warn me about except . . . ."And you, too?" I mumbled.

Then I realized the noncoms were now making an inordinate number of head calls. Caused, no doubt, by the diuretic effect of Douze Marches. Using the useless toilet. Perhaps killing more cockroaches. I waited for the vicinity to clear, closed the door, and wrestled out the radio from behind the commode. As I feared, the wooden packing was well soaked, but I had fortunately replaced the radio in the original, very protective packing after the last use. I slipped the box under my bed while Mama slept.

"What is that?" she mumbled. Couldn't put one over on Mama!

"My worldly wealth," I answered. "Soil from America. For my sleeping place. See how I've watered it to make nourishment."

What a croc! I hoped she'd forget about it.

Then I washed my hands in the brackish water out back. Vigorously.

I returned to my seat across from the general. He continued on as if I had never left. "Oh, and watch out for the *imam*. It is said that he issued a *fatwa* on me."

"I'm sorry." I conjured up my most sympathetic demeanor.

"Grps! Not to worry, Monsieur *le professeur* Américain. The *fatwa* is only that I be shunned. But you be careful of him and his *fatwas*. Even for Christians like us."

"I understand. I will."

"Will you? Good!"

"But will you not take on the Wahidi once and for all?" I couldn't help but ask. This might be the information that would top it all off.

"As for the so-called Wahidi, we are the army to protect the borders against foreign invasion. As we did with Libya. The militia will have to deal with these bandits!" And he seemed to be adamant in his response. Then he rose, but only a bit unsteady on his legs. "For now, Grps! I shall meet and dally with a member of the party for the rest of the afternoon."

At that moment, a subaltern presented himself before the general and saluted as sharply as he was able in his Douze Marches state. "*Mon général*, they are not where we have left them."

"Of course they are, Lieutenant. The Douze Marches has made you forget where we left them," and the two of them marched off to reclaim their weaponry. I feared I knew where they were.

I think I captured the essence of what the general meant in warning me—between the heaving burps. Amazing clarity for a man who had just polished off nearly a fifth of Scotch. (Or did he pour most of it to his ancestors?) Even if not so clear. I attributed it to the fine quality of the Johnny whiskey that Jean had gotten. Or to much practice.

[Note from Aaron Hamblin: I'm not sure where in the chronology this belongs, so I'm inserting it here.] *As for the general, I would not see him for a while. He later sent me one cryptic note that seemed, almost, to be written in code.*

> "*Beware, most of all, of the jealousy and resentment of women.*"

It was a year later that it was said he was assassinated by "pretty

young things." Nor was it for sure "pretty" or maybe "handsome." Male
or female was never made clear.

"Beware." Jealousy and resentment? Or the assassin, perhaps working
for the Wahidi? Or for Colonel Ngokuru's camel militia? Or a poor girl or
boy seeking redemption by responding to the implied orders of the fatwa?

Still, I heeded the general's admonitions.

More or less. [End of insert.]

■ Younis 10

February 1969

It was obvious that Younis couldn't wait to return. He turned up
breathless in my courtyard—in an excited state.

"Lessons first." I felt like a taskmaster.

Then, after the grammatical revelations and grammar drills,
"Where has the story left off, Monsieur Harry? Are Robin and the
men in the festivities?"

"Yes. So all of them, Robin and the Merry Men, are dressed in
a different way over their forest clothes. And their faces hidden by
hoods."

"Why do they do this?"

"In order to slip into the festivities and take part without arrest by
the sheriff. Robin, in disguise, takes part in the archery contest. The
reward for the winner is a fine stallion. Of course, Robin wins the first
place, though, because he is disguised as a mysterious land owner, the
sheriff's men don't know who it is they present the award to."

"As the best archer?"

"Yes, as the best archer. As you may be some day." I got a bit
carried away here, disturbed that I might raise up the boy's hopes,
only to have them shattered by reality.

"Then, I will share all my secrets with you." I think that's what
he said.

It was at that very point that I resolved to break Younis free, especially if I must leave this town. That he will go with me.

■ Another Portent

March 1969

So I timed another walk to school to insure another "coincidental" meeting with the *légionnaire capitaine*. (Yes, all those things were bothering me even more.) I was getting the hang of the salutations, and the handshake was smoother. Still, the morning sun blinded me nearly into a darkness.

He anticipated my questions. "So, from our vantage point, it looks like things are heating up." I was hoping for some sarcasm or an April Fool's joke. There seemed to be neither. "Are you prepared?" he asked.

How prepared? "What should I do?" Not to mention Adoum Justin's likely firing of me for being in the Say Ee Ah.

"Escape. Dig a tunnel out of here. I don't know. See Habert for ideas. But leave, Américain. This is not your fight. Avoid it, much as you have wished."

You can say that again. "This is not my fight. But plane service has been stopped. And the roads are cut off."

"Ah, yes. That is a problem." He did not show any signs of sympathy. And the implication, that I might have been instrumental in bringing this thing to a head, seemed to hang in the air between us after his comment. Or was that my guilty feeling surfacing?

"And the school is still open and running," I added after a moment's silence. "So I am obligated to teach."

"Then teach," he commanded abruptly. I think he was too tired managing his recruits to deal with my search for sympathy. Or a magical way out. For without even a quick handshake, he did an about face to continue on. Marching away in four-four time.

Dig a tunnel?

Nonsense or brilliant?

■ Yet Another of These Portents

March 1969

The night when Terry, Joe, and I were imbibing. Beyond our bedtime. He came to us in his black *jalaba*, out of the dark, and spoke to us:

"*B-ismi-llāhi r-rahmāni r-rahīmi*. You are not of us and will never be. You drink the forbidden tea of joy. Even your accent on our language is not the same. Not of us. And your eyes are of a different brightness, too. Not burned by the sun, winds, and our sand. Rather, of blue. Adorned by a smile. Not full of anger and ferocity. Different. Tinged with curiosity for, rather than fearful of, all things. Not of us. Leave this place now. Thus have I spoken. *Allahu akbar.*"

"What is he saying?" Terry asked.

What *was* he saying?

"In the name of Allah the most gracious, the most merciful. It's the phrase he uses to signal that he is about to say something important. It's sort of like the beginning of a Catholic homily with 'In the name of the Father, Son, and Holy Spirit.' He says we don't have their fierce eyes, or angry looks, or fear."

"We don't?" I think Terry was serious.

"I'm working on it. He's wrong. I get the angry eyes and lose the smile every time I try to mount a camel. This might explain the look and attitude of all these camel riders."

But he was right about "the forbidden tea of joy."

He should have called it the "necessary tea of joy" as well.

■ More Warnings

March 1969

I brought up General Rochedure-Na'ar's admonitions to Michel and Victor.

"Yes." Michel answered. "He warned us as well. He is a fountain of knowledge—I mean when it comes to rumor-mongering—although he would have your head for telling rumors about him."

"He warned us of you especially," Victor repeated.

"Victor!" Michel admonished him with an embarrassed and angry look.

"Warned you of what? That I or we may want to take over this country? Or its hidden resources?" I was really curious about this.

"Yes, for the oil. And that you are Say Ee Ah."

Even if I weren't, good guess. Of course, I'm not. But close. Or lousy spycraft on my part.

"Well . . . ." But Victor seemed puzzled about Michel's admonition and looked around, as if looking for someone to come to his rescue.

"So I should not pay attention to his warnings?" I asked in my confusion.

"Not exactly. That is, the general is what we call ambidextrous. It is said that he and Evian had a romance. But one should not talk of these things." Michel was detouring around my question—and it was also obvious that he was finding this whole discussion distasteful. "Which may account for what I heard were Evian's many visits to Djemélia. Before the uprising got more serious and the roads, more dangerous."

Victor just looked confused.

■ SHG

Mid-March 1969

So we finished what was left of the Scotch. And I sent Jean out to search for another bottle. There was always one more, somewhere. He was more than happy to go on this treasure hunt. And then test and sample the quality of his purchase before turning it over to us.

Meanwhile, I led Alexandru to the SHG compound. To meet Monsieur Boudin. Who had been absent at our last attempt. They met. Salutations all around. The pirates kept in the background.

"Sit down, please, Monsieur . . ."

"Alexandru," I interjected to help him out. He took none too kindly to my attempt to aid him.

"What is your interest in coming to this poor region?"

"Ah. We are doing a survey. Exploring options."

"For oil and gas, no doubt."

"No."

"Barite?"

"Nor that."

"For uranium then."

"We think this is the last stop north, still under government control. We would like a guide who will help give us safe passage to the North, where we can then do some more exploring." He was smooth and noncommittal. That was the first I'd heard about this thing.

When we returned to my *kaz*, well juiced (at least I was), I was just this side of belligerent. "I didn't know you were exploring for uranium. I feel taken advantage of."

"Forgiveness. We must be very cautious. Otherwise some will ask us why we want uranium for. Uranium ore has been discovered in the North. We don't know how much. It may be nothing—or large deposit. I am to explore. Ionatan is trying to determine which *ministre* is responsible for deposits and then attempt to negotiate deals with them."

"Very interesting. Yet you willingly share this information with a stranger such as Boudin." Fascinating.

He deftly changed the subject. "It is said you know this Wahid. His band could give us safe passage. You could be intermediary for us. You could talk him into this job. We will pay well. And we may process to yellow cake there. This means guards and much travel. Of course, we will build the airport."

"Of course. As for being the go-between . . . ."

"But chieftain must help. And warrior is best."

"Of course. They are all warriors. And all think of themselves as chieftains," I added.

"So can you speak to this Wahid?" he implored.

"I will." Thanks, Johnny. Again, I should have gone easy on the Scotch. And at least insisted on a *quid pro quo*.

So now there was another of the reasons to see Wahid. None pleasant, and one may lead to battle.

■   The Menagerie Grows

Late March 1969

First it was a note from General Roche-Na'ar:

> *Salutations. We may need to billet officers of the Army and Militia in and around your house as a step in continuing our campaign against the* Wahidi. *For Colonel Ngokuru and his senior officers. And the French Capitaine.*
>
> *Always at your service, etc. etc. Veuillez agréer mes salutations distinguées.*

Then it was an evening visit from an army *capitaine*. He gave me a smart salute. "I am *Capitaine* Sadakune Pierre. I think General Roche-Na'ar has sent you a note about our coming. We will need this house as a billet for our officers." He looked past me and over my shoulder, to determine whether another, such as Alexandru, was there. Alexandru was out for the moment, already beginning to plan his desert trek. He might return here to have to sleep al fresco.

My nightmare had begun. It was coming true. "Is this absolutely necessary?"

"It is the only place available. The *Nasarah capitaine*, myself, and other subalterns are to be housed with the other Europeans—the

doctor, the school teachers. The rest will sleep outside your domicile."
He was very direct.

"What about the *directeur's* house? Why not billet there?" This
would have been my opportunity to stick one to Partenay.

"None of us dared ask him. He would drink Pernod and harangue
us all the long night. Besides, he has his wife with him. We must be
considerate of that." I later learned that Partenay had invited the
légionnaire capitaine already. Poor *capitaine*. He will be harangued into
battle—as the preferred alternative to being harangued as the guest.

I gave up resisting. "How many of you then?"

"Only five. We can share beds and, if necessary, floor space."

"For how long?"

"Until we receive further orders. But not long, I think."

"Then my home is yours," I said in my very best effort to assume
the demeanor of a welcoming host. "Please come in for a look."

This *capitaine* marched in for a quick look. He smiled always—as
if he was telling a joke. With a "*Monsieur,*" he marched directly to the
other room, the room with my bed and comfort.

"It's not much," I offered, hoping that would encourage him to
change his mind.

"It is perfect, sir. I hope it will only be for one night. Then we'll
move along."

He gave me another smart salute, and before he did his about-
face, the other officers appeared at my door. They each gave me
a smart salute and a crisp "*Monsieur,*" one after the other. Well
choreographed. Then they each shook my hand as if to seal our
agreement. This time I quickly determined that two were regular
army and three, militia (plus the *légionnaire capitaine* who was a bit
of both and who would be moving from billet to billet, for security's
sake). No Ngokuru, I was happy to see.

I chose one of the straw chairs for the night, hoping it would be
the only one. The only night on the straw chair, that is. Hoping only
one night with the snappy officers.

Then all of them disappeared into the night, probably for

Mama's candlelight dinner. I assumed they would be back in time for lights-out.

Whenever that was.

■ The Plan

I was dozing after taking two sips from my faithful glass. In my half sleep, I resolved that he shall go with me. My latest resolution. Perhaps I am too quick to turn my wishes into actions—or, rather, to the statement of future actions. And no Errol Flynn to rescue me.

They marched in, single file, and gathered around the dining table. They were three militia and two regular army types. The *légionnaire capitaine*, my bearer of portents, marched in behind them. They each gave him a crisp salute. Then they lit their gas lamps, spread out a map, and began to discuss options. I was "asleep" in the shadows.

They all spoke in Sara-Ngumbaye at first (perhaps so that they could be sure I wouldn't understand), but then the Sara-Arabic amalgam, and finally French, probably because they came from different language groups and tribes, *and* maybe they assumed the Américain wouldn't understand that, either. The *légionnaire capitaine* knew Arabic. But they were speaking French in deference to the *légionnaire capitaine* who had joined them. By then, I guess I was deemed no threat to them.

I leaned back and feigned sleep in my chosen corner.

"Here it is—this one. The Wadi Abuyad." White Valley. The *capitaine* pointed to a location on his map.

"Why did they choose the low ground?"

"Maybe they thought no one would be chasing them. There's some water there for the horses and camels," a lieutenant suggested.

The *capitaine* seemed a bit doubtful about that assumption. "Or perhaps it's a trap."

"We'll send out our scout tonight. The one with the old camel and accompanying 'wife' on the donkey. It will appear as if he is moving across the desert—heading for Belite. If there's a trap and placements, he'll see signs of them. He'll know what to look for. He'll be a night traveler heading for Belite. Really, his daughter on the donkey. The donkey will have a bell to announce their coming and draw out those waiting—Wahidi guards—if they are there. If they do not return by dawn, we will assume the Wahidi are there and have taken the two riders as prisoners."

"Or killed them," another piped up.

"Yes. Or killed them. If so, we go in and trap them in the valley. Agreed?"

All together, "*Oui.*"

"No prisoners. Nor women nor children killed. Kill only the men. Kill all of the men over sixteen years old. Take no male prisoners but one. Hassan Ibn Jema'a, who calls himself Wahid. Here is the last picture we have of him." He passed the copy of the picture around. From my vantage point I could see that his veil was up.

"But his veil is on—and up," one noted.

"Indeed it is," answered the *légionnaire capitaine*, somewhat impatiently, I thought.

"Then how will we know him?"

"By the fire in the eyes. Also, note the chain and festooning that decorates his turban." Then "Take ears from the dead men for to confirm the count of dead for *Général* Héman."

So I waited impatiently until they were making proper sleep sounds. Then I slipped out and saddled my ersatz chaperon, Omar.

■ A Moment of Courage

Late March 1969

I thought I knew the way. Or Moussa, whoops Omar, would. But it was difficult, in this pitch darkness, to see those tanks, jeeps, and other hardware I had made note of last time.

This was true adventure. True spy stuff.

I didn't like it much.

I needed to either get ahead of the camel-mounted spy, or stay behind him.

The trail was pitch black, and I hoped Omar would find us our way. I also had to listen for the spy's dingling bell or the donkey's braying along this trail. While keeping Omar moving ever so silently. From time to time, I descended Omar and held him tightly around the muzzle. With as much care and affection as I could muster. This was no time for the Wahidi horses, and the spy's camel and donkey, and also Omar, to have a braying macho contest. Or a shout at Satan.

And, by the way, how did the spy know his way? I was mulling over this conundrum when I heard the bell and the donkey's flutter. Somehow, I'd circled around and gotten ahead of the spy. I heard "We must hurry" as I moved to the side, lucky to find a dune high and wide enough to hide Omar and me. Again, Omar was wisely silent.

The spy rode on by me. "Ah," I thought, "he knows where Wadi Abuyad is. It is thought that Wahid is encamped there. And the spy is from this region." This was the only epiphany I would have that week.

He, and "she," or a hooded male child on the donkey, did not see me as they rode by. Slowly.

Their pace was enervating. Too slow. For it was at least ten kilometers more to Wadi Abuyad.

When they, and later we, finally arrived, there was no challenge, no trace of perimeter guards, and no sound of a live encampment. The Wahidi were not there.

The spy moved on by, riding west, probably looking to see whether he had missed the rebel enclave somehow. He listened for the clicking and scraping of weapons. He may have heard a slight noise, for he turned and stopped again.

I waited for him to move on, then I turned north to pass the rear of the Wadi Abuyad on the way towards Wadi Aswad (the Black Valley), where I guessed the Wahidi were encamped tonight. I told

Omar we could sprint now. Or whatever a donkey does when given the spurs.

We did.

■ Next Visit, My Visit

Same night

There was no one in the Wahid Aswad, so I turned back, South, heading for the Wadi Abuyad. I was a bit pissed off. I had been tricked, which might have been the Wahidi's intention. I kicked Omar with my heels, as if the misdirection might have been his fault.

I had affixed a black flag with white Arabic letters and a splash of red like a drop of blood, to the pommel of the saddle. The flag that Wahid had sent me via Rashid. The one that might protect my life, and let them know I was a friendly.

For, as I approached within a half kilometer of the Wadi Abuyad, they swarmed out of the darkness, carbines at the ready, and eyes fierce and angry. Eyes and rough outlines of figures were all I could see. And the glint of carbine barrels.

"*Eshkoon*," I was challenged. "You are the Emricani *Nasarah?*"

"I am. Here is the flag given to me by Wahid himself."

One came very close, close enough for me to see the outline of his dark *jalabah*. "Yes, he said you would come. We saw our flag, or we would have remained hidden. Descend!"

I did. Omar trotted in place nervously but didn't attack the strangers. I said "Easy" to him. Maybe that helped.

"Let us go to Abu Wahid. Leave the donkey here."

The minute I handed the reigns to another one, Omar became more agitated and kicked back his hind legs. He brayed in his anger and frustration.

"Calm your donkey," the man said.

The man holding the reins pulled them hard but had trouble controlling Omar. In a flash, Omar turned, showed the man his back side, and kicked out his back legs. Knocking the unsuspecting man flat.

Another readied his carbine.

"Wait! Wait!" I urged. "I am the only one that can calm him. He won't remain calm in the hands of another."

Still that onlooker chambered a round. All the others started arguing. About how much they would value the donkey. That he was well groomed and clean. Yet that a *Nasarah* might pay a pretty price even for the meat. But that the shot might alert the spy they had just fooled. That they had better use a *kabira* knife.

"Would you kill your own *hamar* and then eat him?" I pleaded. "Or even one of a *Nasarah* or one such as me? Besides, *Nasarah*s would not eat such a one."

We stood there and stared at each other in the blackness. Finally, he said, "All right. He may not even be *hallal*. So you will lead him with you. But keep him calm. No more kicking! And don't let him shit on this pathway."

I whispered a few words to Omar— "Don't kick. Don't shit. Don't piss them off."

He seemed to understand since his ears wiggled in assent—and it seemed he nodded his head. "Good boy," I added.

So we were led through the maze of the encampment to its center and the tent. There was an organizing that cleverly held in the sound of the men sleeping. The camp was shaped like an opera hall, but with acoustics that were arranged to absorb sound. He was truly an engineer.

His tent, on the other hand, was a ragged castoff that had nearly outlived its usefulness. As I would expect.

I recognized Wahid even in this darkness as he stepped gingerly out of the tent—at quick step as if he had not been, nor needed to be, sleeping. A fierce-looking one followed him out, gave me an angry stare, and headed toward the Janjawid encampment to the North. If they were there, none of his wives showed themselves. "Ha! *Saghiri Emricani*! Little American! Why are you out here? And so late."

"Rather, . . . so early." Well, that was a bit brash.

"Yes, *Nasarah*. Saghir, see to the *Nasarah's* donkey."

"He will not obey me, Master. He will kick me again and wake up the camp and alert the spy." The speaker was of the baseball cap, the Kansas City Athletics fan, the one who, as I saw it, had killed Moussa after slicing up his back—the one who was kicked, and who followed us to Wahid's tent—at a respectful distance from Omar. Good job, Omar!

Wahid looked at me curiously. "Hah! Stubborn like his master. Then tie him to that post," he ordered, pointing to the post. "Tell the others to give him sufficient space when walking past him. Fouade, you will guard him." Fouade stepped forward to grudgingly obey.

Then he turned to me. "This one who was kicked looks hugely pissed off!"

"How can you tell, Abu Wahid? Your men, when veiled, all always look pissed off!" It must have been the lack of sleep or the long, irritating ride that made me so bold and brash. And that I was encouraged by Omar. Truly a brave boy, Omar.

"Perhaps they are pissed from riding the camels," I added.

■ The Gordian Knot—or Twist, at Least

"My house has been commandeered by army and militia officers," I began. "They are planning an attack on you. They expect reinforcements soon. They sent a spy . . . ." At that point, I stopped to catch my breath.

"Ah, yes, the one on a camel with another rider, perhaps his wife, on a donkey. I think he's not sure which side he's on," Wahid said.

"How do you know this?" I asked.

"These nomads and locals only travel in daylight. They fear the djinnii of the darkness. They camp and sleep in the night. We thought he might be a spy, but he was making a wicked racket. Why would a real spy do that? Unless he is Say Ee Ah." He smiled conspiratorially. I almost fell for it and was working on a riposte. But he added, "That guy, that 'spy,' is probably intending to play both sides. For the money—the CFA."

"Yes, the Colonel wanted to attack you in the valley. Sitting ducks, he said. But first he wanted to be certain you were in this valley—Wadi Abuyad. He will find out from the spy that you are not. But I'm not sure that you are any safer at Wadi Aswad."

"I will look for another way to fool him. For the moment, do not tell them what you know. Or, if you must, tell them that we have just left the Wadi Abuyad because you may have seen it. Tell them we might do so, that we were circumspect—because we're not sure we trust you. We'll do a double twist. He will assume we will remain at Wadi Abuyad. However, it will appear we have gone to Wadi Aswad. But we will leave a few shiny coins with much of our clothing and some of our cloth tents—the ones the unclean ones have worn and used. The clothing will not be neatly cleaned. When they realize what they're handling, even the gold will strike much fear in them and especially terrify the ignorant among them."

I wasn't sure what story was true, or, if he was truly misleading me—which story to pass on to Ngokuru. I think that was the point. A kind of triple twist I could never unwind with certainty. Too many twists. And turns. For this poor boy.

Well, I told myself, if I must be, I am only the messenger—the go-between. Not mine to unravel. And this was not the Gordian knot. (Though somewhat like it.)

"One more thing. The Bulgarian wants a guide to lead him north."

"Hah! That is our country. One of us will deal with the Bulgarian."

"Yes, but please do not harm him," I urged. "And before I leave, I must see my companions Joe and Terry."

"The clownish ones who ask many questions and render everything a foolish joke?"

"Until the dope wears off," I said.

"Come." We hiked down a gradient to the lowest part of the wadi (where the excrement found its way). This would be the stage were this a true opera hall. And he threw open the flap of one of the tents. "This is *Sidi* Terry. Shall I wake him for you to enquire about his health?"

"No need. Where is the other one?"

He threw open the flap of another tent where, in the shadows, all I could see was a still lump. It produced a lively snore.

I assumed they were both well treated, since they lay soundly sleeping, uninjured and untethered. And they certainly had treated themselves to what was probably the last of the marijuana—probably masking the purtrid scent of the encampment—though that pleasant scent, masking the shit smell, should wear off by late morning.

As for further inquiry, perhaps I should have prodded the still lump after all. But I did not.

"Then you must go back now!" Wahid said. "And don't forget to continue your search for the thief of the betting money." I looked for, but couldn't see, either wink or smile.

How could I forget? And wasn't I speaking to the thief? "Of course, but I may have to explain why I am this night out so late."

"Is your mother awaiting you at your *kaz*? The colonel is your mother then? If so, go rescue Rashid and blame him for your nocturnal wanderings." He began to chuckle.

"No, but . . . ." He had me there.

"Also, write of us after the battle. Not before. But soon. And tell this adventure first.

"So you shall go back immediately, before they awaken. Many thanks for the warning. I will have this one serve as your guard part of the way—up to what is tonight the eighteenth dune." He pointed to the one really pissed-off Wahidi. The one Omar had taken on— Saghir of the Kansas City Athletics baseball cap.

"He'll be pissed off about that and stare fiercely at me the entire way," I blathered. Besides, I thought, I wonder if he know I'm a Cleveland fan.

"Would that you had my faithful nephew, my Rashid, with you.

But you do not. Ah, but how will you know if this one is angry? You said that, when veiled, we all look pissed off."

Point taken.

Point scored.

■ Apostrophe or Epiphany?

I wish it had been learned while imbibing at *Père* Habert's, instead of first-hand from the fierce and angry Saghir. But it was on the journey to the eighteenth dune. That's when I finally knew.

That's when I learned that the shooting and killing of Lièvre and his companion, the event which most riled the government and all the foreigners, was entirely a case of mistaken assumptions, of mistranslation, and of cultural differences. Indeed, what we all believed, were but our thoughts getting too far ahead of the truth.

As near as I could tell, it was all a communication malfunction. That the revolutionists, or bandits, who held those carbines, heard the Doctor say "carabines" and thought he was signaling to the veterinarian travelling with him, to go for his carbine. In fact, he was saying for the Monsieur le Veterinaire Santiago to let go of his carbine. Furthermore, "Lâchez—drop the carbine," was interpreted, in the mind of the rebel, as "take the carbine and shoot the coward, *les lâches*." So the language-handicapped adolescent misunderstood, thinking he heard "Shoot the cowards," and was angry at the perceived insult.

Both of them, the people doctor and animal doctor, were shot dead by the panicky adolescents. Their bodies left to bake and spoil on the road to Ayen Kabir. To rot by dusk. Or until Alain would come to dispose of them. (But thought that his mission was to shoot me.)

Their deaths now became a "Remember the Alamo" *cause célèbre* for the French, the former *légionnaires*, the *parachutistes*, and the Sara-Ngumbayes. Plus anyone helped or cured by the good docteur. The "true" version of the story was no doubt later stamped "top secret" by the government and militia, the better to keep the Caucasians on their guard and more antagonistic toward the Wahidi.

Yet, having explained this, Saghir reined in to face me on my trusty *hamar*. "He was deserving, since he had ravaged the lovely Amina and confused her heart with his *Nasarah* potions," he insisted. "As you do. So I believe I must treat you just as I did him! And this secret will die with you!"

This was a moment I feared most and hoped to avoid. Saghir seeking his personal revenge. He would justify it in his own mind as being for Amina, in the person of himself, but, in truth, it was his revenge against a hated *Nasarah*. Before I knew it, his carbine was readied and pointed at me. At the same time, his Kansas City Athletics cap blew off and away. A portent, perhaps.

"You do not want to harm me, Saghir. I, who am the strong friend of Abu Wahid, your chief."

"I will tell Abu Wahid that you tried to steal my horse from me, and so I had to shoot you."

"Rather you owe *me* a horse, having killed my brave Moussa." I probably should have not made mention of Moussa, although it made him think this one through.

He hesitated. Trying to decipher my jabber.

Meanwhile, I reached for her handkerchief, perhaps to take one last scent of her—or perhaps just to wipe away the sweat flooding from my forehead. "I am not armed," I declared shakily. "I am only reaching for this," I said as I held up her handkerchief.

He gasped as he realized that the filigreed handkerchief had belonged to Amina, and was a sign of her esteem. Though he could have assumed I had somehow taken it from her.

Alain appeared behind him. Seemingly out of nowhere, but really through the last two dunes between which we had just passed. He had his carbine pointed at us. A bit shakily. I wasn't sure if it was pointed at me or at Saghir's head.

"You are called back to camp, Saghir," he said, in a quiet, but menacing, voice. Saghir must have recognized the menace of it, for he lowered his carbine, turned his mount, and sped off back to the Wahidi encampment. Without retrieving the baseball cap that hopped away in the wind.

I raised my hand to thank Alain, but he was already gone.

My mind made an involuntary leap to the sensual gifts of the "lovely Amina," confirmed to be the mistress of Lièvre. (Strange how the mind sometimes works. At least, my mind.) That liaison explained the blue Deux Chevaux. Left there in front of Amina's courtyard by the Doctor Lièvre for safekeeping (and no doubt to keep it a secret from his wife). Now parked in front of Amina's abode, and now, forever in her keeping.

■   But Then . . .

My return that early dawn was eventful.

I found my *kaz* in shambles, destroyed by a furious explosion. Or more than one. Pieces of bodies and uniforms lay strewn about. There was plenty of blood spatter.

Rashid's head rolled and bounced about on the uneven floor. To that familiar arrhythmic beat. His stare fixed on the ceiling, and he smiled as he stared. His turkey-like nose was smashed in, but he didn't seem to have minded.

Upon my arrival, the colonel gave Rashid's head a forceful kick that sent it rolling back and forth. And disrupted the beat.

Rashid's remaining body was nowhere identifiable as one. Its pieces had mixed with those of at least two army officers scattered about. Interesting that the militia officers had been passing the bottle outside when the explosion detonated. And they survived, without injury. I believed I saw remnants of my khaki suit. The one I had worn on special occasions. The one stolen with the first radio.

I was thankfully able to retrieve Younis's *gris-gris* from the mix of bloody entrails. But there was no message inside it.

I went around to the back and made it to the shit hole. Arms folded, I barfed plentifully, though I had not eaten the evening before. For the moment, I restored Younis's *gris-gris* to a towel behind the commode and to its home among the cockroaches. And the piss left by my recent visitors. Praying that Younis would not search for it until I could get it cleaned and back into the red box, and the red box, back into its hole.

Meanwhile, Rashid's head now rolled back and forth, against what little was left of the rear wall. Beating once more to its mysterious rhythm—as if he himself was still beating his head in fury against the wall.

I knew that Miriam was away. That's when it occurred to me that Alexandru was nowhere to be seen. And just then he came out of the smoke and gloom. He looked around and knew immediately what had happened. Knew from his personal experience. Perhaps he had been with Boudin at the moment of detonation. Perhaps with Boudin's pirates. Either way, putting the last-minute touches to his planned venture. All he could say was "Again?"

Ngokuru turned to shout to a figure in the shadows. "Antoine, find the perpetrator of this!" I looked in that same direction, by the baobab, and caught a glimpse of the sky blue uniform and perhaps a smile, before the figure slipped into the darkness of my back yard flora and dunes. I wondered if that truly was Antoine. Or perhaps the other one. Perhaps, this time, he had provoked—their dark angel.

Ngokuru began pacing in the back court, back by the baobab. "This is the work of Hassan Ibn Jema'a. Why did you not warn me?" Lip-curl and eye-twitch in rapid synchronicity.

I had to steady myself, to think more clearly. "I believe this was the work of Rashid ibn . . . whatever. He would not be in there, but to explode his grenades. But yes, it was probably Wahid whom you call by the name of Hassan Ibn Jema'a who put him up to it. Though I know Wahid is now and has been remaining in his own encampment throughout this night. (How would I know that. Unfortunate confession!) But, yes, perhaps he was trying to kill me as well. At least your officers survived." Maybe Rashid's terrorism was timed so I would not be there. Nor the militiamen.

Maybe the contrary.

Ngokuru gave me a how-could-you-know look. I did not satisfy his curiosity. But this was yet another moment to add to his suspicions. Another moment to stoke his anger toward the Wahidi.

And toward me.

■ First (and Last) Warning

Late March 1969

I met Jacques on the road to the Northeast sector. On my way to see Miriam. And, I have to admit, I was also hanging out in those parts hoping to gather some information. And arrow branches for Younis. I was surprised to meet him. At the moment when it was starting to get uncomfortable for *Nasarahs*, given the stares of anger from the populace in this quarter.

"Américain, *ça va?*"

"OK. *Toi?*"

"Not bad. I'm told we will burn this down the day after tomorrow. We've gotten that information to the inhabitants on paper, in French and Arabic, but many seem not to understand. Not to believe us, perhaps."

"Or not able to read. So it's to be the day after tomorrow?"

"So Boudin tells us. Yes. The next day after tomorrow." Jacques looked like he was happily anticipating the event.

"I will wander the sector and see what is known."

"Best to stay out of there. Europeans, us *Nasarahs*, are not very welcome right now." I gave up my "not-*Nasarah*-but-Emricani" mantra. I guessed I would have to be a European, a *Nasarah*, for all time.

"Then what are you doing here? Isn't it dangerous for you as well?" I suggested.

"So it is. I'm leaving here this very moment, since I've done my work." Perhaps mapping and calculating for the burning. Given his smirk, I surmised that he had been with a lady as well.

I hurried taking my leave of him, and heading to Miriam's home. But Miriam's mama said Miriam was at the marketplace, no doubt selling her trinkets and "*jawhira*." Ali was still in school. I asked Miriam's mama if she had heard about the burning the day after tomorrow. I think she mumbled, "No." And lots of other, incomprehensible stuff. I knew that this would forever be the extent of our conversations and mutual understandings. And then I hurried to the oasis, location of the marketplace, to see if Miriam had heard.

She was deep in conversation with Colonel Ngokuru, down at the banks of the trickling stream, and I hid behind a copse. Although I would have been thrilled to overhear their conversation, I assumed they would have halted it in my presence. The colonel gestured forcefully and she, somewhat distractedly. I could catch only "You must!" from him. At one point, he encircled the world with his arms in the Partenay manner, and then he swung around to go, without another word. I waited a reasonably few moments, before approaching her.

"I have heard," she said. "It is rumored. Nothing is certain. Is this thing possible? Can they do this thing? We do not know how to read the papers. Will it be so soon?" Despite her practiced stoicism, she spoke a bit nervously and looked around anxiously. Even frightened— of me, or what I might have seen? Of the "taking" to come?

"Pack and come to my place."

"I must stay in my father's house. This is not a certain thing. These informations are often wrong. Just rumors from Mama's." I felt there would be no point in arguing.

I knew the only recourse was to reach Wahid. To tell him what I had heard. And to radio Norman with what I know.

I met Miriam's brother, Ali, on his way home from the school. "You must find Wahid and tell him this news. Of the burning of the Northeast *arrondissement*. On Thursday. *Alkhamis*. I haven't time to write it in the *gris-gris*." In fact, I sensed that Younis was keeping an eye on the burial location of his prized possession. The best time would be just after the next lesson, but I could not wait. Anyway, Ali was more reliable for carrying oral messages than Rashid. Whose head, by now, was enjoying the prizes of paradise. I hope."You know what you must do. Take Omar to make your way. Wahid should be in the Wadi Aswad by now. Or perhaps the Abuyad. *Allah yakun maeakum,* Allah be with you." Maybe I shouldn't have given Ali location choices.

And it was only later that I realized I had told Ali as if the burning were true and certain. It was not. Also, I may not have used the word for "day after tomorrow" correctly. Or did I say Thursday? I wasn't sure. In my great fear, with too many languages to manipulate. And keep straight. That was another problem with this place. Plus, could Ali remember all this for the time it took to find Wahid? Ali did not return that night or the next day.

[Note from Aaron Hamblin: I'm not sure where in the chronology this belongs, so I'm inserting it here.] Ali later told me that he was made to wait at the Wahidi emcampment as the Wahidi prepared for an "encounter." And he was held so that he could not betray them by "accident"—or otherwise. [End of insert.]

■ Younis 11

Late March 1969

It's obvious that Younis couldn't wait to return. He turned up breathless on my porch. "Where has the story left off, Monsieur Harry? Are Robin and the men in the festivities?"

"Yes. So all of them, Robin and the Merry Men, are dressed in a different way over their forest clothes. And their faces hidden by hoods."

"Why do they do this?"

"In order to slip into the festivities and take part, but avoiding arrest by the sheriff or his many men. Robin, in disguise, takes part in the archery contest. The reward for the winner is a fine stallion. Of course, Robin wins the first place. Though, because he is disguised as a mysterious land owner, the sheriff's men don't know who it is they present the award to. This bothers them and makes them suspicious."

"Please to go on. I will do the English lesson and other things afterward.

"I know who . . . Robin will be awarded as the best archer?"

"Yes, as the best archer. As you may be some day." I got a bit carried away here, then disturbed that I might raise up the boy's hopes, only to have them shattered by reality.

Then, "Younis, come this minute to finish your chores, lazy one!" his mistress shouted. It was at that very point that I once again, for yet another time, resolved to break Younis free, especially if I must leave this town. (And sooner or later I must.) That he will go with me.

■ The Battle Begins—and Ends

Early April 1969

They were given what passed for due warning. From the *sous-préfet*, but passed on for dissemination, by his very nervous and angry (even more than usual) assistants. That the land would be taken over by the government for purposes of exploration and "cultivation." For the enrichment of all. Indeed, eminent domain taking without the niceties.

Few understood. But they began to ask questions. Still, the assistants had already gone, and so the questions remained unanswered. When some of the inhabitants began to move out of their hovels, others caught on. The women were keening, the men helpless in their anger. On the chosen day, it was what seemed to be the Wahidi who quickly surrounded the *arrondissement* to suppress any expressions of anger. Or of revolt.

It came on the morrow, Wednesday, not the day after as Jacques had said. The event occurred so rapidly that the Wahidi had somehow gathered up, so that the militia was not there to repel them. They had no chance, nor the intelligence—that I, or the spy Adin Azuku

Vincent, was to supply—to react and intervene. I would have sent Ali to try to breach the Wahidi line with that news. But he was already being held by Wahid. Too late, I feared. Plus I wasn't sure what to report. Nor to whom.

Something strange was afoot here.

The fires were started before the last denizen was able to move out. Ngokuru had a fondness for flames and heat. He would have enjoyed this. Water, melting the mud and adherences, would have been more efficient to destroy these hovels and melt them away. Nevertheless, rescue water would soak and complete the disintegration of the remaining walls and other structures, when those made homeless tried to extinguish the flames.

I thought I saw Boudin's pirates joining in the melee. The Wahidi exacting their revenge? But the wrong attackers on the wrong victims? This made no sense! Yet, in their midst, you could see the prisoners of Yekbar still wearing their prison stripes, carrying clubs and looking the most vicious of them all. Most confusing!

I rushed to help Miriam and her family. They would lodge with me after all. Despite the lack of a lodging. I rushed to them, to Miriam and the mostly helpless, geriatric mother. We grabbed pots, pans, other cooking utensils, and various items of clothing, quickly, and then we ran.

A panic did start, and so a kind of revolt after all. In their fury, the men who were being displaced, retrieved clubs and *kabira* knives and took after the Caucasians and "Wahidi." They were mostly brought down by batons and some rifle fire.

It was then that I noticed. The boots! The military-issue boots peering out from under these *jalabas*. They were in disguise, the militiamen, as Wahidi! Like (but for the opposite reason) the ploy in the Robin Hood adventure where the Merry Men were in disguise as local denizens. Almost as if the two stories, of Robin and of us, were mirror reflections, one of the other. This one a turning inside out of the Robin Hood theme.

Here the boots told the tale—militiamen under these *jalabas!* To sow confusion and hesitation, among those who rebelled to protect their homes, families, and belongings.

I caught a glimpse of Adin Azuku Vincent, the clumsy militiaman, or would-be assassin (It was he who had "dropped" his carbine during the *légionnaire capitaine*'s drill.), who now fired straight and true. And with ease. But most of them, the militiamen in *jalabas*, in their disguise, did not have their hearts in it. Many militiamen were firing in the air and with tears in their eyes. I learned that most of them were firing rubber bullets and blanks.

We followed Miriam and Youssef through the back alleys and out to the eastern wall. "This way. Left. Then right." Random rounds bounced off the walls near us. But none of us was struck.

With hand signs, Miriam waved us through a breach in the wall and over the surrounding berm, though, even here, there were militiamen at the ready.

The few gateguards on *our* side were motionless with fear. The militiamen on the other side let us pass. Perhaps because of the beautiful woman who led us. Perhaps because of the old lady carrying more pots and pans—who posed no threat and seemed to be moving out as ordered. Perhaps because there was, among this group, a crazy *Nasarah* loaded down with pots and pans (making a terrible, clanging racket).

We climbed up the eastern embankment, slipping in the sand as we hefted our burdens. I helped mother up and across. Then we were in the sweltering desert sand. Firing and screaming in the distance, but nothing much here. There was one baobab not far from the eastern wall where we took some shelter. I dropped my load and turned to run back.

"Where do you go?" Miriam said, a bit of panic in her voice.

"To find Ibrahim. I saw him in there. Fighting for us." [Note from Aaron Hamblin: I'm not sure where in the chronology this belongs, so I'm inserting it here.] I later remembered I had announced my allegiance subconsciously—my declaration of "us." [End of insert.]

"Don't." I didn't know that she cared so.

I'd seen the giant water carrier and prisoner, Ibrahim, in the midst of the rioting, throwing militiamen about like helpless ragdolls. I knew he would soon be overcome. Or shot.

"I must!"

I waded back into the melee, dodging fists and *kabira* knives, ducking to avoid the random rubber bullets—as if there was such a way to duck them. I might have been taken for one of the pirates or other *Nasarah*s allied with the militia. But then I realized that little Youssef had followed me and held my trouser belt.

Several men from the neighborhood tried to protect Miriam's hovel, probably at Ngokuru's orders, but were quickly overcome by *Yekbari* only interested in its loot. Despite its lack of pots and pans. I found Ibrahim there, by what was left of Miriam's hovel, surrounded by the battle. Lying in the dust and dirt, sparks and shards of wood flying about him. Blood was his blanket and also pooled about his shoulders like a pillow.

But, still conscious, he groaned, "Leave me, *Nasarah*-Emricani. My time is gone, so I will kill only other of the militia even if they are Wahidi. By Allah, I will."

"Nonsense. Let me take you to safety." I removed my shirt to staunch his wounds.

I tried to help him up, but he was huge and his weight beyond my strength. Then others saw me using my shirt to staunch his wounds and, assuming I was with them, joined us to drag him until they got him to his feet. We helped him limp into the back alleys. The fire was catching up to us and, meanwhile, the militiamen threw off their disguises and proceeded to hunt "rebels" in the alleys.

I led them all, this second miserable group, to the breach in the wall. We somehow tugged Ibrahim over the embankment and down the other side. The guards did not pay attention to this wounded giant, perhaps out of fear of him. Youssef was with us all the way. Brave boy. Miriam was fiercely angry. With him and with me.

The Yekbar prisoners were gone from here by then. Gone into further hovels to forage for spoils. They were soon followed by the others. By militiamen. I saw them all carry out porcelain, china sets, fine silken robes, and *jalabas*. And the ubiquitous portraits of John Kennedy that they used to wrap the spoils, or proceeded to stab repeatedly into small pieces of paper and cardboard, perhaps for packaging and stuffing. For packaging the silver-plated cups, trays, tableware, and candleholders. And many other items marked with the USA logo. Where will these prisoners' takes find their new homes?

So much for the appreciation for our assistance, as Wahid and Abdel-Hamid had envisioned. (Thank you, Product of the United States of America.) I wondered where the prisoners intended to ensconce their spoils.

We all crawled under a baobab, the upside-down tree. Miriam had wisely brought a large plastic jug of water. Half full. We'd have to ration. There was nothing to do but wait out the conflagration. Nothing to do but let SHG wreak their havoc.

Then we'd slip away, to what was left of my place, in the dark of the night.

Blindly.

■ ## What Could Be Next?

The Wahidi rode out via the Ain Hadjer road (from the west), but they were significantly weakened for lack of Janjawid reinforcements still making their way from the east—and probably thieving and slaughtering on their way. And even the lepers had not got the attack orders.

[Note from Aaron Hamblin: I'm not sure where in the chronology this belongs, so I'm inserting it here.] Then Wahid sent scouts ahead, who discovered that the burning had already taken place (Jacques misled me since the burning took place that Wednesday—not the Thursday—or I got it wrong, or Boudin intentionally misled Jaques. I would never be sure.) And that the prisoners of Yekbar, Ngokuru's gang, were now fully engaged in looting the fallen mud-brick homes.

Wahid, determining that he was undermanned for a full-fledged battle, turned his small group around and headed back to the Wadi Abuyad. [End of insert.]

Wahid was then busy gathering in his Wahidi and lepers at the Wadi Abuyad. Colonel Ngokuru was chafing at the bit, not waiting for reenforcements from Djemélia. He would ride back again with the released Yekbar prisoners to attack the Wahidi and their camp followers at Wadi Aswad. To torture, murder, and loot. To take ears.

So later that same day, Colonel Ngokuru rode out on the Djemélia road (from the south) to complete a rear guard attack on the Wadi Aswad, the alternative Wahidi encampment. He split his force to trap the Wahidi from both sides. But then Ngokuru, sensing an ambush or a trap, chose not to lead his militia into Wadi Aswad. So a contingent of Wahidi waited near the Wadi Aswad to entrap the militia—who never came.

Still, when we got back to what was left of my *kaz*, my surviving militia guests were no longer there. After duty done at the burning, they had immediately ridden out again to stop the Wahidi in their tracks. Out to get ears and blood as well. I heard they would ride all the way to the encampment at Wadi Abuyad—where I had informed Ngokuru they were. . . . Maybe.

But there was no one there. No ears to seize and sever. The Wahidi and lepers must have fled. *"On avait foutu le camp,"* Ngokuru growled. Gone and little clue as to their whereabouts. Wahid left a little gift for the militiamen—the leper tents and clothing. [Note from Aaron Hamblin: I'm not sure where in the chronology this belongs, so I'm inserting it here.] I'm told it took a moment for the Militiamen to realize what they were handling and trying on. "Coins, clothes, and cloth from the unclean!" one yelled. And the others joined in a terrified chorus.

Ngokuru sent out his trackers, but it looked as if the trails had been wiped clean. For miles. No doubt with brush and branches attached to the last wagons out. [End of insert.]

There would be no ears taken this day.

But some might later fall off.

■ The Fifth Visit: His Visit

April 1969

"So your aim is to retake the lands that your family ruled over." I guess I wanted confirmation.

"I had been promised a *présence* to help with the relocation of the peoples of my Northeast *arrondissement*, a relocation to the prefecture lands that would strengthen my claim for it. But that promise was, of course, broken. That is why I questioned you so forcefully when I heard there would be a burning. That is why I believe you have failed me. . . ."

He was starting to anger up in that way of his. As always, he wrapped his veil over his mouth and nose when he was angry—so that only his fierce (perhaps malevolent?) eyes showed.

"I reported the information I had discovered or was given to me. I did not know the day for sure."

He seemed to ignore me, and went on, "In so doing, in not confirming further, you may have taken away the greatest possible source of my people's income, the riches of the oil, that is our right. To be thus enriched by the oil. To live in comfort and peace. Now we must make a war to have our inheritance.

"We ruled this land for many centuries. We had killed or converted all the infidel in it. And *Inch Allah*, God willing, we shall rule again.

"Why did you not warn us?" he repeated.

"I didn't know it would come to . . ."

"You knew enough to warn the *sous-préfet*." He was working himself up again—like a storm—behind his veil.

"How did you know *that*? So *that*, your spy can discover! But not discover the day!" Now *I* was fully paranoid. Plus, I didn't want to implicate Miriam.

"My Alain can discover all things. He is the most valuble of them all! I will never let him go! He is my *almlak alaswd*.

"Also Ngokuru, the evil *capitaine*, knew these things. And the day. And the time. Why didn't you inform me? That's your job."

I was getting worked up as well. (At least Miriam wasn't implicated.) "Excuse me, Sidi Hassan Ibn Jema'a. But Alain gave you the wrong information too. And, by the way, teaching English to the children is my job. Furthermore, your wonderful angel and spy should have told you that Ngokuru is now a colonel, thanks to his heroics at Zenig Etnin, the leper village!"

"In addition, you will choose to trade for the *Nasarah* woman. Thus you will have twice broken our bond. You have betrayed our brotherhood. It is always thus with the *Nasarah*! And Emricani as well!" He was in a really angry, fiery mood. And he was assuming, rightly, that I was leaning toward that solution—to liberate Alice—if I had to choose.

I had no memory of a bond, but "You have broken ours," I pushed back. "You have kidnapped my friends and countrymen."

"Yes, yes, Emricani. I should have known. Emricani, who looks like *Nasarah*. Who speaks like *Nasarah*. Who even worships like *Nasarah*."

"I . . . ." I began to protest.

"Yes, I have seen you with the one who calls himself Father."

"But I do not worship with him. I do not worship with anyone. I am . . . ."

"So much the worse. You will be cursed to hell. And I have offered you the redemption of Islam."

For a moment, I thought this was one of his rhetorical attempts to cool things down. Judging from his look, I couldn't have been more off the mark. "Kill or convert? Here I thought you were Westernized. Secularized. Like us," I went on.

"Ha! No Emricani. I have learned there is a much better way! For I believe *lā ʾilāha ʾillā-llāhu muḥammadun rasūlu-llāh*—that Allah is the one God and Mohammed is his messenger. Write of this!" I watched as he seemed to be taking on a different mode. Like a priest, pastor, or *imam.* Like Father O'Sagarty did sometimes. He *did* calm down. The fierceness seemed to retreat. He looked toward the heavens—entranced.

I was myself nearly entranced. Or just exhausted. "Yes, but . . . ."

But he quickly brought us back down to this world, this here and now. "Emricani, remember. Yes, that I was told you had recited the *Shahadah,* before witnesses. Are you not now one of us, one of the *Mu'minin?*"

Much as I would have liked to, given this heated conversation, I did not counter. That I had fumbled the *Shahadah.* And thus I was no Muslim. But if silence signaled assent, then so it was.

But then, in my panic and to cover my dissembling, my words rushed out. "So the Janjawid say they are messengers of Mohammed. Are they? And then they are your allies. Are you, too, a messenger of Mohammed, and thus carrying the word of Allah?"

"I am a servant of Mohammed and so of Allah. Thus is my *jihad,* my struggle."

For a rare moment, I was speechless as I had never been. I had never seen this rising as a religious one. Again, I missed a critical clue. Somehow. So much for my romanticizing the bandits—or rebels—as like the bandits of Robin Hood. So much for my foolish illusions. If there was a way to misread, it seems I will always find that way. And suffer its result. Perhaps that was what had always been bothering me—since my arrival in this land.

But yet, I had to go on. One more point, "And the lepers, are they too servants of Mohammed? Despite their destiny?"

"Even unto the most afflicted of them."

Even unto the most afflicted of them. Despite their miserable destiny. I had argued with evangelicals in the USA, and with Father Sean O'Sagarty on these very sands. So I knew there was no point to arguing with such believers.

No point.

◼ My Destiny as Go-Between

So I had told Wahid the wrong day of the burning, the day when they could have trapped the militia. But I had given the militia the wrong information about the Wahidi whereabouts. Where they could have been trapped and slaughtered by the Wahidi. So neither would find the other. If luck held, neither would cross with the other and they would continue to use separate roads and paths.

I was the perfect carrier of misinformation in both directions. And so I would be the recipient of Wahid's fiery anger. And I would not have given colonel Ngokuru the location he so wanted, whereby he would free Alice.

The perfect go-between. The perfect traitor. To both sides.

In a vise of my own making.

◼ Younis 12

April 1969

The next time we met, I picked up where we left off. At the festivities where Robin, in disguise, has won the archery contest.

"So Robin Hood wins that contest. Then there would be the horse races. And the Merry Men's best rider was in that race."

"Little John?" Younis asked anxiously.

"Well you know, Little John was not so little. He was really big, almost a giant. Like Ibrahim. Too heavy for the horse, the stallion that Robin had won. Let's say, for the story, that it was Younis of the Good Heart who was the lightest and best rider. He was light like a feather, and Robin's new horse seemed to take to him well."

"Harry . . . Monsieur, was the horse like your Moussa?"

"Very much like Moussa. A strong and valiant horse. Of course, Younis talked to him, the horse, before the race and they—Younis and Moussa—easily won the race. But then, one of the sheriff's guards recognized Younis from the *gris-gris* he wore—the fine leather that, because of his riding, peeked out from underneath his disguise. The guard called for the others and ran to the sheriff. 'Your honor,' he shouts, 'I have seen a rider in the race who is wearing the leather *gris-gris* underneath his coarse robes—and I believe he is one of Robin Hood's Merry Men.'"

"I must not allow my *Yondo gris-gris* to be seen!" Younis exclaimed.

"The sheriff called out 'Bar the gates! Let no one out!' Certainly Robin knew what that meant."

"What did that meant?"

A quick reminder of how the past participle of "to mean" is used. Then Younis asks, "Well, what did that mean? . . . I meant."

"Excellent! It meant that Robin and his Merry Men were trapped within the walls of the sheriff's palace, and that they would have to fight their way out."

"Could Robin not just pay the evil Sheriff off with the prizes just won or with money taken from the rich men?" Younis suggested. Very clever, this one.

"I doubt the sheriff could be bought off. Surely not in front of his men," I reasoned.

"Robin knows this, calls together his men, and tells them, 'We will have to fight our way out. Stalwart men of the forest, you can throw off your disguise garments, the better to fight these sheriff's men.' And they made a plan to surround their enemy."

"So the . . .," I began.

But for the call, "Younis, where are you. You have left work unfinished! Come immediately!"

I understood that he had been in such a hurry to come over that he had neglected his duties. "Go back!" I urged. "Don't forget your tooth stick. We will discover what happened to Robin and his Merry Men the next time."

We will.

■ What Next?

April 1969

I went to visit Mama, to respond to her call, to partake of her fiery sauce, and to survey the damage to Mama's Fine Restaurant. On my day off. None of my accomplices were there.

Through the breakage in the fence, I could catch a glimpse of Amina wrapped in an old abaya and hooded disguise. A militiaman guard stood watch just inside the gate. I heard the women chattering, as I approached the courtyard door.

"What shall I do then? My doctor is gone. I hid away in great sorrow for many weeks at his death. I so miss him and his French ways. But also, I love Hassan Ibn Jema'a, my cousin twice removed. He brings me great excitement. But it can never be. My uncles will never stand for it, no matter how much he steals for me. I like the Emricani, for he is calm and speaks softly. But I could not take him up to spite Wahid. Nor go with him to his homeland. Then there is the policeman, I mean his bro . . . ."

"Sh . . .," Mama whispered. Then, "I think there is someone at the gate." Then "Give yourself to none of them," Mama advised. "In this place, at this time, they will all break your heart. Hassan Ibn Jema'a will never stop his mischief and thievery, and his need for revenge. And you are right that the Emricani will soon leave for Emrica. Especially when the war breaks out. Which will be soon. And where, in Emrica, you would not be happy. Where you would be held in disgrace and shame by the ignorant people there. As for the policeman's bro . . . [inaudible] . . . Give yourself to none of them."

Well I guess that was that. Tell them "*Of one that loved not wisely, but too well.*" That's me.

Then Mama announced, "I have summoned the Emricani to warn him of the attack to come. He will not be surprised. But he will now want to leave this place."

So, at that point, I clapped (as was the custom here) to signal my presence. Suspicious timing, but I wanted to get it over, and then go sulk over this lost love. Mama opened the courtyard door to me. By then, Amina had hidden herself deeply in the damaged kitchen, and the guard at a table, as if he was a patron.

The JFK portrait was gone.

"Emricani. I cannot make sauce. No *w'eke*." She shrugged.

That was all right. I'd lost my appetite in light of the conversation that I had just overheard. I thought about asking for a Douze Marches.

Instead, I stammered. "That's all right. I came in reponse to your message, and to see how you are. And to survey the damage done." She looked much better than the last time I saw her, when she was greatly suffering from her wounds. But her chest, and her breasts, crisscrossed with the bayonet cuts, were still bandaged. Her robe was open so that I could see all this clearly, the breasts having no erotic attraction in this part of the world.

"I am well. The cafe is as you see. No Douze Marches. We still have the view," she grinned. "But they stole away all my pots and pans. And the beer." She gestured an open hand in a half circle, careful not to stretch her arms and cause her wounds to break open and bleed— nor to draw my attention to where Amina was hiding.

"I am glad you are well, mama. I am sorry to miss the *esh b'w'eke* since I might not have another chance to partake," I answered with some sorrow. I was more sorry about her advice to Amina than the absence of *esh b'w'eke* and beer.

"I will see you soon, Monsieur 'arry. To apprise you of the situation and likely forthcoming battles." *Les batailles.*

Or did she say *bottles? Les bouteilles.*

■ The Foolish Game

Then, as my misgivings predicted, Amina became the next "official" pawn in our miserable game. I could only imagine what those slobs might do to her. This was not in my plan. I tried to make some kind of contact, but no one in Dar es Sabir knew anything. Or so they said.

The Wahidi had by now completely cut off the road to Albri with a full-blown checkpoint and, I was told, a pretty good assembly of force. But finally I had a visit. "The colonel says you must see him." Ngokuru himself.

He was looking a bit rough. In mud-caked civilian clothes. I wanted to ask how he got through the roadblock, but he held my eyes with a most fierce, angry stare. Not unlike the one that Wahid bestowed on me. No humor there. These Sara-Ngumbaye rarely fix eyes to eyes when talking to you. I knew something was up.

"Nasarah . . ."

"I . . .," No use protesting. "I am Harry Hamblin."

"I still know who you are. Of course, you are the one who befriends the bandit. Now I know that you are the coward hiding in the leper rags." He recognized me though shaven and shorn. "We have spoken not long ago. I have the other Nasarah, the professeur of Albri, in arrest.

"Then you must un-arrest her."

"And I will when you give me good information about Wahid and the Wahidi. Like where they are now."

"They're at their checkpoint between here and Djemélia. Also, I think, another one between here and Albri." I was stalling. For what, I don't know.

He didn't buy it and, instead, lit a cigarette. He offered me one, but quickly withdrew the offered pack before I could accept. The lip-curl and eye-twitch were enhanced by the smoke of his cigarette. Then the angry stare, the left eye still twitching in rapid time. "The rest. Where are the rest?" he shouted.

"Not a clue. Maybe there are no rest. Maybe there are only those at the roadblocks." I stared at him straight on.

"Nonsense. Get a clue or we'll have to Yekbar her." Yes, sent to Yekbar, for capital crimes like treason and spying. A certain death sentence (though there was no death penalty in this "enlightened country") for even a woman so tough and hardy.

"For what? On what charge?"

"For spying. We know you are all *Say Ee Ah*." He was sure we were CIA. It still took me a moment to translate it in my mind and know his meaning. "We don't have to prove it either. Our laws say that any assumed spy caught will be sent to Yekbar. Final period. Understand?"

I knew it was hopeless to argue this point. This Say Ee Ah attribution. As Mark Twain wrote, "It is easier to fool someone than to convince them that they have been fooled."

"Then take me in place of her." I wasn't usually so heroic. Actually, I wasn't ever so heroic. Not even close. But I figured I had a better chance than her of being freed by our government—given what I knew and did.

"Not a chance. You have feelings for the blond one. Like all *Nasarah*, you lust after her, but also have a great fondness for the beautiful one, Amina. Not unlike mine for Amina. However, Amina will be *my* wife. Yes, I will make it so before you can, and when Hassan Ibn Jema'a is no longer on this earth. (Shades of the sheriff and the lady Marion.)

"You need to tell us where and how to contact the Wahidi. Just give us the locations. Then I will free her. And you may both leave our country."

"Truly, I don't know."

"Then find out." He looked truly exasperated with me. "Or truly, she will be our prisoner. To be sent to Yekbar. Here is a reminder." He handed me a folded note—written as if in code—a note which I still keep. She wrote:

Harry,

By now you know I am under arrest—the militia's prisoner in some kind of deal they want to make with you. I hope you can pull this one off! They've offered me Yekbar as an alternative. Yech! Good luck on your negotiations. And Harry, I'll bet it's time for you to get a haircut. Bang! The whole head! Be sure to face the right way! It is time! I'm sure of it. There is no better time! I'd like to see you and give you one myself! Bang! Be sure to face the right way!"

Love, Alice

All of that about the haircut, especially the last line was certainly in a code of some kind. *"Bang! Be sure to face the right way!"* I wasn't coming up with a decoding though. As usual, no decoder ring available. Maybe she's telling me I must leave her now. Or she, me. "Face right" from her frontage. Right, facing the mountain. Something simple such as she's somehow able to go . . . or wants me to help her go back to Albri, where she can give me a haircut and where I should go. Face right is the mountain and the Mission! Aha . . . The missionaries are going to spring her! They're going to pop that guard over the head and take her up the mountain! *"It is time! I'm sure of it. There is no better time!"* Up to the missionary enclave and sanctuary.

At least there were no censor marks on this note.

"Yet I've done you a great favor by occupying the army general while you swiped his rifles. Is that not enough to free her? Your beloved."

"Not yet enough! Find where he is!" Again the hand slapped the table—not far from my face.

"Alice gives excellent haircuts," I tried in desperation.

"Maybe she can entice him to us with the offer of a haircut. Like the biblical Samson." I was surprised he played along with my sarcasm this far.

"American aid. Rice for your people. Weapons for your militia!"

"Yes. The Ruskiyés have already offered such for the Wahidi."

"All right. And if I find out, you will free Amina into my care?"

There it was. Thus my choice, given that he had Alice as well. The choice of which one I would bargain for. (Assured that Alice will be well cared for by the missionaries.) Thus, Amina. I looked for some kind of guarantee.

"You have my word. My sworn word. By Allah."

"Great! Are you a Muslim then?" *Inch Allah.*

"Today I am." He was getting even more irritated with me. I knew by his deadpan stare, but also with the rapid eyelid flutter—as rapid as the flapping of a humingbird's wings—that this was as good as it would get. My hope was to find at least the location of a satellite camp, if not Wahidi HQ, from Jean. Or from Wahid himself. My regret was that I could no longer exchange it for the information I would have given Wahid before the burning of the Northeast *arrondissement.* I'd have to reveal something else. Something better.

"Wadi Aswad." There. That's better.

That's something else. Indeed it is.

"Also, write of us after the battle. Not before. But soon," Wahid had intoned. Almost singing it.

Make it almost like a song. Of heroism.

As in times of old.

■ Younis 13

April 1969

When Younis came next, after our salutations, I asked, "Is your work done?"

"For today, Monsieur. I have served the *soupée* and the Master is asleep from the beer he has consumed. But I must still beware as the Mistress is angry with the children—because of her anger with the Master. For the beer he has consumed. Not allowed for *my* people. Yech."

Secretly, I would have been delighted to join old Jacob in a Douze Marches. "Ah, so you might be called back."

"Yes, Monsieur Harry."

"Well, heed this. Here is the vocabulary for this story.

"Robin knows they have been discovered because of the *gris-gris* peeking out from Younis de Bon Coeur's disguise." I was definitely ad-libbing this part.

"I am truly sorry," Younis said with a pained look.

"Don't be. It was destined to happen.

"Robin calls together his men, and tells them that 'We will have to fight our way out. Stalwart men of the forest, you can throw off your disguise garments, the better to fight these sheriff's men. And then on to victory!'" I too was taken away by the romance of the battle, and the story came out even more rapidly. "And so they made a plan to surround their enemy. Even though the enemy outnumbered them greatly. But they also had tunnels dug for their escape. And for other things. You see, here in the picture is the entrance of the tunnel."

■ Strange Bedfellows?

April 1969

It was then that I determined that a healthy exchange of intelligence would increase our credibility and veracity. Mine and *Père* Habert's. But I had to wait out many a night of excessive drinking with my colleagues and others to get him alone. And often he would retire before the rest of us.

Finally, my time came. "Monsieur *Père* Habert, as you may know, as part of my job I regularly report back to my headquarters in Djemélia. Mostly on educational issues, but also on political issues since they often impinge on our functioning."

"Ha! I know that."

Whoops! I was tempted to ask how he knew, but didn't. "Well, I understand that you too have contact with an agency in Djemélia, and that perhaps some of the information we send is similar in scope."

"Ah, you mean like what you communicate to your HQ by that late night, ha!—perhaps I should say *early morning* radio?" His eyebrows raised.

Double whoops and shit for good measure! "What gave you the idea that I communicate with them, other than face-to-face?"

"Ah, come now 'arry, you know I have close contacts with the Third Para."

"Then they know about the radio?" But I only feigned surprise. So this was both good and bad. It confirmed that Third Para had stolen the first radio and was listening in. As I thought. But it also confirmed that *Père* Habert was well informed about it. And probably already plagiarizing or embellishing my somewhat, sometimes misleading and exaggerated reports for his own duties and purposes.

"So I trust you are the only one here that knows of this?" I prayed.

"The only one."

"And do you agree with my reports—their accuracy and conclusions?"

"Mostly. Mostly the reports are very good. But I have other sources to round things out." He poured us each another glass.

Bingo. "And I was going to ask, therefore, if we could share information." I held my breath.

"It would be my pleasure. Ha! And it's only fair. On condition that you don't reveal my sources. Nor will I, yours, when it's me doing the reporting. And if you realize, then, ha!, that your reports must necessarily follow mine in time. Unless, I decide vice-versa. You see, 'arry?"

"I can do that," I agreed.

I noticed he peppered his speech with "Ha!" which I assume may be a characteristic of his regional patois. Or from acid reflux. Encouraged by his renown Scotch.

"Ha! Then we will have the advantage of verifiability between our agencies. Does that sound like a good proposition?" he asked.

"Very much so," I agreed.

"And, I think, just like what you intended to propose. Ha! That is, as soon as the others left."

Sharper than I thought. "You have me there."

"And I thought *un homme de qualité* like you would be more than a volunteer teacher." He gave me a half smile. "You *are un homme de qualité*, aren't you?"

"I hope so." I tried to sound sufficiently self-assured. Ha! Everyone seems to think that being a teacher ranks low on the worthiness graph. Maybe it's best that I took this moonlighting job. (Yeah, kidding.)

"Not that there's anything wrong with being a teacher! Just watch out for our friend, the Indian. Ha! We don't know who he might be working for."

"I will."

"And our other friend down the road." He pointed toward Ivan's *kaz*. "No more trips to the outback with him. To the lepers and others," he counseled. "As you probably know, they are with the rebellion. Ha! The contagious enemy. And the *docteur* may be with them as well. The Soviets would be happy to supply arms to the rebels. Ha! As well as to the government. The Soviets need the oil dollars that this country may yet get. For now, they can be paid with CFA money for the arms sold to these ones."

Maybe they had a deal with Wahid. A-ha! Through the lepers.

"I know." Actually, I didn't until now. But this was certainly part of the game. And another great tidbit for colonel Ngokuru. "Even unto the most afflicted of them," I thought.

"Then let me seal our bargain with a glass of whiskey. You may have one too," he added. "Ha! *A-allez!*" Then he smiled to signal his sarcasm.

I tried to smile as well. We toasted to our future.

And that we might survive it.

■ A World Below

Père Habert suggested I follow him into his house. Unlike the rough-hewn exterior of mud-adobe, and wood, plus walls topped with broken glass on the outside, the inside was well finished with smooth, painted walls and even floorboards. Of course, the ubiquitous portrait of John Kennedy was even here. There was no receiving room—the courtyard served that function—but a well-equipped kitchen and sleeping rooms for each of the four, or was it five, kids? And the interior corridor was much longer than the outside suggested. With a back courtyard equipped with WC and modestly hidden shower.

I was duly impressed. "I am duly impressed," I offered.

"I'm pleased that you are. But there is one more thing. From this room . . . ." He waved me into a storage room and pushed some heavy furniture to the side.

There he pulled up what seemed to be a cellar door, and we peered down below using his flashlight.

"You are one whose discretion I can trust. Ha! Let me show you this."

I followed him down a rickety metal ladder about six feet. There was a cozy spherical area large enough to hold four or five people. Or more, if some were kids.

And Modou had been right. I had another *aha* moment (or should I say Habert's rhetorical "Ha!" moment?) when I saw loam-like dirt and then clay deep beneath the several feet of sand and dried earth. I remembered that Modou had stated with utmost certainty that "beneath this awful sand, it is like loam and fresh earth as in days gone by. Not this desiccated desert." I would tell him what I had found. But only just before he sees it.

Solidity rather than the constant moving current of sand. Solidity beneath the sand. And richness beneath the dryness.

"As you can see. This is where I hide the important things. This is where I keep my stores of Scotch. And Pernot. And from time to time, bottles of fine wine." Then I understood how Jean was always coming up with a fresh bottle of Scotch. At bargain prices. Also, wrapped in soft cloth, what looked like M1s—Karibiner 98 and MAS Modèle 36 bolt actions. Many of them. Left over from the Algerian War? And another of his secrets.

"I am astounded."

"Yes, so we are prepared, should things take a turn for the worse. We can exit by crawling beneath our enemy. There's one more thing." He turned away from me, put felt guards on his knees, then fell to his knees, and began crawling through a tunnel of which the ceiling was held up by a variety of wood slats and baobab branches. "This goes to a property behind our cottage that we own and rent out. Just at the foot of the Jumeaux. The exit is from a room like the one above. Do you want to see it?"

How could I refuse—and still be a respectful guest?

We crawled for what seemed to my knees like an eternity. We passed three areas with unopened bottles, rifles wrapped and covered, and metal ladders. I assumed that these were exits along the way. For the more claustrophobic among us. We ended at a spherical area not unlike the one under his cottage. More cleanly wrapped rifles and a large pile of grenades. There was a similar metal ladder.

"This way." He climbed the ladder and pushed hard on the wood atop. The cellar-like door opened to a musty smelling room cluttered with broken objects. A storage room with an attached (although unworkable) WC with modern-looking accoutrements.

As I rose from the tunnel, through a kind of WC storeroom with an impressive allotment of Scotch, I could see through a hazy, dusty window that we were not far from the town wall but closer to the foot of Jumeaux. Closer to where the two mountains met. Strange to locate such a modern WC (but with no water pipes) so far from living quarters. Bringing back fond memories of that time of my own, sometimes failed, rush to my WC.

"This is for our protection. From them. Should they rise up in their resentment." He gestured back toward the town. "Like the Tuaregs have done or the Wahidi, for example. As you have seen with the tragic grenading. I have made it for my family. We can even hide and eat and drink down here, only coming out in the dark. But you may need it sooner. With your charges. What I will call your pilgrims—whites, Ngumbaye, Arabs, and others.

"As if you were going to Mecca. Should you leave, I may put out such a story. Ha! That their influence has converted you all into Moslems intent on making the *hajj* as soon as possible. In this lifetime, given the vagaries of life here. Paid for, Ha! By USA! That may slow them down for a while—and buy you some time.

"But do not tell of me and mine, *whoever* wins the next battle. For there will surely be another after that. And yet another." He smiled.

He then resumed his thoughts on the tunnel and our escape. "You see, it is but a short distance to the foothills from here. And the rebels are gathering north of town. They may leave these southern walls and exits, where we would be exposed, unattended. And I suspect that it may soon be time for you to go away from here."

For the first time, I was truly frightened by this prospect. Because he seemed better informed than the rest of us. Because he knew how to read the tea leaves—especially those prepared by his wife, Batila.

"You truly think so?"

"I have seen this before, this restlessness and gathering. The resentment melding into a misplaced energy. The Wahidi, Tuareg, even Janjawid from the east. The burning only inflamed them. Pardon the inexecrable pun."

"But won't you need it to flee? You and your family?" I was truly concerned for him.

"And we will, if the time comes. For you can see how they are like children, children who ride horses and camels and can shoot rounds. Dangerous, troublesome children."

But he was more interested in showing off his workmanship and his heroism. "You see, this tunnel took me ten years to make. Ten years on my knees. Ha! You see how they are so." He pulled up his pant legs to show me knees swollen by arthritis and legs scarred from so much crawling, as well as from past desert war machine gun fire.

"In the chance that this may happen. I have only had to use it once. Maybe I will soon say *twice*."

"Yet with all the walking above it, don't you fear a collapse."

"There is not much walking above. Besides, I spend hours down here shoring it up. I even use water, and mud-cake, and cement, when available, to solidify the walls and ceiling. And I reinforce it regularly. Come now, we'll take the easy way back and sip the whiskey."

"And the people who live here?"

"They know. But they are Batila's family and, so, trustworthy."

Trustworthy. Like me?

■ Where's Wahid When I Need Him?

April 1969

The conversation with Jean did not go well. "Where can I go to find Wahid and his followers?"

"He will come to you, as he always does."

"But I have urgent news for him. I must see him immediately. I'm told he is not at the Wadi, though most of his troops have returned there."

"Then I will get the news to him."

I was getting a bit frustrated. "Via your Arab telephone? It will be completely garbled before he receives it."

"Ah, Monsieur, you don't trust me?"

"Not at all the case. I do trust you, but not the system."

"I do not know the exact location, Monsieur."

"You can guess it then."

"I would not even attempt to guess, Monsieur."

"You could at least give me hints, Jean."

"I would not know how to make a hint, Monsieur."

I knew that once he started throwing in the Monsieurs—with regularity—that the discussion was closed. I would have to approach Wahid himself—myself.

April 16, 1969

 Aaron,

  Yes, I'm fine. I may be coming home sometime soon.
I guess mom and dad will be thrilled. My ~~employers~~
employer won't be. I think it's caused by the content of
these returned letters. Supposedly lending credence to the
notion that I am CIA. Imagine that!
  So I'm waiting for a shoe (or two) to drop—which
is an appropriate metaphor since, among the Bedouin
Arabs, a sign of anger and insult is to throw your shoe at
the despised one. They would throw them in this land,
as well, but shoes don't come cheap around here, and few
can afford to lose them.
  I'll try again with this one, this letter, and see what
happens.

 Your brother, Harry

■ Plot in the Making?

 I got back to the remains of my *kaz* from *Père* Habert's in relatively short order. Night had fallen, and Alexandru had the two petrol lamps lit. Or Jean had.

 I was startled to find Akhween of the *kh* uvular (or is it velar, fricative?) and Alexandru deep in conversation. In French. "I . . . am I interrupting something? Should I wait outside?"

 "Not at all, 'arry. We are planning our trip north. Akhween has found a solution and volunteers."

 "Volunteers? How convenient. Why not Modou?" I was slightly perturbed, but couldn't think of a good reason why I should be. Unless I wanted to give Modou a chance to get out of town a bit. Get some sunshine. Get jumped by Wahid, and such.

"I didn't ask him," Alexandru answered. "I think I would do better with a native, one who speaks their language naturally and natively."

He moved smoothly to another concern. "Well, of course they'll want to be paid. Unfortunately, these gentlemen have no bank accounts so, we figure, I'll have to have money orders sent from Djemélia. Meanwhile, I have given them a down payment. All that is left to me." I wondered what he had to trade.

It was only when I saw them later that I realized the two escorts would be Saghir and Abdelsalam. But I didn't warn Alexandru—perhaps because I was still peeved with him for my not being included in the planning of, or reason for, his trek. I did not remind him that his escorts most likely had killed Lièvre and Santiago. And, almost, me.

Abdelsalam. Whose French was shaky. And Saghir. Whose brain was shaky.

07/06 03:16:WTF:ALXDRUJOURNYG4ORE:WI2WAHID*I*BA DGUYS:HH:STOP

■ Another Warning

At first light, he was already there, our *imam*. Or is he an *ulema?*—a man of great learning? So he clapped before coming to our doorstep. His intelligence system seemed to me to be uncanny. Not your Arab telephone.

And so he began his "homily":

"*B-ismi-llāhi r-raḥmāni r-raḥīmi.* Do not go there, *Nasarah.* Not there. Not up and down the rolling dunes to Faya. It will change your life forever. Forever. Or you will have no life. No life, *Nasarah.* The sand will burn your eyes. Your tongue will dry up and wither, for there will be no water—even if you take plenty enough with you. The easy things—your very breath—will be no more. Go to your home. Thus have I spoken. *Allahu akbar.*"

Spoken to me, meant for Alexandru, I guessed. He may have

thought he was being merciful. He could not in good conscience allow the *Nasarah* to go off into the fierce and deadly desert (the so-called "desert of death"), not without this forewarning. Thus had he so spoken.

Allahu akbar!

■ More Signs and Portents

April 1969

Not two days later Alexandru stumbled into the forecourt and collapsed into the sand and gravel. We lifted him to a chair, cleaned his sand rash and the blood where sweat kept it from drying, and waited.

He resumed breathing normally, then told this tale. "I believe the escorts Akhween arranged for me were those same teenage brigands you once pointed out—the ones who had killed Lièvre and his partner. I should have remembered your warning.

"We had gone about sixty kilometers with these Wahidi escorts, when a dozen others, Janjawid by their headpieces, appeared in a cloud of dust. There seemed to be many more on the hills—at the horizon. They grabbed our camels and bags of water. Of course, they mounted my Land Rover. To steal it as well. My so-called escorts joined with them, firing their rifles everywhere and yelling a torrent of words where only 'Wahid,' 'Wahidi' and 'Janjawid' were discernible to me—and then rode off."

It seems that Wahid had used the Janjawid as messengers—to signal to the two escorts to do their worst and return to the gathering Wahidi encampment. Akhween may have set it all in motion. Or Boudin. Or both. They might have been intending to kill Alexandru and steal from him.

"The idiots shot our camels—who made a frightening, anguishing, groaning racket." So Alexandru adorned himself with the blood of a wounded camel, played dead, and, after their cursory search, the Janjawid took what very little money he carried, then took the millet, and took the unharmed horses and camels as well. After that, they lost interest and rode off. Toward Dar es Sabir or, more likely, to one of the many Wahidi encampments nearby. The gang up on the hills followed parallel to them.

When they were all of them gone, Alexandru rode a screaming, wounded camel, the only one still living, until it collapsed about twenty kilometers from Dar es Sabir. Then he was fortunate to be found by a group of Bedouins who took him to Dar es Sabir and who shared their water and a camel.

He was fiercely sunburned, breathing with difficulty, but still coherent. He was lucid enough to borrow money from me to pay the Bedouin, who were waiting patiently just outside the forecourt, since his little money had been taken by the thieving Wahidi and Janjawid.

It was obvious, when he began rambling more, that he was succumbing to heat exhaustion. We tried to get him to lie quietly in my bed. He rambled on for a while.

"It's all right," he said. "My people are used to such disappointments. And, remember, we are the people who always keep a bag packed. Always at least one bag packed. For our inevitable need to escape. Everywhere we are.

"So next time we will approach the Faya from the northern side. From Libya. Or Algeria. Anyway, had I succeeded in getting to our destination, I would have been likely stranded and victim of someone, maybe even of these Palestinians. . . . Don't write a report on me," he asked of me.

So that's when I was sure Alexandru's brains were getting scrambled—by the roasting sun and the life-threatening trauma. "There will be other ways, other times. . . ." he mumbled. Then he fell into a troubled sleep.

I paid the Bedouin with the month's salary I had just received from my own HQ.

As Alexandru slept, I pondered these events. I wondered if Boudin might have orchestrated them—to delay or even finish off

Alexandru's search for . . . whatever it was. Yes, for uranium. Yes, his were the musings of the paranoid—or perhaps of one who sees clearly. And if that was Boudin's intention, it was successful, in a way.

Or maybe that Wahid, on his own initiative, had suddenly recalled Alexandru's "escorts." And sent for the Janjawid as well. Who only stopped for a moment before doing their patron's bidding? Wahid, calling for them, to begin preparations for the seizure of Dar es Sabir?

So I must think how to warn Ngokuru. Without actually warning him. That is, without all the details. Blame it all on the Janjawid? But enough information to free Alice and Amina. So I would tell him the story of Alexandru's encounter—skewed so that he might draw the "correct" conclusions from it. Unless he already knew.

Always trying to keep my ace. Always holding on to at least one thing. Yet my mind was still a spinning cauldron of conflicting assumptions.

"Prepare your militiamen for a likely Wahid attack in the coming days."

07/06 21:42:WTF:ATCKBYW@DARIMMINENT:MUST FLEE:HH:STOP

■ *Fatwa: A Ruling of the Wise*

April 1969

First it said, "*B-ismi-llāhi r-raḥmāni r-raḥīmi,*" on crumbled copybook paper.

Then it was launched: "*Asmanoon. [Hear us]—You are a strange and difficult people. You send soldiers to kill us by war or by disease. Then you send others to minister to our needs. Needs created by your very soldiers and greedy ones. Still, we starve and die in many numbers.*

"*Thus we banish all Nasarah from this place, this country, forthwith. Go to your home.*"

No clarification of what "this country" is. No mention of Emricani. Maybe we were exempted.

Maybe.

Who then betrayed us? Who would issue this *fatwa*? "Who issued this thing, Antoine?"

His eyes were shaded but their whites peered out at me from under his rakishly adjusted cap bill. He maintained that perpetual grin. "Who but the Wahid or his minions. . . . Perhaps our *imam*. He who is established as an *ulema*, a legal scholar, as well. I am but the messenger. I did not see who delivered this to my doorstep."

He of the black *jalaba*? I doubted that. More likely the *imam's* assistant—he who was so disgusted that I couldn't even make the *Shahadah*. "Why?"

"Ah, *Nasarah* Américain, you must ask me such things?"

"How shall we be protected then?" So the pincer was closing in. Look what I had wrought. The insurgents—Wahidi—had called me out and the militia soldiers were convinced I was with the insurgents. Who knew what the army thought? A fine cock-up, this.

"There is no way out, but that you too must go away from here," I urged him.

He did not see it all. "No. . . . Listen, Mons . . ." Antoine began.

". . . the children. . . ." I emphasized.

"We ourselves will care for them!" He too was emphatic. "We are the police chief now and must watch over them!"

"The camel soldiers will recruit them, or the Janjawid will kidnap them, turn them into murderers and rapists!" I was soon caught up in my little paroxysm of fury. I could see that my behavior and my words shocked Antoine, but I could not forbear. "Monsieur *le chef* Antoine, let's take them out now. Take them away from here, down to Albri, or to the caves in the Jumeaux. . . ."

"And you think they wouldn't search us out there?" he interrupted. "That those Naringar who live in those caves could be trusted? That they wouldn't go running to the camel soldiers? Or Wahid? Or both?"

"Then where?" In fact, we hadn't seen any Naringar in the caves or nearby. Perhaps he was only testing me. Testing my veracity.

He neatly dodged that question. "But I would be aiding you in kidnapping them." Still the half grin, and his face at that angle, as if looking up to me. As if I were of greater height. And, thus, his better.

"Just tell me where and I will do it alone." Or with the help of Leonard and Godin. I hoped.

Antoine seemed to read me well. "The other Américains would come to your aid? They would risk this?"

"I don't know."

I did not.

■ One More Time; One More Try

May 1969

The message I did not want to receive:
WTF:OSREMAININPLCE:LN:STOP

I took these messages, the statements and responses, to Habert for his inspection and, I hoped, his concurrence. "I would not have sent these quite yet. Ha! Not yet, though it may be time for you to go. Despite your HQ's admonishment." That's all he offered.

Then I had one more conversation with Antoine. The one I felt would be the clincher.

He gave me the opening. "The winner of this war will need police," he assured me, and perhaps himself as well. Again he turned his head to the side and bent his knees slightly. To effect subordination, and as if he were looking up to me? "They will need a chief such as me even more—to keep the order. To protect the children."

"If the Wahidi and Janjawid win, they will impose their own order. They will make their own laws including the *Sharia*." I emphasized the *Sharia* part. "They will appoint their own policemen who will certainly not be trained in France." Or in traffic management.

"So they will," he agreed. "But, still, I am chief."

"Are you prepared to enforce the *Sharia?*" I asked him, as if in challenge or reprimand.

"I do not know that body of law."

"Antoine. . . ."

"Yet, though I am not so prepared, I will learn it."

"Instead, come with us."

Out of character, Antoine let fall this propensity to be obdurate, and decided immediately and firmly that he would go with us. [Note from Aaron Hamblin: I'm not sure where in the chronology this belongs, so I'm inserting it here.] Of course, I would realize it later. It was Alain who spoke to me, and who would travel with us. Alain, Wahid's *almlak alaswd*. I should have recognized him. [End of insert.]

■ *Yondo*

"It is *Yondo*, Monsieur 'arry. Our test to join manhood." I thought that in our world there is a test for manhood also done with many cuts—the fight or flight—mostly of the mental kind of . . . of tests. For example, much like our American football or SATs. So Younis had his test as well.

"*Yondo?*"

"The beginning. Our beginning. When we are welcomed into and become to manhood."

"And, then?"

"We must all go. All of us."

"All of you?" I guess I was being unduly persistent.

He nodded. "But I have no father to 'deliver' me."

"Can I 'deliver' you then?"

His eyes lit up but he gave me no answer. I pursued a different angle. "So all of your tribe receive those scars that represent *Yondo*."

"All of them." Younis was very certain.

"Then how is it that there are at least two men among the militia recruits who speak at least some Sara-Ngumbaye but bear only two scars on each cheek. Only two such scars." I was thinking of Akhween as well as that recalcitrant recruit, Adin Azuku Vincent.

"It is not possible." He was emphatic and certain. "Unless they are perhaps very young Ngumbaye like me."

"I saw it with my own eyes."

"Then they are not of us."

"Indeed?"

He turned away as he puzzled over this anomaly. Then he repeated with greater certainty, "They must not be of us."

"How is that?" I pressed.

"Then they are spies for the Wahidi. Probably Narangar posing as Sara. To fool the recruiter who might not know. As Merry Men who had infiltrated those who were attending the festivities." He turned back to look at me—with that look of certainty and finality. Plus, proud of the reference to Robin Hood that he had made.

"Who look and speak somewhat like a Sara, Sara-Ngumbaye?" I pressed even more. "Is it possible?"

"Yes. It must be."

So, confirmation. That there *were* spies in the ranks. As I already knew. Spies for Wahidi. Spies who may now be excised. If, or when, I tell Ngokuru. It may even accelerate their demise.

Or ours.

■ *La Notion Américaine*—Part II . . . or So

May 1969

La Notion Américaine, The American Idea—Part II. This peace overture got right to the point. That is, the fair (Notion Part I), having failed to pacify the two sides (a naive notion, he once said), it was more essential than ever to arrange a truce meeting between the two sides.

I made the proposal to the half-juiced dancers at the next Saturday night soirée.

"The fair and race did not bring peace," I began.

"You can say that again!" someone piped up.

"So I believe we must arrange a truce between the two sides, and a peace conference between their leaders." I thought that was a reasonable *notion*.

All the while, the *imam* was happy that the crazy dancing had halted, and he was able to collect more *zakat*, the charity (from those who would be made to feel guilty in their drunken state), at this more calm and subdued town party. (Unlike the other, wilder *soirées*.) At the same time whispering and nodding something.

"Good luck on that one!" I guess that call-response guy was feeling Douze Marches but good.

"I propose arranging such a meeting. What do you say?" It was as if I was asking for a show of hands.

Not too many hands showed. Only a few brave souls. Perhaps touched by the Douze—or other substances.

"OK. Who will approach Colonel Ngokuru with this proposal?"

"Why don't you do it, *Américain*?" Same guy. Probably loaded.

"Why don't you?" I was tempted to respond. But instead, "I am not well liked by the colonel. He would refuse my ideas."

"I can see why," the smart-ass popped up.

"I will approach Wahid if someone will take on the colonel," I offered.

That's when a voice from the back announced, "I will." It was Lieutenant Vincent in civies. Lieutenant Vincent of the Leper village burning. "I have the colonel's ear more than anyone." As well he should—the colonel having a soft spot for ears.

■ Spies Abound . . . in Battalions

I also put in the next message that there was at least one, maybe two, Wahidi spies in the colonel's battalion.

07/08 03:20WTF:2WAHDSPIESNMILITIA:HH:STOP

If the *Third Para* was truly reading our messages, they will have learned that the Wahidi are informed of Ngokuru's intentions, and will ambush the militia force sent to Wadi Abyud the next time. They will inform Ngokuru, and so the militia and their colonel, knowing this, will abort that mission. And that is exactly what the militia did.

Brilliant! Sometimes I can be a quick study.

Instead, they took hostages for *real* this time. No more house arrest for Alice. (The missionaries' plan to spring her had been foiled.) A real jail cell now. The other hostage seized by the militia was Amina. Bad choice. I thought we could not negotiate in this manner.

So the Wahidi did likewise. I confess that I may have suggested that approach to Wahid. A hostage for a hostage. Bad idea.

The situation became crazier. Like all things in this country, things became exaggerated. One always had to be two and two was always four. And so on.

We tried to negotiate, but no one could find a counterpart to negotiate with. Ngokuru had officially arrested Alice and Amina. To be tried and judged. Another bad choice. (He didn't take Miriam, so it might not have been *me* he was pissed off at.)

In retaliation, I suggested that Wahid take a hostage as well. Wahidi captured Terry *and* Joe when they once again attempted to rescue their poles, satellites, and doo-dads by going out via the northern road. Captured when they arrived back at the northern gates—having torn back as they were shot at by those ruffians. Terry's usual luck. Unintended consequences for all of us.

"Our third attempt should be charmed," I could imagine Terry saying to Joe. "Three times must be a charm." But three times were no charm for him.

Nor for Modou either, I might have added. Who likewise could no longer go up the Jumeaux and back.

And for all this, I realized I was no practiced diplomat.

■ Diplomacy in Action

May 1969

Then Ngokuru changed his mind about throwing Alice into a cell, but kept her under house arrest. In Modou's house. Safe for Alice. I was still furious about the taking, blamed myself, and hoped for a quick and easy solution—that would release her. I guess I hoped for a Wahidi victory at first, although I realized that, given the Janjawid-Wahidi alliance, she could be taken even further from a safe return.

So I insisted on seeing Ngokuru, finally succeeded, and tried another tack. Anger. "Look, Alice as a hostage isn't going to get you anywhere, since neither she nor I can help you find Wahid. Why don't you form a small band of trackers? Do what you did at the Zenig Etnin, the Leper village. Make villagers somewhere tell you. Burn their entire village if they won't?"

"I don't know. You are beginning to sound like me, *Corps de la Paix*. Also, I've heard that the Lepers are now encamped with the Janjawid. We may have contributed to that alliance. Plus, those fuckers don't care who they ally with." I wasn't sure if he meant the lepers or the Janjawid. "But we don't want to anger other villages and so increase the rebel forces."

"You would be better off threatening to try someone the Wahidi care about. Someone Wahid cares about. Who would then force others to give up the information? Someone he or they love," I added.

"And who would that be?" he asked but already knew very well.

"Perhaps it is, indeed, Amina bint Mohammed al Jema'a." There. I said it. In the open and with emphasis. There it was. My choice. Alice over Amina.

"Interesting idea. As you may know, I already have Amina under arrest." The eye-twitch was gathering steam. It seemed to be going even more rapidly. Definitely eighth-note timing—if that was possible. "Under the watchful eye of Alain."

"On what pretense? Your wife-to-be?" I asked.

He was taken aback by that suggestion. Or that I suspected it.

But I pushed on with my previously formed justification or, rather, my tendency to slide into sarcasm. "Indeed. She is of the same tribe as Wahid. Even a close relative? Is she not therefore suspect as a traitor or spy? Isn't she likely to know Wahid's current location? Did you not have Alice held for the same accusations—betrayal and suspected Say Ee Ah?" There I was, myself, in full betrayal mode. Though it was destined to happen, I told myself.

To rescue Alice.

■ Beggars' Symphony

May 1969

His eye was a symphony of twitching. "Interesting idea."

I held my breath.

"You know, in the end we have all our own people at heart. Really, 'amblin. It is for their own good that we face off the bandits."

"By burning off their villages? By killing their afflicted ones?" I should have kept my mouth shut.

"Enough." He slammed the flat of his open hand on the interrogation table. "We killed no one!"

"A goat. And two, rendered earless." I guess I couldn't help myself.

"No location information from you, no yellow hair. Your decision."

"I have no more information to give you," I said. Stupid outburst. Weak supplication. At that moment I realized that, had it not been for my nationality or, perhaps, the color of my skin, I would have suffered a more rigorous and painful interrogation.

Adin Azuku Vincent, my diplomat assistant when we rescued the two couples, was sent to Ngokuru as the spy. I was told that, under duress, he insisted he had not been alone. He insisted that Akhween and perhaps "another" were his partners in spying. But I am also told that people will say anything under torture.

To stop the symphony of pain.

■   Yet Another Visit: His Visit

May 1969

As for me, I waited for my night visitor. Jean or Ali would facilitate it. And sure as the blue moon will eventually rise, he appeared behind my back-court some evenings later. In the shadows. Behind the first dune. Carbine resting on his thighs as he sat in the sand.

"What is this good news I'm told you have for me?" he asked, without the *pro forma* salutations. He seemed unusually pressed for time.

I, on the other hand, tried to stick to protocol. "*Salaam aleikum*, Sidi Wahid. It has been a good moment since I saw you. I trust you and all about you are well. I am glad you could come here to meet with me."

"Then what is this thing I must know?" He rolled his carbine nervously on his thighs.

"That the colonel wishes to speak with you. To negotiate a cease-fire. To determine a way to preserve the town and protect its citizens from devastation." I tried to sound calm and at ease.

"He should have thought of that before the burnings and the killing of my beloved cousin, and the attempts to murder us."

"He claims he did not kill Rashid. That Rashid blew himself up. With the grenades you had given him to show off with." I was astonished that he could so reverse the story. "I saw the dead ones myself. Perhaps I was targeted as well."

"He lies. The colonel's officers beheaded him and then blew up your *kaz*. Probably at the Colonel Ngokuru's orders. Or the army's." His veil was up. His eyes flashing. Flashing more anger than I had ever seen.

"With their comrades inside? Two of them were also killed." I was beside myself. Amazed at his stubborn denial.

"Yes, they would indeed effect such a conspiracy, even against their own. I am told the three survivors were the camel militiamen.

The two inside, therefore, regular army. It is so. A *Nasarah* would not understand this."

"Unlike you, Sidi Wahid, the colonel must take his orders from the President of the Republic. Who sees the oil under the burnt-out *arrondissement* as a blessing. A blessing for the people." I tried to gather in and control my frustration. "Who sees you as bandits and thugs."

"We want our land, our province, back. Whatever may be beneath the ground. And to worship as we please."

And to accuse the Colonel Ngokuru for Rashid's death. And to have Amina.

"Then see if we can begin the process with a truce meeting with Colonel Ngokuru. Negotiate that you can worship as you please and have rule over the Faya Prefecture." I was making this up—making it up as we went along. Isn't that how it works?

"The *sous-préfet* would give us these things? Ngokuru would give us these things? Ha!"

I dodged the question. "Can I offer you drink or sweets?" I know it was a terrible segué, but it was all I could think of. "Or a taste of the *Nasarah's* tea?" Bad form?

"Now he has taken Amina, my betrothed," he carried on, as if we were still in full discussion on the previous topic.

"*Was* your betrothed," I corrected.

"You have betrayed her, and so all that we have had—the two of us." He extended his hand, palm up, to indicate me—not Amina. Perhaps he was reading more into the relationship between Amina and me than I expected. Or perhaps it was the relationship between him and me. I should assume it was the latter.

"You and me?" I must have enhanced his self-image, probably with the Robin Hood analogy. Or the "loan" of Moussa.

Veil slowly down. Sort of wandering down. "I have loved her and offered the bride-price to her parents. They died before they could accept it."

"I understand that they refused it." I was treading deep waters with him at this point.

Veil up. "They would have come around. They would have accepted it. As soon as I told them she is my beloved, my first-wife-to-be, as well.

"I must go back to our encampment. Now. I am told the militia are watching you. To pass your house from time to time. To follow you where you go. To see what you do. Spies are there, even among the ragged people." Who may have been enjoying our repartee. "Meanwhile, I will consult with my council. But now, before the militia come here, I must go."

"And I, with mine." I meant with Lieutenant Vincent. For, in reality, we still didn't have an agreement from the colonel.

Not yet.

■ Younis 14

May 1969

"So the fight began. Robin rushed to the gates on the stallion where, after arrows were shot at him—but missed—and a brief sword fight ensued, the guards there were overcome. He then opened the tunnel entrance, and Will Scarlet crawled out from outside the castle wall."

"Why did Will go through the tunnel? Where did he go, Monsieur 'arry?"

"Ah, that's the crux of it. For, in a short time, many, many other men began to pour in behind Will and then through the gates (once they were opened by the tunnel crawlers) into the palace yard."

"Who were the many others, then?"

"Why all the slaves, servants, and peasants from the surrounding towns and provinces."

"Why did they come?"

"Because they had been badly treated by the sheriff and his men. Like Robin, many saw their land and belongings stolen away. Now, Younis, the numbers and the fight were in Robin's favor. Gradually

Robin's men and the fellow slaves, servants, peasants, and yeomen took over the sheriff's palace."

"As will our beloved Wahidi," Younis nearly shouted out.

"As may our beloved Wahidi," I forced myself to respond—with no suggestion of skepticism.

"And then?" Younis was tapping his foot in anticipation.

"And then, instead of being arrested, Robin Hood and his Merry Men arrested the sheriff, and threatened to throw him into the dungeon. They freed the lady Marion and the friar, by peaceable negotiations. It was said that they had been treated well." I guess I was being more than forgiving towards the sheriff and his minions.

"And then the friar, the holy man, performed the ceremony that married Robin and Marion. After that, using the sheriff's festivity preparations for what was to be his marriage to Marion, they all celebrated. Later, Robin was rewarded with a knighthood, a special honor, by the king, returned from his own adventures (who had a quarrel with the sheriff as well.)"

"And . . .?"

"What if Robin really just wants his land back? He could care less about the other dispossessed or the lawmen, who were said to have treated Marion and the friar well. What if all this were true, Younis?" I couldn't resist inserting a bit of my own skepticism at this point. A hint of my developing belief in likely motivations.

"Then I would not follow him . . ."

"Well, we can't be sure how this story ends. So this is our end of this story. Any way that you want it to end. You make your own end."

"Then I would have a happy ending. A happy ever after."

"Me too! You are surely Younis le bon Coeur! And there are many songs about Robin's heroism.

"But there are many more such stories! I have this book of all these other stories about Robin Hood, and other heroes. *The Black Knight, The Count of Monte Cristo,* and many others. But, like you, I must work, and don't have time to tell them all to you. You will have to read them yourself."

Younis looked troubled. "Still, I will be there to help you," I assured him. *I will be there, if our escape plan is successful.*

■ Negotiations

June-July 1969

The negotiations for the time, place, and manner of the truce meeting were argued at length. Wahid did not want to move the encampment nor show it to the enemy, and Ngokuru did not want to go too far from the town. So, at my suggestion, a place halfway to the Wadi Aswad was finally chosen.

I suggested that masses of men from each side could eventually result in a full-fledged battle. So it was agreed that only the principal and his second would be present. It was like taking a page from the Dueling Code of the seventeenth or eighteenth century. And I would be the intermediary—if needed.

The date didn't matter so much, except that Wahid insisted on using the Muslim lunar *Hijri* calendar. So we compared it with the Gregorian calendar, year from our Lord's birth to year from *Hajj* (when Mohammed reached Medina)—month of *Muharram* (a month when no war is permitted unless one is attacked), which Ngokuru would respect. Then we did the appropriate math, 1969 to 1385 (I thought), and dates of the rising moon, and eventually settled on corresponding dates.

All this entailed running back and forth between principals and *imam*s with suggestions and requests. (From all who lent us the wisdom of propitious dates.) Again, I was the middleman. So I consulted *Directeur* Partenay for some time off to perform these tasks. Also, Ngokuru was said to have consulted his ancestors and the *griots*.

If all this can be done, why not peace between these two parties? Anyway, the Wahidi had to wait until *Muharram* ended for the battle to commence. So during that month might be a good time to have peace talks.

I thought I was getting better at this negotiation and peace making stuff, and I was feeling heady.

But I also had no doubt that, soon, I would be given to realize that those heady feelings are not meant to last.

Meanwhile, on the ninth and tenth of Muharram, the most orthodox Moslem students were spitting into their cups. Fasting. So as not to swallow even their own saliva. The cups were on their desks. But the spit often close to, or in, my eyes.

As the practice of the fast demands.

◼ The Truce Meeting

May 1969

The time and day of the peace meeting came. From meeting detail negotiations to this point, there were no incidents. All was quiet. I was feeling the peace talks were going to go well. Signs and portents? Quick study, me?

The parties arrived, mounted, principals and their seconds. The Wahidi black flag with white "Akbar" and red drop, and the militia's white flag of truce. Wahid's second was that dope Saghir, who nearly got Alexandru killed and probably killed Lièvre and Santiago—because he couldn't interpret the meaning of *lâche* in context. Ngokuru's was Lieutenant Vincent of the leper storehouse-burning, ear-taking, potion-consuming, and potion-gagging.

The two principals grappled with their hands, each as if the other one had a communicable disease. Finally, hesitatingly, they shook hands. Weak start.

Mounted on Omar, I stayed back out of hearing range, and the wind picked up and made the hearing even more difficult. The interaction seemed to be picking up as well—more movement and animation. Whoops! More angry gestures.

As things seemed to get more heated, they signaled to call me over. Both of them. Simultaneously. Not a good sign.

Wahid first exclaimed, "He will not free Amina as a sign of goodwill."

Ngokuru responded, "Not until you give us the spy in our ranks. The second one."

Wahid: "I must deny there is such a spy. But even if there were such a one, I could not condemn my brother to be *Yekbaré*. Or worse."

Ngokuru: "How can we have peace, if the movements of the militia are always known? And then acted upon? Besides, if you are granted your prefecture, your spy might soon be freed from Yekbar."

Me: "You must, each of you, give up something." I tried to pronounce the cliché forcefully. I guess I hadn't thought this part through.

Wahid: "But, it is he who provoked Rashid, antagonizing him, and so led to his death!"

Epithets followed. Louder. More forceful.

Ngokuru (interrupting): "But . . . I wasn't even there . . . I did not provoke. It is he who enabled the execution of Lièvre and Santiago!" More epithets. Even more forceful.

There was much anger. If their cheek skin had been of a lighter hue, they would have been red with fury.

Me: "You must compromise." I pronounced it in French and searched my mind frantically for the Arabic equivalent.

Wahid: "But not on this matter . . ." More epithets, even more forcefully shouted.

Ngokuru (interrupting): "But not to sacrifice . . ."

It has been noted that bad things and bad events are often the result of a moment's inattention.

So it was at that moment when the idiot Saghir, the Wahidi *mashutin* (the Wahidi nut case), the horse murderer, the assassin, the former owner of the Kansas City Athletics baseball cap, fired off his carbine. Lieutenant Vincent had only a pistol held in his right hand. That was the arm that the bullet smashed through. He dropped his pistol. Saghir, the nutcase, Kansas City Athletics fan looked surprised and shocked at what happened. Who? Me?

It was good fortune that it was not Ngokuru who had been wounded.

"I thought he was about to shoot you, O Lord Wahid," Saghir, the horse murderer or *mashutin,* or human murderer—take your pick—tried to justify his action.

Lieutenant Vincent was groaning and making intermittent screams. Somewhat histrionically I thought. There was a bit of blood. Maybe more than a bit.

"I must take the lieutenant back to the clinic," Ngokuru shouted. On the cusp of violent anger. "These discussions are finished." He leaned to put an arm through Lieutenant Vincent's left arm. To keep him steady. They wheeled and rode off. No pretense at salutation.

Wahid did the same with but a look of irritation—more like disgust—aimed at Saghir. I rode behind the colonel and lieutenant, tempted but not daring to ask when (if) we could resume these discussions.

As we galloped past the third or fourth dune, we heard a single rifle shot. I guess that was my answer.

Meanwhile, Lieutenant Vincent's blood decorated, then was swallowed by the sand.

I guess this diplomacy stuff is even harder than I thought.

■ Had I Lost My Way?

June 1969

Ultimately, I thought, it was my decision—Alice or Amina, Terry and Joe or Akhween. I was truly losing my balance. And, yes, I would fall either way. And get invited to leave. For the USA or Yekbar.

"We must choose," Wahid insisted. But he had already decided in favor of his cousin. Yet I realized that, for all my professed love for her, I could not . . . I would not choose her.

Wahid also had said many times that he would never give up his favored spy, Alain, who could move back and forth from Wahid encampment to Dar es Sabir—and, so, scoop up all the rumors and likely militia movements and plans, sometimes from his brother, sometimes *as* his brother—and did all Wahid's bidding. He was also one of the chosen snipers, though his shooting accuracy was reputed to be the same or worse than Antoine's.

I suggested giving up Adin Azuku Vincent's partner who had probably been "made" via Alain's talkative, rogue, kidnapper friends anyway.

"We must give them the spy," I argued with Wahid. "The spy is not of much use to you, as you have often said." The spy for Amina? But then what will the Wahid do with Terry and Joe who, never freed of their "captivity" inside Dar es Sabir, were now prisoners left to the mercy of the angry Wahidi. And Ngokuru is now left with Alice, to do with what he will, as I could only imagine.

So I was overtaken by events and paralyzed by the dilemma. A dilemma in part of my own making.

I drank my way through a good part of another bottle of Johnny.

■ Advisory Council (of the Roundtable)

Late June 1969

We gathered on the makeshift patio behind what was left of my *kaz*. Where I often tutored Younis. I brought out the surviving chairs and stools for them to sit on. I found myself in the middle of a half-circle of my friends, to ask their advice. Regarding my dilemma.

Chivalrous councilors of the round table.

I withheld booze until I'd gotten some sensible suggestions.

"What would you do?" I asked Godin.

"I would make bargain to insure that Alice and Amina are nourished, given shots, protected from disease. Also, for this, as Wahid wishes, the spies be given over and Amina could be freed.

Not Americans though. This would be for those two governments to negotiate at later time. Also make sure captives would receive vaccinations. And watch for venereal disease."

Big help. Note the self-serving politics of letting negotiations take place "at a later time." And what were the chances of contracting venereal disease?

"And thus abandon Terry and Joe to the custody and tender loving 'protection' of the Wahidi? Or even to Yekbar?" I asked.

"Rush them and kill the leader," counseled the *légionnaire capitaine*.

"And risk getting the hostages killed? What would you do *notre trés sage juge?*"

"I would see that the kidnappers are brought to trial."

"Perhaps, some day. But in the meantime, Terry, Joe, Adin Azuku Vincent, and Alice and Amina languish at their captors' mercy?" I responded.

"Yes, we often hold prisoners in jail before trial. No *habeas corpus* here. And if there were, no one would pay attention to it." From a national *juge*. Rumored to be in line for a ministerial post. *Ministre de la Justice*.

"So what would you do, Father O'Sagarty?"

"Administer last rites." If he hadn't offered up his broad, Irish grin, as well, I would have taken him at his word.

"You have a plan B?"

"Ah, Harry, you've encountered the central dilemma of our lives. That whatever path we choose, we are eventually met with debilitating consequences, we are. We have a saying in Ireland . . . but I can't recall it just now." He'd probably been tasting of his store of fine Irish libation before he got here—making him even more loquacious than usual.

"The dilemma is fourfold. It would have been bad enough if the two sides had kidnapped one to hold hostage, but each has taken two. Why is that? And of the four hostages, they are all innocent of any wrongdoing, are they not?"

I was getting pissed, as I usually was when Sean O'Sagarty began his "mystery" responses.

". . . And that is the central dilemma or mystery itself. We are, none of us, innocent. All are conceived in sin. Some of us are thus punished before others. The so-called 'innocents' may meet our Lord and Maker first, but will receive the greatest rewards." He must have prepared this recitation in advance. Or delivered it before today.

"Then what's the point, Sean?"

"Point of what?" He truly didn't know the intent of my question.

"Point of living and trying to help our fellow man." I was starting to get really pissed off.

"Yes, that is the great dilemma itself, isn't it? The point is a mystery known only to the Lord and his Son." Boy, he could sure spin a story.

"We just went round in a vicious circle. The point can't be known, and that's the point?" If it hadn't been for the greater problem, I'd be really getting furious at his disingenuous double-talk.

"That's the reason for the need for faith. If you had it, you would understand these things."

"How does that help my friends?"

A histrionic shrug.

Big help.

"What would you do, Modou?"

"Give me Scotch before I answer," he ordered. Then a rueful, but unfathomable, smile. I broke my own rule and brought out a bottle. He drank a large swig, pulled himself straight up in his chair, and answered (the others eyed the bottle longingly). "I would lie to each side and tell Wahid that Ngokuru wanted the other spy, call him Spy B. I would then tell Ngokuru that Wahid wanted Amina freed.

"You know that both will do the contrary. Wahid will free Terry instead. Ngokuru will free Alice."

"But under flag of truce, each leader would know that they had been duped. Terry would not pass for Spy B nor Alice for Amina," I pointed out.

"Hope that Alice wears the *Hijab* or headscarf. That Terry wears his usual baseball-type cap with the bill well pulled down on his head, as the spy may often do. Or, better yet, a blue veil as a Tuareg would do.

"Arrange it so that Terry and Alice are too far away when they're freed to be recognized. Perhaps at separate banks of the Wadi Abuyad. Give each one a place marker for the prisoners to go to. Where the liberated ones would have to climb around dunes. Riders, who know not what to look for other than the expected gender, would go out to rescue each one behind a dune and take them back to their respective organizations. Meanwhile, attendants for each side would be retreating. By the time the two leaders saw the truth, it would be too late. They would be 'stuck' with the *fait accompli*."

"You may never cease to amaze me," even though I thought this plot was a bit—maybe even totally—off the wall.

It seemed to me that he took a slight bow.

"So, my colleagues. What do you suggest?"

"That we buy Wahid off?" Michel answered. "Surely CFA. Or dollars. To buy arms."

"I doubt that. Though he might be tempted, he could not accept money now that he has made his demands known. Not in front of the Wahidi," I answered. Then "Victor?"

And Victor neatly summed it up. "Call out the *Troisième Parachutistes*."

The other suggestions were even less useful. Even when later plied with "Russian tea." Or Scotch.

It was good that Partenay was not there.

■ Diplomatic Negotiation, Diplomatic Results

July 1969

We finally freed Alice by continual "negotiations." I had to throw in the ace I had been holding for a critical need—I surmised that this was the "critical need." So Ngokuru freed Alice, and Wahid, Terry.

For I had also reminded Ngokuru that, "If not, you and your militia battalion will feel the full weight of the United States Government. On you. Here." I think the reminder of the C-130 helped.

I had been saving that one. I tried to include Amina in the deal, but Ngokuru resisted. "She is not *Américaine*. The Ooo-es-Ah will not care about her captivity. Only Wahid will. And he must offer the spy in trade as well."

And so it was agreed to leave Alice and Terry (but not Joe) away from the camps or town. Nor at the place of truce. So they left them on the road to Albri. Towards the northwestern foot of Mt. Jumeux. Hog-tied, and much bruised, and bloodied.

Both were dumped to the ground by the militia and Wahidi. Disheveled and distraught. At least Alice had not been raped.

I think.

Thus they were freed. At first, neither would share in our usual banter. Perhaps blaming me for all these events. And they would be right. Both would seldom talk about their ordeal, and, then, only in the vaguest terms. And Alice was never as light-hearted nor as optimistic as before it.

She refused to decode her message—the lines *"I'll bet it's time for you to get a haircut. It is time! I'm sure of it. There is no better time! I'd like to give you one myself"*—to see if I got it right. She answered only that, if I didn't understand it, it was my loss. Whatever *that* meant. And I knew by her response that she would never again give me a haircut.

Alice insisted on going back the short way to Albri—immediately. To her *kaz*. To recover. Ali would serve as escort and interpreter. We would later come to get her there. (As Modou once had promised.) Perhaps by air.

But, as it happened, the road to Albri was also much blocked by Wahidi. So Ali brought her back to my place. But she opted to stay with Modou. And, thus, she might learn all his secrets.

Terry opined about Joe. I promised we would repatriate him.

And all this was not my first inkling that it would soon be our time to leave this place.

Soon.

The vise was closing.

■ Modou Comes Through

June-July 1969

"So you see, Harold," Modou had said, "That is the only place. This is our Plan B. If Plan A, the airlift out of Dar es Sabir to more friendly land, is not possible, we will go out via the mountains. The camel-mounted militia will fall back, as they must protect their rear from the Wahidi, and will only be able to follow us on foot—if at all. They may, however, send the Yekbar prisoners on foot and unarmed. Or lightly armed. We will have to outrun them. We will find water in the wadi in the cleavage on Jumeau and then, in the underground streams on the high plateau. And," he had added, "come, Harold, look into this." He had led me to a tiny, hidden entrance, where I had to stoop low to gaze into its green-black shadows. Maybe here is where we could sleep.

"That is the place," he then pointed southwest. "Out there, beyond the Jumeaux, is a great sandstone plateau with figures like statues and ancient cave drawings. Where a helicopter can land. The helicopter will pick us up there, southwest," he pointed toward the stone plateau, "then on to Djamé from where we can then find transport to Albri. To rescue Alice—if need be."

"Complicated. How do you know these things?" Perhaps he had a radio.

He chose not to answer. I had always been disturbed by his mystery. Noted that he never invited me but to the "courtyard" of his *kaz*. Never inside. To learn his secrets. It was as if each one of us had our secret. As if each one of us had been selected by our respective master to watch and verify the other one. But I didn't know which of us were so selected. Nor who I could safely lie to.

Instead, I asked, "Then why not go directly to Albri after we are aboard? Fly from here?" For Wahid had by then given Alice and Ali special dispensation—to pass to Albri—where she would pack her things and stand by for evacuation. So she did. By borrowed jeep that she used her charms to wrangle. [Note from Aaron Hamblin: I'm not sure where in the chronology this belongs, so I'm inserting it here.] *I later learned that Alice went to Albri, but unexpectedly returned. With all her suitcases. Brave girl!* [End of insert.]

"Because of this rebellion, it is said that the Janjawid have received heat-seeking anti-aircraft guns from the Russians in the environs of Albri. I think they are called SAM missiles. Also XM148 grenade launchers. So they are not permitting your aircraft to approach those places. C-130s might be able to outwit them. But not helicopters. Too slow and even too predictable."

"Why helicopters at Ennedi then?" I asked.

"Because of the dunes, rock monuments, and sand, a C-130 can't land there and certainly can't take off from there. But heat-seekers are not within range yet," he answered—with certainty, as if he had been apprised of these things beforehand. Quite sometime beforehand.

"Amazing! No electricity to inhabitants, but state-of-the-art weaponry!"

"Indeed, Harold."

"Then you or they will not risk leaving *us*, but you will, Alice. She is expendable!"

Modou looked blank for a moment. Then "Better rescue the most than only one."

"Better some men than an intelligent, resourceful, beautiful, woman? Whose choice? This sequence of rescue?" But I was immediately sorry that I had said this.

"Oh, Harold." And his features were more rueful than usual. But then he returned to a more commanding attitude. The stronger version of Modou. "You must apologize!" he commanded.

"I'm so sorry. Then we'll go out of the country from Djamé? Via Djemélia International Airport?" I rattled on, playing out the scenario to cover my indiscretion. "We can disguise as aid workers to board a Red Cross plane out to the Cameroons."

"Ah, you have no passports with visas. They are being held by the *Département de l'intérieur et de tourisme*. But we can be managing a relatively small plane. Or, perhaps, a C-130 with Red Cross supplies. Even so, they will have to come in from a great height, straight down, to confuse the heat-seekers. First from Djemélia to Albri, then back to Djamé. Then we can sneak you out of here, perhaps on that same C-130. That is Plan C, the Djemélia plan."

"And straight up upon exiting?"

"Of course."

"And you?"

"I must remain in Djemélia." He did not look too happy about this prospect. "The consequence of my life that has been a total fuck-up." Now I understood better why he gave me the parchment to hold onto.

"What about Omar, Kalb, and even Chien?" I was giving myself time to think.

"They have no visas either, Harold. Or even passports," he said, smiling again, though again ruefully. "Nor permits. We must let them go in the valley at Ennedi or, better, in the fields here or around the airport in Djemélia."

I made no protest but would deal with Kalb, at least, later. I would not sacrifice him as I had Moussa.

"So, it is understood," I said. "We will take Hank and Earl's C-130 to Djemélia.

"Failing that plan A, we will execute Plan B. It sounds like you have planned this well," I said to cover my frustration. I could not fathom all of us, host country nationals and *Nasarah*s, achieving that mountain. On foot.

"You see, Harold, our embassy and organizations are caring for you. And perhaps for me."

"Of course for you. And, as for Plan B, I will lead on the escape and ascent, and you will then lead us out from the summit of Jumeaux, through the descent, and out to the destination—the great sand monuments." So we made the plans—Plan A (by plane) and Plan B (on foot)—almost a by-the-way exercise. How to make a precipitous exit without being seen by one side or the other? Since we didn't know who was most likely to be gunning for us.

Thanks to *Père* Habert. And for his tunnel for escape—Plan B. Also, thanks to the decoys, though they might not understand that they were decoys—Father Sean O'Sagarty and his flock.

"Better rescue the most than only one."

WTF:ASKHANKEARLFLYUSTOMECCA714:HH:STOP

I had bypassed Habert's consent with this message. The *Third Para* would relay it to him.

Yet, still, for the actual escape from Djemélia, there was no thought-out plan C.

■ The Day Before the Planned Departure— Without the Students

July 1969

They somehow knew. And at the end of classes one day, the 21st of Muharram, they gathered around me so that I could not escape. Of course, with all that had been said and done, I panicked at first.

"*Monsieur le professeur,*" a student of the *quatrième* intoned. He advanced toward me with a mysterious package in hand. I reflexively retreated a step or two. Shades of Rashid. He continued until we were face-to-face and, practically, foot-to-foot. "*Monsieur le professeur,* we are not able to go with you. But we will remember you always. And we will remember the English. . . ."

"As strangely as you may speak it."

"Ah, yes, as strangely as we may speak it. Especially without your tutelage," he answered, without a moment's hesitation. "Please open this package. This is from all of us. A token of our appreciation. And we hope you will come back soon. As soon as this battle is ended. As soon as this war is done."

At that point, I opened the carefully wrapped parting gift, and took out the book. Weatherworn and much handled, but still in fine condition, and with the gold page-edging still not worn off. I opened it gingerly to discover a Koran with the Arabic on one side, the even-numbered pages, and the French translation on the face page, the odd-numbered pages. The Arabic was in a simple, *hijazi* script, readable for me.

I was truly moved by this gesture, and I think I showed it. The students, mostly Muslim, recited the *Shahadah* while in their circle around me. "Thank you," I said, with, maudlin as it may seem, a lump in my throat. "I will treasure this always."

And I will.

■ The Day Before the Planned Departure— *Sous-préfet* on his Knees (Figuratively)

A visit I least expected. Though I should have.

Early morning. I was in what was left of my *kaz* figuring out what to pack and what I must give up. There wasn't much left to plow through after the explosion. Still, at that moment, I was contemplating whether to ship or to give up the fertility statue, the woman on a birthing stool with a corn-eating monkey on her head, when the least expected happened. The *sous-préfet* appeared at the broken doorway with his minions, those who seemed perpetually at odds with the world. Or at least with the *Nasarah* world. He commanded his minions to stay outside, but came himself through the former doorway. Into my former bedroom, where I was packing. Or, rather, determining which artifacts to box and send by post to Cleveland.

"Excuse me, Monsieur *le professeur*," he began, in a near whisper. "I must speak with you." I assumed he meant me, though his eyes seemed to focus, through his Coke-bottle glasses, on the remnants to my right. He was festooned in his most beautiful robes of purest azure.

"Please. I can invite you to sit, but on my bed, since only it survived the explosion." Of course, I wanted him to feel some guilt for the bombing. At least a failure of rigorous policing by his administration.

He sat. Stared beyond me, to my right, as he gathered his thoughts. "I must go to Djemélia on government business," he finally said. So he knew or guessed well that Djemélia was our destination.

"Of course," I replied in my most diplomatic tone.

"There are no commercial planes flying, and all roads have been blocked by the bandits."

"Yes," I said in a noncommittal near whisper.

"But it is said that you depart tomorrow for Mecca."

"We shall." Still noncommittal and in a stage whisper.

"By plane, or that you will travel over the Jumeaux on foot."

"We shall."

"Then . . . ." And here it was obvious he was having difficulty getting the words out.

"Yes?" I asked in my only effort to help him.

"May I join your pilgrims then?"

"Are you planning to bring Lady Fatima with you?" I had to ask.

He thought this one through. Perhaps trying to decide. To decide which answer would be best. Then, "Only me."

"None of your efficient, diplomatic, and friendly assistants?

"None of them."

"Then it is yes, but with a condition." Now I was on a roll. "You must use your high-level influence to insure that we—those of us who choose or are chosen to go—insure that we can fly out with the next American AID or other flight, avoiding inconveniences of passports and other papers. To Cameroun. Or Sudan. Or other neighbor. Can you do that?"

"I will do my best," he replied.

"Your best must be to so ensure our departure," I hammered in a louder voice. "No excuses!"

"I will."

"Or stories of your dalliances and negligence will be spread."

"Yes. I will, Monsieur."

"Yes. And you will." So much for my first try at being a tough guy.

■ My Best (My Only) Gift

I rushed out to place the fertility statue, the woman on a birthing stool, as a shrine, in the stinking hut, his crypt. In front of the baby. An apt tribute which would remain long after the unnamed "he" was only bones. Blended with the rotten tomato soup leaking from its broken cans.

So I named him Mohammed. I remained there only to repeat the *Shahada* as fast as I could say it. To escape the crypt as fast as I could.

Very fast.

■ The Day Before the Planned Departure— Colleagues on Their Knees (Literally)

They also came in the early morning, Michel and Victor, as I was still packing my knapsack for tomorrow morning's escape. Rather, "escapade," as the *légionnaire capitaine* might say. They were looking a bit washed out and definitely in a supplicating mood.

"You must . . .," Michel began.

". . . take us with you!" Victor rushed in.

"If I say we're all full up?"

"You can't be," they both chimed in. In perfect harmony.

"All tickets sold. Plus this plane don't carry no ramblers, no thieves, no liars, no hightoned gamblers," I sang in English. This might be one definition of torture. Repayment for all those rapid blah-blah conversations, the contents of which I will never know.

"You can't be. There's always room for one more," Michel insisted.

"Yes, one more. But what shall I do about two more?"

Michel looked glum. Victor wasn't sure he got it, but snickered anyway.

"Together, the both of you choose which one," I added and went back to my packing.

They argued vehemently, each one attempting to indicate their greater value, hence their better worth to go with us.

"I am *militaire*."

"I too am *militaire*."

"I teach history and music."

"I do math and science."

"I can do all those things."

Michel repeatedly argued that Victor would take up the space of two by himself. Victor responded that Michel should not count since he could sit on his, Victor's, lap.

I let them go on a while as I worked to suppress a laugh. "All right," I relented. "But only if, when we're on foot, such as in Plan B, you take the rear guard to signal us if the Janjawid or Yekbari are coming. Or that you've been shot."

"We will. What is Plan B?"

"A hike over the mountains."

"I will even bring my old, but workable carbine," Michel offered.

It was agreed, and we sealed the bargain with a Johnny Walker. I was keeping Johnny in business these days.

■ The Day before the Planned Departure— without Ibrahim

"You should come with us. Yekbar inmates will be too occupied with looting still, and prison officials won't miss you for many days.

Especially, since I won't be asking for you. And I surely won't be. By the time you are asked for, you will be long gone." I was practically pleading with him. With Ibrahim, the prisoner.

"How do you leave?" he asked.

"Via plane or Jumeaux."

"Who goes with you?"

"Idriss family, three students who must escape because they are Sara-Ngumbaye, Alice (the teacher from Albri), the Isrea . . . Bulgarian, little Younis (the slave), Michel and Victor (the *professeurs*), plus Modou Chaterjee, our leader, perhaps the Russian doctor Ivan Godin, our Jean, perhaps the *légionnaire capitaine*."

He thought for a long moment. "All gentle to me. Even the royalty of Idriss. And you have been a gentle master."

"Good. I will supply you with *Nasarah* clothes that we can make fit. . . . Then you'll come with us." I was hopeful.

"I will not," he said firmly.

I was stunned. "W . . . wh . . . what have you got to lose?"

"I am in your debt," he reminded me.

"Then I owe you once more. In your world, I am now responsible for you." I knew I was starting to tear and red up. To surprise him with my emotion.

"Please master. That is Ngumbaye rule and law. I am not Ngumbaye. I will stay here." I could see he was intent. Perhaps playing on my ignorance of custom as well. "How do you go?" he asked.

I felt I had a flicker of hope. I explained the whole plan to him. Even the tunnel part of Plan B. My vocabulary, in this mélange of patois and Arabic, was weak in places, so I used hand and body language. I think he got the idea.

"Master, you will come out at the far end of the tunnel, at the lone, useless toilet before the path up the *jabal* of the two tits?"

"Yes." He knew his way around. More than I thought.

"Then they will surely see you, those of Yekbar or the Janjawid, or both, and chase you for your riches."

"We will have only the clothes on our backs and in our pack. We hope to make our way enough before they can catch up to us." I was beginning to doubt my own plan.

"At least one of you may have treasure as well. I will remain and fight them off."

"I . . . I cannot let you do this thing," I stammered. I could not imagine what he meant by "treasure," since we would have only our packs.

"You will be too far away to deny me," he said.

"You will surely be overwhelmed and killed by those thugs."

"I will surely hold them off and stop them from going forward. The *Yekbari* have no weapons."

"Why do you do this?" By now, I had forgotten my question about "treasure."

"I owe my soul and body to you. And your kindnesses to Moussa, though you could not save him. Besides, I am angry at the burning, at the militia, at the way they have recruited the inmates of Yekbar."

"Yet your shoulder has not healed," I tried, in desperation.

"I am well again. Totally so."

I could see he was determined in his decision. His decision to stay and, so, to die. I had never known one like that. "Then take tea with me."

He laughed heartily and said "Ah master, I would be pleased to take of the *Nasarah*'s tea, the Russian's tea, with you."

And so we did.

■ The Day before the Planned Departure— with or without Bernard Partenay

As always, the Deux Chevaux coughed and spit as it came around his courtyard to a sudden halt in front of me. No Fatima descended. Rather, only Partenay slid out to wish us well on the day before our rumored departure.

His lips twitched and his mouth moved in silent pantomime—as if, I thought, in supplication.

But when he spoke, he did so in a manner not previously known to me—in a voice barely above a whisper, and with a modicum of consideration. I could read it as an acceptance of his fate.

And no coughing in imitation of his Deux Chevaux, nor any rancid breath from too great a dose of wine or beer. "On your trip, I wish you well, Américain."

"And I, you, as well, Monsieur. I hope we go by plane so that you and Hélène can go with us."

"And I might as well suggest that you take Monsieur Modou with you, since he, too, has been expelled by Adoum Justin."

"What do you mean by 'he, too'?" I couldn't help but ask.

"Why, as you were, Monsieur. Were you not told?" He appeared truly surprised. Nor did he seem to relish telling me.

"I was not. I was not told." Expelled. I might as well kiss any *Corps de la Paix* or government service good-bye. "To be expelled from this paradise?" That's when I surely knew this was no game—that I'd better hightail it for the low country before Yekbar comes calling.

"*Oui*, so it is. Take him with you. In fact, take all of those of us who wish to go." I assumed he meant the other *professeurs*. "If not by plane, we will remain, left to ourselves by all of you—as I had abandoned my sister these many years ago! Despite her cries—as the bombs came raining down." He was in tears now. "Now it is my turn." Thus he confessed what he would never say when in his normal (inebriated) state.

Then, with fewer tears, he announced, "We, Hélène and I, are destined to stay here, I think. If we must, if the plane does not come, we will stay here, last bastions and sole guardians of our civilization."

Was he serious? Last bastions? Perhaps.

Then, after a moment's hesitation, a wistful half smile. "I wish I could be with you if you must go with Plan B, and my wife as well, Monsieur. But we would never make the climb and only slow you down."

At that moment, she appeared at the unshuttered window. Yes, she was withering away here, her last, sad days spent in desert fiery heat, filth, and sand. And for me, as an image at the glassless window, red-eyed and ever waiting. I thought, for just that moment, of the dying child thrust into my care, my Mohammed, and what they could have done for him.

I gave her a feeble wave and, him, a sort of pat on the back. "Wish your wife, Helène, well. I'll miss her set table."

"She will be pleased to hear that. *Adieu*," he murmured. Unto God.

"*Au revoir*," I replied. Until we meet again.

He turned and shuffled toward his house. Then turned suddenly toward me, smiled, and said. "*Et bien, oui, au revoir.*" And so. Until we meet again.

■ The Day before the Planned Departure— without Father Sean

"OK, Father, we've had our arguments. But now is no time to dwell on those. You must come with us."

"You flatter yourself, Harry, that I dwell on those things. But, as you know, I must stay here with my flock."

"But much of your flock is going with me."

"Sure, there will be a few. But the rest are remaining here. I can't abandon them, can I? It is my sacred duty to remain with them, it is. Besides, if a battle starts, I will take the little group out through the breach you showed me on the northern wall. 'Miriam's breach,' as you call it. None shall harm a priest and his adherents. I will decorate all the others with crosses, even if they are not Catholics. That will make them appear Christian. We'll await the end of the battle, then return to help the wounded and administer last rites.

"And if, for some reason, these ones should kill me, Harry, there is no higher calling than to sacrifice one's life for the life of others." Then he added, "*Dulce et decorum est pro hominem mori.*"

"I think it's '*pro patria mori*,' I had to remind him.

"Perhaps it is. Would you like me to hear your confession before you leave?" He had to ask.

"Only one thing. Forgive me, father, but in my arrogance I may have interrupted the balance of things." And so on. I didn't bother to even cross myself, and I think he sensed that I thought these words had fallen into the deaf sands. Where they would be covered up by the the winds and dunes. Soon and forever.

I finished. Since I was no believer, he commanded no penance. "Alright, then. Someday you will accept the mystery of faith. In the meantime, let's take a quaff of God's own holy water before we part company." With that suggestion, a flask swiftly appeared from beneath his cassock.

"My thoughts exactly," I agreed.

"An Irishman's handcuffs, this," he joked, pointing to the whiskey.

And a priest who was always prepared. Still, we had no glasses, so we clinked his cross to the flask, "*Saliente*," and we each took a nip of fine Irish whiskey directly from the flask.

"One more—for the road as they say." So we did one more—a bitter swig for me this time—but a fitting breakfast before our precipitate departure.

"God keep you then," I said, violating my own argued precepts.

"Thank you, Harry. And you as well."

I shook his hand and turned on my heels, rewarded then with a bitter taste welling up—from my own guilt. And fear. Fear for all of us.

As if in response to those fears, shouting arose immediately. From different parts of town and outside the walls. The two sides and their partisans, I supposed. Screaming to scare the enemy. And perhaps test the others' determination. It would be a sleepless night and a very early gathering to make our escape.

We will, each escapee, go off singly or in pairs so as not to arouse suspicions and, so, to avoid the curfew guards making their rounds.

Then take the path to the airport. Just before dawn. We rehearsed this once to test the enforcement of the curfew. There were enforcers on the sandy paths and in doorways. But Ibrahim would stand lookout for us.

This was Plan A.

So among the *Nasarah*, we would leave Father Sean, *Père* Habert and the *légionnaire capitaine*. But not the Russian, Godin. We would gather in Tom, Dick and Harry *Hajj*. Plus four students including three southern Sara-Ngumbayes and Mohammed Idriss. Holding hands in pairs. In the Ngumbaye fashion.

Leaving the others to their destinies.

Forgive me Father . . . I needed yet another drink.

[Note from Aaron Hamblin: I'm not sure where in the chronology this belongs, so I'm inserting it here.] *I am told by a student letter dated 10/10/70 that Father Sean O'Sagarty led the "decoy" of students to the north wall breach heading for the baobab tree where—thanks to Miriam—her family, Ibrahim, and I had found refuge. I have just learned that they had been slaughtered by Janjawid. I could only imagine him bidding his followers, fakirs, the unbelievers, and Mu'minin, the believers, to kneel and pray before their beheading. But the Muslims with him would rather fight than submit. And perhaps they did.* [End of insert.]

■ **The Day before the Planned Departure— without the *Légionnaire Capitaine*, But With the *Capitaine's* Best Friend**

July 1969

"The rumor of your escapade, or should I say escape, has spread," he joked. At least I hoped he was joking.

"Far and wide. Via Arab telephone," I joked back. "Then they'll never get it right. For they will say that we are on our way to a pilgrimage, to Mecca. Are you coming with us?"

"You know that this old soldier cannot. I must remain with *my* 'students.' Who are, in fact, my new graduates, or will be, since they are soon to be put to the final test. Féroce would be a great warrior here, but I do not want him to be slaughtered by these madmen. You must take him with you. Free him into the wilderness when you can."

"But I . . . ." I could think of a million reasons why I should not and could not.

"I know I'm asking much. I know that you would prefer not to. But my luck may have run out. I may sacrifice more than an arm this time. I want to know that he is free and in no danger. I'll give you two days' raw meat to keep him fed and happy. You'll know he's happy by the speed of his growling. Faster means unhappy. Pissed off.

"Slowly, like this—Grrrrrr . . .—means he's normal. I would not say happy. I'll talk to him, explain all to him, before you go."

"Wouldn't he rather give me a smile if he's happy, a scowl if he's not?"

I knew this was difficult for him. That Féroce meant more to this soldier than one would have expected. Than his command. He tried to smile.

"And, as thanks, I offer you my *képi*." I knew the great value these officers placed in their *képi*. "This is not to be argued or discussed. He will be a great warrior for you, should you need one. And, as the Sara have it, he will protect your soul. I'll bring him to you before the dawn."

I tried to collect my thoughts. "We depart before dawn. Tomorrow, before dawn." I wanted to say more but couldn't put it together in time. "From the airport, or, if that fails, from *Père* Habert's home." Then "With your 'students,' watch your back. There is a traitor among them."

He seemed not to register the warning, for he said only, "Féroce will be with you then." He marched off in his usual four-four cadence. With Féroce, who had been polite and quiet during our entire conversation. Perhaps Féroce had been listening intently. It was a significant moment for him.

I would have the *guépard*.

And the *kepi*—perhaps for Féroce to sleep on. Scent of his old friend.

As a last resort.

■ The Day before the Planned Departure— with or without Ivan Godin?

July 1969

"How did you know we were going?"

"The news is everywhere. And I must be with you. My *chefs* have ordered me so." He pronounced "*chefs*" the American way.

"The news is everywhere?" I was not amused.

"Yes. That you are to make the pilgrimage. To Mecca. The *Hajji*. Only I know is for other destination."

I was a little shaken that the Arab telephone might really be functioning. Maybe I should put out via Arab telephone that we left yesterday—or will be leaving the day after tomorrow. That sort of misdirection worked for the burning of the poorer *arrondissement*.

But I carried on with the more important business at hand. "How did they order you? They have not been here in weeks. Not since the troubles began," I persisted.

"Yes, they have so commanded."

He wasn't answering my question. I wanted to know how he communicated with his "*chefs*." "Yes, but how did they communicate with you, if they did not see you face to face?"

"I am ordered to go. It would be best, it will only be possible, if I go with you."

"But what if you are *Kah Jay Bay*? The *Komitet Gosudarstvennoy Bezopasnosti*? I was showing off to keep him honest. "Or the *Jay Er U* (GRU). We would then be sworn enemies!" I couldn't resist pulling his chain.

"*My chefs* would protest that."

"Even if we are *Corps de la paix?*"

"Even that."

He lost his smile. He turned away from me. "*Der'mo!*" I think he said. And some other words that sounded like expletives. But, then, even the quietly spoken Russian often sounds to me like a run of shouted expletives. How could you tell?

He turned back to me. I tried to maintain a fierce and angry look. That the desert ones did so well. But I almost smiled.

"By radio."

"What?"

"I make radio with them. With *chefs.*"

I almost asked him if he had to get up at 3 a.m. to send his messages. But I refrained. "Then you *are* a spy," I said as forcefully as I could. Oh great! Yet another one listening in to me. I had no idea! Or didn't want to.

"'arry, I am eyes and ears only." Where had I heard that before?

"And mouth, too, if you send communications by radio. Do you tell them stories about me?"

"Only how you are so funny when you drink much vodka. And your voice for singing is so flat after the drink of fine whiskey that you bring me."

So Johnny Walker Red was considered fine whiskey in his community. Things are surely tougher than they let on in the good old CCCP. "That's all?" I was wondering about the quality of his USSR-made vodka. Plus I thought I sang pretty well. Well, you can't expect good taste from a Commie.

"That I hear you are fine teacher. That you have lady friend. I am forbidden such. So that I assume that, since the lady is not forbidden to you, then you cannot be a spy. Even eyes and ears. Or this lady would be your *kompromat.* But that . . . ."

"Yes?"

"But that you have made fine friends with the Wahid."

"Tell your *chefs* that." I tried to make it sound as if my decision depended on his response to my order.

"I will tell them this truth, 'arry. What I should, as eyes and ears, have done."

"Word of honor?"

"As an honorable Russian officer." He let slip the "officer" part. "As all Russians," he added, "I am *prizyvnik*. Then *"Ya vsego lish' sluga Sovetskogo Soyuza,"* he exclaimed, shaking his head. [8]

"Then be at my *kaz* before dawn. Pack light. Also, we are not armed. And bring bottles of vodka."

"*Spaciba*. Thank you, 'arry. What shall I do with the radio?"

"Smash it so that the pieces are unrecognizable. Then bury the pieces deep under the *kaz* or *clinique* where there are loose foundation stones." Urging him to this was a slightly dirty trick, since I was taking my radio with me. I wasn't going to risk another ribbing from Hank and others for losing this one.

"Tomorrow, before dawn, at your home," he confirmed. "*Spasiba*. And 'arry, you Americans are not as bad as they say."

"Then tell your *chefs* that we are all geniuses. Gifted with perfect eyes and ears. And a great capacity for drinking."

"I cannot lie that way. Besides 'arry, *da*, I knew all the time. But I did not tell them. . . . *Spaciba*."

■ The Day before the Planned Departure— without Miriam

"Then it was you."

"Yes, Monsieur, I am the one."

I slumped into the nearest chair. "You reminded Ngokuru about my friend, Alice, and you suggested the taking of Amina, of the family of Wahid, as well."

---

[8] *"I am but a servant of the Soviet Union,"* I think. I'm not sure if I captured his statement correctly in Russian, but pretty sure of the translation.

"Yes, I saw that you loved the yellow-haired one. I told him that the she was here. So that he might arrest her. With the others. Yes."

"And Amina?"

"She is of Wahid's tribe, their princess, and so a likely traitor." She had simply confirmed to Ngokuru what he already knew. What I had said as well. We were in it together, Miriam and I.

"You seemed to have planned it all very well." I was astonished. Ever astonished—naïve and callow, Wahid had said. Indeed I was. A veritable fifth column! In my bedroom. (Well, the general had warned me.)

I couldn't help but ask, "Why did you do this thing?"

"They would all take you from me. Like Monsieur Evian was taken from me."

"And Terry and Joe?"

"I saw them here once. Another time, you described them to me with excitement in your voice. I thought they would take you away as well. Because they are Emricani, like you. And they also seemed to be like the cowboys and fierce warriors—like the *Nasarahs* that burned us out." Terry and Joe might be pleased with that description. "Ali knew the way to Wahid and took to him my advice."

"That was the way. I didn't know you cared so much for me." I did not read the tea leaves well. Or at all.

She gave me only that look—that she accepted her fate without question. Without anger or fear. Without joy or sorrow. An absolute beauty, she was.

I rose and slapped her once. Good and hard. For a moment, I even thought that it was too bad I didn't have that Alsacian brute, Heinrich, to do this work for me. She maintained the same look.

"Why? Why?" I cried out. I was beside myself with anger. At her and, most of all, at myself.

She surprised me with her answer. "Ngokuru ordered me to do it. To be with you and to tell him all things. For to keep our grandfather's house. To spy on you. As Moussa David had done with Evian. As *I* had done with Evian. As Moussa was to do with you."

"So Ngokuru had you spy on me as Moussa did on Evian. Moussa was killed, perhaps for his pederasty, or his wish not to spy, or bad reporting." It was coming together for me now. How they did not want me to view the body. Especially if his privates had been stuffed in his mouth. Or if he was much diseased.

"Yet you still lost your home." I was barely in control enough to get the words out. There was no longer love or passion. I had been thoroughly taken.

A long silence followed.

"Then he betrayed you as you have betrayed me," I said, with the anger now mixed with great sadness.

"Yes. For our home was anyway destroyed."

"Still . . . . So now you must live in what is left of my house even if I am no longer here." My mind was racing, searching for a solution, an answer.

"Still, the *sous-préfet* will throw us out if he knows you will not be here. Then we would become without home. Another reason why you must stay."

"Or the Wahidi might do worse, if they were to take this town and find out you served Ngokuru. And the *Nasarah*."

"Yes, they would kill me. Perhaps stone me for lying with you, a *Nasarah*." Now, finally, she was in tears. Or nearly.

"For have I not told you before this? That, in my tribe, when you accept a gift or favor from one, that one has touched your soul and so owes you gifts or favors for the rest of his life. You gave me, and my mother, and my brother Ali domicile after we were burned out by the other *Nasarah*s. So you have touched our souls. Thus you must take care of us for the rest of our lives. Or yours."

The rest of our lives. I could imagine her and her family ensconced in the USA. Actually, I couldn't.

Then I had a flash of reasoned memory. "But you saved me and so touched my soul by leading me, us, through that breach in the town wall. So are we not quits?"

Maybe a *double touché*. Or, possibly, a strike two.

Her silence may have meant assent.

Now she knew I would go.
Without her.

■ Get This

I sat down at the radio to launch a note. The night before our rumored departure. I might as well confess the whole confused and intertwined spy circus. From my skewed point of view. So I wasn't thinking very clearly. In my hurry, I again bypassed Habert, and, in the middle of my coding, I received a message back:

"WTF:2CONFUSMSGS@ONCE:STOP."

I stopped. I didn't know who this receiver and sender (who did not sign) was. Or what his coding meant. It may have been our interceptor exposing himself. ("Highly irregular," the British would say.) And the listener was announcing that we, two of us, were sending at the same time. But Habert's would be in French, mine in English. So the second sender was sending in English as well. Terry, Joe, Modou, or Alice? I waited five minutes, then resumed with only "WTF:UPRISGSOON:HH:STOP"

Highly irregular.

■ The Departure

July 14, 1969

To always expect the unexpected. Like the body slam from a French paratrooper. Like the death of a joyful student. Like the sudden victory, then demise, of a favorite gelding.

Expect the unexpected—like I never did.

I should have known better than to expect Leonard. Or Earl and Hank. When I saw the big airplane.

There was a big airplane, all right, but with the wrong markings.

Markings of the national flag. And heavily armed indigenous soldiers guarding its perimeter.

So much for Plan A. Or was it B? Or even C? I was losing track.

Of course, as General Rochedure-Na'ar stepped down via the mobile stairway, the guards came to rifle-ready. With a smart clack. Even I stiffened to attention. From old habits. Really.

I was only glad I was first. Or second. Well, first enough to warn the others.

Or, I thought, Antoine could. He had actually preceded me and now lingered by Chien. He gave General Rochedure-Na'ar a smart salute. As the general, in all his heft, stepped onto the tarmac, Antoine came up beside me.

"When I've engaged the general in conversation, try to slip away and warn the others," I whispered to Antoine. "Especially Partenay and his wife."

"Aha, Américain, it is good of you to greet us. Happy *Fête Nationale*. At least in France!"

"It is good of you to come. What brings you back to Dar Es Sabir?" I was a bit fearful of his answer.

"Not to see you off. Very bold of you to plan so. But, indeed, it is you and your fellow 'pilgrims' that we most need at this point. As you may have seen, the army has been engaged to fight alongside the militia. We are their allies. And you are ours."

"You are ours" reverberated. "But Allah waits for no one," I intoned, reaching for a voice both solemn and sanctimonious.

"We will render unto God what is God's. But first we must do God's work. Mecca and the Kaaba will wait."

"But . . .," I sputtered.

"So thousands of others will take your place at the Kaaba. You will not be missed. Come, walk to town with me. You need not be afraid. I have my guards, as you can see."

Yes, the indigenous soldiers that were so disciplined and so armed, the Nationals who were guarding the perimeter of the plane, were at all sides of us. He need not be afraid. As for me, these guys still scared the shit out of me. It would have been less so if they'd shown less nervous fear themselves and had but moderated the scowls they seemed to insist on bearing. And done away with the aviator sun glasses.

But, as we walked, the general complimented Antoine for running ahead to announce his coming. "And put off the rest of you pilgrims from coming for nothing. Except that I might have thereby identified all of you. But never mind. It will all come out."

So he had it all figured out. Smart guy. Good intelligence. "So what do you plan to do with us?" I had to ask.

"Why, nothing. Just to keep you around to show that the *Nasarah* and even refugees are with us. With the *Armée Nationale*. On film."

"I guess I'd better hone my acting skills."

"Yes. And meet me at the town center. At 08:00 the day after tomorrow morning. With your French *Nasarah* colleagues. And the Libyan who is in the best shape. But not the Indian *pay-day*. Or any blacks. Even the *sous-préfet* would put the newsmen off. And you, being an Américain *Nasarah* . . . ."

"I am no *Nasarah* . . . ."

"Yeah, yeah. And you, being Américain, will be best of all.

"Or . . . at a later date we can round up all the pilgrims and send you and them, sooner than anticipated, to their various makers. So you are the star and the key!"

Now I am a propaganda shill as well. Who woulda thought. Not my momma. Well, Plan Alpha-numero whatever was now in effect.

Such as it might be.

■ The Day before the Next Planned Departure--Dry Run

July 14, 1969

It was on a dry run for plan B that Abdel-Hamid caught me. I had made sure Miriam did not follow me but hadn't expected this

324 David Michael Litwack

one. Me alone, fortunately. Fortuitous really. I had just climbed out from the tunnel—and exited through the fake WC belonging to Batila's relations.

He was with another sufferer. The two were assigned to patrol this area from the southern wall of the town to the Jumeaux—at dusk when they would be less well seen. They were menacingly and well armed. Putting to good use the new carbines courtesy of *Père* Habert, me, Clive, Grace, etc., and, of course, themselves. Most scary as they appeared even more scarified in the waning daylight. And probably not caring who they frightened or shot.

He recognized me immediately. "Ah, *Emrican* who will bring us great gifts. Friend of our lord, Wahid. *Keef halekum.* How do you do?"

"I am well. And you?"

"I am Abdel-Hamid, chief of the unclean band. Formerly tribe of Asouyé Kerem. You have visited my village twice and eaten and drunk tea with us, the unclean. And I took you to retrieve the hostages from the renegade Wahidi. Maybe they were Janjawid. Do you remember me?"

"How could I not? How could I not remember such wisdom?" It was Father Christmas, all right. But despite the jolly countenance and roundish shape, he looked even worse, even scarier, in the fading daylight.

"This is my cousin Esmir ibn Mohammed el Faya who is also of the unclean."

As if I couldn't tell.

"We are searching for escapees or attempting escapees who may be trying to leave this town for Albri. Around the Jumeux. That they might go for militia reinforcements. Is that your destination?"

"No. I am just for an afternoon walk." I was pushing it.

"Hmm. Likely story. Is that the toilet you would use for such a walk. It's in a strange place," he pushed on.

"In fact, the WC is a storeroom as well. Where I keep my whiskey. It is attached to the town ramparts and it is under the tree in a good, cool place. I have just stopped for a taste. Would you and Esmir like a taste?"

"Of course." He was always good for a merry drink. "Where is such a bottle?"

"Give me one minute to retrieve it." They looked at me with some uncertainty, then shrugged simultaneously to indicate "Why not."

I hurried back to the WC, removed the commode, and climbed into the tunnel. Fortunately, I had noticed a case of bottles not too far from this exit. I brought one bottle back, a Johnny Black. One of the *Père's* better bottles.

"Ah-hah! Thank you beneficent *Emrican*." We opened it and we each took a practice swig. I didn't mind the other drinkers, but I would have preferred a dash of soda. I needed to keep that Idriss soda-making machine more at hand. Or get my own.

"Why was this bottle not yet opened? Did you not drink from it?" Abdel-Hamid asked. Always attentive, always on guard.

Esmir repeated, "If you came and drank some, why has this bottle not yet been opened?"

"Ah, Abdel-Hamid and Esmir. For such as you I would bring a special, unopened bottle! The whiskey is better this way. For everyday whiskey, I drink the red label. For you, I have brought out the black label, a superior brand."

"That such would be so." Abdel-Hamid was beginning to feel good.

Esmir, on the other hand, was less accustomed to this *Nasarah's* drink. He felt queasy and proposed to use the toilet. "I must use your *merde* facilities. I will be careful to avoid the bottles." He barfed just in front of the WC, then went in to satisfy his other end. I was glad that at least we had left a bucket of water there for him to cleanse himself. In the desert Arab way.

After some moments of loud, forceful flatulence, he stumbled out, fell down next to Abdel-Hamid, and uttered, "The mechanism does not work. Fortunately there was a bucket of water. For good manners." Then he flopped down and immediately dozed off.

Our only exit from the tunnel and WC was thus twice fouled. I reminded myself not to touch his left hand.

"He is not accustomed to such fine whiskey," Abdel-Hamid assured me. "He was once a faithful Muslim." Then he took another grand swig. "This is Allah's reward to him for that faithfulness," he said, gesturing to his scars and lesions.

I walked gingerly around his sacrilegious mutterings.

We talked about the imminent battle, and I pressed him on how it might be avoided. Plus the fate of the *Nasarahs*.

He asserted that the attack could not be avoided and would occur as soon as the northern and western sides of Dar es Sabir were in a vise. The Janjawid or Wahidi would soon cut off the eastern part as well. No mention of the southern wall. "No one can escape the attacks. No one will," he assured me. "But the Janjawid will slay the Fakir who do not convert on the spot. The Wahidi will not be so . . . demanding."

Very reassuring. "*Inch Allah*, I am reassured. I will suggest that the *Nasarahs* go to the west and south of the town. Or convert on the spot." My fate seemed destined toward the south, toward Albri and Djemélia beyond.

But, just in case, I'd review the *Takbir* and *Shahadah*.

Then I knew this was the moment to raise my newly-fashioned proposal. "I will bring you a fine Deux Chevaux, a blue one, if you can drive it. In turn, I will ask you first to care for Jean's Omar the *hamar* and another one until we come for them." I had brilliantly determined that these donkeys wouldn't fit through Habert's tunnel.

"Ah, thank you, Emricani, for this auto. This is the first of your gifts. It is as Wahid said. I know that you will bring us a cure for this curse—a lake of raisins, many virgins for our pleasure, and beautiful cups of hand-shaped silver when you return. Besides, Esmir has yet all his hands and fingers. He will make a good driver. I will show him how."

"Wonderful. But to insure I will return, you must do two things for me. On this day I will put out such things as a wheelbarrow which you will find just outside the wall—along with Omar the *Hamar* and the other donkey called Evian, which will be tied up to the barrow. Take all of it, with the donkeys and wheelbarrow attached to the back bumper of your Deux Chevaux, to a place at the northern foot of the Jumeaux. Tie the donkeys. Hide all. Until we, the pilgrims, come.

"If you are stopped by your allies on the way, tell them you are fulfilling your patrol duties, and tell them you are also in search of caves in the rocks and land that might supply good charcoal because your current supply is running out. Running out, as the sand takes over your village repositories and fertile woodland."

"So I may employ my acting and lying skills?"

"Absolutely. And to great effect.

"Lastly, place the car at the breach of the southern wall. Halfway through the wall. Out of sight from the curfew guards and others."

"What breach?"

"The one that Omar will make with his hind legs," I said.

"You ask for us to have adventure. This we can do." He seemed to really anticipate this adventure. Good thing I got him juiced up first.

Then I laid the big one on him. "On the first day of the battle, take the Deux Chevaux and drive it north, passing the western wall to the Faya road north. Try to avoid the battle zones, but, if necessary, show your compatriots that you are taking the car to provision the northern fighters. I will put in some food and this fine whiskey for the drinkers among them. The whiskey will make them brave in battle."

And stupid. I would also have to give up most of my supply of C rations and other canned goods. But, in return, the drunk warriors are likely to stumble, their guns misfiring. "Go as fast as you can. You may be chased. If so, gather your greatest speed to outrun the horses and Land Rovers of the Wahidi. If you do these things, it will be a great favor for me and you will keep the first of many gifts that the Emricani plan to bring to you when we return."

"Again, I will act!" Abdel-Hamid shouted with unfeigned joy.

"Yes. As if in the *Américain* movies!"

The ruse was a bit weak and not well thought out, but it would delay the trackers and followers a bit—until we were well on the mountain path toward its summit.

"Then we can keep this car, yes?" Abdel-Hamid was truly excited about this possibility.

"It will be yours. I will bring all this to you tomorrow, the last day of the month of Muharram."

"You do us great honor, unclean as we are. The whiskey will be the best gift of all," Abdel-Hamid said.

Esmir barfed his consent.

■ Teenage Memories

July 14-15, 1969

Esmir and Abdel-Hamid accompanied me back through the western gate in their role as perimeter guards. All the way back to the remains of my *kaz*.

I had jumped a car using ignition wires one time in my life. Long ago. I would try to remember the match. (Not to mention how to do stick-shifting afterwards.)

So I sneaked back out of my remainder of a *kaz*, past Miriam and her family, in my most Western clothes and in the company of my leprous escorts. The Western clothes, because I feared I would otherwise be taken for a town denizen in my brown *jalaba* and perhaps summarily shot for breaking curfew. The *prokaza* ones left me by Amina's courtyard.

I found the blue Deux Chevaux parked in its usual place. The doors had no locks. I ever so quietly felt around to remove the steering panel and retrieve the wires. Then I noticed a key hanging from the sun visor. With it, the car started. Good thing, too. Since I wouldn't have to explain to Abdel-Hamid how to jump-start the engine.

It purred quietly. Ok, not so quietly. So I pumped the gas pedal, shoved it directly into second, and shot off down the street amidst puffs of smoke and an infernal racket.

In the rearview mirror, I could see a figure, bare-chested, but wearing sky-blue police uniform pants, coming out the door of Amina's courtyard, just as I swung left around the corner and toward the gate of the western wall—the gate I had often taken Amina through. I hoped that the sloppy guards would still be there. Sloppily sleeping. As for Amina and her "guest," I was too much engaged to think about it until much later.

Shots were fired as I neared the wall—from behind me. The guards awoke as I sped-through the western arch and away from the wall. They didn't fire, the guards. The car barked and screamed, amplified by the echo of the outside wall. Then no shots came from any direction, and I turned south on the Albri road and drove on to the agreed meeting place.

Abdel-Hamid and Esmir were at our agreed-upon meeting place. I let Esmir drive, while I sat next to him and gave advice and directions. He drove in his meandering and sloppy way, anyway. We parked under an acacia tree which would keep the car cool. Well . . . cooler.

I folded the keys into Esmir's hand, and we agreed on a time and this place to provision the Deux Chevaux and lead out the donkeys. Done and successful, I took a swig from the whiskey we had buried under the tree, then slipped through a small breach where we would later bring provisions and the donkeys. The donkeys, Omar and Evian—whom I will use to create a large wall hole with their hind legs—by teasing their hind ends with *cram-cram* and pissing them off until they have kicked the wall in.

■ Message for History

July 15, 1969
I'm glad it was in Morse. Less dramatic:

"WTF:NO HANKEARLABANDNGSHIP OVRJUMOCRW INCREAS:HH:STOP:"

First response:

"WTF:BECLERWATSHIPWATCRW:GOD:STOP"

Second (almost simultaneous) response:

WTF:NOSTANDFAST:LN:STOP

I puzzled over the signature of the first response. No clever laugh verbiage followed. Then it occurred to me—he had been reading my Morse all along. Asking those odd questions that, when I answered them, I got a query from HQ, "YTHISPERTIN?" As if I was having a serious, one-on-one conversation, but with two different players. With Leonard Norman and with . . . GOD . . .

Gerard Olivier Dubois! (When I received this signature before, I had assumed this was Leonard only joking.) Sometimes, I was communicating perhaps with Gerard alone. Or with him perhaps working with or for the SDECE. And it was then that I knew that the morning café slam had been well planned. Gerard Olivier Dubois— *Gerard, Corps de la Guerre.*

"WTF:SOISSAGE:HHDELAPAIX:STOP" I signaled to Gerard. "Be careful."

I wondered how many others he had slammed into to ensure he got the right radioman. Or woman. From Dar es Sabir and, perhaps, other hotspots. I wondered why he chose this moment to reveal himself.

Then another one:

"WTF:WHRETOTHEYCOMFM:GOD:STOP."

So I replied:.

"WTF:NO&WBUTJANJAWDCOMFMEA:HH:STOP"

Thus was I complicit.

It may later be written so.

◼ The Killer Winds

July 15, 1969

If we hadn't enough troubles, the threat of early Harmattan-like winds hung over the town. That would bring the announcing locusts as well. Who would come like a cloud one day, darkening the entire sky. Or like a blizzard in the northern USA winter. And a great roaring sound made by thousands of flutters in synchrony. Upsetting everyone. Bringing on nosebleeds in some. (The thought of which brought on to me the vision of Lièvre's half face.)

And welcomed by the attackers as a diversion that would hide their movements. Just the kind of maneuver Wahid had become known for.

The wind would blow itself out in a day or two. The sand will have reconfigured itself. The locusts would depart at the head of the fleeing wind. Those locusts that were dead from impact would lay everywhere, even in the *kazes* and hovels where they will have squeezed through boarded-up windows and doors. Then to be fried, salted, and eaten for the next few days as appetizing snacks.

With the streaming hordes of these locusts and the fierce winds—a perfect day for an attack.

A perfect day for an escape.

◼ The Next Dawn of the Escape

Morning of July 16, 1969

I was determined to check out the airfield again before leaving. One more time. From somewhere on the dark road, the miserable

Chien joined me. He walked along side me, but at a respectful distance.

He had somehow calculated the date of the last passenger flight to come, six weeks ago. Even given the General's surprise arrival. And he was still faithful to that master whose return he forever awaited.

The disciples of the cult, awaiting the likelihood that the plane of riches would come this day, had also gathered in a corner of the field.

As for me, I always thought of Earl and Hank's plane as the bringer of mixed gifts, of Western food and drink, but also spy equipment. But, most of all, as the body carrier, the funeral plane, the carrier of death.

I paced off and measured the airfield while I waited. Then, I reassured the cultists who were waiting as well. That I would come back. That the plane was coming. Sometime. With all that was promised. But not today.

Nothing came. Chien lay down and whimpered. I gave a nostalgic salute. I could wait no longer, and I set off to return. To escape. Another way.

■ A Letter Never Sent

July 15, 1969

Aaron,

Something dangerous is brewing but I can't write about it since even the last letter to you was returned by the censors. Maybe all of my letters to you have been, and will be, censored and never sent. Just as well. There are things about me that, in my lifetime, you may never know.

I may have been responsible for the disappearance— or worse—of the lovely Amina or the telecom American, my friend, the quiet one, Joe. The Militia thinks I'm a

spy. The rebels are pissed off at me. Big time! I'm not
sure what I'll do next.

Harry

■ The *Nasarah* Crawl

July 16, 1969

Perhaps no more or less than we deserved. We began our crawl, one by one, with great effort—given our sleepless nights and nervous fatigue. Alexandru and I spurting ahead—"crawling point," you might say. The uncles, Tom *Hajj*, Dick *Hajj*, and Harry *Hajj*, struggled in the middle. Over the hot, pure urine that Kalb was leaving us all, as he ran back and forth excitedly, fighting his way over each of us. Each of us his personal fire hydrant. The wages of stealth.

Féroce made no leavings—just growled his way through. Behind us. Much to our terror. His growl was neither fast nor slow. But he made us crawl faster.

Terry yelled and shouted about his minion, Joe, the entire way— that Joe was lost and we would be leaving him to the whims of the Wahidi. And he accused me of saying Joe would be there for this escape, which I never did. Well, perhaps I implied such when I had said "He will have joined us . . ." But I also added (perhaps in a lower key), ". . . in spirit, until the rising here is finished." I may have suggested that we would return to find him when we could.

I should have learned about suggestive promises made. And promises kept. Or not kept.

Antoine (I was beginning to suspect this was Alain, but why would he want to join us except to betray us?) was in a particularly bad mood. He complained about the animals, their filth, leavings, and irritating behavior. Kalb did not take it personally and kept up his energetic sprints and nervous incontinence.

Michel and Victor watched our rear, just behind our *Imam* who had come as well.

To give us spiritual strength . . . and guidance.

Not to mention the gifts of yesterday from Esmir, waiting for us at the end of our desperate crawl.

Actually, two gifts.

■ *Gris-gris* (for Good Luck?)

July 16, 1969

We were through the tunnel with Terry's shouts echoing back almost to the entry, but now he was hoarse and somewhat subdued—and soon had no tunnel echo to amplify his voice—before Younis shouted out "My *gris-gris*! I forgot my *gris-gris*."

"You're wearing it," I said, my ears still echoing from Terry's shouting. We all turned our attention to Younis. Even Terry.

"Not this one. The one for *Yondo*. From my father. The one I buried!" He was trembling and in tears. "I must have it, or Allah will punish me tenfold." Tenfold of what, I wondered. "I must go back for it!"

"If you do that, the Master or Mistress will probably catch you and punish you for your absence—or for your attempted escape! You will not be able to do this journey. You will not be released from slavery. You will never escape! Unlike Robin! Or Will Scarlet!" I too had forgotten the *gris-gris* cum "messaging pouch!"

"Will Scarlet came back," he retorted defiantly.

I was still working up my best lines. But he was insistent. "I must go back to retrieve it!" he repeated.

"You cannot go back!" I was equally insistent.

Younis was beside himself. He continued shouting and nervously pacing at the foot of Jumeaux.

"I will retrieve it," I finally said. I dared not mention that I had left the forgotten *gris-gris* behind the dysfunctional commode (where

I'd previously hidden the radio) after its recovery in the detritus of the *kaz* bombing. "Modou will lead the expedition in my absence."

Now Modou was in a bit of a panic. "But Harold, we agreed that I am to take charge only on the descent—to meet the US forces. What might happen to you? They have militia guards posted all around the town!"

"Just be sure you hide well behind these large boulders. Leave the donkeys in plain sight, since they should not draw any suspicion. It'll be fine. I'll be back soon."

"Stupid superstition," Modou exhaled, eyeing Younis.

Then I pivoted towards Younis. "Younis, is the *gris-gris* in the red box that you buried?" Though I knew I would have heard from him had he moved the box and found it empty.

"The same," he answered more calmly.

"Buried in the same place. Where you last buried it?" I thought I'd better make sure. Make sure he thought it was where he left it.

"Yes." By the time he answered, I was back in the fake WC and climbing down the shaky ladder.

I hurried as much as my bruised and tunnel-rashed knees would allow, passing all the storage bins on the way. And Kalb's messes. I exited on very sore knees and with wet hands, at *Père* Habert's storeroom. *Père* Habert was just rising from his bed as I came though his house.

"Dawn is upon us!" he remonstrated.

"Yes, one thing forgotten! Hands too soiled to shake bonjour . . .," and I rushed off to my *kaz* and its back forty. I had to walk. I could not run, for fear I would alert the militia guards.

I found the place where the ground had been disturbed, and dug madly. I found the red candy box, then groped behind the commode, found the *gris-gris*, shook the mud and scraped Rashid's blood off as best I could, tossed it inside the red box, and rushed to return to the mountain with the box and its contents. I noticed that the master and mistress were not home after all. All was closed up and there was no shouting for Younis. Of course. I realized that they must have gotten wind of the impending battle and were probably hiding out in one of the wadis. I should have observed them more attentively as my sentinels, my warning canaries.

I gathered up the red box and *gris-gris*, then ran back, past the woman with the alms basket. Past the woman formerly, but no longer, with her starving child.

Still, I was amazed at their strength and resilience. Past the *mutilé de guerre*, the likely spy. Spying on me.

For the last time.

But I did not stop to offer alms as I usually did, only to throw the rest of my change on the ground among them. That they might fight over the paltry coins.

"It sounds warlike out there," I yelled to *Père* Habert just as he came into the hallway. "Best of luck," I cried.

"And to you," he shouted back as I was about to open the first hatchway to the tunnel. I heard gunfire—not backfire—just as I was about to shut the door. Hoping that no militia guards would harass *Père* Habert about the stupid *Nasarah* who had passed that way.

Just then two guards were at his forecourt demanding to see the *Nasarah* that had entered his premises.

I climbed back out, closed and covered the entry, and was then stopped by those guards, who seemed to be waiting for me.

"What are you doing, *Nasarah?*" one asked me.

"I am not a *Nas* . . . ." (Ah, never mind. This was not the moment!) "I am going to retrieve my escaped donkeys," I responded. "I have awaited the end of curfew, and now I must bring them back." I smiled and tried to look complacent.

"But we asked this of the unclean Abdel-Hamid and the unclean Esmir. They tell us the donkeys are theirs."

"Ah. I loaned them to the unclean. So that they might gather wood to make charcoal. Now I must retrieve them."

"Where have you come from?" Just what I was afraid of. Being forced to divulge the presence of the tunnel.

"I was just arranging this for my militia friends." I reached down for a Johnny, fortunately within reach. They jumped as I did so but did not aim their carbines. I handed the bottle to them. "Here. You may want to examine it to prove its authenticity."

"The two of them conferred in a mix of Arabic and Sara. Guard 1: "Shall we let him go?"

Guard 2: "He looks stupid enough even to violate the curfew."

Guard 1: "Or drunk. In fact, the curfew is lifted with the dawn. I wonder what is in that red box."

Guard 2, reverting to French: "Yes and he wears the dress of the *Nasarah*. The *général* was clear about these types." Then he turned to me. "What is in that red box?" he asked me as he shifted his carbine—possibly one of those I had helped purchase to rescue the French and British hostages. Fitting poetic justice that I should die by my own rescue ransom payoff.

"A *gris-gris*," I answered and held the box open.

Guard 2: "What do you need a *gris-gris* for?"

Me: "It is a gift from a student."

Guard 1: "Ah, then you had better use it to say your prayers." Then he turned to his mate and reverted back to Arabic to add, "I think he is the *professeur* of English and perhaps the procurer of young boys. No doubt one of those boys gave him the *gris-gris*."

Guard 2: "Yes, he could be that one, that Evian. Let's kill him, then. We can say he was drunk and violated the curfew. He will be a prize for us."

So I had to interrupt: "I'm not the procurer of boys though I am the *professeur* of English," I declared between rapid gasps—gasps of the terrified.

Guard 2: "Ah, you speak our Arabic. The procurer of boys did not. That is a good thing."

My thought: "I thanked my stars that I had learned the *Shahadah*. And I then recited it without a mistake. Perfectly. Thus, before these two Moslem witnesses, I was unofficially (or maybe officially) converted."

Guard 1: "Yes, a good thing. He is of the *mu'minīn*. Let's not kill him. This time."

Guard 2: "Let's not, this time. *Amshi!*" he shouted at me. *Get out of here.* "Too bad," he said to his partner. "He has big, outsized ears. The *général* would have appreciated them."

I *amshid*. This time hoofing it over the open plain to the foot of Jumeaux—all in plain sight. Thank Allah for the gathering locusts homing in—like the fog of sand. Still, I must have looked odd, running among the locusts, my legs shaking so. Or, as if there was something lodged n the seat of my pants. Perhaps there was.

This adventure impressed upon me the vagaries of life. And the stupidity. . . . Ah, never mind.

"Stay where you are," I cried to the hiding pilgrims. "Until those two guards are out of sight! I will brush the donkeys in the meantime."

The two guards finally made their way. Past the faux WC and then behind Balita's family's home and out of sight. To secure the parade ground once again.

I was back to my charges, and I suggested they start climbing the first rocky outcrop to the mountains. Younis got down on his knees and kissed my right hand—the hand soiled by the leavings of Kalb, Féroce, and Esmir—a veritable cocktail—as I handed him the box.

He examined the *gris-gris* and proclaimed for all to hear, "Even your blood, spilled on these. For me. I may be forever in debt to you! Master!" The blood was, more likely, Rashid's.

■ The Beginning of the Ending: But Tempus Is Fugiting

We had not gotten anywhere yet. As it was customary, at the beginning of such an assent, that the *imam* say a brief prayer for the travelers. So he did.

"*B-ismi-llāhi r-raḥmāni r-raḥīmi*. I am your spiritual guide and your servant. I am beholden to your kindness and of that toward our son Moussa Daoud. It is my debt to you, the *Nasarah* who is not *Nasarah*, who is Emricani, which makes me to violate my oath. The oath of my forebears. The oath that told me to allow fate to intervene and destiny to make the way. But this, as Allah wishes. May they all be well, wherever they go. Thus have I spoken. *Allahu akbar."*

With that, we were on our way.

■ The Ascent

Despite the rough climb, not much of a mountain really, but the highest point in this sea of sand═even a bit of vegetation to hold down the coal-like rock and black gravel. We planned to trek for at least twelve hours, with the acacias and rocks tearing at our hands and our clothing.

Uncle Tom *Hajj*, Yusef Idriss *Hajj*, was in and out of the wheelbarrow pulled by Omar. When out, with the help of his "servants," he was weaving with the exertion and could easily lose his balance and, so, his life. Idriss Mohammed moved well—but his Uncle Dick *Hajj*, Daoud Idriss *Hajj*, was also straining.

The donkey, Omar the *Hamar*, was doing fine—even carrying the radio and with Alice riding him side-seated from time to time. And even with the added load of the bagged C rations and spam (thanks Air Force—I won't tell anyone it's pork). Omar, even pulling Uncle Harry *Hajj* in the wheelbarrow, was a champ. (It was agreed to leave Evian, the other donkey, to wander in the foothills. Behind us. Anyway, I'd had enough of Evian in all his guises. But, characteristically, Evian still insisted on following us, lagging well behind and carrying nothing.)

Then the other students. Two Southern ladies whose fathers were Sara functionaries and who, therefore, might be in danger from the Wahidi, and three Sahel young men, also in ethnic danger, plus Idriss Mohammed, and the Idriss body guards.

Idriss Mohammed carried a box on his back like a pack which I assumed contained the gift of the *tarboosh*. (Not a good idea to wear it, since its shiny filigree might serve as a convenient target. But still, he did.) Of course, I wore the the *légionnaire's képi*—also a convenient target. The painted head of Modou's Shiva, his androgynous, four-armed carved wooden idol, peeked out of the knapsack on his back. I could see the tiny woman reclining on Shiva's head and his half-moustache on the male part of its face. I thought these colors might be brightly visible to those below.

Alexandru was in good shape and took long strides just in front of Jean and Younis who took good strides with the *guépard* Féroce between them. I dropped back to walk with Modou. The *sous-préfet*, not so good, lagged behind. Behind him, Godin pressed on with determination, one time mumbling, "*Ni shagu nazad*—not one step backward," as I am told Stalin ordered with these words (regarding the siege of Stalingrad) in the Great Patriotic War. But from Stalin's point of view, we might still have been going the wrong way. Still, in this way, Godin encouraged the *sous-préfet* to keep moving.

■ The Attack Is Not Postponed Due to Inclement Weather

From our high point, we could see the miniature figures and clouds of smoke—the ants firing at each other. It was apparent that Mohammed the giant had kept the hordes who saw us from climbing after us. Whichever force they were. Whichever riches we were thought to carry. And I think they had given up on, or never even started, following us as they now faced a more proximate and dangerous enemy.

The red and blue, crammed into a crevice, caught my eye. I don't believe in coincidences, nor in the minds of wind spirits. But it nevertheless was, as I realized on approaching it, the lost cap of our now-deceased Kansas City Athletics fan. Blown here from the dunes where Saghir thought to end my life. Perhaps brought here by a wandering soul, even a mate or partner for Féroce.

And so I became a sort of traitor to the *légionnaire capitaine*, donning the baseball cap to replace his *képi*.

Then, announcing the Harmatan, that horde of locusts swooped low and in seeming formation, often covering the view below us. A few had ambitions to go higher, but most of those flattened themselves against the rocky wall and outcropped, serrated stone. We were also scratched and startled by them from time to time.

For his part, Evian behind us floundered and finally, confused or overwhelmed by the locusts, tumbled off the pathway into the precipice, with one last bray. Our first loss.

■ Dangerous Paths

Then the road itself. No more than five feet wide in some places, it was well cleared of brush. Terry and Joe had carved out a decent path to move and place their poles. They used donkeys to carry those poles, and they smoothed out the irregularities in the pathway so that the pole-bearing donkeys could more easily make their turns. Each pole deposited in line of sight to its predecessor.

But stubborn donkeys would sometimes refuse to move, sensing danger. They had to be urged on and encouraged. Our Omar was gently urged on by Alice's whispers. The pole-carrying ones were not. Now I understood why the work had been taking so long. No Alice in the work crew to urge their donkeys on.

For it would have taken more than twice as long and required twice as much work to move the poles around rather than over the Jumeaux. Terry and Joe had to make the choice—around or over. Was it their fate (the fate as in the *imam*'s prayer?) to lose—to make what might be described as the losing choice? Or not?

The drop-offs on the right were intimidating and terrifying for those who fear heights. I score high in that category. And in places, these were great heights. I glued myself to the left wall at these points, and throughout our escape up these mountains.

■ Omar the *Hamar*

Omar pulled the wheel barrow carrying Uncle Harry *Hajj*. With Alice sometimes riding him as well.

Alice whispered often to the donkey. Into his ear. As I wish she had done to me. Each time that he halted, sensing danger, she would say something to him that would spur him on. As he had done with Amina. This one liked girls, Omar the *Hamar*. And so he was as sure-footed as, and more daring than, I would have expected him to be. And less stubborn, with Alice's encouragement, even where the track was rough and the road narrow.

■ Rest Area 1

We dragged through part of the first night, moving much more slowly than Modou and I had when we were only the two of us. This time, we often had to retrace our steps to help the fatigued and weakened ones. Also, the Arabs and Sahelians remonstrated, fearing the *djin* of nightfall and darkness. Nevertheless, we pushed on, using my petrol lamp until the kerosene was gone and then my flashlight until the batteries were dead. Finally, up a piece by the moonlight. Then we stopped—signaled by Jean—for a respite until dawn.

On the morning of the second day, soaked in our sweat, yet thankful for the more temperate breeze, we reached a point where we could step down into a trickle of water—into a sort of wadi below. I was thankful that the sounds of the clash and clang of warfare no longer reached us.

■ More Trekking

Below, I could make out the scrambling of ant-sized figures—through and beneath the smoke that billowed from weapon fire and the frenetic flight of the locusts.

And behind us all was my friend, the conflicted and sometime shadowy *imam*, dressed, as always, in his black *jalaba*. No one could remember giving him an invitation or permission to join us. There was fear he might betray Habert's tunnel. So at the last minute we gave him the meeting place, only then realizing that he could just as well march across the desert to the foot of Jumeaux without there being any suspicion on the part of the militia or Wahidi. After all, he was the *imam*. "Thus have I spoken." Yet he could have been lost among the horde of locusts or the terrible winds.

We rested. But only a moment's respite.

■ Yet More of Trekking

Some would have died on the climb.

Partenay would never have made it. I myself came to curse every cigarette I'd ever smoked, every whiskey, beer, or wine I'd ever drunk. Especially in the last few days. And we pushed on.

Bending unbreakable thorned branches that were tearing at our left, then jagged, stony outcrops, pummeling us on the left and, at our feet, on the right. Still, we could not have gone around the other way, around the mountain—on the lowland—without meeting the militia, or *Yekbari*, or the Wahidi, or the Janjawid. This way would give our US Cavalry time to gather and meet us . . . .Or Lièvre's assassins.

It was warming at the second dawn, but there was still a bit of dew on the wild branberries—the so called acacia—as much as there would ever be. And we chewed the moisture-laden twigs and even the bark from the grewia plant that grew plentifully among the gravelly stones. These kept us hydrated. As did our sips of rationed water.

It was good that we started so early to gain some height before the searing sun was in full mode. And before the Janjawid, especially the Janjawid, discovered our attempt at escape—or our "escapade" as the *légionnaire capitaine* might have called it.

I watched Alexandru, still leading the way, with Jean and Younis a mere step behind. All walking point, with no fear of the *guépard*, the beast that slouched and loped between them. I was touched that Younis wore "our" bow and carried his homemade arrows, even on this rough climb. I carried the books and comics in my backpack.

As for Jean, even when I was looking to hire what the French colonials called a "boy," I remember being struck by those certain qualities in Jean. But Younis? Brave lad.

Jean himself stated how he had worked for others and how he left Evian when he realized what the man was doing with his students. (Hell of a way to raise their grade averages, Terry would say.) Jean put his moral sense before his means of livelihood and didn't brag about it. Now, here he was, walking second point, over the Jumeaux, leading us to liberation, and fearless as he went forward. Surely now, I realized how young, callow, and naïve he must have found me.

With Alexandru. With Younis. With the *guépard*, Féroce.

■ Under Fire

Bullets pinging like gravel on steel. Many around Idriss Mohammed and me. He was now wearing the beautiful *tarboosh*, I, the *légionnaire capitaine's képi*. In our colorful hats, I realized that we, or rather our headpieces, may have been drawing fire.

"They're too far to fire on us . . .," I had assured everyone. But maybe I had spoken too soon. The bullets were a bit below us, careening off those stony outcrops. And ricocheting at us. I hated my helplessness, my inability to anticipate and ward off the deadly missiles. Truly symbolic of my life here. But as long as we *heard* them firing . . . .

OK, the *képi* was what was probably attracting their attention and drawing their fire. Quick study, me. It was then that I suggested to Mohammed that he remove the beautiful *tarboosh* that he had donned to better care for it. I removed the *képi* and shoved it inside my khaki shirt, partner to the KC Athletics cap thus *stored*. No more bull's-eyes for the Janjawid—or whoever was down there. Its scent would keep Féroce enamored with me.

■ Abandoned (by the "Messenger?")

Halfway to the summit, the *imam* had announced "Now I will return to Dar es Sabir."

"Stay with us,' I shouted.

"I cannot. I have my people to pray with." Shades of Father O'Sagarty. "Come here again, Emricani, come to us as our brother. And bring gifts for our afflicted ones."

"It's too dangerous to descend, *Imam*," I shouted above the locusts' wing claps, like thunder, and the wind.

"One more word," he shouted. *B-ismi-llāhi r-rahmāni r-rahīmi.* You must tell our story. How we suffer as the desert creeps south to us and takes away our nourishment. How the Southerners enslave us. Tell them! Thus have I spoken." And so he began his descent, his return to Dar es Sabir and his house of prayer. In the belief that they, none of them, would harm an *imam*. "*Allahu akbar.*"

Though perhaps to be abandoned yet again by his one God.

So he, too, the *imam*, might turn out to be another one of our decoys.

At the peak, we reached a point where we could step down into another wadi below on our left, where there was also but a trickle of water that had collected from the only rain yet this "rainy" season.

For the "spring" comes late to this land, if you could call it spring at all. Cooling, dripping rain is the only sign—and it sometimes comes only once—perhaps for an hour. As if the rainy season, for but an instant, remembered its name. Then the "spring" as suddenly vanishes. One moment of the rain. Another moment of wishing us good luck.

The water sieved down a hospitable rocky outcrop. We knew for sure that we were no longer in the harsh, angry desert. We sat.

■ Rest Area 2

The cave, to our left, was mostly hidden by the rocky outcroppings, and it had been gone over by archaeologists who no doubt found signs of previous inhabitants and artists. Prehistoric Man, but perhaps more recent inhabitants.

And yet, even more recent, twentieth-century visitors, judging by the Douze Marches and cheap wine bottles and other detritus. Will future archaeologists and anthropologists search out these mysteries? Will any of them draw the parallel between Douze Marches and the twelve steps of AA fame? (Will it by then be "Weed & Heroin Anonymous" or WAHA?) Anyway, what wag came up with that beer appellation? (An American, of course. Working for Budweiser who had the license for beer sales in this lost country. He must have thought the humor would be appreciated. But it was, to date, probably not noticed and not understood. The *etiquette*-label showed twelve stairs climbing to a celestial abstraction.)

The first twenty feet of the cave were open to the sun at sunset and afforded a good view of the desert and town. In those times, thousands of years ago, that frontage may have offered a high, well-placed lookout. Overlooking the sandy desert and tiny oases of the time. Or, as we are told, there may have been even higher, more fertile ground below us in those ancient times.

Turning west, I could see the dry, sandy desert studded with tiny dunes and, furthest to the southwest, I thought I could even make out the great red rock and sand monuments of Ennedi, their guardian formations and surrounding desert plain. Our way out.

We sat, drank the water, broke out some C rations. I demonstrated how to use the keys to open the C ration cans.

"What is this 'Spam'?" Idriss Mohammed asked. "What means this word 'pork?'"

The success of my English teaching. "Ah, but the sausages of the dead cow." I spoke in English (perhaps I have now made it the *lyingest* of all these languages) and thus told everyone that the Spam was a derivative of beef sausage called "pork," so as to assuage their religious concerns. Also, I mumbled to make my explanation even less coherent. But Moudou, the half-practicing Hindu, made a face and barfing noise. No one paid attention.

So we ate voraciously, scraping the last bits from the tiny cans. Leaving those cans for future anthropologists to puzzle over as well.

As the sun descended, the *juge* and I began our conversation. Briefly interrupted by Antoine in Modou's face, in fierce remonstrance. "See how much quicker it would be to take this path rather than the one you have chosen?"

"But that one is harder to descend on, especially for the old ones, and we are more likely to meet the militia, Janjaweed, or Wahid or others at its base," Modou retorted.

"Wahid at its base," Antoine mimicked. Uncharacteristically angry and in full attack mode.

Uncharacteristic for Antoine, but very characteristic for Alain. Slow-study-me should have noticed the personality difference sooner. For it was Alain, while Antoine remained behind "to protect the children." Of course! As he would and *must* do. Brave man. Heroic.

"Then you take that road," Modou challenged. "And meet us at Ennedi!"

"Modou," I said, "don't provoke him."

Alain shouted "I don't provoke! I don't provoke!" But he was definitely taken aback by the challenge, and retired to the cave to consider that option. He then polled each of us to guage whether others would join him on that road. Given no takers, he retired to sulk at a spot in the cave.

"No," he shouted angrily from within the cave. "It is truly that I must go to Mecca. To become a hajji. Before I fall in battle. For I have said the *Takbir*. I am truly of the *mu'minīn* now!" Good answer. Good way to avoid the looming battle. Then, "But I don't provoke!"

"Then why did you come with us? To spy for Wahid?" I couldn't help but ask.

"To go with you to Mecca. To make the hajj. Also, I saved your life twice and now I must protect your hajj." I think he was referring to Antoine's disruption of his (Alain's) intent to kill me. Or perhaps the confrontation with Saghir. So it would be that Alain saved my life. But only once, if memory serves.

"So it should be. Get on with you!"

Almlak Alaswd.

■ The Judgment

This time the *juge* explained to me that he grew up an orphan, adopted by Fulani *griots*, storytellers, but was then educated by Swiss missionaries. He became a famed orator in this country—in French. "Then I studied the law and came to this point."

Probably for the look of sophistication, he broke out his pipe, filled it with imported tobacco—or maybe Terry's stuff judging by the *juge*'s nonstop chatter from that point.

"I should have remained behind to preside over the judgment of those who caused this destruction."

It seemed that he was wracked with guilt. "Which side?" I asked.

"Ah, yes, which side to be judged? The losing side?"

"But the winning side might not recognize you as a *juge*."

"Ah, yes. But then they might."

"Still on your cock-up accusation, *Monsieur le juge*?" I asked.

"That all this was caused by a secret, Yankee incursion."

And so he orated some more to me, challenged me on the Vietnam incursion, and ended with a look at me—indeed, of blame and condemnation—before declaring, "If you are remembered by history here, 'arry, history will not be kind to you."

Nice finale to an exhausting day and evening.

■ Sweet Dreams

"At sometime, Harold, I will tell you of the rugby slam I received from a young sergeant of the *Troisième Parachutiste*. I thought it was by accident since he apologized profusely. Then we made acquaintances and exchanged stories about telecommunications. You see, Harold, now I am wondering if he is not listening to me, maybe even watching us. This is what I have feared since that intentional slam and meeting." Again, the rueful smile.

"You sound paranoid," I mused. In fact, his story sounded very familiar. But I was too tired to offer Modou my similar story, much less any analysis, understanding, or sympathy.

So, at that point, I whispered that this Spam was truly pork so he could eat it. I gave him what I had saved for him. But I wasn't sure he would eat. In fact, his lethargy and fatigue suggested not.

Then I urged that we all try to sleep—well against the left hand wall if not in the cave. Backs against the wall, half of them were already dozing off. Already well ensconced in their chosen bed of rocks smoothed by the work of Terry and Joe.

No one but Modou, Alain, Younis, and I volunteered to try out the cave. The rest feared snakes and bats. The four of us, plus Féroce and the dogs, were too tired to care. Chien went deep into the cave—as far away from Modou as he could go. Féroce lay a few meters beyond us, his snoring much like his perpetual growling. Happy or angry? Who could tell?

Modou and I spread our sleeping bags at the entrance. As far from the path's edge as comfortable. Before I dozed off, I mumbled to Modou "You were right. There is a richness beneath the sand. A fertile soil like gold itself. Perhaps this is what Kahina meant. There are no shifting sands there, but only stillness. You were right."

He only grunted, turned over, and, I think, began to weep.

Michel and Victor took turns standing guard for us.

■ In Your Dreams

Deep in my dreams, I thought I heard something. A holler or a scream. Perhaps a wolf in the valley. Or a warning from the djinnii. I lurched up, then realizing I had to relieve myself. I crawled about, making my way to the mouth of the cave, looking for a spot that would make sense—a drop-off that I could use with a minimum of disruption and so as not to soil our sleeping places. At the cave mouth, and beyond, the earth was dry and not slippery. I turned left, took one step, and realized I was too near the precipice. Where Modou had nearly tumbled last time. A close call.

I turned right where there was an easier path to the wadi far below. I used that. I went back to my blanket. I noticed that Modou's sleeping blanket was ruffled. One of his notebooks lay on top of the carry-bag that served as his pillow. Probably he went to explore the internals of the cave. Searching for parchment. Or doing the same thing I had just done. Taking a piss. He knew where to go.

I dozed off again, but it seemed like only for a moment.

Then, in the deep night, well before the dawn, Younis pulled me out of the comfort of my rocky bed and out of hearing of the others. "Here is the secret of those I once promised, Master Harry, for I know the guilty one."

"Guilty of what?" Given my exhaustion, I was caught totally off guard.

"Of the theft. Of the betting money, the 135,000 plus CFA stolen during the fighting at the fair."

"The fair fight? How would you know this?"

"I was told by a witness who saw the money scraped away during the confusion of the fighting." He was trembling with excitement.

"Who then?" I was a bit on edge and had to force myself to keep my voice down.

"It was the *juge*. The very one who is with us now."

"What the witness probably saw was the *juge* scraping away the money to protect it."

"If scraping only to preserve the money, where is it now? With the money, he can go West, go home, where he is a singer, a griot, perhaps a descendant of holy ones, a speaker of 'truths,' so I am told. Or go to see America."

"Why did you wait so long to tell me?" I was rightly perturbed.

"I was not so sure. Besides, it was your Emricani who seemed to be arranging it all and sharing of the money. (I then knew that Terry and Joe had indeed arrived a day early—to arrange the *juge*'s visit or immigration details.)

"Still, I was not sure. Not until I remembered that a sheaf of what could have been CFA bills peeked out from his knapsack as we climbed. He quickly stuffed them back into the knapsack. I think I was the only one who saw. Also, this was the only time to speak to you in quiet and private." He was definitely sorry to bring me this news. As if the guilt were his.

"I will attempt to resolve this," I told him. Though I had no idea how. I spent the remaining time until dawn watching the *juge* sleeping on top of his lumpen knapsack, watching the lumps which served as his pillow. And perhaps his fortune.

So did Kalb, who arose with me several times so I could train him to sniff at the *juge*'s knapsack and pretend to seize it—after I had pointed to it repeatedly, with encouragement in my whispering.

But in the night, Kalb did not uncover the money—or anything else.

The next time I awoke, from a doze, in the near dawn, I stepped out of the cave entrance. Carefully. The sky was clear, and I could see down to Dar es Sabir, which looked like a miniature townscape from here. Complete with the fog caused by weapons firing. Like a railroad layout from Lionel—without the train tracks and trains.

But populated by scurrying, ant-like battalions.

[Note from Aaron Hamblin: I'm not sure where in the chronology this belongs, so I'm inserting it here.] And here's the way I later learned that things lined up: The Militia had its contingent plus the recently released *Yekbared* felons. The Militia reinforcements from Albri had not materialized. In fact, it might have been them we saw crawling toward Dar es Sabir from the southeast. Very slowly and perhaps with little enthusiasm. The Wahidi had its contingent plus the Jinjaweed and, for added color, the lepers of the Prokaza village. The numbers seemed to add up evenly with the Wahidi outnumbering the militia by just a few more (counting the lepers). [End of insert.]

■ *Le Corps de la guerre*

So in the early morning, it had already begun—or it appeared so—even though the night had been a quiet one.

Above the smoke and din of battle, we could see at least three military planes speeding from the south toward Dar es Sabir. We turned to watch them. They weren't looking for us. And their cargo was soon dispatched. *Troisième Parachutiste* jumpers beginning their descent.

They jumped from one plane at a time, in sequences of three from each plane. And then over again. It looked like they were aiming towards the south end of the town, but away from the Wahidi attack coming from the north and west. They were coming to reinforce the camel militia. And perhaps to show them how it was done.

I was mesmerized by the mushroom-shaped gray-white silk opening, it seemed, so near us. Just across the sky from us. In the bright blue dawn, like flower petals sailing in the wind. Gerard was no longer a *bleu-bite*, he said.

One was lost. A chute that didn't open. What we call a "bounce." What the Third Para would call a *chandelle romaine*. I hoped it was not Gerard. I may have hoped it was Heinrich the Brute, if he had survived Habré's stabbing. We couldn't distinguish the paratroopers on the ground for all the smoke.

The planes had lightened themselves of their load and were turning back. One was wounded by a heatseeker. To us, the contact was silent. Only the sight of a fiery eruption and the wounded airplane. On returning, the planes seemed to hover over us, and then passed. Mohammed was sure that one of them tipped his wing toward us. Wishing us *bon voyage et bonne chance* perhaps.

■ Three Lost

But suddenly, it was done. Whether by accident or with design. A loud clap—then he was taken by Chien's anger and broken heart. Chien, who blamed Modou for the disappearance of his master. I was knocked off my feet as he rushed by me.

They left me to explain it all as best I could.

For at the clap, perhaps a gun shot, Chien had stormed out of the cave, let out a whimper, then a long, protracted growl and tumbled over the precipice—perhaps to join the master he had so longed for. To join Evian.

Yet he took with him the despised Modou whom he had seized by an arm in his iron jaws as he sped through and out the cave. Antoine, ah no, Alain was at the entrance to the cave, staring with an angry smile at the scene in front of him. The scene he may have provoked. If ever he provoked. Holding his (or Antoine's) police-issue revolver. Then he turned to take the steeper, more crooked path toward the fate that may have been awaiting him below. "Wahid below! Don't provoke!" he shouted. We were still in too much shock to even notice.

Modou had probably been exploring what Chien deemed his territory without his permission. I guess I had saved Modou's life for what seemed to have amounted to only a few more seconds. For all that, he was carried to the precipice and beyond, but remained in total silence. As for Chien, his life of the *Akita* of everlasting loyalty had exhausted itself.

Plus, in the excitement, Féroce had been aroused and chased the two, grabbing onto Modou's leg with his carnivorous teeth. Perhaps to rescue him. But all three tumbled over the precipice with Modou's hand seizing the ledge—but only for a fleeting second.

Féroce's roar carried to us for a moment. Then, a terrifying silence.

It was the dramatic denouement to three lives of sadness and loss. (And it was just like them to dramatize it so.)

In a delayed reaction, Kalb had let out a cry as he too lunged toward the ledge—the *juge's* pillow, the knapsack, in his bite—to follow his friend Chien. He might have gone over, if I hadn't grabbed his tail and yanked him backward onto safer ground.

But the knapsack was lost. We could see pieces of paper, no doubt CFA, flittering out as the knapsack fell that long distance. At that moment, Terry yelled a loud and dramatic "No!" So much for the *juge's* trip to the *Ooo Es Ah*. So much for the carefully wrought "arrangements." So much for finding the truth.

Thus we experienced our second, third, and fourth casualties—one taken down, I'll report, by a ricocheting bullet, two by a faithful dog. In truth, all by their pain and desperation.

Really, I'll only report two lost. No mention of Féroce. No one would believe that story anyway. I tossed his master's *képi*, given me for taking Féroce with us, over the ledge to join him. And I also would report the loss of the *juge's* "diary," despite the attempted retrieval by little Kalb.

Most of our fellow pilgrims were already awake—and witnesses to the "accident." They were "shocked!" Ivan was at the precipice, downtrodden that he was no longer able to aid and cure. But he did notice, and later mentioned, another figure, swathed in white linen, at the bottom of that ravine. Likely, the shrouded corpse of the despised Evian.

Chien could have waited until more of the audience had fully awakened for more dramatic effect. But still, there were sufficient witnesses. I was sorry Modou could not have chosen the holy Ganges for his last statement and for his last moments.

So I believe it had been a sign when he entrusted me with that ancient piece of parchment and left his diary that, in his mind, summarized his life's accomplishments. I should have seen it coming, but we all had our minds on the probable dangers of the *guépard*.

[Note from Aaron Hamblin: I'm not sure where in the chronology this belongs, so I'm inserting it here.] And yet another loss for Terry, if I understood the dynamics and dramatics. For now I understood that the early arrival of Terry and Joe had been to conclude the travel and visa arrangements for the *juge*. And the theft of the betting money, to be used by the *juge* as the payoff for this service and for the voyage. Our escape was a convenient means to cover the theft. I would some day understand it all. And why the *juge* walked away from us. And the truth he thought he would find in the USA. [End of insert.]

The *juge*, who had been watching his knapsack disappear in a daze, then turned and headed back down the pathway. Terry ran after him. They held an animated conference. Much gesticulating. Then the *juge* moved on down the mountain, and Terry returned to us. "He's going home," Terry told us.

"To meet his maker," I thought. No one good-humored enough down there to put up with his challenges and insults.

Then, for the first time on this journey, Alice came up to me. Her face flushed and the tears flowing freely. She stared at me a moment, then blurted an angry "You again! Are we all so cursed to know you?" Then she turned to join the others. Perhaps to ignore me for the rest of this trip—and even for the rest of our lives.

For all of this, I felt as I did when I lost Moussa. But this time, without the tears. Still, sometime later, this memory might suddenly surprise me. To roll down my cheeks. To dampen my shirt. And my day.

■ Sightseeing

Looking west, with the morning light mostly to our left and behind us, I stared at the dry, sandy plain studded with what seemed to be tiny dunes but which I knew were gigantesque. And, furthest to the southwest, I thought I could even make out the rest of the great sand monuments, their guardian formations, and the surrounding desert plain. The sun was no longer so blinding. I could see it all. Not in black and white. In color. Modou's dream. Our way out.

Turning northwest, we saw the morning's first explosions. It must have been the Third Para setting them off. Taking down the buildings now occupied by the Wahidi and their fellow travelers, buildings both sacred and secular, town section by town section. The mosque and house of justice which held the *zakat*, the charity donations, as well. And did not touch the social center—the perhaps someday-to-be-redubbed "national theatre" that Abdel-Hamid so coveted.

■ The Feints

So the feints must have worked. There was no one on the mountain trail behind us. Abdel-Hamid and Esmir to the northwest in the speeding blue Deux Chevaux and Father O'Sagarty with his flock (and others) to the northeast. Both serving to mislead by drawing the combatants away from the route of our escape.

As for Abdel-Hamid and Esmir, the Prokaza brothers, no one would touch them or even get near them when they were stopped. Who would? [Note from Aaron Hamblin: I'm not sure where in the chronology this belongs, so I'm inserting it here.] As I later learned, they went back to their Prokaza village with their surviving townsmen to await the great Emricani gifts of grapes and dates and virgins and hand-wrought silver cups and other, even better, automobiles. Perhaps also, with medicines that would cure their ailment. [End of insert.]

[Note from Aaron Hamblin: I'm not sure where in the chronology this belongs, so I'm inserting it here.] But later I also learned that Father O'Sagarty had not survived. I imagine that he offered his life to the Janjawid to save his flock. I imagine that he prayed so first. Before they beheaded him. His prayers may have gone unanswered. For he may have died first and did not see the subsequent slaughter. Death first would have been the only reward given him by his merciful God. [End of insert.]

■ On the One Hand, On the Other Hand

Yes, to my own surprise, I turned the other way. That is, I climbed back to the peak a short distance behind us, swooped up Kalb in one arm (I had taken the radio in the other), looked back once, then headed down the way we had just come. Alexandru would lead them the rest of the way. In fact, he was first to shout "C'mon Harry!"

I kept on, all right. Though I waved once but didn't turn to look. "I just remembered," I shouted back. "I scheduled my audition and rehearsal this morning! It's my great cinematic opportunity!" I doubt they heard me.

Jean ran down to catch up with me. "Where are you going, Jean?"

"I am your servant, Monsieur. I must follow you."

"As my last command to you, I order you to rejoin the escapees. I can no longer employ you. You must go back to them!" I shouted. "Be sure to take *Hamar* where your journey ends.

I think he was truly taken aback. Never expecting to be laid off. Or sent away. We stared at each other for a long moment. I offered my hand as a sign of friendship. He ignored it, petted Kalb, turned on his heels, and climbed to rejoin the others.

The descent was as difficult as the ascent. I had to seize the acacias, grewia, and outcropping rocks to prevent a disastrous slide.

But I had plenty of time to think it through. This whole story.

And, with only the sounds of my steps on the rocky path and my strained breathing, the memories came flooding back. Every moment with every step—how it began . . . how it transpired . . . and how it has ended.

And so perhaps I can finally be objective and see them equally and as equals—the colonel, he of the lip-curl and eye-twitch, and the rebel bandit who, when angry, wrapped his veil across his face so as to show only his fierce and angry eyes.

Perhaps I now hated them both equally. For having disappointed me so. For failing to play the roles I attributed to them. Perhaps this is what had been bothering me most. This perfect symmetry . . . of recalcitrance and self-aggrandizement.

■ Home Sweet Home

I returned to my *kaz* safely. No Wahidi or militia to block my way. Ibrahim had done his job. An army contingent was waiting to escort me to my *kaz*. As if they knew I would be coming. Strange. The town's atmosphere was calm and quiet . . . for that moment.

I returned "home." To Miriam's joy. We celebrated carnally . . . in the open remains of the *kaz* structure, in the open sight of the world.

I did my film act for the general—in French and English—about all the comforts of Dar es Sabir—for Nasarah Westerners and tourists. And, for that, I was reinstated as a *professeur* at the collège in good standing. Rewarded for my upright dialog acting or performing horizontally in my bed, I will never know.

The students were more than surprised at my rapid return and probably sorry they had spent their small fortunes on that beautiful Koran.

Well, it didn't last long. A telex came from Adoum Justin closing the school for the remainder of the school year (about a week) and freeing me to go to Djemélia.

WTF:IM RELEASED FMCOLLEGE.PLSADVISE:HH:STOP.

WTF:STAYPUTWAIT4ER:LN:STOP.

The general and his C130 then moved on, as the second battle threatened to get underway. No medal for this one perhaps.

Earl soon arrived in an old (and somewhat rickety) Piper Cub. He greeted me with "Congratulations! I'm to take you back. And you'll still be alive!" *He* even sounded surprised. I made sure Hank saw that I still had the radio. Hank gave me his usual look but said nothing. No name tag either. He was armed. An M1.

"Sorry you had to make this trip," I said. "Especially in this!"

Miriam was sorry I was making the trip as well. For the first time, I saw tears running down her cheeks.

"We'll fly low, below their radar, enough to confuse them!" Earl said.

We did.

The flight was nerve-wracking but good for sightseeing. Close to the ground except when we spotted rebels. Or bandits. Or militia. Earl had us shift seats now and then. I guess to balance our weight.

We arrived safely to find out that my "pilgrims" had just left. Minus those lost and minus Alain. For Algiers. And safe haven. Perhaps Alain went to Mecca. To consecrate his soul. Before the next battle.

In the meantime, I think the sand continues to reclaim what once had been its own.

End Notes

[Later inserts:]

[The Good News: I later learned that a national theatre was built in the Social Center of Dar es Sabir, where Abdel-Hamid became a local comedian and star. Maybe telling Prokaza jokes. Maybe, stories and plays about the magical, dusted *esh b'weké* that rendered a prowess beyond belief.

And that nearly fifteen years after we slipped away, Younis had become a world-class archer for the USA team under the mystifying alias "Abu Robin." For that, I suppose that I deserve to feel somehow responsible—and with the satisfaction of a proud teacher . . . or father.

I took Idriss Mohammed with me on my venturesome journeys. As I promised the Uncle *Hajjs*. For the beautiful *tarboosh* that I always wore at Mohammed's urging.

The Not-so-Good/Bad(?) News: No one can say for sure, rather no one will say for sure, how Wahid met his end. But his death a few years after we slipped away, in the Wahidi capital of Dar es Sabir, resulted in the eventual dissolution of the Wahidi into other rebel groups and tribal warrior cults. The special forces, an offshoot of the militia company led by a General Ngokuru and trained by the Troisième *Parachutiste*, have received credit for Wahid's elimination. So far, none of that force has given an interview or written an article or book about the exploit. Nor has any journalist. I think Gerard Olivier Dubois could give me the truth. Perhaps some day.

Other candidates for his killing include the National Militia, the National Army, a disgruntled follower, or a jealous betrothed. I prefer to believe the latter. That it was indeed Amina, being finally liberated by Ngokuru after her many refusals to him, and enraged by all the failures that surrounded her, who took it all out on Wahid. Taking her last, best revenge—for the betterment of us all—or in our honor.

I was later told that, meanwhile, the Wahidi had been driven back several times. Fought to a standstill. And so these battles were destined to take place all over again. And again. And again.

"Write of us after the battle," he said. "Not before." After which battle? Perhaps, someday I'll return to see the results, the story of battle, of the winners and losers, For myself. [End of later inserts.]

All this awaits another telling. Another story.

■ Postscript

January 1, 1970

Wouldn't you know it: I have been given a Certificate of Merit for bravery beyond the call . . . signed by my congressman—who I doubt could ever find Dar es Sabir, or even the Sahel, on a map of Africa.

The certificate is for helping the Idriss brothers, Tom, Dick and Harry, and nephew Mohammed, escape and survive. I later learned that President Mugabaye had made an unfortunate deal with Gaddafi to lock the brothers up, to Yekbar them, as spies! So I had saved the remnants of a regime. Perhaps for better days. No one mentioned my Oscar-meriting performance on camera—probably because it never received its deserved acclaim. Hollywood never called me.

And this entire situation began to clarify for me. For I learned that having these many spies yielded a protection—a good way to confuse the enemy and keep him ignorant of means and methods. One, to watch the militia, another, to watch the towns people, a third to watch the enemy, another, to watch the other enemy, and one to watch it all. Eyes and ears everywhere. Truly, the CIA's James Angleton's "wilderness of mirrors." Plus, by spreading the information gathering around, they created a synthesis that would deliver the truth of things. I learned this, but still don't believe it so.

I was certified as brave. They don't have a certificate for naïve or callow. And so I have something to frame as an exaggerated testament to those times.

In discussing stories he'd heard, where the storyteller was the hero and central figure, Hemingway once said that his usual response was to discount the storyteller's professed level of bravery by about thirty percent. It struck me as a fairly sensible rule of thumb, and I've since found it quite useful, particularly in my own case.

And particularly when the drinks are flowing freely and the tales grow tall.

Nevertheless, I also often recall the warning that I could have heeded. *If you are remembered by history here, history will not be kind to you.* I should frame this as well.

But I know that, in this case, history won't give a shit.

■ *Post-Post Script*

January 2, 1975

My excellent copyreader has noticed, and you no doubt have as well, that throughout this narrative, I did not name the country where I was posted and where these events took place. I assumed it would be recognized. Yes, it could be Chad, it could be Niger, even Mali. I was asked (implication— "ordered") by my former directors not to mention its name in anything written, in any memoires. So I gave the characters and places fictitious names. Except for mine. I was warned that to betray our secrecy might mean the surrender of my certificate. The only testament to what little courage I may have had.

Or this story could have taken place in a land of my imagination, with all those fright-inducing attributes of the Sahel—and filled with all those things I most fear.

Aaron's Note: There is more to come . . .

Printed in the United States
By Bookmasters

Printed in the United States
By Bookmasters